Praise for Elin Hilderbrand's

Winter in Paradise

"What do you do once you've become queen of the summer novel and mastered the art of the Christmas novel? You start a new series, of course! The incomparable Elin Hilderbrand brings us to St. John for the first novel in her new Paradise series...Another compulsively readable hit by Hilderbrand."
— Brenda Janowitz, *PopSugar* 28 Best New Books to Curl Up with This Fall

"With great verve, Hilderbrand has done it again with her latest, *Winter in Paradise,* the first book in a planned trilogy. She is witty and engaging, and she keeps her readers intrigued with a memorable set of characters...As always, she delivers a story with much detail, weaving her characters and plotlines expertly...Be prepared to read a fast-paced and entertaining novel for several hours, which will keep you longing for the second in the series." — Vivian Payton, *Bookreporter*

"As she does in her books set on Nantucket, Hilderbrand excels at establishing a setting (the food! the luxury! the sea turtles!) that will inspire wanderlust...Hilderbrand is the queen of the summer blockbuster; her fans will be thrilled that she's taken on winter." — Susan Maguire, *Booklist*

Winter in Paradise

ALSO BY ELIN HILDERBRAND

Winter in Paradise

A Novel

Elin Hilderbrand

Little, Brown and Company

New York   Boston   London

To Matt and Julie Lasota

St. John was a place I used to visit — but then I met you and it became home.

———————————

Copyright © 2018 by Elin Hilderbrand
Excerpt from *What Happens in Paradise* copyright © 2019 by Elin Hilderbrand

Little, Brown and Company
Hachette Book Group
1290 Avenue of the Americas, New York, NY 10104
littlebrown.com

Little, Brown and Company is a division of Hachette Book Group, Inc. The Little, Brown and Company name and logo are trademarks of Hachette Book Group, Inc.

The publisher is not responsible for websites (or their content) that are not owned by the publisher.

Printed in the United States of America

Originally published in hardcover by Little, Brown and Company, October 2018
First Little, Brown and Company mass market edition, August 2020

CW

10 9 8 7 6 5 4 3 2 1

ATTENTION CORPORATIONS AND ORGANIZATIONS:
Most HACHETTE BOOK GROUP books are available at quantity discounts with bulk purchase for educational, business, or sales promotional use. For information, please call or write:

Special Markets Department, Hachette Book Group
1290 Avenue of the Americas, New York, NY 10104
Telephone: 1-800-222-6747 Fax: 1-800-477-5925

AUTHOR'S NOTE

This is the first novel I've written that isn't set on my home island of Nantucket. Instead, it's set on an island I consider a home away from home, my happy place and my refuge: St. John, USVI. I started going to St. John in the spring of 2012, and I have been back every year since for a five-week stretch to finish up my winter books (every book in the Winter Street series was completed there) and to start my summer novels (I wrote large sections of *Beautiful Day, The Matchmaker, The Rumor, Here's to Us,* and *The Identicals* there). Over the years I got to know some of the islanders, and that's when my love of St. John was cemented. I have always maintained that, ultimately, the places we love are about people.

As many of you know, both the United States Virgin Islands and the British Virgin Islands sustained massive damage during Hurricanes Irma, Jose, and Maria in the fall of 2017. I worried I would not be able to return to St. John in the spring of 2018, but by mid-March, the island was ready for me and I returned, jubilant and grateful.

The island is not the same. There are areas of complete devastation, homes lost, trees that look like badly broken bones. Many of the island businesses, places I really and truly loved, either shut down temporarily or closed for good. During my stay in March and April of 2018, the island's two biggest resorts, the Westin and Caneel Bay, were out of commission. But the spirit of St. John remained. People were upbeat and forward-looking. The island thrummed with the spirit of regeneration. I had a wonderful and magical five weeks, as I always do.

I've set this in January 2019 but as if it's January 2017, before the hurricane. There are shops, restaurants, and hotels mentioned that are no longer in business. I felt that to write this novel effectively, I had to write about the St. John I had known and loved, and not complicate the narrative with details of the storm. The storm may yet surface during this trilogy, but it does not in this book. I would like to acknowledge the loss and the hardship that my beloved island and its people suffered—and I want to laud the entire community for its selflessness, cooperation, and bravery. You are an example to us all. God bless you.

The good news is that St. John is ready for you to come back or visit for the first time. It's still paradise, all the more beautiful because of what it has endured.

PART ONE

Stateside

IRENE: IOWA CITY

It's the first night of the new year.

Irene Steele has spent the day in a state of focused productivity. From nine to one, she filed away every piece of paperwork relating to the complete moth-to-butterfly renovation of her 1892 Queen Anne–style home on Church Street. From one to two, she ate a thick sandwich, chicken salad on pumpernickel (she has always been naturally slender, luckily, so no New Year's diets for her), and then she took a short nap on the velvet fainting couch in front of the fire in the parlor. From two fifteen to three thirty, she composed an email response to her boss, Joseph Feeney, the publisher of *Heartland Home & Style* magazine, who two days earlier had informed her that she was being "promoted" from editor in chief of the magazine to executive editor, a newly created position that reduces both Irene's hours and responsibilities by half and comes with a 30 percent pay cut.

At a quarter of four, she tried calling her husband, Russ, who was away on business. The phone rang six times and went to voicemail. Irene didn't leave a message. Russ never listened to them, anyway.

ᴗne tried Russ again at four thirty and was shuttled *straight*
ᴛo voicemail. She paused, then hung up. Russ was on his phone
night and day. Irene wondered if he was intentionally avoiding
her call. He might have been upset about their conversation
the day before, but first thing this morning, a lavish bouquet
of snow-white calla lilies had been delivered to the door with
a note: *Because you love callas and I love you. Xo R.* Irene had
been delighted; there was nothing like fresh flowers to brighten
a house in winter. She was amazed that Russ had been able to
find someone who would deliver on the holiday, but his inge-
nuity knew no bounds.

At five o'clock, Irene poured herself a generous glass of
Kendall-Jackson chardonnay, took a shower, and put on the
silk and cashmere color-block sweater and black crepe slim
pants from Eileen Fisher that Russ had given her for Christmas. She bundled up in her shearling coat, earmuffs, and calf-
skin leather gloves to walk the four blocks through Iowa City
to meet her best friend, esteemed American history professor
Lydia Christensen, at the Pullman Bar & Diner.

The New Year's Day dinner is a tradition going into its seventh
year. It started when Lydia got divorced from her philandering husband, Philip, and Russ's travel schedule went from
"nearly all the time" to "all the time." The dinner is supposed
to be a positive, life-affirming ritual: Irene and Lydia count
their many, many blessings—this friendship near the top of
the list—and state their aspirations for the twelve months
ahead. But Irene and Lydia are only human, and so their conversation sometimes lapses into predictable lamentation. The

greatest unfairness in this world, according to Lydia, is that men get sexier and better-looking as they get older and women… don't. They just don't.

"The CIA should hire women in their fifties," Lydia says. "We're invisible."

"Would you ladies like more wine?" Ryan, the server, asks.

"Yes, please!" Irene says with her brightest smile. Is *she* invisible? A week ago, she wouldn't have thought so, but news of her "promotion" makes her think maybe Lydia is right. Joseph Feeney is sliding Irene down the masthead (and hoping she won't notice that's what he's doing) and replacing her with Mavis Key, a thirty-one-year-old dynamo who left a high-powered interior design firm in Manhattan to follow her husband to Cedar Rapids. She came waltzing into the magazine's offices only eight months ago with her shiny, sexy résumé, and all of a sudden, Joseph wants the magazine to be more city-slick and sophisticated. He wants to shift attention and resources from the physical magazine to their online version, and, using Mavis Key's expertise, he wants to create a "social media presence." Irene stands in firm opposition. Teenagers and millennials use social media, but the demographic of *Heartland Home & Style* is women 39–65, which also happens to be Irene's demographic. Those readers want magazines they can *hold,* glossies they can page through and coo over at the dentist's office; they want features that reflect the cozy, bread-and-butter values of the Midwest.

Irene's sudden, unexpected, and unwanted "promotion" makes Irene feel like a fuddy-duddy in Mom jeans. It makes her feel completely irrelevant. She will be invited to meetings, the less important ones, but her opinion will be disregarded. She will review layout and content, but no changes will be made. She will visit people in their offices, take advertisers out to lunch, and chat. She has been reduced to a figurehead, a mascot, a pet.

Irene gazes up at Ryan as he fills their glasses with buttery chardonnay—the Cakebread, a splurge—and wonders what he sees when he looks at them. Does he see two vague, female-shaped outlines, the kind that detectives spray-paint around dead bodies? Or does he see two vibrant, interesting, desirable women of a certain age?

Okay, scratch desirable. Ryan, Irene knows (because she eats at the Pullman Bar & Diner at least once a week while Russ is away), is twenty-five years old, working on his graduate degree in applied mathematics, though he doesn't look like any mathematician Irene has ever imagined. He looks like one of the famous Ryans—Ryan Seacrest, Ryan Gosling. Ryan O'Neal.

Ryan *O'Neal?* Now she really *is* aging herself!

Irene has been known to indulge Lydia when she boards the Woe-Is-Me train, but she decides not to do it this evening. "I don't feel invisible," she says. She leans across the table. "In fact, I've been thinking of running for office."

Lydia shrieks like Irene zapped her on the flank with a cattle prod. "What? What do you mean 'run for office'? You mean *Congress?* Or just, like, the Iowa City School Board?"

Irene had been thinking Congress, though when the word comes out of Lydia's mouth, it sounds absurd. Irene knows *nothing* about politics. Not one thing. But as the (former) editor in chief of *Heartland Home & Style* magazine, she knows a lot about getting things done. On a deadline. And she knows about listening to other people's point of view and dealing with difficult personalities. Oh, does she.

"Maybe not run for office," Irene says. "But I need something else." She doesn't want to go into her demotion-disguised-as-promotion right now; the pain is still too fresh.

"*I* need something else," Lydia says. "I need a single man, straight, between the ages of fifty-five and seventy, over six feet tall, with a six-figure income and a sizable IRA. Oh, and a sense of humor. Oh, and hobbies that include grocery shopping, doing the dishes, and folding laundry."

Irene shakes her head. "A man isn't going to solve your problems, Lydia. Didn't we learn that in our consciousness-raising group decades ago?"

"A man *will* solve my problems, because my problem is that I've got no man," Lydia says. She throws back what's left of her wine. "You wouldn't understand because you have Russ, who dotes on you night and day."

"When he's around," Irene says. She knows her complaints fall on deaf ears. Russ joined the Husband Hall of Fame seven years earlier when he hired a barnstormer plane to circle Iowa City dragging a banner that said: HAPPY 50TH IRENE STEELE. I LOVE YOU! Irene's friends had been awestruck, but Irene found the showiness of the birthday wishes a bit off-putting. She would have been happy with just a card.

"Let's get the check," Lydia says. "Maybe that barista with the beard will be working at the bookstore."

Irene and Lydia split the bill as they do every year with the New Year's dinner, then they stroll down South Dubuque from the Pullman to Prairie Lights bookstore. The temperature tonight is a robust thirteen degrees, but Irene barely notices the cold. She was born and raised right here in eastern Iowa, where the winds come straight down from Manitoba. Russ hates the cold. Russ's father was a navy pilot and so Russ grew up in Jacksonville, San Diego, and Corpus Christi; he saw snow for the first time when he went to college at Northwestern. Privately, Irene considers Russ's aversion to the cold a constitutional inferiority. As wonderful as he is, Irene would never describe him as hearty.

Lydia holds open the door to Prairie Lights and winks at Irene. "I see him," she whispers.

"Don't be shy. Order something complicated and strike up a conversation," Irene says. "It's a new year."

Lydia whips off her hat and shakes out her strawberry-blond hair. She's a pretty woman, Irene thinks, and, with the confidence she's displaying now, not at all invisible. Surely Brandon, the fifty-something barista with the thick spectacles and the leather apron—better suited to welding than to making espresso drinks—would be intrigued by Professor Lydia Christensen? She coauthored the definitive biography of our nation's thirty-first president. Herbert Hoover has gotten a bad rap from history, but most Iowans are kindly disposed toward him because he was born and raised in West Branch.

As Lydia marches to the café, Irene floats over to the new fiction. She loves nothing better than a stack of fresh books on her nightstand. What an enriching way to start the new year. Irene spent her New Year's Eve taking down all of her holiday decorations and packing them neatly away. She left the boxes at the bottom of the attic stairs. Russ is due back late tomorrow night or early Thursday morning, he said, and once he returns, he will be fully at her disposal. He left for a "surprise" business trip two days after Christmas. The man has more surprise business trips than anyone Irene has ever heard of and in this case, he was leaving Irene alone for New Year's. They had quarreled about it the previous afternoon on the phone. Russ had said, "I'm fully devoted to you, Irene, and I strive to see your point of view in every disagreement. But let's recall who encouraged whom to take this job. Let's recall who said she didn't want to be married to a corn syrup salesman for the rest of her life."

Their conversation, repeated for years nearly verbatim, ended there, as it always did. Irene *had* pushed Russ to take the job with Ascension, and with that decision came sacrifice. Russ is away more than he's home, but he does call all the time, and he sends flowers and often leaves her a surprise gift on her pillow when he goes away—jewelry or a pair of snazzy reading glasses, gift cards to the Pullman, a monogrammed makeup case. He is so thoughtful and loving that he makes Irene feel chilly and indifferent by comparison. Also, and not inconsequentially, his new job affords them a very nice lifestyle, luxurious by Iowa standards. They own the Victorian, with its extravagant gardens and in-ground swimming pool on a full-acre lot on Church Street. Irene had been able to renovate the house exactly the way she dreamed of, sparing no expense. It took her nearly six years, proceeding one room at a time.

Now the house is a showpiece. Irene lobbied to have it featured in the magazine, but she encountered resistance from Mavis Key, who thought it would seem like shameless self-promotion to splash pictures of their own editor's home across their pages. *Talk about navel-gazing,* Mavis had said, a comment that hurt Irene. She suspects the real problem is Mavis's aversion to Victorian homes. Like Irene, they are out of fashion.

Mavis Key can buzz right off! Irene thinks. Irene's house is a reflection not only of years of painstaking work but also of her soul. The first floor has twelve-foot ceilings and features arched lancet windows with layered window treatments in velvet and damask. The palette throughout the house is one of rich, dark jewel tones—the formal living room is garnet, the parlor amethyst, and the kitchen has accents of topaz and emerald. There are tapestries and ornate rugs throughout, even in the bathrooms. Irene's favorite part of the house isn't a room per se but rather the grand staircase, which ascends two floors. It's paneled in dark walnut and at the top of the second flight of stairs is an exquisite stained-glass window that faces east. In the morning when the sun comes up, the third-floor landing is spangled with bursts of color. Irene has been known to take her mug of tea to the landing and just meditate on the convergence of man-made and natural beauty.

Irene supervised all of the interior carpentry, the refinishing of the floors, the repairs to the crown molding, the intricate painting—including, in the dining room, a wraparound mural of the landscape of Door County, Wisconsin, where Irene spent summers growing up. Irene also handpicked the antiques, traveling as far away as Minneapolis and Portland, Oregon, to attend estate sales.

Now that the house is finished, there is nothing left to do but enjoy it—and this is where Irene has hit a stumbling block. When she tells Lydia that she needs "something else," she isn't kidding. Russ is away for work at *least* two weeks a month, and their boys are grown up. Baker lives in Houston, where he day-trades stocks and serves as a stay-at-home father to his four-year-old son, Floyd. Baker's wife, Dr. Anna Schaffer, is a cardiothoracic surgeon at Memorial Hermann, which is a very stressful and time-consuming job; she, like Russ, is almost never around. Irene's younger son, Cash, lives in Denver, where he owns and operates two outdoor supply stores.

Neither of the boys comes home much anymore, which saddens Irene, although she knows she should be grateful they're out living their own lives.

There was a moment yesterday around dusk when everyone else in America was getting ready for New Year's Eve festivities—showering, pouring dressing drinks, preparing hors d'oeuvres, pulling little black dresses out of closets—that Irene was hit by a profound loneliness. She had spoken to Russ, they had quarreled, and right after they hung up, Irene considered calling him back, but she refrained. There was nothing less attractive than a needy woman—and besides, Russ was busy.

Irene plucks the new story collection by Curtis Sittenfeld off the shelf; Curtis is a graduate of the Iowa Writers' Workshop, which Irene happens to believe is the best in the country.

She hears Lydia laughing and peers around the stacks to see her friend and Brandon engaged in conversation. Brandon is leaning on his forearms on the counter while the espresso machine shrieks behind him. He hardly seems to notice; he's enraptured.

So much for being invisible! Irene thinks. Lydia is glowing like the northern lights.

Irene feels a twinge of an unfamiliar emotion. It's *longing,* she realizes. She misses Russ. Her husband spent years and years gazing at her with love—and, more often than not, she swatted him away, finding his attention overwrought and embarrassing.

Irene is distracted by a buzzing—her phone in her purse. That, she thinks with relief, will be Russ. But when she pulls out her phone, she sees the number is from area code 305. Irene doesn't recognize it and she guesses it's a telemarketer.

She lets the call go, disappointed and more than a little annoyed at Russ. Where *is* he? She hasn't heard from him since midafternoon the day before; it's not like him to go so long without calling. And where is he this week? Did he even tell her? Did she even ask? Russ's "work emergencies" take him to various bland, warm locations—Sarasota, Vero Beach, Naples. He nearly always comes home with a tan, inspiring envy from their friends who care about such things.

Irene notices the time—nine o'clock already—and realizes she has forgotten to call Milly, Russ's mother. Milly is ninety-seven years old; she lives at the Brown Deer retirement community in Coralville, a few miles away. Milly is in the medical unit now, although she's still cogent most of the time, still spry and witty, still a favorite with residents and staff alike. Irene visits Milly once a week and she calls her every night between seven and eight, but she forgot tonight because of her dinner with Lydia. By now, Milly will be fast asleep.

Not a worry, Irene thinks. She'll stop by to see Milly on her way home from work tomorrow. It'll be a good way to fill up her afternoons now that her hours have been cut. Maybe she'll take Milly to the Wig and Pen. Milly likes the chicken wings, though of course they aren't approved by her nutritionist. But what are they going to do, kill her?

The idea of Millicent Steele being finally done in by an order of zippy, peppery wing dings makes Irene smile as she chooses the Curtis Sittenfeld stories as well as *Where'd You Go, Bernadette,* by Maria Semple, which Irene had pretended to read for her book club half a dozen years earlier. With the house finished, she now has time to go back and catch up. Irene heads over to the register to pay. Meanwhile, Lydia is still at the café, still chatting with Brandon; her macchiato lets off the faintest whisper of steam between them.

Lydia turns when she feels Irene's hand on her back.

"Are you leaving?" Lydia asks. Her cheeks are flushed. "I'll probably stay for a while, enjoy my coffee."

"Oh," Irene says. "Okay, then. Thanks for dinner, it was fun, Happy New Year, call me tomorrow, be safe getting home, all of that." Irene smiles at Brandon, but his eyes are fastened on Lydia like she's the only woman in the world.

Good for her! Irene thinks as she walks home. It's a new year and Lydia is going after what she wants. A man. Brandon the barista.

The wind has picked up. It's bitterly cold and Irene has to head right into the teeth of it to get home. She ducks her head as she hurries down Linn Street, past a group of undergrads coming out of Paglia's Pizza, laughing and horsing around. One of the boys bumps into Irene.

"Sorry, ma'am," he says. "Didn't see you."

Invisible, she thinks.

This thought fades when she turns the corner and sees her house, her stunning castle, all lit up from within.

She'll light a fire in the library, she thinks. Make a cup of herbal tea, hunker down on the sofa with her favorite chenille blanket, crack open one of her new books.

Maybe the "something else" she's seeking isn't running for office, Irene thinks. Maybe it's turning her home into a bed-and-breakfast. It has six bedrooms, all with attached baths. If she kept one as a guest room for family, that still left four rooms she could rent out. Four rooms is manageable, right? Irene has a second cousin named Mitzi Quinn who ran an inn on Nantucket until her husband passed away. Mitzi had loved running the inn, although she did say it wasn't for the faint of heart.

Well, Irene's heart is as indestructible as they come.

What would Russ say if she proposed running an inn? She guesses he'd tell her to do whatever makes her happy.

It would solve the problem of her loneliness—people in the house all the time.

Would anyone want to come to Iowa City? Parents' weekend at the university, she supposes. Graduation. Certain football weekends.

It has definite appeal. She'll think on it.

When Irene opens the front door, she hears the house phone ringing. *That* will definitely be Russ, she thinks. No one calls the house phone anymore.

But when Irene reaches for the phone in the study just off the main hall, she sees it's the same 305 number that showed up on her cell phone. She hesitates for a second, then picks up the receiver.

"Hello?" she says. "Steele residence."

"Hello, may I please speak to Irene Steele?" The voice is female, unfamiliar.

"This is she," Irene says.

"Mrs. Steele, this is Todd Croft's secretary, Marilyn Monroe."

Marilyn Monroe, Todd Croft's oddly named secretary. Yes, Irene has heard about this woman, though she's never met her. Irene has only met Todd Croft, Russ's boss, once before. Todd

Croft and Russ had been acquainted at Northwestern, and thirteen years ago, Russ and Irene had bumped into Todd in the lobby of the Drake Hotel in Chicago. That chance meeting led to a job offer, the one Irene had been so eager for Russ to accept. Now Todd Croft is just a name, invoked by Russ again and again. The man has become synonymous with the unseen force that rules their lives. *Todd needs me in Tampa on Tuesday. Todd has new clients he's courting in Lubbock.* "Todd the God," Irene calls him privately. And yet everything she has—this house, the swimming pool and gazebo, the brand-new Lexus in the garage—is thanks to Todd Croft.

"Happy New Year, Marilyn?" Irene says. There's a hesitation in her voice because Irene can't imagine why Marilyn Monroe—Irene has no choice but to picture this woman as a platinum blonde, buxom, with a beauty mark—would be calling. "Is everything…?"

"Mrs. Steele," Marilyn says. "Something has happened."

"Happened?" Irene says.

"There was an accident," Marilyn says. "I'm afraid your husband is dead."

AYERS: ST. JOHN, USVI

Servers across the country—hell, across the world—regard New Year's Eve with dread, and although Ayers Wilson is no exception, she tries to keep an open mind. It's just another night at La Tapa, the best restaurant in St. John, which is the best of the Virgin Islands—U.S. and British combined—in Ayers's opinion. Tonight, for the holiday, there are two seatings with a fixed menu, priced at eighty-five dollars a head, so in many ways it'll be easier than regular service and the tips should be excellent. Ayers will likely clear four hundred dollars. She has no reason to complain.

Except...Rosie is off tonight because the Invisible Man is in town. This means Ayers is working with Tilda, who is not only young and inexperienced but also a relentless scorekeeper, *and* she has a crush on Skip, the bartender; it's both pathetic and annoying to watch her flirt.

The first seating, miraculously, goes smoothly. Ayers waits on one of the families who came on her snorkeling trip to the British Virgin Islands that morning. The mother looks like a woman plucked from a Rubens painting, voluptuous and redhaired, with milky skin. She had wisely spent most of the day under the boat's canopy while Ayers snorkeled with her two teenagers, pointing out spotted eagle rays and hawksbill turtles. Now the mother tilts her head. She knows she recognizes Ayers, but she can't figure out how.

"I'm Ayers," she says. "I was a crew member on *Treasure Island* today."

"Yes!" the mother says. The father grins—kind of a goofy guy, perfectly harmless—and the kids gape. This happens all the time: people are amazed that Ayers works two jobs and that she might appear in their lives in two different capacities *on the same day.*

Ayers's other tables are couples who want to finish eating so they can get down to the Beach Bar to watch the fireworks. In past years, Ayers has managed to squeak out of work by quarter of twelve. She and Mick would change into bathing suits and swim out to Mick's skiff to watch the fireworks from the placid waters of Frank Bay.

Ayers and Mick broke up in November, right after they returned to St. John from the summer season on Cape Cod. Mick, the longtime manager of the Beach Bar, had hired a girl named Brigid, who had no experience waiting tables.

Why on earth did you hire her, then? Ayers asked, but she figured it out in the next instant.

And sure enough, there followed days of Mick staying late to "train" the new hire, whom he later described to Ayers as "green" and "clueless" and "a deer in the headlights." On the third day of this training, Ayers climbed out of bed and drove down to the Beach Bar. It was two thirty in the morning and the town was deserted; the only vehicle anywhere near the bar was Mick's battered blue Jeep. Ayers tiptoed around the side of the building to see Brigid sitting up on the bar counter and Mick with his head between her legs.

Ayers hasn't been to the Beach Bar once since she and Mick split, and she certainly won't go tonight. She has bumped into Mick—alone, thankfully—once at Island Cork and once, incredibly, out in Coral Bay, at Pickles in Paradise, the place "they" always stopped to get sandwiches (one Sidewinder and one Sister's Garden, which "they" shared so "they" could each have half) before "they" went to the stone beach, Grootpan Bay, where "they" were always alone and hence could swim naked. Ayers had been stung to see Mick at the deli—he was picking up the Sidewinder, which was funny because she was picking up a Sister's Garden—and she could tell by the look on his face that he was stung to see *her.* They probably should have divided the island up—Pickles for her, Sam & Jack's for him—but St. John was small enough as it was.

Ayers has also seen Mick driving his blue Jeep with Brigid in the passenger seat—and worse, with Mick's dog, an AmStaff-pit bull mix, Gordon, standing in Brigid's lap. Gordon used to stand in Ayers's lap, but apparently Gordon was as fickle and easily fooled as his owner.

Tilda taps Ayers on the shoulder and hands her a shot glass of beer, which Ayers accepts gratefully.

"Thanks," Ayers says. "I need about forty of these." They click shot glasses and throw the beer back.

"Yeah, you do," Tilda says. "Because *look.*"

Ayers turns to see Mick and Brigid walking into La Tapa, hand in hand. Clover, the hostess, leads them over to Table 11, in Ayers's section.

"No," Ayers says. "Not happening. No way."

"I'll take them," Tilda says. "You can have Table 2. It's the Hesketts. You're welcome."

"Thank you," Ayers says. The Hesketts own a boutique hotel in Chocolate Hole called St. John Guest Suites; they're lovely people, with excellent taste in wine. It's a good trade, and very kind of Tilda, although a part of Ayers, of course, would like to wait on Mick and Brigid and dump some food—ideally the garlicky paella for two—right into Brigid's lap. She's wearing white.

What is Mick *thinking*? And why isn't he *working*? It's New Year's Eve, he's the manager of the Beach Bar, it will be mayhem down there, even now at a quarter to ten. How did he get the night off? The owners *never* give him holidays or weekends off. And why isn't *Brigid* working? Why did they choose La Tapa for dinner when they both knew Ayers would be here? Are they looking for trouble? Because if they are, they found it. Ayers's nostrils flare and she paws at the ground with one clog like an angry bull.

She steps into the alcove by the restroom, pulls out her phone, and texts Rosie. *Where are you? Please come save me. Mick and Brigid are here at La Tapa for second seating!*

A few seconds later, there's a photographic response—a table set for two with a bottle of Krug champagne in an ice bucket.

In the background is the Caribbean, scattered with pinpricks of light—boats heading over to Jost Van Dyke for the invitation-only Wheeland Brothers concert. It has been rumored that Kenny Chesney might sit in for a song or two.

Ayers studies the picture, trying to get an idea of where the Invisible Man's house is. Looks like somewhere near Cinnamon Bay. Rosie refuses to disclose exactly where the Invisible Man lives or even tell Ayers his name. He's very private, Rosie says. His business is sensitive. He travels a lot. Apparently the house is impossible to find. There are lots of places like that on St. John. Rosie stays with the Invisible Man when he's on-island, but otherwise she and her daughter, Maia, live with Rosie's stepfather, Huck, the fishing captain, who owns a house on Jacob's Ladder. It's a strange arrangement, nearly suspect, and yet Rosie seems content with the way things are. Once, after service, when Ayers and Rosie were drinking upstairs at the Quiet Mon, Rosie confided that the Invisible Man paid for all of Rosie and Maia's living expenses, including Maia's tuition at Gifft Hill School.

Ayers makes it her New Year's resolution to find out more about the Invisible Man—at the very least, to figure out where he lives.

She tucks her phone away and heads out to the floor to studiously ignore Mick and Brigid and to hear which fabulous wine the Hesketts are going to end their year with.

After her shift, Ayers greets the new year with a bottle of Schramsberg sparkling rosé, sitting on the west end of Oppenheimer Beach. Because of the wind, she can actually hear the music floating over from Jost. There's a group of West Indians down the beach, drinking on the porch of the community center. At midnight, they sing "Auld Lang Syne." Ayers texts Rosie. *Happy New Year, my friend. Xo.*

Rosie responds immediately. *Love you, my friend.*

At least Rosie loves her, Ayers thinks. That will have to be enough.

It's ten o'clock the next morning when there's a pounding on Ayers's door. She hears Mick's voice. "Ayers! Wake up! Open up! Ayers!"

She groans. Whatever he wants, she doesn't have time for it. He sounds upset. Maybe he got fired, maybe Brigid broke things off, maybe the new year brought the crystal-clear realization that the biggest mistake he ever made was letting his relationship with Ayers go up in smoke.

Ayers rises from the futon and staggers toward the front door. Her head feels like a broken plate. After the Schramsberg on the beach, there had been some shots of tequila here at home, as well as a forbidden cigarette (she quit two years ago but keeps a pack stashed on top of her refrigerator in case of emergency). She needs a gallon of very cold water and fifty Advil.

She swings open the door. There's Mick, with tears streaming down his face. The sight renders Ayers speechless. Mick is a douche bag. He doesn't cry. Ever.

"What?" she says, though it sounds like more of a croak.

"Rosie," Mick says. "Rosie is dead."

CASH: DENVER

After meeting with his accountant, Glenn, at Machete Tequila + Tacos, it becomes clear that Cash is going to lose not only the Cherry Creek store but the one in Belmar as well. All Cash can think is: *Thank God.*

Now he can go back to being a ski bum.

He hadn't really wanted to go into business in the first place, but he had grown tired of receiving envelopes in the mail from his father, with newspaper clippings meant to be encouraging and helpful about young men "just like you" who had stumbled across a way to turn their life's passions into income-generating ventures. Russ was also keen for Cash to "finish your education," and so sometimes the envelopes included advertisements for online college courses or the myriad offerings for nontraditional students at the University of Iowa. *You could live at home!* Russ wrote, and Cash would picture himself trapped with his parents in the suffocating ornateness of their Victorian house. Because Russ was so rarely home, Cash suspected that Russ's true motivation was to have Cash care for his mother and grandmother, chauffeur them to the Wig and Pen, play Bingo with Milly and the other extreme-elders at Brown Deer. No thank you. When Cash talked to his father on the phone, Russ would end each conversation by gently pointing out that sooner or later, Cash was going to need to think about health insurance, a retirement fund, having an infrastructure in place so he could start a family.

Like your brother.

Russ had never actually uttered this phrase, but Cash heard it as the subtext. Cash wanted to point out to his father that while Baker *used to* work the Chicago futures market, and while he *used to* make a ton of money, he now sits at home in Houston, day-trading in his boxer shorts and smoking more weed than Cash could ever hope to get his hands on in *Colorado,* where weed is *legal.* Baker only has two claims to actual legitimacy: He cares for his four-year-old son, Floyd (although Floyd goes to Montessori school every day from eight thirty to three), and he keeps house for his wife, Dr. Anna Schaffer, who has turned into a legitimate Houston superstar. She's the Olajuwon of the cardiothoracic surgery scene.

Cash lets Glenn, the accountant, pick up the tab for the four Cadillac margaritas and order of guac—fifty-seven bucks— and then the two men walk out to the parking lot together. Cash wonders if he will be able to keep his pickup with the name of the store—Savage Season Outdoor Supply—painted on the side. It's an eye-catching truck, made even more gorgeous with his golden retriever, Winnie, in the back.

He fears the truck will be repossessed, like the stores. The bank is coming in the morning. Right now, he needs to go to both stores and empty the registers. There is two hundred and forty-five dollars in the Cherry Creek store and a hundred and eighteen dollars in the Belmar store. This and Winnie are all Cash has left to his name.

He has a rental apartment on 18th Avenue in City Park West but he hasn't paid his rent for January so he envisions a middle-of-the-night pack up and escape to Breckenridge. Jay, who runs the ski school, will be thrilled to have Cash back. Unlike every other twenty-something kid in the Rocky Mountains, Cash knows how to ski as well as snowboard. This means Cash can teach the trophy-wives-of-tech-moguls who want a hot instructor way more than they want to make turns, and it also means huge tips from the moguls who want their ladies taken care of while they go ski the horseshoe bowl on Peak 8.

It's all going to work out, Cash thinks. Losing the stores is just a bump in the road.

As Cash turns onto Third Street, he puts both of the truck's windows down. Winnie automatically sticks her head out the passenger-side window and Cash sticks his head out the driver's side.

He's free!

No more standing behind the register selling Salomon boots to some Gen Z executive in from Manhattan who says he's heard hiking Mount Falcon is "lit," no more biting his tongue to keep from telling Executive Boy Wonder that he could hike Mount Falcon in the Gucci slides he came in wearing. No more worrying about inventory or deliveries or if Dylan, the kid Cash hired to "manage" the Belmar store, was filching from the register in order to pay his oxy dealer.

He's free!

His father will be *very disappointed.* Russ was Cash's only investor, and all of that money is now gone, with absolutely nothing to show for it; it's as though Cash has blown it all on a very expensive video game. Cash will have to call his father and tell him—before he finds out another way, such as an email from the bank. Any other father would be angry, but what Cash knows will happen is that Russ will tell Cash he's "let down," which is so much worse.

Cash will also have to hear from his brother, Baker. Baker didn't like it when Russ "handed" Cash the stores, and he predicted Cash would fail within two years. *Why doesn't Cash have to work for what he gets, like everyone else?* Baker had thundered when he'd found out what was happening. *He won't appreciate the opportunity he has unless he's earned it himself.* In essence, Cash had rolled his eyes at his older brother and chalked the rant up to jealousy. What he wished he'd confided to Baker was that he didn't *want* the stores. They weren't so much *handed to* him as *foisted upon* him by their overeager father. Now that Baker's prediction has come true—the stores are gone, Cash sunk them, and he feels little, if any, personal loss, because his sense of self wasn't vested—Cash will have to endure the inevitable *I told you so.*

Cash loves his brother, in theory. In practice, he can't stand the guy.

In a rare show of courage—probably fueled by the Cadillac margaritas—Cash picks up his phone and dials his father's number. It's eight thirty here, nine thirty at home, ten thirty on the East Coast. Cash isn't sure where his father is this week, but he hopes the late hour works in his favor. His father likes to have a bourbon or two most nights. He hopes that it's one of those nights, and that Russ's mood is buoyant and he and

Cash can laugh off the train wreck of two stores and a two-hundred-thousand-dollar investment as a valuable learning experience.

The call goes to voicemail. Cash experiences a rush of relief that leaves him dizzy.

A few seconds later, his phone lights up and the relief quickly turns to dread. Then relief again when Cash sees that it's not his father calling back. It's his mother.

His mother! Cash hates reverting to the behaviors of his adolescence, but he decides in that instant that he will tell his mother about the stores going under and he will let Irene tell Russ. He can even tell Irene *not* to tell Russ — he can pretend he wants to break the news to Russ himself, but Irene won't be able to help herself. Those two are typical parents; they tell each other everything.

"What's good, Mama?" Cash says. "Happy New Year."

"Cash," Irene says, "where are you?"

Something is wrong with her voice. It sounds like she's being strangled.

"I'm pulling into my driveway," he says. "Just me and Winnie." Now is not the time to explain that he's going to pack up all of his worldly belongings and head for the mountains; somehow, he senses this.

"Cash," Irene says.

"Yes, Mom."

"Your father is dead."

Cash's first thought is: *I don't have to tell him about the stores.* Then, the cold, sick meaning of the words hit him. His father is dead.

Dead.

But . . . what?

"What are you talking about?" Cash says. "What do you mean?"

"There was an accident," Irene says. "A helicopter crash, in the Virgin Islands..."

"The Virgin *Islands*?" Cash says. He's confused. Are the Virgin Islands even a real place? He thinks they *are* real, but they sound fake and he would have a hard time finding them on a map. Are they in the Caribbean, or farther south, like the Falklands? And what do the Virgin Islands, wherever they are, have to do with his father?

A *helicopter* crash? No, there's been a mistake.

"St. John, in the Virgin Islands," Irene says, and her voice is full-on quavering now. Cash shuts the engine of his truck off and releases a long, slow stream of air. Winnie lays her head in Cash's lap. It's amazing how much dogs understand. Cash has seen and heard his mother cry on plenty of occasions—all of them happy, every tear a tear of joy and wonder. She cried when Baker and Cash graduated from high school, when Baker and Anna had Floyd, she cried every Christmas Eve when the church choir launched into "O Come, All Ye Faithful." But Irene Hagen Steele didn't cry over disappointment, or even death. When her parents died, Irene handled it with a solid midwestern pragmatism. Circle of life and all that. She arranged for proper Lutheran funerals and covered dish receptions afterward. She didn't cry.

This, of course, is something else entirely.

"St. John," Cash repeats. "In the Virgin Islands."

"Your father was in a helicopter crash," Irene says. "It crashed into the sea. Three people were on board: your father, the pilot, and a local woman."

"Who *told* you this?" Cash asks.

"Todd Croft's secretary, Marilyn," Irene says. "Todd Croft, your father's boss."

"Was Dad in the Virgin Islands *working*?" Cash asks. The exact details of his father's career have been hazy ever since he switched jobs. When Cash was young, Russ worked as a salesman for the Corn Refiners Association. Then, when Cash entered high school, Russ got a different job, a much betterpaying job working for Todd Croft, who owned a boutique investment firm, Ascension, that catered to high-end clients— international soccer stars and the like, though when Cash asked *which* soccer stars, Russ claimed he wasn't at liberty to say. Russ's job was to keep the clients happy, do interface, provide a personal touch, whatever that meant. All Cash knows for sure is that they went from being the middlest of middle class to people who had money. "Having money" meant Irene could buy and renovate her dream house; it meant no college loans; it meant Russ had seed money for Cash's doomed business venture.

"I'm not sure," Irene says. "Todd's secretary, Marilyn, told me your father has a 'concern' there. She told me your father owns *property* there."

"Property?" Cash says. "Does Baker know about this?"

"I haven't talked to Baker yet," Irene says. "I called you first."

Right, Cash thinks. Their family, like every family, has its allegiances. It's Irene and Cash on one side and Russ and Baker on the other. Irene called Cash first because they're closer—and also because she fears Anna, Baker's wife.

"Maybe Baker knows what Dad was doing in the Virgin Islands?" Cash says. His father is dead. Could this possibly be *true*? His father was in a *helicopter crash*?

"I have to fly down there," Irene says. "I can't get there tomorrow. I'm leaving Thursday morning out of Chicago. I'm not sure what to do about your grandmother. This will kill her."

Cash does some quick mental calculating. It's an eleven-hour drive from Denver to Iowa City. If Cash grabs his things from the apartment and the money from both stores, he'll be on 76 by ten o'clock. Even with stops, he should be pulling into his parents' driveway before noon.

"I'm going with you," Cash says. "I'll be at your house tomorrow and I'm going down there with you."

"But how can you get away?" Irene asks. "The stores…"

"Mom," Cash says. "Mom?"

"Yes," she says.

"Call Baker," Cash says. "But don't tell anyone else about this yet. Don't call Grammie. I'll be there tomorrow. I'll help you. I'm on my way."

HUCK: ST. JOHN

Any day on St. John is better than a holiday, if you ask Captain Sam Powers, known to one and all as "Huck." Huck's first mate, Adam, is twenty-seven years old, and all he can talk about on their December 31st afternoon fishing charter (a couple from Albany, New York, and their college-aged daughter, who hasn't been off her phone since getting on the boat) is how he can't wait to go to Drink for the big party that night.

They have a ball drop and snow, and everyone is served drinks in real glasses instead of plastic cups.

"You should come with me," Adam says to the college-aged daughter. (Maybe she's older, Huck can't tell, but he thought he was clear with Adam: pursue girls who show an interest in fishing! This girl, who is scrolling through her Instaface account, is attractive, sure, but she doesn't even seem to realize she's out on the water, for Pete's sake. If it were up to Huck, he'd turn around and take her back to the dock.)

The girl raises her eyes to look at Adam, who is elbow-deep in a bucket of squid, baiting the trolling lines. "Ah-ight," she says.

Is that even a word? Huck wonders.

"Yeah?" Adam says. "You'll go? It won't get good until about ten, but we should plan to arrive around eight, eight thirty."

"We have a dinner reservation at eight in Coral Bay," the girl's mother says. The mother is attractive as well, but she isn't interested in fishing either. She brought a book—something called *Lilac Girls.* Huck isn't against books on his boat; in fact, there was a period of time when he believed that a person reading brought the fish. Huck likes to read himself, though never on the boat, but at home in his hammock, yes. When LeeAnn was alive, she got him hooked on Carl Hiaasen, and from there it was an easy jump to Elmore Leonard and Michael Connelly. Rosie is always telling him he should try some *female* writers, and he promised her he would read anything she put into his hands, as long as it didn't have the word *girl* in the title. *Gone Girl, Girl on the Train*—and now look, *Lilac Girls.* The mother—Huck has forgotten her name; he only retains the names of people interested in fishing—seems pretty engrossed, however.

"Dinner reservation?" Dan, the father, says. Dan is a name Huck remembers because Dan wants to catch fish and Dan is paying for the trip. Dan works for the state government of New York—Huck shudders just thinking about it—but he is now on his Caribbean vacation and he wants to catch a fish, preferably a wahoo or a mahi. Huck assured Dan that would happen even though he's been experiencing something of a dry spell. He hasn't had a decent haul since the high season started.

Huck has decided to stay inshore—one look at the mother and daughter told him they would *not* be up for the forty-minute ride south to blue water—so wahoo and mahi are out of the question.

"Yes," the mother says. "We have an eight o'clock reservation at Shipwreck Landing."

"Good place," Huck says.

"But I want to catch a fish and grill it up," Dan says. "That's what we agreed on."

The wife shrugs. "If you catch a fish big enough to feed the three of us, I'll cancel."

"Count me out," the daughter says. "I want to go to the party."

Huck will have to reprimand Adam for starting this mess. He doesn't get involved in other people's family drama. He focuses all of his emotional energy on his own girls—LeeAnn's daughter, Rosie, and Rosie's daughter, Maia. Maia, at age twelve, probably qualifies as Huck's favorite person in the world.

Now there's a girl who loves to fish.

Huck's mind wanders as it tends to when he's captaining his boat, *The Mississippi*. People always ask if he's from Hannibal or Natchez, St. Louis or New Orleans, but the answer is no. Huck's nickname was given to him his first week in St. John, twenty years earlier at the bar at Skinny Legs, by a West Indian fella named Rupert, who is now Huck's best friend. Rupert saw Huck's strawberry-blond hair and the nickname fit somehow. Rupert hooked him up with a boat for sale — a twenty-six-foot Regulator — that had been bought by a kid on the island who lost his shirt gambling in Puerto Rico and needed to sell it quick for cheap. The boat had been named *Lady Luck*, but Huck changed it immediately to *The Mississippi* to match his new identity.

Who wants to drink from real glasses? Huck wonders. He can do that at home. His favorite thing about this island is that it's a barefoot, casual place; there isn't a pretentious thing about it. After a full-day charter, Huck likes to hit Joe's Rum Hut for happy hour — he gets a planters punch or the local beer — and he wanders to the waterline of Frank Bay for a cigarette, then he heads down to Beach Bar with his drink and he's allowed to finish it there before he buys his next drink. He knows everyone and everyone knows him: Huck, captain of *The Mississippi*. It doesn't matter that he hasn't had a decent catch since Halloween. He always has clients because he's connected. And he also happens to know what he's doing.

Huck will spend tonight with Maia because the Invisible Man is on-island. Sometimes, when the Invisible Man is here, Maia will go along with her mother, but tonight is New Year's Eve. The Invisible Man hasn't been here for New Year's Eve in four years, and so Rosie planned a special night of champagne and romance.

Fine. Huck can think of no better person to ring the new year in with than Maia. Huck will stop by Candi's on the way home and pick up some barbecue.

He anchors the boat at the edge of Mandal Bay, off the north coast of St. Thomas, and helps Adam bait the hooks. The air has been crystalline since Christmas, and today there isn't a cloud to be seen. The sky is a deep, painterly blue. There are supposed to be thunderstorms tomorrow morning but there's no sign of them now.

"Who's casting?" Huck asks. Dan already has his rod at the ready. Mrs. Dan is reading, and the daughter is on her phone. Huck looks between the two of them. Nothing.

Hey, Huck wants to say. *You're in the Caribbean! Look at the string of palm trees backing that platinum beach over there. Look how clear the water is. Days don't get any more picturesque than this. Now, let's catch some fish.*

Adam taps the girl's shoulder. "You want to try? I can cast it for you."

"No, thanks," she says. She does manage to tear her eyes off her screen long enough to offer him a smile. "This is my dad's thing."

How can Adam possibly want to take this girl on a date? Huck wonders. He doesn't bother asking the wife if she wants to fish. He just casts the line himself.

New Year's Eve doesn't change his luck. Dan catches two blue runners and a hardnose. He's getting visibly discouraged; he's a hunter with a family to feed. Then, blessedly, he reels in a small blackfin tuna, which will be at least enough for him and

Mrs. Dan. This does double duty of making Dan feel like a success and getting the daughter off the hook for dinner.

"Everyone happy?" Huck asks. He doesn't wait for an answer. "Okay, let's head back in."

The town of Cruz Bay is more frenetic than usual. People are flooding the streets, plastic cups in hand, wearing shiny hats and feather boas; women are in black velvet dresses even though it's eighty-one degrees. Huck couldn't be happier to get in his truck, stop by Candi's for one order of ribs and one of chicken, extra comeback sauce, one side of pasta salad, one of slaw and one of plantains, then coax his aging truck up the series of switchbacks that comprise Jacob's Ladder.

"Come on, chipmunks," he says, as his engine growls in its lowest gear. He started saying this to amuse Maia when she was little—she loved thinking about a pair of little furry animals eagerly powering the engine of Huck's truck—and now when he says it out of habit, Maia rolls her eyes.

Maia is standing in the driveway wearing denim shorts that she made herself the old-fashioned way—by taking scissors to a perfectly good pair of jeans—and a gray t-shirt on which she painted what Huck refers to as an iguana on acid: the bugger is a swirl of seventeen different colors. Maia's hair is out of its cornrows in a bushy ponytail, which is how Huck likes it best. She must be 99 percent her father, whom Huck has never had the pleasure of meeting, but she was gifted with the milk-chocolate eyes of Huck's late wife, LeeAnn, which is another reason why Maia is Huck's favorite and basically can do no wrong.

"Hey, Nut," he says. "Nut" is short for "Peanut," which refers to a birthmark Maia has on her shoulder. She still tolerates the name, though maybe not for much longer. "Joanie went home?"

"Yes, but I was invited there overnight," Maia says. "I texted but you didn't answer. Drive me?" He can see the uncertainty on her face. She knows that they had plans and that she's now breaking them to go to Joanie's. What she doesn't know is whether he's going to be relieved about this change of plans—because he wants to drink some beers and fall asleep in his hammock long before midnight—or upset, maybe even angry.

She's getting older, Huck thinks. Her legs are long but still as straight as sticks; she remains a little girl for the time being. Anyone with one good eye can see what's coming down the road: bras, boyfriends, broken hearts, bad decisions, maybe not quite as bad as the ones her mother has made, he hopes.

Joanie is a good kid with nice parents. Both the mother and father are marine biologists who work for the National Park Service. They are avid hikers, naturalists, vegans. Huck can't imagine what they're having for dinner, but whatever it is, Maia will be wishing she stayed home for ribs and chicken.

He nods at his passenger seat. "Let's go," he says.

LeeAnn believed that everything happens for a reason, a theory that Huck only half agrees with, because some moments in this life seem random and senseless.

But he is very, very happy that Maia is at Joanie's house the next morning.

* * *

Huck spends his New Year's Eve eating both the ribs and the chicken and drinking a cold six-pack of Island Hoppin' IPA, then wandering down the street to have one drink with the neighbors, a local family made up of Benjamins and Singers—they're having a full-on shindig with a roast pig and home-made moonshine. Huck gets a good tip from Cleve Benjamin: there has been a school of mahi hanging six miles offshore, in the same place for the past three days. Cleve has the coordinates written in his phone; he shares them with Huck.

"There's enough fish in that spot to fill your freezer chest until *next* Christmas," Cleve says.

Huck is grateful for the information and feels lucky to be trusted and liked by his West Indian neighbors. He's accepted because he was married to LeeAnn—some of these folks grew up with LeeAnn out in Coral Bay, others knew her from church or worked with her at the Myrah Keating Smith Community Health Center, still others are distantly related to her first husband (Rosie's father), Levi Small, who left the island long ago and has never come back.

Huck wanders home and takes his last long look of the year over Great Cruz Bay; he can hear music wafting up from the Westin below. Then he goes inside and falls asleep.

He intends to sleep in but is awakened at seven by the fore-casted thunderstorm, and then he can't go back to sleep, so he gets out of bed and fixes himself a New Year's breakfast of hash—made from potatoes, onions, peppers, and some of the leftover barbecued chicken—and throws two fried eggs on top. He reads his book, *The Late Show,* by Connelly. He stops every few pages to wonder about the wife from yesterday—if she enjoyed the fish or if Dan cooked it for too long and ruined it. Huck then wonders about Adam and the daughter. Did they have fun at Drink? Did Adam get lucky? Or did the girl have too much champagne, as most amateurs do on the final night of the year, and spend her night crying or puking? Huck bets on the latter.

He is having a cigarette on the front porch when the police pull up. He thinks for a second it's about Adam. But they ask him to go inside and then they tell him: there was a helicopter crash early that morning in the waters north of Virgin Gorda.

Rosie is dead.

BAKER: HOUSTON, TEXAS

Anna makes two New Year's resolutions: She's going to spend more time at home with Baker and Floyd, and she's going to become friends with at least one of the other mothers at Floyd's Montessori school, the Children's Cottage. She hands Baker a page from her prescription pad (Dr. Anna Schaffer, MD) with the two goals written down.

1. More time at home
2. Friends

Baker finds he has follow-up questions. Does "more time at home" mean she'll have sex with him on days other than his birthday and their anniversary? Does "making friends" mean that some of the "at home" time will be spent on "girls' night out," or in long phone conversations listening to Delia, mother of Sophie, air her grievances against Mandy, mother of Aidan?

Baker folds the paper in half, kisses it, and puts it in his jeans pocket. It's appropriate that Anna wrote her resolutions on the prescription pad, because their relationship is sick. These two actions will heal it, he hopes. "Good for you," he says. "What should we do today?"

A look of panic crosses Anna's face. She's a beautiful woman, with flawless olive skin; she has impenetrable brown eyes and long dark hair. She exudes serenity and, beyond that, competence. She's a natural-born perfectionist, at least when it comes to cardiothoracic surgery. It's only her personal life that she has trouble navigating.

"Today?" she says. She checks her phone. "I have to go to the hospital."

"It's New Year's Day," Baker says.

"It's *Tuesday,*" she says. "I have rounds."

"But...," Baker says, waving the page from her prescription pad in the air.

"Am I supposed to tell Mr. Kavetsky, who just had a triple bypass, that I can't check on him because I have to...what? Do a gouache project with my husband and four-year-old? Watch *Despicable Me 3* yet *again?*"

"You haven't even seen it *once!*" Baker says. His voice is defiant, verging on bratty. *He* sounds like a four-year-old. But come *on*! For Anna to represent herself as someone who is routinely subjected to children's movies is downright unfair. She *never* watches movies with Floyd; she hasn't seen *Despicable Me 3*—or numbers one and two, for that matter. On the rare occasion she does sit down with Baker and Floyd to watch a movie, she falls asleep in the comfy womb of the leather gel recliner, leaving Baker to answer Floyd's rapid-fire questions about the intricacies of character and plot. Floyd, like his mother, has a finely tuned intellect, but it's as if after physically giving birth to Floyd, after donating the genius half of his DNA, Anna decided her job was done. First, she turned the care and feeding of Floyd over to a baby nurse for the staggering fee of three hundred fifty dollars a day, and then, when Anna was done "breastfeeding"—she nearly always pumped milk, was a fiend about it, in fact, insisting that it was much more "efficient" than latching Floyd onto her actual body when he was going to switch to the bottle eventually anyway— they hired Maria José, a nanny from El Salvador. Maria José and Anna didn't see eye to eye (Maria José held Floyd all day long, and in the evenings, when Anna came home from the hospital, Floyd was set down, and he would cry)—and so Maria José was dismissed.

Then Anna hired Svana, from Iceland, who drew Floyd a bath that was too hot and scalded him the color of a lobster, necessitating a trip to urgent care. Good-bye, Svana. At that point, Baker was looking for a job in private equity, but he kept getting to final interviews and not getting hired—he suspected that Houston firms tended to hire Texas boys, especially those who had played high school football—and since Anna's career provided plenty of money, Baker thought, why didn't *he* stay home and care for Floyd? He could day-trade while Floyd napped. Day-trading encapsulated everything he loved about his field—it was a game, a gamble, a risk, a thrill—and he was good at it. He was also good at parenting. The love and joy and wonder he felt when he looked at tiny baby Floyd—a person, another *person,* he had helped create— was nearly overwhelming. Why would he pay someone else to care for their child when he could do it himself?

Anna had put up the predictable arguments: Staying home with Floyd wouldn't provide Baker with any intellectual stimulation. *You'll be bored stiff,* she said. He would be like the unfulfilled housewives of the 1950s. He would choose something inappropriate to fill his time—internet porn or marijuana, or an affair with one of the mothers he met at the playground. He would get so far behind in his career that he would never catch up. What would Baker do when Floyd was eighteen and headed to college? Even three years hence, when Floyd went to preschool, too much time would have passed for Baker to seamlessly reenter the world of high finance. He would become depressed, smoke more weed than he already did, get addicted to pills.

Baker had assured Anna at the time that she was being melodramatic. But now Floyd is four years old, and while he is a very bright, curious, and well-adjusted kid, it's true that Baker's decision to stay home has created issues. First of all, Anna has grown so comfortable with their new roles that she has nearly checked out of family life altogether. Secondly, whereas Baker has *not* become addicted to internet porn or had an affair, he does smoke a fair amount of dope, and he has developed very close friendships with a group of mothers, all of whom have sons and daughters at the Children's Cottage. His clique includes Wendy, Becky, Debbie, and Ellen. They are all

single mothers—three divorced and one single by choice—
which is how they became friends in the first place. They have
more or less adopted Baker as their "school husband." He cov-
ers their kids when they have work emergencies, he fixes things
around their houses, and he gives them free investment advice.
He suspects that the other mothers—the married mothers—
are critical of the relationship between Baker and his school
wives, but it wasn't until the Holiday Sing that he realized just
how jealous and vile women could be. One of them cornered
Anna in the bathroom and told her she was very "evolved" for
letting Baker have a "harem."

Anna had not been amused. Baker assured her the friendships were just that and not one thing more. He informed
Anna that if she wanted to put an end to the vicious gossip, she
should show her face around school more often. She should
make some friends of her own, which was how she arrived at
Resolution Number Two.

"Why can't someone else cover your rounds?" Baker asks
now. "Why can't Louisa do it?" Louisa is another surgeon in
the practice, Anna's closest friend. It feels like Anna is forever
going in to cover *Louisa's* patients; surely Anna is due a return
favor?

"Louisa is busy," Anna snaps. "We're all busy."

"I won't make you do gouache," Baker says. It's a very cool
painting technique that Wendy taught him; she makes her
own greeting cards and wrapping paper. "Or watch *Despicable
Me 3*. I thought we could go to the park. It's beautiful out..."

"I'm sure Floyd will love it," Anna says. She grabs her bag
and smiles. Smiles are what pass for kisses these days. "I'll be
home by six. We can get pizza!" She says this, apparently not
recalling that Baker has bought a roast he'd planned to serve

with Boursin potatoes and sautéed asparagus. Anna isn't impressed by Baker's efforts in the kitchen. In her world, each dawning day is merely another chance to eat pizza.

"Okay," Baker says. He watches Anna's back disappear through the door—and at that moment, he knows he has no choice. He has to ask for a divorce.

Divorce, he thinks as he waits at the bottom of the big slide for Floyd. It's such a dark, ugly, complicated word.

Floyd comes whooshing down, his bangs flying. He's such a *good* kid, so cute and perfect in his boyness. "That was my tenth time down," Floyd says. "Let's go to the swings."

Always ten times down the slide, no more, no less, and slide always precedes swings, where Baker is allowed to push Floyd seven times—then Floyd takes over under the power of his own pumping legs. Baker senses some OCD tendencies in the rules Floyd sticks to at the park, although the jungle gym is a free-for-all and Floyd is very sociable and can make friends with other children in an instant, as he does today. When he's finished on the swings, he joins a game of tag, leaving Baker to lie back in the grass and let the mellow January sunshine warm his face.

Divorce.

Divorce Anna.

Will she even *notice*? She'll move out and rent one of the condos across the street from the hospital. She'll have no problem paying for the house and for Baker and for Floyd. Baker has a tidy sum in the bank as well; his luck this past year playing the market has been tremendous. All will be well. Baker's only concern is that Anna will *never* see Floyd if they don't live in the same house. And yet isn't that exactly why Baker should get out? What kind of mother doesn't love her own child? That may be too harsh. Certainly Anna *loves* Floyd. But does she *like* him? Does she enjoy one single thing about being a parent?

Baker sits up on his elbows and watches Floyd, running and laughing, right in the thick of it with a bunch of kids he just met. He's so happy and carefree. Can Baker really be considering putting the kid through the emotional trauma of a divorce? Anna's parents are divorced. Her father has been divorced *twice*. And so that is her idea of normal. But Baker's parents have been happily married for thirty-five years. Baker knows that Irene and Russ will see his divorce as a failure. *He* will see it as a failure.

It's a new year, Baker thinks. And Anna *did* make the resolutions, which is a promising start.

He'll give it more time, he decides. Maybe she'll surprise him.

Anna doesn't make it home by six, although she does call. "I'm going to be another hour," she says. "Just order the pizza without me."

Does she ever get tired of disappointing people? Baker wonders.

"Will do," he says. He won't order pizza, but neither will he go to the trouble of making the roast. Floyd has asked for pancakes for dinner, and pancakes he will get. Baker makes bacon and squeezes some fresh juice. Why not?

"Would you mind staying awake until I get home?" Anna asks. She sounds almost nervous, and Baker gets a flutter of excitement in his stomach.

"Absolutely," he says.

That simple question changes the whole tenor of the evening. Anna wants him to stay awake. She wants to spend time with him. She wants to…connect, maybe. He'll give her a massage, he'll draw her a bath, he'll wash her hair, he'll do anything she wants. He loves her so much. At times, it's like loving a shadow or a hologram. But not tonight.

Baker makes big, fluffy buttermilk pancakes and crispy bacon, and he gives Floyd two cups of juice, even though that's a lot of sugar before bed. He cleans the kitchen, does the dishes, sends Floyd down the hall to brush his teeth. He helps Floyd get into his pajamas and starts reading him *The Dirty Cowboy.* It's a long book, and Floyd falls asleep on page six, as he always does. Baker eases himself off the bed, turns on the night-light, and slips out of the room.

This is the time of night when he usually takes a few hits off his bong, but he won't tonight. He needs to stay awake!

He cracks open a beer, gets himself a bowl of Ben & Jerry's Red Velvet Cake ice cream—which his single-by-choice mom-friend Ellen turned him on to (she eats "like a long-haul trucker," in her own words)—and switches on the TV to get a recap of the bowl games. He's…just drifting off when he hears Anna coming through the door. He sits bolt upright. He's awake!

"Hey, babe," he says. "I'm in here."

He hears Anna in the kitchen, rummaging through the fridge, opening the cabinets. He hears a cork being pulled from wine. A few seconds later, Anna comes into the den. She lets her hair free of her elastic, takes a sip of wine, and regards him with an expression he can't read. Interest? Curiosity? *What does she see when she looks at him?* he wonders. Well, he's slouched on the sofa with an open beer and half a bowl of melted ice cream on the table next to him, so she can hardly view him as a sexy world conqueror.

He sits up straight, moves over, pats the sofa next to him. He is soft with forgiveness. It's as easy for him to fall into his chubby-hubby stoner-dad role as it is for Anna to default to her super-busy achieving spouse. He's guilty of smoking a joint and falling asleep on the sofa most nights. He's as much to blame for their disconnect as she is.

She reaches for the remote and shuts off the TV. In the six years of their marriage, eight years together, Baker has never known Anna to watch a single minute of television.

"How was work?" Baker asks.

"I'm leaving you," Anna says.

"What?"

"I'm in love with someone else," Anna says. "And it's beyond my control so I'm not going to bother apologizing for it."

"Oh," Baker says. "Okay." He looks at his wife. With her hair down and loose, she is at her most beautiful, which he feels is unfair, given the circumstances. But then, too, Baker experiences a strange sense of inevitability. He knew this was coming, didn't he? Earlier today, when he had thought about divorce, when he had all but decided on it, in fact, it was because he *knew* this was coming. Anna doesn't love him. She loves someone else. But who? Who is it?

"Who?" Baker says. "Who is it?"

"Louisa," Anna says. "I'm in love with Louisa."

She's in love with Louisa.

Anna doesn't bother giving him time to process, to react, to emote. No. She takes her wine and leaves the room.

Baker sinks back into the Baker-shaped and -sized divot on the couch. His phone rings. It's his mother.

His mother? No. He can't possibly speak to his mother right now. Briefly, he wonders if Anna called his parents to inform them she was leaving him, then decides the answer is no. Anna and his mother don't have a relationship. And Russ once naively referred to Anna as a "smart cookie," and Anna hasn't spoken to him since.

The house phone rings and Baker wonders who on earth would be calling the house phone at ten o'clock on New Year's night. The ringing stops. Anna calls down the hall. "Bake? It's your mom."

This is not happening, Baker thinks. Now he has to get on the phone and make at least sixty seconds of pleasant conversation without letting his mother know that his life is dissolving like an aspirin in acid. His wife is in love with her esteemed colleague, Louisa!

"Hey, Mom," Baker says, picking up the phone in the kitchen. He hears Anna hang up. "Happy New Year."

"Baker," Irene says. She's crying. So obviously Anna *did* tell her.

"Mom, listen…" Baker scrambles for a way to talk Irene off the ledge. She was born and raised in Iowa. She's the editor of *Heartland Home & Style.* Do they even *have* lesbians in the heartland? Baker doesn't mean to be a wise guy—he obviously knows the answer is yes, and Irene and Russ live in Iowa

City, which is pretty much the People's Republic of Iowa, but even so, he worries this is really going to upset her. Confuse her. She's going to ask *why* Anna turned into a lesbian. She's going to ask if it's Baker's fault.

"Baker," Irene says. "There was an accident. Your father is dead."

PART TWO

Little Cinnamon

IRENE

She wrote down everything Marilyn Monroe told her. There was a helicopter crash. Russ and a local woman and the pilot left from a private helipad at seven o'clock in the morning on Tuesday, January first. There had been a thunderstorm; the helicopter was struck and it went down somewhere between Virgin Gorda and Anegada. Anegada had been the apparent destination, Marilyn said. The helicopter wreckage had been recovered, as well as the three bodies.

"Mr. Steele's property manager traveled to the British Virgin Islands to identify the body," Marilyn said. "And Mr. Croft has arranged for cremation."

"Wait," Irene said. "What?" She knew that Russ wanted to be cremated, it's what they both wanted, but did this mean...? "Am I not going to *see* him again, then, before...?"

"I'm sorry, Mrs. Steele," Marilyn said. "You're going to have to trust Mr. Croft's judgment on this. The body needed to be identified as soon as possible, so Mr. Croft requested that Mr. Steele's property manager do it. Time was of the essence, and a decision had to be made."

"I don't understand!" Irene said. "Shouldn't *I* have been

the one to make the decision? I'm his wife. Who is this so-called property manager? What does that even mean? I don't understand!"

"I know this is coming as a shock," Marilyn said. "Beyond a shock. Again, you'll just have to trust that Mr. Croft took the appropriate measures."

Trust Todd Croft? He was a man Irene had met briefly only once, a man who had controlled their lives for thirteen years. And it wasn't even Todd himself telling Irene that Russ had died in a helicopter crash between Virgin Gorda and someplace else, a place Irene had never heard of, but, rather, his secretary, Marilyn Monroe. It was like a joke, a prank, a bad dream. Irene had gone so far as to pinch the soft skin on the underside of her wrist, hard, to make sure she was awake and cogent; that Ryan, their handsome server, hadn't slipped something into the Cakebread chardonnay earlier.

Marilyn was telling Irene that some "property manager" had ID'd the body and that Todd Croft had given the okay to cremate it. Time was of the essence and Irene would never see her husband again. "Why was Russ in the Virgin Islands?" Irene asked. "He never once mentioned the Virgin Islands. Was he there for work?"

"He had concerns there," Marilyn said. "He owned a home there."

"A home?" Irene said. "My husband did *not* own a home in the Virgin Islands. I would obviously know if he owned a home. I'm his *wife*."

"I'm very sorry," Marilyn said. She paused. "Mr. Steele owns a villa on St. John."

"A villa?"

"Yes," Marilyn said. "If you have a pen and paper, I can give you the specifics…"

"Pen and *paper*?" Irene said. "I'm flying down there."

"That's not advisable…," Marilyn said.

"You can't stop me," Irene said. "Russ was my *husband*. I've lost my *husband*." Does this secretary, Marilyn Monroe, *understand*? Irene briefly, fancifully, thinks about the husbands of the real Marilyn Monroe. Arthur Miller. Joe DiMaggio. Someone else. "I'm going down there to see about this so-called home. Because, frankly, this all sounds suspicious. Are you sure we're talking about Russell Steele, of Iowa City, Iowa? Originally from…" Where was Russ born? She can't remember. "Are you *sure*?"

"Mrs. Steele," Marilyn said. Her tone of voice made it sound like Irene was being unreasonable. "There's a woman who will meet you at the ferry if you insist on making the trip. Her name is Paulette Vickers. Her number is 340-555-6121. She'll take you to Mr. Steele's villa."

Irene's head was spinning. She had drunk too much of the Cakebread chardonnay. Dinner at the Pullman with Lydia, Brandon the barista at Prairie Lights—all of that now seemed to belong to a different life.

"I'm very sorry, Irene," Marilyn Monroe said, more gently now, and then she hung up.

Cash arrives at noon the next day. Irene wakes up sprawled across the purple velvet fainting couch in her clothes, Winnie licking her face. She languishes in the warm, wet love of her son's dog before she comes to full consciousness. Slowly she opens her eyes and sees Cash's expression, and she remembers.

Russ is dead. Helicopter crash. West Indian woman, a local, dead, and the pilot also dead. Villa. On a scrap of paper on the coffee table is the phone number of someone named Paulette. Also on the paper is Irene's flight information.

Cash has always been a free spirit, but he does a remarkably good job of taking charge. First, he sits next to Irene on the fainting couch and holds both her hands in his. He's expecting her to cry. She keeps expecting herself to cry, to gush like a dam breaking—her husband of thirty-five years is dead!— but nothing comes. She doesn't believe it. It makes no sense. There's been a mistake. Russ is in the Virgin Islands and went on a helicopter ride to an island no one has ever heard of with a local woman? And what did Marilyn Monroe say about a villa? What *is* a villa, exactly? Irene pictures a vacation home, a tropical vacation home. Marilyn had called it *Mr. Steele's home.* Which makes no sense. Russ's home is here, on Church Street. He and Irene talked about buying someplace up in Door County once Milly passed so that they could have the boys and their families come visit. Irene had pictured waterskiing, trout fishing, big family dinners around a harvest table, lighting sparklers out on the porch while they listened to the loons. She envisioned a silvered, aging version of her and Russ, side by side in rocking chairs. But that image implodes like a star.

"Milly," Irene says. They need to tell Milly.

"Not yet," Cash says. "First we're going to worry about

you." He looks at the paper on the coffee table. "These are your flights? You booked these?"

Irene nods. She booked the flights last night, although it now seems like a dream. Making plane reservations to St. Thomas has no basis in Irene's reality. (She had discovered that she couldn't fly to St. John, because St. John has no airport. Private helipads, yes, but no commercial airport. She had to take a ferry from St. Thomas.) And yet she had done it. She flew Chicago to Atlanta, and then Atlanta to St. Thomas, on Delta. She has booked herself coming back a week later, and that seems surreal. Who would Irene *be* after a week in St. John, collecting her husband's remains? Because she certainly can't do it and stay the same person she is now.

"I booked them," she says. "I have to be in Chicago tomorrow by nine."

"I'll drive," Cash says. "I'm going to book myself on the flight as well. Myself and Winnie. And I'll tell Baker to meet us in Atlanta."

"With Floyd?" Irene asks.

"No, Floyd has school. He's staying home with Anna. It'll be just you, me, and Baker. And Winnie."

Irene nods. There are so many things to think about, but none come to mind. "This woman, Paulette, is supposed to pick us up. Would you call her and let her know we're coming?"

"I will," Cash says. "I'm going to bring you ice water and aspirin. I'm going to make coffee. Can you handle toast?"

"I cannot handle toast," Irene says. She takes a deep breath and looks around the impeccably furnished amethyst parlor. How many hours did she slave over this room, this house? For the past six years, she has been married to this house. Russ came second; he used to joke about it. When she was in a good mood, she told him she was feathering their love nest. When she was in a bad mood, she told him he was never home anyway, so what did it matter if she was preoccupied?

Only now does she realize how little attention she actually paid him—the particulars of his work, where he was and what he did. When she talked to him on Monday afternoon, what had he said? He had a dinner meeting with clients. He wasn't sure if he would be able to stay up until midnight. He loved her.

Had he been *lying*?

Russ's villa. The Virgin Islands. A local woman.

Yes, he'd been lying.

When Cash comes back in with Irene's coffee, she says, "I haven't told anyone except you and Baker."

"Good," Cash says.

"I haven't told my friends. I haven't told work. I haven't told Milly. What am I going to tell Milly?"

"Let's do this," Cash says. "I'll call the magazine and tell them there's been a family emergency and that you'll be out the next week or so."

Irene nods. Work is the least of her worries, because, of course, she has just been demoted. The magazine will be fine without her. She doesn't care about the magazine. She doesn't care about anything except…this. This. Russ, he's gone.

"We can't tell Milly," Cash says.

"We can't *not* tell Milly," Irene says.

"Let's tell her together when we get back," Cash says. "We can't tell her and then leave."

"That's right," Irene says. "We can't tell her and then leave."

"Call her tonight, as usual," Cash says. "Tell her we're taking a surprise vacation."

A surprise vacation, Irene thinks.

* * *

It's a blur, all a blur, until the plane lands in St. Thomas and the other passengers erupt in applause.

Irene peers out the window. St. Thomas has verdant hills — green and lush, dotted with brightly colored buildings, yellow and pink, the color of sand, the color of shells. The water is... well, it's the brilliant turquoise you see in advertisements. Yes, St. Thomas is supposed to be a place that makes you clap and cheer.

"It's so...pretty," Irene says.

"Anna and I honeymooned on Anguilla," Baker says. "It looked like this, only flatter."

"That's right, you did," Irene says. She remembers being nonplussed when Baker and Anna chose Anguilla. Irene and Russ had offered the honeymoon as a wedding present — anywhere they wanted to go, anywhere in the *world* — and they had chosen Anguilla. It had seemed so...*unimaginative* to Irene. But Baker had said that Anna wanted to stay close to home. She had wanted sunshine, massages, a constant flow of alcohol. She didn't want to *tour* anything.

Irene, if she had her druthers, would vacation in Europe — France, Switzerland, England, places with history, places with culture. And so that was what she and Russ had done: a week in London, a week in the Cotswolds, a week in Provence, in Paris, in St. Moritz. Or they went to Colorado and skied. Irene harbors a natural prejudice against the Caribbean. Why is that? She thinks back on a trip to Jamaica when the boys were young, eight and ten, maybe nine and seven. This was before they had money, so they had booked a mediocre hotel near the airport. It had rained all week and they had barely left their rooms. Russ had finally given the boys money to go to the arcade in the hotel lobby. Baker and Cash were down there for a couple of hours—Irene had napped—and then she had woken up, alarmed to discover they still weren't back. Russ had gone down to check on them and had come rushing up, frantic. The kids were *gone*.

Irene can still recall the sheer panic she felt then. It had been like falling into a hole with no bottom. They had alerted hotel security, who had directed them to a shantytown right across the street from the hotel; sometimes women infiltrated the lobby and convinced hotel guests to shop for souvenirs. They found a mishmash of shacks with corrugated tin roofs; it was noisy in the rain. There were women cooking and men playing cards and children and chickens running around, plenty of children, so it wasn't sinister, by any means, but it had seemed so to Irene—a rabbit warren of foreignness that had swallowed her sons. She lashed out at the men, screaming, *Where are my children? My sons?* Her voice was accusatory, when really the only person Irene could blame was herself. She had been *napping*—and now her boys were gone.

They had turned up, of course, almost immediately. They were listening to a gentleman with long, graying dreadlocks play the guitar in one of the shacks. Irene had grabbed Baker so fiercely she'd nearly wrenched his arm out of its socket.

That had been it for Irene and the Caribbean. She had smiled politely whenever anyone said they were headed to Barbados or Aruba or the Dominican Republic, and she had probably said, "I'm sure it will be wonderful!" But in her head, she had been thinking, *Better you than me.*

And now here she is. They have to descend a set of stairs onto the tarmac and then walk into the terminal. The air is warm, humid, sweet-smelling. Irene is wearing a white short-sleeved blouse and a pair of khaki capri pants, sandals, sunglasses. She knows what she looks like to everyone else.

She looks like a woman taking a vacation.

AYERS

Helicopter crash off Virgin Gorda, three dead: Rosie, the Invisible Man, the pilot, whose name was Stephen Thompson. Ayers doesn't know if he was white or West Indian.

"They think the helicopter got hit by lightning," Mick says. "Did you hear the storm this morning?"

Ayers had been woken up by the thunder, but then she'd fallen right back to sleep.

"What do I do?" she asks Mick. "Where do I go?"

He holds his arms out to offer her a hug and she accepts. Out the front door she sees Gordon sitting patiently in the passenger seat of Mick's blue Jeep. No Brigid, thank God. Although what does Brigid matter anymore? Ayers thought Mick dumping her for Brigid equaled heartbreak, but now Ayers understands a new definition of heartbreak.

Rosie is dead.

"I have to go to Huck's," Ayers says.

"I'll drive you," Mick says. "Let's go."

Huck lives up Jacob's Ladder, a series of switchbacks so steep that Ayers's head lolls back and she feels like she might swallow her tongue. At the last turn before Huck's duplex, the cars are lined up: two local police cars, pickup trucks, a Jeep that belongs to Huck's first mate, Adam, a car from U.S. Customs and Border Control.

Walking down the street are the West Indian women — many of them friends of LeeAnn's, Ayers knows — some of them carrying covered dishes, some carrying flowers, one holding a Bible aloft. It's as busy as downtown during Carnival. One thing about a close-knit community like St. John: no one endures a tragedy alone. Ayers had experienced the celebration of LeeAnn Powers's life five years earlier; she hadn't realized until then that dying could be beautiful and filled with love.

LeeAnn had been sixty years old when she died, a newly retired nurse practitioner and a grandmother. She'd had congestive heart failure, so her death hadn't been a great surprise. Rosie, Maia, and Huck all had time to say good-bye.

Rosie's death is something else entirely, but the support and prayers will be great, maybe greater. Many, if not all, of these women watched Rosie grow up; a handful probably cared for her while LeeAnn worked nights and weekends up at Myrah Keating and over at Schneider Regional Medical Center on St. Thomas — until Captain Huck swept LeeAnn off her feet and married her.

Mick hits the brakes before ascending the final hill, and Ayers sees the uncertainty on his face. Do they belong here? They're locals, but they aren't native islanders; neither of them has family here, or roots. They merely have jobs. Mick has managed the Beach Bar for eleven years; Ayers has waited tables at La Tapa for nine years and been a crew member on *Treasure Island* for seven. She has never had anyone close to her die. What's the protocol?

If Ayers were to list anyone as a family member on this island, it would be Rosie. Would have been Rosie. And Maia and Huck. So, yes, Ayers is going up to the house. If she *doesn't* go, what would Huck think?

"Park up there," Ayers says, indicating a spot mid-hill. "We can walk the rest of the way."

"You go," Mick says. "I'll wait here until you want to leave. Or, if you decide to stay for a while, text me and I'll come back for you later."

Ayers nods and rubs Gordon's bucket head. She has missed him, and when human words and emotions fail, animals still provide comfort.

She climbs out of the Jeep. It's broiling in the sun, and Ayers's stomach roils with last night's tequila and that stupid cigarette. Her best friend is dead. Ayers stops. She's going to vomit or faint. Her vision splotches. One of the West Indian women—Dearie, she has a beauty shop up behind the Lumberyard building—takes Ayers's hand and all but pulls her up the hill.

"Ayers!"

She sees Huck hurrying off his porch, where a group of men—some white, some West Indian, some in uniform, some not—are gathered. A West Indian woman named Helen— she was LeeAnn's best friend—emerges from the house with a pot of coffee and starts filling cups.

"Oh, Huck," Ayers whispers. She stands with her arms hanging uselessly at her sides, tears streaming down her face as he gathers her up in a hug. He's a big bear of a man with a bushy reddish-gray beard and the ropy, muscled forearms of a fisherman. He's missing half his left pinky thanks to a feisty barracuda. He's an island character, nearly an icon. *Everyone* knows Huck, but few love him like Ayers does, and like Rosie did. He was more a father to Rosie than Rosie's own father, and the same can probably be said for Ayers.

"Is it true?" she asks.

He lets her go. "It's true," he says. His eyes shine. "Helicopter went down. They were headed over to Anegada for the day, I guess."

Ayers has questions. "They" means Rosie and the Invisible Man, but why did they take a helicopter and not a boat, like normal people? Too slow, she figures. Helicopter is faster and makes more of a statement. What happened? Who was this pilot, Stephen Thompson, and did he not check the weather report? Aren't there *rules,* the FAA and whatever?

But those questions don't matter.

"Maia?" Ayers asks.

"She's at Joanie's," Huck says. "I talked to Joanie's parents. They had planned to take the girls to Salt Pond and then to hike Ram's Head in the late afternoon once it cooled down, then have dinner at Café Concordia. I told them to go ahead with their plans. Maia may end up hating me for it, but I want her to have today. I'll tell her when she gets home. I was hoping you would be here when I tell her. She likes you. What does she always say? You're like her mom, but…"

"But better," Ayers says. "Because I'm not her mom."

"She's going to need you now," Huck says. "She's going to need you a whole lot."

"Okay," Ayers says, but she can barely get the word out because she's crying too hard. *It's fine,* she thinks. She'll cry now, she can fall to absolute pieces now, but there's a twelve-year-old girl depending on her to be strong, and, dammit, Ayers isn't going to let her down.

CASH

Cash treats his mother like she's made of bone china. She's not, he knows—she has kept a stiff upper lip thus far, and she looks pulled together. Her chestnut hair is in its usual fat braid with a swoop of bangs that dips toward her right eye. For Cash's entire life, his mother's hair has looked exactly the same. They used to tease her about it, but now Cash finds it soothing. If Irene braided her hair, some essential part of her is intact. He can't imagine what must be going through her mind. It's bad enough that Russ is dead, but to die in such a dramatic, suspicious way, in a place none of them even knew he was, and then to find out that he has "concerns" and owns property here? It's also an unusual burden to be on such a somber mission in such an achingly beautiful place. It's bright, sunny, and hot. The air is crystalline, and the water is turquoise, more beautiful than any water Cash has ever seen. The islands are green and mountainous—volcanic, he learned, when he did a little research. There are enormous yachts anchored in the harbor with people out drinking, barbecuing, playing reggae music. The ferry is abuzz with excited tourists talking about fish tacos at Longboard and snorkeling at Maho Bay. Cash picks three seats on the far right side of the boat. He and Baker have barely spoken a word to each other since meeting up in Atlanta; Russ's death hasn't changed the fact that Baker is one of Cash's least favorite people on planet Earth.

They take the seats on either side of their mother, buffering her. Winnie hangs her head over the lower railing, panting at the ocean. She's a mountain dog; this is all brand-new to her.

It takes only twenty minutes to reach St. John. Cash has

read that it's a smaller, more rustic cousin of St. Thomas. There are no traffic lights, no chain stores, and only one small casino, The Parrot Club. Seventy percent or more of the land on St. John is owned by the National Park Service. It's for hikers and snorkelers, birders and fishermen, people who love the outdoors. Cash likes the sound of it.

Or he would, under other circumstances.

Cash had spoken with Paulette Vickers on the phone. She told him she was the property manager of Mr. Steele's villa. The phrase "property manager" triggered a memory of something Irene had told him.

"Are you the one who identified my father's body?" Cash asked.

"That was my husband, Douglas," Paulette said.

"And your husband knew my father? Knew what he looked like? And my father was dead? And the man who was dead was actually my father, Russell Steele?" Cash had paused. "I know these questions sound strange. It's just that I'm in a state of suspended disbelief."

Yes, yes, she understood, she said. Though how could she, possibly? Paulette said that she took care of maintaining the villa in the summer months, when Mr. Steele was away, and that Douglas did all the handyman work. When Cash had asked how long his father had owned the villa, Paulette had been slow to answer. She said that she had "inherited" the villa from another property manager three years earlier. She wasn't certain when Mr. Steele had bought the villa; she would have to check the files.

"All right, I'll wait," Cash had said, and Paulette had laughed.

"How are you related to Mr. Steele?" Paulette had asked. "Marilyn, from Mr. Croft's office, said only that a family member would be calling."

"I'm his son," Cash had said. "His younger son. My brother will be coming as well, and my mother, Irene. Mr. Steele's widow."

This had elicited a long pause from Paulette. "I see," she said.

"Is there a problem?" Cash asked. He meant aside from the obvious problem that his father was dead under mysterious circumstances.

"Not at all," Paulette said. "I didn't realize Mr. Steele had sons, but then again, he was a very private person. He liked to keep a low profile, to be 'invisible,' he used to say. The villa, as you'll see, has everything: a pool and a hot tub, a shuffleboard court and a billiards table, multiple decks and outdoor living spaces, nine bedrooms, seven of them en suite, and, of course, a private beach. There was no reason for him to leave the property, and he rarely did."

Cash's head was spinning. Nine bedrooms? A shuffleboard court? A private beach? It just wasn't *possible.* Cash thanked Paulette, gave her the details of their travel, and hung up.

Cash and Baker help their mother off the ferry while Winnie goes nuts, pulling on the leash, intrigued by so many new smells. Cash sees a West Indian woman in a purple dress waving at him. Is that Paulette Vickers? How would she have recognized him? He wonders if Paulette had been *friends* with Russ, if maybe Russ had shown Paulette pictures of his family at home. But then Cash remembers that he told Paulette he was bringing his golden retriever.

He strides up to her and offers his hand. "Paulette, I'm Cash Steele. Can we get into your car and away from here with minimum fanfare?" It has only just occurred to Cash that there might be some attendant celebrity to being the family of the man who died in the helicopter crash on New Year's Day.

"Yes, of course," Paulette says. She waits, smile plastered to her face, while Irene and Baker approach, and then she offers Irene her hand. Irene stares.

"You knew my husband?" Irene asks. "You knew Russ?"

"Mom, let's get to the car," Cash says.

Baker smooths things over by taking Paulette's outstretched hand and saying, "Very nice to meet you. Thank you for coming to get us. What a beautiful island."

Cash gives Baker a hard stare. It *is* a beautiful island, but it hardly seems appropriate to say so.

Paulette, although she must realize that the three of them are numb with shock and grief, prattles on about the sights as though they are run-of-the-mill tourists. The town is called Cruz Bay, it's where the "action" is, the shopping, the restaurants, the infamous Woody's, with its infamous happy hour.

Happy hour? Cash almost interrupts Paulette to remind her who she has in her car, but his mother puts a hand on his arm to silence him.

Winnie's head is out the window, and Cash decides to follow suit and turn his gaze outward, tuning out Paulette. Baker can handle her.

The "town" is maybe four blocks long. It's understated and laid-back. There are restaurants with outdoor seating under awnings, bakeries, barbecue joints, shops selling silver jewelry, renting snorkel equipment—nothing gaudy or overbearing.

They pass public tennis courts and a school with children in yellow-and-navy uniforms out on the playground.

"The children are just back to school after the holiday break," Paulette says. "I have a son at that school. He's six."

"I have a son who's four," Baker says. "He's back in Houston with his mother."

Cash supposes he should be grateful that Baker's an extrovert; he will be the goodwill ambassador and Cash will tend to Irene. The family joke has always been that Cash is the daughter Irene never had; it doesn't bother Cash because he's secure in his masculinity. He knows his strengths: he's sensitive, thoughtful, introspective, a nurturer. And Baker is alpha, or he was until he married Anna. She definitely wears the pants in that family—hell, the whole tuxedo—but Cash is relieved to see that Baker has retained his charm.

Out of town, the road grows steep and curvy. Paulette is pointing out trailheads, talking about hiking, about the three-thousand-year-old petroglyphs of the Reef Bay Trail.

"Very famous," she says. "They're what St. John is known for."

On either side of the road is dense vegetation. Everything here is so green and alive, Cash can practically hear it growing. At the crest of a hill, Paulette pulls over to the shoulder. Below them is a crescent of white beach backed by palm trees. It's the most picture-perfect beach Cash has ever seen. It's so beautiful it hurts.

"That's Trunk Bay," Paulette says. "Perennially voted one of the best beaches in the world."

"Great," Baker says, nodding. He pulls out his phone, and Cash wonders if he's going to take a *picture,* but no, he's just checking the time. "Paulette, you are so kind to serve as our tour guide, and I hope you don't think I'm being rude when I suggest you take us right to my father's property. We've been traveling since early this morning."

"Of course," Paulette says. "I just thought since you were unfamiliar with the island, you might want to see what all the fuss is about."

They couldn't have sent anyone less sensitive, Cash thinks. And yet he doesn't want to alienate Paulette because she is, right now, their only link to Russ's life here.

Paulette pulls back onto the road. She's at ease on the windy, twisty, steep terrain, where there's zero room for error. One side of the road is unforgiving mountain face, and the other side is a dramatic drop to the sea. Paulette waves to the drivers of the big open-air taxis that pass them — too close for Cash's comfort — in the oncoming lane. She stops to talk to one of the taxi drivers. They speak some kind of island patois; the only words Cash recognizes are "invisible man." *Is that what they call Russ?* he wonders. He peers discreetly at his mother. Her eyes are closed.

Finally, Paulette slows down, puts on her blinker, and turns. They drive up a series of hairpin turns. The road is deserted and it's shady; there are driveways, but no houses are visible. At the end of the road is a high gate with a sign that reads: PRIVATE.

Baker laughs. "Is this where Kenny Chesney lives?"

Paulette punches a code into the keypad and the gate swings open. Cash nudges his mother awake. He knows she's tired, but she has to see this. It's like something from a movie. This is his father's *villa,* his *father's* villa, on an island in the Caribbean. Cash can't help thinking that there has been a mistake, a very large, serious, and yet simple mistake. A man named Russell Steele did die in a helicopter crash north of Virgin Gorda, but it was a different Russell Steele. Their Russell Steele—husband, father, connoisseur of arcane trivia and corny puns, fan of the Beatles and *The Blues Brothers,* is still alive somewhere, schmoozing with clients in Sarasota or Pensacola.

The driveway is long, surrounded on both sides by evenly spaced palm trees, each of which has a spotlight at the bottom. When they reach the house, Cash takes his mother's hand.

"We're here," Paulette says.

They all climb out of the car. Baker lets out a long, low whistle. He has absolutely no impulse control.

The property is…stunning. They're way, way up high, with hundred-eighty-degree views of the water and the islands beyond. Paulette leads them up a curved stone staircase to a mahogany deck, where she turns with her arms open like a woman on a game show, as if to present the view.

"That's Jost Van Dyke and, next to it, Tortola."

"What?" Irene says.

"The British Virgin Islands, Mom," Baker says.

Paulette guides them around the outside of the house. The grounds are impeccably landscaped with bougainvillea, frangipani, banana trees, and tall hibiscus bushes. There's a round aqua pool with a slide down to a second, free-form, dark-blue pool. A few yards away is a separate hot tub, water bubbling, surface steaming. There's a covered outdoor kitchen with a granite bar, a grill, an ice machine, and a glass-fronted refrigerator displaying a variety of Italian sparkling waters. Cash shakes his head. This isn't his father's house. Russ drinks tap water.

Paulette opens a sliding glass door and they all step into the house; after the heat outside, the air-conditioning is delicious. The ceiling of the living room is peaked, with thick beams jutting from the center like the spokes of a wheel. They wander into the enormous eat-in kitchen and Paulette says, "I'll let you explore in peace. I'll be on the deck if you have any questions."

"Which way to the master bedroom?" Irene asks. "And is there a study?"

"The master is at the end of that hall," Paulette says. "Mr. Steele's study is attached. All of the other bedrooms are upstairs, and there's a lower level with a billiards table and a wine cellar. That level opens up onto the shuffleboard court below. And the steps to the beach. There are eighty steps, just so you're aware."

"I'm going down to check that out," Baker says. He looks at Cash. "Do you want to come?"

"I'll go with Mom," Cash says. He can't let his mother walk into the "master bedroom" — presumably where his father slept — by herself.

Baker cocks an eyebrow, a signature expression of his, and Cash remembers just how much his brother irks him. Cash resents Baker's confidence, his smug self-assuredness, his aura of superiority. Baker is the worst kind of older brother—all alpha dominance, no support or advice. But the most frustrating thing is that despite this, Cash yearns to be just like him. "This place is unbelievable," Baker says. "And I do mean *unbelievable*." He lowers his voice. "It can't be Dad's. They have the wrong guy."

Cash doesn't comment, though he happens to agree. He trails his mother down the long hall to the master suite. In the bedroom is a king bed positioned to face the water through an enormous sliding glass door. There are two walk-in closets — empty, both of them: Cash checks immediately — and there's a huge marble bathroom with dual sinks, a sunken soaking tub for two, and a glassed-in shower. There's a paneled study, which is where Irene has chosen to start poking around. The top of the desk is clear, so she's rifling through drawers. Cash, meanwhile, pokes through the bathroom. There are a couple of toothbrushes and a can of shaving cream, but nothing else in the way of personal items.

The place feels *staged*. It feels *cleaned out*. If Russ had been living here or even just staying here—Irene said he'd left Iowa on December 26—then wouldn't he have left behind clothes, a razor, aftershave, reading glasses?

Cash opens the dresser drawers. Empty. That's weird, right? He goes over to the bed and opens the nightstand drawer. He startles as if he's found a disembodied head.

There's a photograph staring up at him. It's a framed photograph of Russ with a West Indian woman. They're lying in a hammock. Cash turns around. It's the hammock that's hanging out on the deck right off the master bedroom. Russ is wearing sunglasses and grinning at the camera and the woman is snuggled up against him.

Cash casts about the room for a place to hide the photograph. He can't have his mother see it.

He stuffs it between the mattress and box spring, then sits on the bed and drops his head in his hands. His unspoken suspicions have been confirmed: Russ had a mistress, most likely the woman who was with him on the helicopter. The bigger shock, perhaps, is seeing a picture of his father in this house. This is real. This is his father's house. His father is dead.

Cash wants to laugh. It's absurd! He wants to scream. After all of Russ's gentle prodding for Cash to finish his education and establish an "infrastructure," it turns out his father's own infrastructure was built of lies! He had a *secret life!* A fifteen-million-dollar villa in the Caribbean and a West Indian mistress!

What else? Cash wonders. What else was Russell Steele—a

three-term member of the Iowa City School Board while Cash was growing up — hiding?

He pokes his head into the study, where his mother is sitting at the desk, staring out the window.

"I'm going out to get some air, Mom," he says. "I'll be right back."

"Was there anything in the bedroom?" she asks.

"Not really," Cash says. "This is like the house of a stranger."

"Well," she says.

He finds Paulette out on the front deck, reciting a shopping list to someone over the phone. When she sees him, she hangs up and lights a cigarette. He's encouraged by this gesture. He needs to talk to the real Paulette Vickers.

"So, what do you think of the house?" she asks.

"I have some questions." His voice is low. He leans his forearms on the railing and she follows suit. Together, they gaze out at the vista — the glittering aquamarine water, the lush green islands, the sleek boats that must belong to the luckiest people in the world. Maybe Paulette takes this landscape for granted, but for Cash it's like discovering another planet. "I'd like to talk frankly, without my mother present."

"I'll answer what questions I can," Paulette says.

"This is my father's house?"

"Yes."

"Where are all of his things? His clothes, for example? His shoes, his bathing suits, his deodorant? It's as anonymous as a Holiday Inn."

"Nicer than a Holiday Inn," Paulette says.

"Please don't dodge the question," Cash says. "If he was staying here before he left on that helicopter, where are his things? Did someone go through the house?"

"I did," Paulette says. "I had strict orders from Mr. Croft's secretary to rid the house of all personal effects." She pauses. "So as not to upset you. Or your mother."

"So where are they?" Cash asks.

"Packed up," Paulette says. "Mr. Croft sent someone to collect them this morning."

"Did he," Cash says. "Does Mr. Croft have a house on St. John as well?"

"Not to my knowledge," Paulette says.

"What does that mean, not to your *knowledge*?" Cash says. "You're a local with a child in the schools. You work for a real estate agency. It seems like you would know whether or not Mr. Croft has a house here."

"Down here...," Paulette says, "a lot of the high-end properties are owned by trusts. People come to the islands to *escape,* Mr. Steele."

To *hide,* Cash thinks.

"Can you tell me where Mr. Croft does live?" Cash says. "Where is his business located?"

"Again, I'm not certain..."

"Paulette," Cash says. He feels himself about to lash out at her. She seems nice—lovely, even—and he can't understand why she's giving him the runaround. "I'm sure you can see that we're grieving. My brother and I lost our father, my mother her husband. If he'd died of a heart attack at home, this would have been tragic enough. But he died *here,* in a place we didn't know he'd even visited, much less owned property in. The details we've received are sparse. Part of the way the three of us are going to process our loss is to find out exactly what happened. We need to talk to Todd Croft."

"That would be a start, I suppose," Paulette says.

"Do you have a phone number for him?"

Paulette laughs drily. "For Mr. Croft? No, I'm afraid not. I've never met the man. I've never even spoken to him on the phone."

"You're kidding," Cash says.

"I deal with his secretary," Paulette says. "Marilyn. She called your mother, so your mother has her number."

"But it's Mr. Croft who pays you," Cash says. "Right?" He nearly says, *It's Mr. Croft who pulls the puppet strings.* He pulled Russ's, or at least that was how it had seemed.

"I was paid by Mr. Steele directly," Paulette says. "In cash. And occasionally by Mr. Thompson."

"Mr. Thompson?" Cash says. "Who is Mr. Thompson?"

"Stephen Thompson," Paulette says. "He was their associate."

"Their associate," Cash says. He feels like he's on a detective show, only he's the new guy, first day on the job, trying to figure things out. "Do you have a number for Mr. Thompson, then?"

"I do," Paulette says. She stares at the glowing tip of her cigarette.

"Paulette, again..."

"Mr. Thompson is dead," Paulette says. "He was the pilot."

"He was the pilot," Cash says. "And the third person who died, the local woman, she and my father...were involved?"

"I'm not comfortable discussing that," Paulette says.

"I have a photograph of them together," Cash says. "It was in the drawer of the nightstand."

Paulette exhales a stream of smoke and casts her eyes down.

"What's her name?"

"Again, Mr. Steele, I'm not..."

"Paulette," Cash says. "Please. *Please.*" His voice breaks, and he fears he's going to cry. He wants to go back to New Year's Eve, or even to New Year's Day, to the mortifying and yet inevitable conversation with Glenn the accountant. He wants his father to be alive. Cash will confess his failure with the stores and he *won't* go to Breckenridge to waste away the rest of his young adulthood. He'll enroll at the University of Colorado, Denver. He'll get a degree. He'll make something of himself. But he wants his father back. His desperation creates a sour taste in his mouth and he inhales a breath—the honey scent of frangipani combined with Paulette's secondhand smoke.

Paulette looks at Cash. She must sense his pain, because her brown eyes well with tears. "Rosie," she says. "Rosie Small. She was the daughter of LeeAnn Powers, who was married to Captain Huck. LeeAnn died five years ago." Paulette taps her ashes into the bougainvillea below. "There's going to be a memorial service tomorrow at the Episcopalian church, with a reception following at Chester's Getaway. If you go to either the service or the reception, you'll find people who can tell you more. But I'd advise you to be discreet. And to go with an open mind and an open heart. Lots and lots of people on this island loved Rosie Small. And almost no one on this island knew your father. Like I said, he preferred to remain invisible."

Cash turns around to face the house. "And we can stay here a few days?"

"As long as you want," Paulette says. "It's yours now."

"Okay, thank you, Paulette," Cash says. "Really, thank you."

"God bless you boys," Paulette says. "And God bless your mother."

HUCK

Joanie's parents, Jeff and Julie—they are a self-proclaimed "J" family—pull into the driveway at six o'clock on the dot. Huck somehow managed to get everyone out of the house except for Ayers. She is sitting at the counter, wringing her hands and staring at a bottle of eighteen-year-old Flor de Caña rum like she's drowning and it's a life raft. Huck nearly suggests they both do a shot to fortify their nerves, but then he thinks better of it.

As his grandfather used to say: hard things are hard. Huck has done plenty of hard things in his life. He was drafted into the Vietnam War right out of high school. He had been born and raised on Islamorada in the Florida Keys, so he thought the U.S. Navy would be a natural fit, and he was happy because in the navy, you didn't get shot at. But choice was for those who enlisted, not for those who got drafted, and the powers that be placed Huck in the Marine Corps. His first year in Vietnam was spent facedown in the mud, in the jungle, in the rice paddies, fearing for his life every second of every day, developing an addiction to nicotine that he still can't shake.

Later, years after he got home, he had to put his then-wife, Kimberly, into rehab for drinking and serve her with divorce papers.

He buried his sister, Caroline, who died of brain cancer at forty-one, and his mother, who died of heartbreak over Caroline, and eventually his beloved father, the original captain, Captain Paul Powers, who had run a fishing charter out of Islamorada for fifty years and whose passengers had included Jack Nicklaus and Frank Sinatra. He had taught Huck everything he knew about fishing and about being a man.

It was after his father died that Huck moved to the Virgin Islands, where life was easy for a long time. He bought his boat, started his business, and met and married LeeAnn Small, an island treasure. Huck would name burying LeeAnn as the hardest thing he'd ever had to do, but only because he had loved the woman so damn much.

This would be harder.

Maia comes bounding into the house, her skin burnished from a full day outside, even though Jeff and Julie are fastidious about sunscreen and bug spray. The smile on her face is proof that he was right: she had a happy day. Maybe the last happy day for the rest of her childhood.

He doesn't want to tell her.

Maia sees Ayers and goes right to her for a hug. Huck catches Ayers's expression over Maia's shoulder; her eyes are shining. He doesn't have but a few seconds left before Ayers breaks down.

They should have done the rum shot. He's shaking.

"Maia," he says. "Please sit."

She pulls away from Ayers and looks at him wide-eyed. "Are you *mad*?" she asks. "You *said* I could go."

"I'm not mad," Huck says. "But would you please sit down? Ayers and I have to tell you something."

"What?" Maia says. She is standing, defiant now in her posture.

Ayers reaches out to take Maia's hand.

"There was a helicopter crash north of Virgin Gorda," Huck says. "Maia, your mother is dead."

There is a blankness on Maia's face and this, Huck thinks, is the soul-destroying moment: Maia taking in the words and making sense of them.

Then, Maia starts to scream. The sound is raw, primitive; it's the sound of an animal. Ayers pulls Maia close and tears stream down Huck's face and he thinks, *Hard things are hard,* and *Please, God, do not give her anything harder than this.*

The screaming morphs into crying, great ragged sobs, seemingly bigger than the girl herself. Huck goes for tissues, a glass of ice water, a pillow in case she wants to punch something. He and Ayers had made a pact that they would not shush Maia or tell her everything was going to be okay. They were not going to *lie* to the girl. They were going to let her take in what she could, and then they were going to answer her questions as honestly as possible.

The crying ends eventually. Ayers leads Maia to the sofa, and Huck plants himself in the chair, within arm's reach. He had been over at Schneider hospital with LeeAnn when Rosie gave birth to Maia. He had been the third person to hold her, red and wriggling and utterly captivating. If Huck were very honest, he would admit to feeling a quick stab of disappointment that the baby hadn't been a boy. Huck had imagined a grandson to take fishing. But Maia stole Huck's heart that first moment in his arms, and he decided that she would make a better mate anyway. The men in LeeAnn's family were either weak or absent. It was the women who were strong.

Maia blows her nose, gets a clear breath. Her face, which had been so radiant when she walked in, is now mottled, and, if Huck isn't imagining it, her dainty features have instantly aged. She suddenly looks seventeen, or twenty-five.

"Helicopter," Maia says. "So she was with my father. Is he dead, too?"

"*Father?*" Ayers says.

"Honey," Huck says. "She was with her...her friend. The one who comes to visit." The man's name is Russell Steele. Rosie told Huck the guy's name when he first came on the scene, a few months after LeeAnn died, but Rosie kept the relationship private. The fellow showed up one or two weeks a month, November through May; he had some big villa on the north shore. Huck had a pretty good idea which road it was, though he'd never been invited to the house and he'd never met the guy. Maia, he knew, went to the house sometimes when the man was on-island, though there were plenty of occasions when Rosie had asked Huck to cover so that she and her mystery lover could have some privacy.

Huck won't lie: the arrangement had troubled him. He had expected at least an *introduction*. He had expected, if not a weekly barbecue, then an invitation for a beer. But Rosie had been both stubborn and contrite when it came to the Invisible Man. She was very sorry—and Huck could see on her face that the emotion was genuine—but she wanted to keep her relationship private. The island was small, she had been born and raised there, everyone had always been right up in her business, and she just wanted one thing that would not be discussed and dissected by the community at large.

Huck had suspected this was not how Rosie truly felt. He had suspected that her plea was on behalf of the Invisible Man.

Which meant, of course, only one thing: he was married. Or he was one of those bastards who had a girl like Rosie in every port. International finance was his business, Rosie said, which meant, of course, only one thing: he was also a criminal. You want an honest business? Go out on a boat, catch a fish, and eat it for dinner.

But the Invisible Man should not be confused with the Pirate, which is what Maia is now doing. The Pirate was some other white fella who came in on his buddy's yacht, hot on Rosie—this was back when Rosie was cocktail waitressing at Caneel Bay—knocked her up and left without a trace. Rosie called him "the Pirate" because he'd stolen her heart.

And her dignity, LeeAnn had said privately to Huck.

Rosie had fallen hard for the Pirate in the four days they'd spent together. It had been over a long weekend—Presidents' Day in February. And then Maia had been born on November 15.

"If by 'friend' you mean Russ, then, yes, he's my father. Was my father. Russell Steele. So they're both dead?" Maia holds Huck's gaze. "They're *both* dead?"

"Yes," Huck says. He wonders if there's something he doesn't know. He wonders if Rosie let the Invisible Man *adopt* Maia at some point over the years without telling anyone. Without telling him. He knows the Invisible Man pays for Maia's expenses, including her tuition at Gifft Hill, but Huck had thought that was a gesture, possibly even a payment in exchange for Rosie's discretion. Rosie still had a job, paid her own bills, lived under Huck's roof whenever the Invisible Man was away, which was a lot. Had Rosie been hiding something *that* big? How had she pulled it off, legally, without someone in the courthouse in Charlotte Amalie blabbing? It eventually would have gotten back to Huck.

Impossible, Huck thinks. They must have just started calling this Steele fellow Maia's "father."

"So I'm an orphan," Maia says. "I have no one."

"You have me," Ayers says. "You're always going to have me."

"And you have me," Huck says. He gets down on his knees before Maia, which seems fitting because he has done nothing for the past twelve years so much as worship this child. He knows she's too young to understand the quality of his devotion—and this is probably for the best. She doesn't need someone to worship her. She needs someone to love her, clothe her, feed her, teach her right from wrong, someone to set limits and provide opportunities, someone to believe in her and be her champion.

And that person will be Huck. He will be her Unconditional. He will be her No Matter What.

BAKER

Anna did Baker a favor before he left. She filled a prescription of Ativan for his mother.

"I bet you she won't take them," Anna said. "But it'll be good to have them just in case."

It turned out Anna knew Irene better than Baker imagined. She did refuse the pills at first.

But Thursday night, when the sun is dropping like a hot coal into the Caribbean and Irene has refused Baker's offer of dinner three times, she says, "I think I'd like to try sleeping. Can I see those pills?"

"Do you want the master bedroom, Mom?" Cash asked.

"Heavens, no," Irene said. "I'll take one of the guest rooms upstairs." She offered them both a weak smile. "That's what I am, a guest. A guest in your father's house."

Cash helped Irene get situated upstairs while Baker checked the contents of the kitchen. Paulette had said it was "well-stocked," and she also said that she could arrange for a private chef if they so desired.

"No private chef," Baker said. "I don't think my mother wants any strangers in the house."

"The landscapers are scheduled every Friday...," Paulette said.

"Please," Baker said. "If you would just tell everyone to give us our privacy for a week..."

"Of course," Paulette said. "Call if you need anything."

Now, Baker inspects the fridge and cabinets. "Well-stocked" is an understatement. The fridge is filled with steaks, hamburgers, pasta salad, deli meats, fresh vegetables, milk, eggs, and a giant bowl of tropical fruit salad. The bottom shelf holds four flavors of local beer. The cabinets contain enough pasta, cereal, and canned goods—including, curiously, six cans of SpaghettiOs—for a small family to survive a nuclear fallout. The SpaghettiOs remind Baker of Floyd, and he thinks to go out on the deck and call home, but honestly, the only positive thing about this whole surreal trip is that he's able to leave his own problems behind. Or, rather, his "own problems" become what is happening here. His father is *dead.* Right? Baker hasn't been able to feel the reality of Russ's death, however, because nothing about this *makes any sense.*

Take, for example, the wine cellar. Russell Steele was a man who liked his Leinenkugel's, his Bud Light, and his scotch. Baker has no memory of Russ *ever* drinking wine. Champagne, maybe, at Baker and Anna's wedding. One sip. The person who liked wine in their family was Irene. She drank chardonnay from California. Her everyday wine was Kendall-Jackson, her favorite splurges Simi and Cakebread. Curiously—or not?—Baker had found one case of both Simi and Cakebread in his father's wine cellar, almost as if he were expecting Irene to visit.

Cash comes down the stairs just as Baker is cracking open what he believes to be a well-deserved beer, and he reaches into the fridge to grab one for Cash. Cash takes it from him and nods toward the pool.

"She's asleep," Cash says. "The pill knocked her right out. Which is a good thing, because I need to talk to you."

They go out to the swimming pool and sit with their feet in the shallow end. The gurgle of the fountain will drown out their voices in case Irene should appear.

"What is it?" Baker says.

"He had a mistress," Cash says. "A West Indian woman. I found a picture of the two of them in the master bedroom."

Baker takes a sip of his beer. It's good, but not quite good enough to distract him from this crushing news about his father. Is *nobody* as they seem? Does *everyone* have nefarious secrets? Okay, obviously something was going on with his father, and it occurred to Baker that the "local woman" in the helicopter was, perhaps, a damning detail. But that was only a maybe. She could have been the *pilot's* girlfriend, or a tour guide, or one of Russ's clients.

"Let me see this picture," Baker says.

Cash disappears into the house, returning with a framed photograph of Russ and a truly stunning West Indian woman, lying together in a hammock.

There is no misreading the photo.

What strikes Baker is how Russ looks. He's wearing sunglasses so it's a bit hard to tell, but the father Baker knows — the goofy midwestern salesman always ready with a quip or pun — has been replaced by a man who looks sophisticated, worldly, and most of all, confident. When Baker and Cash were growing up, Russ had been like nothing so much as a big, eager Saint Bernard who faced each day with the same quest for attention, love, reassurance. He had a list of DIY projects that he liked to tackle on the weekends. He would go in to wake the boys up on a Saturday morning, calling Baker "buddy," and Cash "pal," as he did their entire lives, but they wouldn't stir. Russ would then take a seat at Baker's desk and wait. When the boys finally woke up, he would jump up with a childlike enthusiasm. Baker understood his father's eager-to-please, don't-rock-the-boat attitude to be the result of his childhood. He had moved every eighteen months, and the quest to be found likable and to be included was constant. But Baker won't lie. Both he and Cash found their father's obsequiousness off-putting, nearly cringeworthy. There were a lot of shared eye rolls.

Once Russ got his new job, he had a new luster, certainly; there was suddenly a *ton* of money. But Russ's attention was still so intense — possibly even more intense because he was around less frequently — that sometimes Baker and Cash wanted to deflect it. They thought their father was a nice enough guy, but ultimately they preferred the cooler, more reserved presence of their mother.

This man in the photograph with the open-collared tomato-red shirt and the "I've-got-the-world-by-the-balls" smile is a stranger.

"Has Mom seen this?" Baker asks.

"No."

"Good."

Cash stands up. "I'm returning it to its hiding place."

"Get two more beers," Baker says. "Please."

Baker grills up six cheeseburgers, and he and Cash fall on the food as they used to when they were teenagers—without thinking, without conversation. Then they sit, with their empty plates before them, staring at the twinkling lights of Tortola in the distance. Baker wonders if he should tell Cash about Anna. Cash is, after all, his brother, though they aren't close; they don't confide in each other. Baker has long viewed Cash as a little punk—that was definitely true all through growing up—because Russ and Irene coddled him. And he had spent his adult years freewheeling, which always seemed more like freeloading: sleeping on his buddies' couches out in Breckenridge, teaching skiing for a pittance because the job came with a free season pass, living off the food that his roommates who worked at restaurants brought home.

Baker and his parents had been unimpressed. But then what did Russ go and do? He bought Cash a business! Handed him the keys to two outdoor supply stores! Baker had really kept his distance then, because the demonstration of blatant favoritism was so egregious. Baker had always been able to speak frankly with his father, and he nearly told Russ that sinking two hundred grand into any business Cash was going to run was as good as sending it to a Nigerian prince.

The only time in recent history that Baker had seen Cash in a more favorable light was when he had taken Anna to Breckenridge to ski, back when they were dating. Anna had been uncharacteristically effusive in her praise of Cash. She loved that he got them access to the back-of-the-mountain trails. She loved that he was dating the hostess at the hottest sushi restaurant in town and then scored them a table in the window at eight o'clock on a Saturday night.

Your brother knows everyone, Anna had said. *He's like the mayor.*

Six months later, Baker had grudgingly asked Cash to serve as best man in his wedding.

"I really wish we had some weed," Baker says now. "I need to relax. My heart has been racing since Mom called with the news. Maybe I should take one of Mom's Ativans."

Cash takes an audible breath, as though Baker has startled him out of a waking sleep-state. "Wait," Cash says. "There's more to the story about the woman Dad was seeing."

"Right," Baker says. He'd dropped the thread of their earlier conversation. The woman in the photograph.

"I asked Paulette about her," Cash says. "The woman's name was Rosie Small. There's a memorial service being held tomorrow at the Episcopal church, followed by a reception at a place called Chester's Getaway."

Baker nods. Todd Croft arranged for Russ's body to be cremated.

As for a funeral service...Irene wants to wait until they figure out what's going on before they even tell anyone that Russ is dead. They can't very well tell everyone they know that Russ was killed in a helicopter crash in the Virgin Islands when they have no answers to the inevitable follow-up questions. Baker has scoured the internet—there has been no mention anywhere of a helicopter crash in the Virgin Islands.

Baker notices Cash looking at him expectantly. "What?"

"We have to go tomorrow," Cash says. "To either the service or the reception."

"Why?" Baker says.

"To find out who this woman was," Cash says.

"I'm not sure that's a good idea," Baker says. "What would that accomplish?"

"There are so many questions," Cash says. "How did Dad meet her, how long have they been together..."

"Who cares?" Baker says. "Think about it: What is it going to benefit you or me to know the answers? She was a woman Dad was screwing down here. How will it help to know any more?" Baker leans in and lowers his voice. "How will it help Mom? The answer is, it won't. We need to get Dad's ashes and leave. Put this house on the market, if it's even ours to sell."

"Paulette said it was ours," Cash says. "I'll ask her to produce the deed. Mom will have to call her attorney and have him check Dad's will. If Dad owns this house outright and the will leaves everything to Mom and the two of us, then it would be ours to sell."

"You sound like Jackass P. Esquire," Baker says.

"We need to find Todd Croft. See what he can tell us about Dad's business. It wasn't just a 'boutique investment firm,' Baker."

No, Baker thinks. This became evident the second they pulled into the driveway of this house. This is a twelve- or fifteen-million-dollar property. If Russ did own it outright, then he was into something far bigger than he claimed to be. Shell companies, offshore accounts, hiding money, cleaning it, the things you see in movies. He had access to a helicopter.

"I really think we should leave things be," Baker says.

"I don't," Cash says. "I'm going to either the service or the reception tomorrow and you're coming with me. I'll let you pick which one."

"Reception," Baker says. "Obviously. Because there will be alcohol."

"People will be more likely to tell us things," Cash says.

Things we don't want to know, Baker thinks.

At one o'clock the next afternoon, they find themselves in one of the two gunmetal-gray Jeep Saharas that belong to their father, driving to a place called Chester's Getaway off the Centerline Road.

They told their mother they were going on a top secret investigative mission.

"We can't tell you anything else," Baker said.

"I don't want to know anything else," Irene said. "Do what you have to do. I have my own list."

Baker thought his mother looked marginally better. She had finally slept, for a full twelve hours, and then she'd eaten a few chunks of fresh pineapple and a bite of toast.

"What's on your list?" Baker asked.

Irene blinked. "I'm going to call Ed Sorley, our attorney, and ask him to fax me a copy of your father's will. I'm going to call Todd Croft and I'm going to call Paulette. I was in no shape yesterday to ask her any questions, but today I want to appeal to her, woman to woman."

Baker kissed his mother on the forehead. She was a strong woman. She should be falling apart, but instead she had made a list.

"Call if you need us," Baker said.

There are cars lined up for hundreds of yards before they reach the entrance to Chester's and so they have to turn around, double back, and park at the end of the line. They arrive at Chester's at the same time that a bus lets off a load of people—a mix of young and old, white and West Indian, most of them somberly dressed.

Chester's is a two-story clapboard building set off the road and painted ivory and dusty pink. The parking lot has been taken over by a tent. Billowing out behind the tent are clouds of barbecue-scented smoke. Somewhere, a steel band is playing.

"It's good that it's crowded," Cash says. "We won't stick out."

"Let's get a drink," Baker says. It feels wrong to be here. They didn't know Rosie Small. They are the sons of her lover, the man who was taking her to Anegada, and who was indirectly responsible for her death. Surely there are people in attendance—possibly a lot of people—who believe Rosie's death is Russ's fault.

The place is too packed for there to be any kind of receiving line, thank God, which was another reason for avoiding the service. Cash seems to think everyone here is just going to offer up all kinds of information, but Baker isn't so sure.

Baker asks a gentleman in a fedora where the bar can be found and the gentleman says, "Drinks inside but you got to pay. Food outside is free. Pig roast and all the sides, including Chester's johnnycakes. You ever had Chester's johnnycakes?"

Baker sidles away without answering. "The bar is inside," he says to Cash.

"It's hot," Cash says. He's pink in the face and sweating. He chose to wear a long-sleeved plaid shirt and a pair of jeans. Baker is in khaki shorts and a navy polo. They both look... well, the word Baker wants to use is *white*...he doesn't mean Caucasian, exactly, but rather pale and out of place, like they've just parachuted in from the North Pole. Only half the people here are West Indian, but the other white people here look tan, weathered, well-seasoned.

The inside of Chester's is mercifully cooler, and Baker immediately feels better because the bar is the kind Baker would seek out if he had time to seek out bars. There's a long counter, a few tables, a sticky concrete floor, and a room through the back that has a pool table and a dartboard. Chester's Getaway has clearly seen dramas more interesting than the one he and Cash are presently living, or at least Baker would like to believe this. Two TVs hang over the bar, but they're both shut off. The line for a drink is three deep, and Baker decides to exercise his privilege as older brother.

"You wait," he tells Cash. "I'm going to wander."

"Wander *where*?" Cash says. "There isn't room to think in here, much less *wander.*"

"Over there," Baker says. He nods vaguely in the direction of an easel displaying photos. *Celebrating Rosie,* it says in bubble letters across the top. Baker hands Cash a twenty, since his brother is perpetually low on money. "And get me two beers, please, when it's your turn."

Cash shrugs and tries to shoulder his way closer to the bar. Meanwhile Baker shuffles over to the sign and the photos, wondering if there are any photos of Rosie Small with their father. There's a woman standing next to the easel behind a small table where she's encouraging people to sign the guest book.

"Hello," she says to Baker. "Would you like to sign the guest book?"

Baker's mouth falls open. It's not just that he's unsure of what to say—*No*, the answer to her question is definitely *no*, he does not want to sign the guest book—it's that she is the prettiest woman he has ever seen. Ever. She has blond ringlet curls and a smile like the sun. She's a natural beauty, and above and beyond that, she looks *nice.*

Anna is striking, certainly. There have been times in the past eight years when Baker hasn't been able to stop staring at her. But this woman affects Baker differently. She's lightly tanned, with freckles across her nose. She wears no makeup. She has blue eyes and straight white teeth. She wears five or six silver bracelets and a simple black jersey dress that clings to her slender frame. Looking at her fills Baker with wordless joy. She looks like hope.

I'm in love with you, he thinks. *Whoever you are.*

"Sure," he says. "I'd love to sign the guest book."

He accepts the pen from her, wondering what name he can possibly sign. He stalls by locking eyes with her and saying, "Can I get you a drink or anything? You seem to have pulled the short straw, being stuck back here in the corner."

"Oh," she says. "It's fine. Chester is keeping me in rum punches." She holds up a plastic cup containing an inch of watery pink liquid, a maraschino cherry, and an orange slice. "He'll be back soon, I'm sure." She sets down the cup and offers a hand. "I'm Ayers Wilson, by the way. I was Rosie's best friend." She tilts her head. "I don't think I recognize you. How did you know Rosie?"

"I…uh…I didn't, really," Baker says. "I came with someone who knew her. My brother. He's at the bar, getting me a beer, I hope."

Ayers laughs. "Nice brother," she says. "How did he know Rosie?"

"Um…," Baker says. "He worked with her."

Ayers's eyes widen. "Really?" she says. "Who's your brother? Is it Skip? Oh my God, that's right, Skip's *brother* from LA, right? But, wait…he's…she's transitioning to a woman. That's not you, I take it."

"No," Baker says. Just like that, he's been caught. "Actually, my brother *is* at the bar, but he didn't work with Rosie."

Ayers shakes her head. "Don't tell me," she says. "You guys are crashing, right?"

Baker sighs. "Kind of."

"Here on vacation, saw the crowd, smelled the pig roast,

and figured why not?" Ayers gives him a pointed look and he feels like an idiot. Before he can decide if he should tell her who he really is, she shrugs. "I honestly don't blame you."

"You don't?" Baker says. "I didn't want to come. My brother insisted."

"I'm actually happy to meet a complete stranger who has nothing to do with any of this," Ayers says. "Half the women here are pissed that I'm doing the guest book instead of Rosie's third cousin or Maia's preschool teacher, and as if that's not bad enough, over there in the doorway are my ex-boyfriend and the tramp he left me for."

Baker looks toward the doorway and sees a chunky guy with a buzz cut and a woman in her twenties who has seen fit to come to a memorial reception without either washing her hair or wearing a bra.

He turns back to Ayers. He's still holding the pen.

"Just write your name," Ayers says. "I'll remember you as the crasher and that'll cheer me up."

"Okay." Baker says. He writes: *Baker.* Then he hands the pen back to Ayers.

"Baker," she reads. "Well, Mr. Baker, it was nice meeting you."

"Baker is my first name," he says.

"Gotcha," Ayers says. "You're afraid to write your last name in case I call the police? Or do you go solely by your first name, like Madonna and Cher?"

"The latter," he says. She's flirting with him, he thinks. He stands up to his full height and squares his shoulders.

"Do you want to come outside with me and have a cigarette?" she asks. "Or are you horrified by a woman who smokes?"

He would follow her to East Japip to drink snake venom,

he thinks. He answers by scooting the table aside so she can step out. "Lead the way," he says.

She navigates around the crowd to the back of the tent, where a West Indian man with an orange bandana wrapped around his head is tending to the pig. There's a rubber trash can filled with beer and ice. Ayers grabs two, then says to the man, "You forgot about me, Chester. I'm taking these."

Chester waves his basting brush in the air. "Okay, doll."

Ayers leads Baker to the edge of the parking lot, where there is a tree with a low branch big and sturdy enough to sit on. Ayers pulls a pack of cigarettes out of a little crocheted purse that hangs across her body and lights up. "I'm horrified by people who smoke," Ayers says. "But my best friend just died and so I'm going to give myself a pass for a while to indulge in some self-destructive behavior." She hands the cigarette to Baker. "Want to join me?"

"Sure," he says. He inhales and promptly coughs. "Sorry, I'm out of practice. I haven't had a cigarette since I was fourteen years old standing out in back of the ice rink. It's been only weed for me since then."

This makes Ayers laugh. "So where are you visiting from, Baker?"

"Me?" he says. "Houston."

"Houston," Ayers says. "Never been. Are you a doctor? You look like a doctor."

No, he nearly says. *But my wife's a doctor.*

"I'm not a doctor," he says. "I used to trade in commodities but now I'm kind of between jobs. I do some day-trading and I'm a stay-at-home dad. My son, Floyd, is four."

"Floyd," Ayers says. "Cool name."

"It's making a comeback," Baker says. "Your name is pretty cool."

"My parents are wanderers," Ayers says. "They travel all over the world. I was named after Ayers Rock in Australia, which is, apparently, where I was conceived. But since then the rock has been reclaimed by the Aboriginals and now it's called Uluru. And so I am now politically incorrect Ayers."

"It's pretty," Baker says. *You're pretty,* he thinks.

"So what brings you down here?" Ayers asks. "Vacation?"

How should he answer this? "Not a vacation, exactly," he says. "I'm here with my mom and my brother."

"Family reunion?" Ayers asks.

"I guess you could say that."

"Are you married?" Ayers asks. She blows out a stream of smoke and looks at him frankly. Something inside of him stirs. Someday, he thinks, he will be married to this girl right here, Ayers Wilson. And they will remember this, their very first conversation, sitting on a low tree branch outside Chester's Getaway during the funeral reception for her best friend, who also happened to be Baker's father's mistress.

"I was," he says. "I mean, technically I still am. But my wife found a girlfriend. She announced two days ago that she was leaving me for her colleague, Louisa."

"Ouch," Ayers says.

"Don't feel sorry for me," Baker says. "It's nothing compared to what you're going through."

"That's right," Ayers says. "Thanks for reminding me."

"I heard your friend was in an accident," Baker says. He wants to tell her who he is, but he's afraid she'll run off and he'll never see her again. "What was she like?"

"Rosie? She was…she was…she just *was*," Ayers says. "You know how sometimes people just click? And there's no reason for it? Rosie and I were like that. I met her working at La Tapa."

"La Tapa," Baker says.

"It's the best restaurant on the island. When I first got to St. John, it was the only place I wanted to work, but places like that can be hard to break into. I was very lucky to get hired and even luckier that Rosie took me under her wing. Rosie was a local, she's born and raised here, her parents were born and raised here, and her grandparents. There was no reason for her to befriend me, some white chick who shows up for the season to get in on the good tips, then leaves. But Rosie was nice to me from the very beginning. She was protective. She showed me where the quiet beaches were, she introduced me to a guy who sold me a pickup truck for cheap, she took me to Pine Peace market and introduced me to her mother and her step-father and just generally treated me like a long-lost sister."

"Wow," Baker says. He's moved by this and he wants to ask some strategic follow-up questions. Was she seeing anyone? Had Ayers known Russ? But at that moment, Baker looks up and sees Cash headed toward them, holding two beers in each hand.

Baker shakes his head at Cash in an attempt to convey the very important message: *She doesn't know who we are!* But Cash looks too hot and pissed-off to care about secret codes.

"Why the hell did you *vanish* like that?" Cash asks. "You expected me to find you all the way over here?"

"That's my fault," Ayers says, dropping the butt of her cigarette into her now empty beer. "I led your brother astray. Sorry about that."

Cash hands Baker two of the four beers and takes a long swallow of one of the beers he's holding. He seems like he's making an effort to regroup. "It's fine," he says.

"Cash, this is Ayers Wilson," Baker says. "Ayers is a friend of the deceased…"

"Best friend," Ayers interrupts. "Your brother admitted that you two are crashing."

"Um…yeah," Cash says.

"It seems like there would be better ways to spend your precious vacation days than attending a local funeral lunch," Ayers says. "Though Chester's barbecue is pretty good."

"Vacation days?" Cash says, and he gives Baker a quizzical look.

Ayers takes the awkward moment of silence that follows—during which Baker is silently imploring Cash to just *go with it*—as an opportunity to stand up. "I should get back to my post," she says. "And back to my grief, although God knows that's not going anywhere." She offers Baker her hand. "Thank you for allowing me to escape for a few minutes. Maybe I'll see you again before you leave."

"I hope so," Baker says. "What's the name of the restaurant where you work?"

"La Tapa," she says. "Right downtown, near Woody's."

"Woody's of the infamous happy hour," Baker says.

Ayers touches a finger to her nose. "You got it. And hey, go get yourself some barbecue. Anyone gives you trouble, tell them you're with me." She vanishes back into the crowd.

"What was that?" Cash asks, once she's gone. "You told her we were on *vacation*?"

But Baker is too lovestruck to answer.

IRENE

She's relieved when the boys leave the villa because she needs time and space to think, really think, and she needs room to process. There are two weighty issues Irene has to deal with. One is Russ's death, and the other is his deception.

Because this house, this island, is a very large, very real deception. Russell Steele, Irene's husband of thirty-five years, was a liar, a schemer, and most likely a cheat. Irene doesn't know what to say—words fail her, thoughts fail her, and the boys seem to expect both thoughts and words, some expression of pain, some expression of anger. But Irene is so befuddled she can't yet identify pain or anger. Her interior life is a barren wasteland.

She thinks back to the woman she was before, even hours before that blood-chilling call from Marilyn Monroe. She had been consumed with her problems at work, the demotion, the magazine moving off in a flashy new direction without her. She had gone to dinner with Lydia. Lydia had said, *You wouldn't understand because you have Russ, who dotes on you night and day.* Irene had deflected the statement, saying, *When he's around.* But she had thought, then, that Lydia was right: Irene did have a doting husband and she didn't properly understand what it was like to be alone.

Irene Hagen first met Russell Steele at a bar called the Field House during Irene's senior year in college when the University of Iowa played Northwestern in a snowstorm and that snowstorm turned into a blizzard and I-80, which led back to

Chicago, was shut down, effectively stranding all of the North-western fans in Iowa City. There had been a rumor circulating among Irene's sorority sisters at Alpha Chi Omega that the Northwestern boys were looking to hook up simply so they would have a place to sleep that night.

Only a few minutes after Irene heard this rumor, she felt a tap on her shoulder. "My name is Russell Steele," Russ said. "Would you allow me the honor of buying you a drink?"

Irene had scoffed. The guy was cute—brown hair, brown eyes, hooded Northwestern sweatshirt, *clean-cut*, her father would have said—and he had a beseeching look on his face, but Irene suffered no fools.

"No, thanks," she said, and she turned back to her friends.

Russell Steele had walked away. The jukebox, Irene remem-bered, was playing "Little Red Corvette," and Irene and her friends had stormed the dance floor. When they returned to their spot at the bar, there was a drink waiting for Irene. At that time in college, she drank something called a Lemon Drop, because she had an idea that vodka was less fattening than beer. Vanity came at a price: Lemon Drops at the Field House cost five dollars, a relative fortune.

"From that guy, over there," the bartender said. "The enemy."

When Irene looked, Russ waved.

He had stayed on the other side of the bar the rest of the night, and when it was time to go home, she had gone over to thank him for the drink.

"You didn't have to do that," she said.

"I know," he said. "But you're pretty and a way better dancer than all your friends."

"You're only saying that because you want a place to sleep tonight."

"I'm saying it because it's true," Russ said. "I'll be fine on a park bench tonight."

Irene had sighed. "You can sleep on the floor of my room," she said. "But I want you out by nine and if you touch me, I'll call security."

"Deal," Russell Steele said.

Russ had spent the night on Irene's dorm room floor—she had grudgingly given him one of the blankets and pillows from her own bed—with his arms crossed over his chest, like he was sleeping in a coffin. It was weird, Irene had thought, but also sort of endearing. At nine the next morning, when he was on his way out to catch his ride back to Evanston, she gave him her phone number. She figured she would never hear from him again, but he had called that very night, and the next day, he sent a bouquet of white calla lilies. He had noticed a poster of white callas on Irene's dorm room wall.

Because you love callas and I love you. That was what the card on the flowers said that had arrived on New Year's Day. Russ had been dead by the time those flowers arrived.

Irene thinks back on her marriage. Had she ever had reason to doubt Russ's honesty, or his fidelity? No. Russ's dominant trait had been one of utter devotion; he had never been one to flirt with other women. If Irene complimented a certain woman's figure or sense of style, Russ would say, "I didn't notice." And Irene believed him.

There was a way in which their marriage had been divided in half. The first half of their marriage, they had been normal, hardworking midwesterners, trying to raise two boys. Russ had his job selling corn syrup, and Irene was a full-time mother who picked up freelance editing work once the boys were in school. They lived in a nondescript ranch on Clover Street, a cul-de-sac east of the university, close to the high school. Irene won't lie: those had been lean years. She might even characterize them as tough. If Irene and Russ wanted to do anything fun or special—even a night out to dinner at the steakhouse in the Amanas—they had to budget. When Irene's minivan died, they had to ask Russ's mother, Milly, for a loan.

When Russ got the job offer from Todd Croft, it had seemed nothing short of a miracle, or like God's benevolent intervention finally lifting them up. Suddenly there was money—so much money! They were able to send Baker to Northwestern without taking out any loans. Then they were able to buy the fixer-upper of Irene's dreams on Church Street. A scant year after Russ got this new job, Irene was offered a full-time editorial position at *Heartland Home & Style.* Between the renovation and the new job, she had been so consumed, so *busy,* that she had barely taken notice of the dark side of their good fortune: Russ became less like a man she was married to and more like a man she dated whenever he was in town. But she had liked that, hadn't she? It had been nice to have Russ out from underfoot, to have freedom and autonomy when it came to making decisions about the new house, which was especially sweet since she no longer worried about their finances. Irene had been complicit in the change in their relationship; she had preferred their new situation to the slog of everyday married life. Irene's friends and coworkers asked why Irene never joined Russ on his business trips. He was in Florida, right? Didn't Irene want to enjoy the sun?

Irene used to answer, "I'll join him one of these days! I just need to find the time."

Deep down, she knew she should have been asking Russ questions: How did he like the new job? What were its downsides, its challenges? She should have kept track of where he was on certain days, who his clients were. She should have made plans to travel with him. But she didn't. And that's really all she can say: she didn't.

And so, as much as Irene wants to believe that Russ was an evil, deceptive charlatan with unfathomable secrets, she understands that she was partly to blame.

She is disturbed that Todd Croft made the unilateral decision to cremate Russ's body. He should have asked her permission. He should have given Irene control.

Baker spoke to someone at border control and discovered that because the crash happened in British waters, the British authorities — Virgin Islands Search and Rescue (VISAR), in conjunction with Her Majesty's coast guard — needed to give the FAA the authority to investigate the cause of the crash. But there were loopholes and regulations, as with any bureaucracy.

"I can't tell if they're giving me the runaround or if it's just a lot of red tape," Baker told Irene. "I haven't talked to the same person twice, so I don't have an ally. I did find out that the pilot's name is Stephen Thompson and he was a British citizen. The helicopter apparently belonged to him. So it's a British helicopter with a British pilot that crashed into British waters."

They are essentially being held hostage here as they wait for the ashes and the findings from the crash-site investigation. The only upside is this gives Irene time to do some detective work. She sits down at the desk in Russ's study. There is noth-

ing in any of the drawers but pens and some paper clips, nothing on the shelves but one lonely legal pad. Someone came in
and removed everything else.

The phone on Russ's desk works, and once the boys have
left, Irene dials the 305 number that Marilyn Monroe called
from on Tuesday night. Area code 305, she now knows, is
Miami. This, at least, makes a certain kind of sense.

The phone rings three times and Irene's stomach clenches.
She will demand to talk to Todd Croft. She deserves answers.
She deserves *answers*! What kind of business was Russ involved
in? What was going *on* down here? She fears Todd won't
tell her.

The phone clicks over to a recording, telling her that the
number she has dialed is no longer in service.

No longer in service.

Somehow, Irene isn't surprised.

She tries Paulette's cell phone next but is shuttled right to
voicemail. There's a magnet on the refrigerator from the real
estate company that provides a phone number.

A woman answers on the first ring. "Afternoon, this is Welcome to Paradise Real Estate, Octavia speaking. How can I
help you?"

"Yes, hello," Irene says. "May I please speak to Paulette
Vickers?"

"Paulette is out of the office today, I'm afraid," Octavia
says. "Would you like her voicemail?"

"It's urgent," Irene says. "Is there any way I might speak to
her in person?"

"I'm afraid not," Octavia says. "She's at a funeral. I don't
expect her back in the office until tomorrow morning."

Funeral, Irene thinks.

"Okay, Octavia, thank you very much," Irene says, and she hangs up.

Funeral for the local woman, Irene thinks. The local woman who was in the helicopter with Russ and the British pilot, Stephen Thompson, flying at seven o'clock in the morning from St. John to an island in the British Virgin Islands called Anegada. Who was this local woman?

Irene isn't naive. There is no possibility that Russ lived in this house by himself, without a companion, without a woman. Irene thinks back to the day before, when Cash was searching the master bedroom. He told Irene he'd found nothing, but Irene knew he was lying.

Winnie comes banging into the study, panting and wagging her tail, sniffing at Irene's knees. Irene rubs Winnie's soft butterscotch head and says, "Come with me."

She and Winnie enter the master bedroom, and Irene says, "What are we looking for, Winnie? What are we looking for?" She stands in the middle of the room and inhales, trying to divine something, anything, using her intuition. Someone came through the house and cleared it out, sweeping away all of Russ's dirt.

But something—Cash had found something. He had that expression on his face, feigned innocence, like when he used to hide his one-hitter in his varsity soccer jacket, and years before that when he finished an entire box of Girl Scout cookies—Caramel deLites—by himself and then stuffed the box deep in the trash.

Stuffed the box deep in the trash.

Irene looks around the room for hidden nooks and crannies. She checks the drawer of the nightstand: empty.

She sees Winnie nosing the bed. Is she picking up a scent?

Winnie seems pretty interested, nearly insistent, her nose working into the gap between the mattress and the box spring.

"What are you doing?" Irene asks. She lifts the white matelassé coverlet—she has to admit there is a freshness to the decor of this house that is a nice alternative to the heavy, dark furnishings of home—and slips her hand under the mattress. Bingo. She feels the edge of something.

She pulls out a frame. A photograph.

Oh.

Oh no. God, no.

Irene sits on the bed, her hands shaking.

The photograph is of Russ with a beautiful young West Indian woman. They're lying in a hammock, their limbs intertwined. The woman's skin is the color of coffee with cream, and next to her Russ is golden, glowing. He looks healthy.

He looks happy.

Irene lets out a moan. She can't believe the agony she feels. Russ had another woman, a lover. More than a lover: Irene can tell from the ease and familiarity of their pose, from Russ's smile, from the woman's eyes shining. They were together, a pair, a couple. They were in love.

Irene wants to smash the glass. She wants to go onto the balcony and throw the offending photograph as far as she can into the tropical bushes below.

But she needs it. It's evidence.

Irene is mortified to think that Cash has seen this photo, this proof of his father's secret life. It conveys failure—on Russ's part, certainly, but also on Irene's part. She wasn't sexy, desirable, or enticing enough to have kept her husband happy at home. This photograph is proof.

Irene screams until she feels her voice reach its ragged

edge. It feels so indulgent, so childish, but it's also the release she's been waiting for. Russ was *cheating* on her, living with someone young and beautiful, having sex with her, laughing with her, kissing her, eating meals with her, curling up in a hammock with her, falling asleep next to her. For how long? For years, Irene has to assume. Every single time he told her he was "working" in Florida or God knows where else, he was here, in this house, with this woman. The depth of Russ's lies takes Irene's breath away. Hundreds of lies, *thousands* of lies. He had professed his love for Irene daily, every single time she spoke to him on the phone. He had told her he loved her so often, she had stopped hearing it. She thinks of the airplane he hired to drag a banner around Iowa City on her fiftieth birthday. At the time, Irene had been embarrassed by that blatant show of devotion. What she hadn't realized, of course, was that Russ was trying to compensate. He hadn't hired the airplane because he loved Irene and wanted everyone to know it; he'd hired it because he felt guilty.

And did this woman know? Irene wonders. Did she know that Russ was married and had two sons? Did she know that he lived in a Victorian house in Iowa City, Iowa? Had Russ shown her pictures of Irene? It's too heinous to contemplate. Irene cries, she *wails,* and Winnie starts to bark, but Irene can't stop. She's grateful that the boys are gone so she can just let go. She was such a trusting fool.

She thinks back on the many hours that she spent comforting Lydia when Lydia found out that her husband, Phil, philandering Phil, was cheating on her. Phil worked as the head of security for the University of Iowa. One night, he answered a call from a freshman named Natalie Mercer, who was receiving calls on her dorm room phone. The caller kept saying he was watching her, he could see what she was wearing, he was coming to get her when she least expected it. Irene could remember Lydia relaying these terrifying details to her, back when Natalie Mercer was a faceless university student. Phil ended up catching the guy, a doctoral candidate in psychiatry, of all things. He was expelled from the school and this was, in theory, a happy ending. Peace was restored; Phil was a hero. But then, over a year later, when Lydia sensed the temperature of her marriage cooling to a suspicious low, she did some snooping—and what did she find? Phil's cell phone documenting a lurid affair with Natalie Mercer that dated all the way back to the day Phil caught the caller.

Irene remembers feeling disgusted with Phil, but also—in her most private thoughts—a bit incredulous that Phil had been conducting an affair for over a year and Lydia hadn't noticed.

Compared to what Russ has done, Phil having an affair with a student seems almost quaint.

Irene and Russ were married at the First Presbyterian Church in Iowa City in 1984, when they were fresh out of college. They had been together for a scant year and a half, since that football game in the blizzard. Russ's father, the navy pilot, was dead by then, but Milly was there to represent the family. Milly and Irene had hit it off from the moment they met. Because Russ had grown up in so many places, he didn't have any longtime childhood friends or neighbors or members of the community attending the wedding, the way Irene did. He had Milly and Milly's two sisters—Bobbie and Cissy, whom Russ called "the aunties"—and there were also a bunch of Russ's friends and fraternity brothers from Northwestern. Nothing about Russ's background had seemed unusual, and certainly not sinister.

Irene and Russ had said their vows and kissed at the altar.

There had been a reception at the Elks Lodge, where they ate filet mignon and cut the cake and danced to "Little Red Corvette," and then after the reception, Irene and Russ ran through a shower of rice to get to the getaway car. They drove to the Hancock House, a bed-and-breakfast in Dubuque, Iowa, where they were given a suite with a library, and a claw-foot tub in front of a fireplace in the bathroom, and it was in this moment that Irene fell in love with the style and decor of Queen Anne houses. She said to Russ, "I want us to live in a house just like this one."

Russ had laughed nervously. They were renting a one-bedroom apartment in University City. They were kids. They had, Irene sees now, barely known each other then, the newly minted Mr. and Mrs. Russell Steele.

Irene had grown to know Russ the only way it could be done—by putting in the time. She had learned how Russ liked his coffee, how he liked his eggs, the way he brushed his teeth, the sound of his snoring, the habits of other drivers that made him angry, the actors he admired and found funny, the way he whistled "Penny Lane," only that song, when he was doing small home improvement projects. Irene knew his shoe size, his jacket size, his waist and inseam measurements. She knew how he had voted in every election. She knew his first, second, and third favorite flavor of ice cream. She knew he would get forty pages into a book and then abandon it, no matter how good it was. She knew that he had spent his childhood as a constant outsider because he moved so often. She also knew he never felt like his father loved him. Russ's father was a military man, a fortress, with a mind and heart that were impossible to penetrate. Irene knew that, because of his father, Russ had never wanted to serve in the military. In fact, if Irene were to disclose Russ's biggest secret, it was that he had sabo-taged his chances of getting into the U.S. Naval Academy by intentionally missing his interview.

That, as it turns out, was not his biggest secret.

Irene howls. There are so many thoughts that pierce her, not least of which is her own blindness, her own myopia, her own pathetic, middle-class, middle America view that mar-riages are meant to last forever, through the bad times, through the boring times. They were Russ and Irene Steele, parents of Baker and Cash, owner of the stunning Victorian on Church Street. They were good, God-fearing, straightforward people. Not people with scandalous secrets.

Finally, Irene stops crying. She wears herself out. She must have worn Winnie out as well, because Winnie has fallen asleep in a sunny spot on the floor.

Irene regards the photograph. Russ has a lover, an island girl. It seems less awful than it did forty minutes earlier. One thing Irene has learned in her fifty-seven years is that no mat-ter how hideous something seems at first, with the passing of time comes habituation and then acceptance. What Irene is living through now is abhorrent. But the world is filled with deceptions and betrayals—nearly every life has one—and yet the sun still rises and sets, the world continues on.

She sits up. The water out the window seems to wink at her, and not in a wicked, I-seduced-your-husband sort of way but in a benevolent way.

What did Paulette say? Eighty steps down to a private beach. Okay.

* * *

Irene decides to go barefoot. The stone steps turn to wood, they meander down the side of the hill until the vegetation clears and Irene steps onto a tiny, perfect crescent of white sand beach. The sand is like sugar, like flour, like talcum. She stoops to pick some up and rub it between her fingers. Is it real? Yes.

There are three teak chaises on the beach with bright orange cushions. Irene tries to imagine Russ lying on one of these chaises, with his girlfriend next to him. *And who would the third chaise be for?* she wonders.

Today it's for Irene. She lies back in the sun, absorbing the heat, which feels like a miracle after the icy winds of Iowa City. She can't stay here long, just another minute; wrinkles are multiplying on her face by the second, she's certain. Her breathing is almost back to normal. Her eyes are sore but dry.

Russ had a lover.

Deep breath.

Okay.

Irene gets up and walks to the water's edge. The color is halfway between blue and green; it's not a color found elsewhere in nature, except, in rare and wonderful cases, in people's eyes. Tiny waves lap at her feet. The water is soft and just cool enough to be refreshing. When Irene had packed, back in Iowa, the idea of bringing a bathing suit had briefly crossed her mind, part of some kind of mental checklist, but she hadn't been able to imagine circumstances in which she would want or need one. She looks both ways. This beach is secluded from view. There are a few boats on the horizon, but no one can see her here.

Irene shucks off her clothes and stands naked on the beach. Is she invisible? She feels quite the opposite. She feels exposed. Let the world see her drooping breasts, the dimpling at her thighs, the cesarean scar eight inches across her lower abdomen.

She steps into the water and all she can think is how good it feels, the coolness enveloping her. She swims out a few yards.

This is the same water that claimed Russ. Russ is dead. That's the next fact Irene has to grapple with. He's gone. He's never coming back. She will never see him again. She can't ask him why he did what he did, where she went wrong, where they both went wrong. She can't scream at him and he can't apologize. There is nowhere to put her fury, no one to answer the question of *why.*

Irene lies back in the water, floating, looking at the cloudless bluebird sky, and thinks, really *thinks,* what it was like for Russ in that helicopter. Irene has never been in a helicopter, but she has a vague notion that it's loud. Russ was probably wearing a headset. Did he see the storm approaching? Did he see flashes of lightning or hear thunder? Was he scared? When the helicopter got hit, did it go into free fall? Was it terrifying? Did Russ have a second or two when he knew they were plummeting, when the earth was getting closer and closer? Did his heart stop? Did he have any thoughts? Did he think about Irene and the boys? And what about impact? Did he burst into flames? Did he lose consciousness? Did he drown?

Irene sets her feet on the firm, sandy bottom and wades toward shore, until her toe hits something solid. She bends down and picks up a smooth gray rock the size of an egg. She drops the stone from hip-height into the water and watches it sink.

Russ's body had been lying at the bottom of the sea like that rock.

Her heart shatters. The tears she cries now aren't of anger

or indignation but of pure sadness. Russ is dead and the woman, his lover, his love, is dead. Dead. Never coming back.

I will forgive them, Irene thinks. *I will make myself forgive them if it's the last thing I do.*

Irene dries off in the sun, puts her clothes back on, and faces the eighty steps she has to climb to get back to the villa.

The woman in the photograph is young, thirty or thirty-five. She must have family, parents. And Irene is going to find out who they are.

AYERS

She wakes up the morning after the funeral hungover, no surprise there. She has to go back to work at La Tapa at four o'clock and she's due to crew a BVI charter on *Treasure Island* the next day. Her best friend is dead but that doesn't change the fact that Ayers has bills to pay.

Maia, she knows, has bravely decided to go back to school on Monday. Gifft Hill is nurturing, a nest, and all of Maia's friends are there. Her teachers will care for her and keep her busy. If she needs to take a break, she'll take a break. If she needs to cry, she'll cry. There's no point staying home to wallow, Maia said, sounding a lot older than twelve.

There's no point staying home to wallow, Ayers thinks, and so she ties up her hiking boots and throws a couple bottles of water and a baggie of trail mix into her small pack and she climbs into her truck.

She drives down the Centerline Road past mile marker five and parks. She's going to hike the Reef Bay Trail today, all the way down and all the way back up. It's not her favorite hike on St. John—it's popular and sometimes overrun with tourists—but it has the payoff of the petroglyphs carved into the rocks at the bottom of the trail, and today Ayers wants to put her eyes on something that has lasted three thousand years.

The first time she hiked this trail, nearly ten years earlier, she was with Rosie. It was their first date.

As Ayers starts down the path, she remembers Rosie asking her, *So what's your story, anyway? Where are you from and how did you end up here?*

As always, Ayers had hesitated before answering. She envied people who had *grown up* someplace—Missoula, Montana; Cleveland, Ohio; Little Rock, Arkansas. Ayers had been home-schooled by her parents, both of whom suffered from an acute case of wanderlust. She had lived in eight countries growing up and had visited dozens of others. To most people, this sounded cool, and in some ways, Ayers knows, it *was* cool, or parts of it were. But since humans are inclined to want what they don't have, she longed to live in America, preferably the solid, unchanging, undramatic Midwest, and attend a real high school, the kind shown in movies, complete with a football team, cheerleaders, pep rallies, chemistry labs, summer reading lists, hall passes, proms, detentions, assemblies, fundraisers, lockers, Spanish clubs, marching bands, and the dismissal bell.

What had she told Rosie? She had told her the unvarnished truth.

My parents were hippies, vagabonds, travelers; we lived out of our backpacks. My father did maintenance at hostels in exchange for a free place to stay, and my mother waited tables for money. We lived in Kathmandu; in Hoi An, Vietnam; in Santiago, Chile. We spent one year traveling across Australia, and when we finally got to Perth, my parents liked it so much I thought we would stay, but then my grandmother got very sick so we went back to San Francisco, where she lived, and I thought we would live in San Francisco because my grandmother left my father money—a lot of money. But the only thing my parents ever wanted to do with money was travel, and so we moved to Europe—Paris first, then Italy, then Greece. We were living in Morocco when I turned eighteen and I had applied to college without their knowledge—Clemson University in South Carolina—and I got in and I went, but I had to pay for it all myself and I worked two jobs in addition to studying, which left me no time for fun. I hated it in the end and so I dropped out and started working the seasonal circuit. I spent my summers in New England—Cape Cod, Newport, the Vineyard—and winters in the Caribbean. I spent last winter in Aruba and a guy I met there told me about St. John. So here I am.

Holy shit, Rosie had said.

I know, Ayers said. *I know.*

Ayers makes it to the bottom of the hill in no time. The trail is steep and rocky but well maintained and shaded by a thick canopy of leaves all the way down, though the sun streams through here and there in a way that turns the air emerald. Ayers is so dehydrated from the night before that she sucks down her first bottle of water in one long pull. She should have brought more than two bottles. What was she thinking? She considers her trail mix. She hasn't eaten much of anything since hearing the news; not even Chester's barbecue appealed to her.

Rosie is dead. When Ayers gets to work at four, Rosie won't be there. Her name will be off the schedule. There will be a new hire by Monday. At La Tapa, Rosie is replaceable. But not with Ayers.

Ayers hikes up to a small outcropping of rocks to see the petroglyphs. They've had rain recently—the thunderstorm that killed Rosie—so the markings in the stone are easy to see. Ayers gets up close and focuses on them. So old. So permanent. Ayers could leave St. John today and come back in fifty years and they would still be here.

Rosie had a tattoo of the petroglyph above her ankle that Ayers had always admired. *Get one,* Rosie had said. *We can match.* But Ayers had felt funny about appropriating the symbol as her own. She hadn't *grown* up here; she had merely *shown* up here. She somehow didn't think she had earned it.

Maybe now, though.

One of the rogue thoughts Ayers has entertained in the past few days is that of leaving. Without Mick and without Rosie, she wondered, what's the point?

The point, she supposes, is that St. John is as much of a home as she has ever had.

Besides, there's Maia to consider now. Ayers can't leave Maia. If Ayers is going to make a change, it should be the opposite of leaving. She needs to stay here through the year—endure the hot summer, pray through hurricane season.

There's only one other person at the petroglyphs, a guy with bushy blond hair and a gorgeous golden retriever. He looks like a hard-core hiker: he's wearing cargo shorts and a pair of Salomon boots. He's studying the petroglyphs with an intensity that discourages conversation, but the dog runs right over to Ayers and buries her nose in Ayers's crotch.

"Aw, sweetheart," Ayers says. She pries the dog's snout from between her legs.

"Winnie!" the hiker calls out. Ayers looks up and he smiles. "I'm sorry. I sent her to finishing school but still she has no manners."

"Not a problem," Ayers says. "That's the most action I've gotten in weeks."

The hiker blushes and Ayers congratulates herself on being truly inappropriate. Then she takes a closer look at him. She has seen this guy before, but where?

"Do I know you?" she asks.

"No, I don't think so," the hiker says. "I just got here a couple days…" His voice trails off. "Oh, wait."

Wait, Ayers thinks. She assumed he'd come into the restaurant or maybe even been a guest on *Treasure Island*, but no, she met him *yesterday,* at the reception. "Yeah," Ayers says. "I… you… were at Chester's, right? With…?"

"My brother," the hiker says. "Baker."

"Right," Ayers says. "Baker." She had liked Baker. He was super-handsome, tall, charming. She had thought maybe she had actually *met a man* at Rosie's funeral reception. She had thought maybe he'd been a gift from Rosie.

But Baker was a tourist and Ayers tried to stay away from tourists. This was advice she had received from Rosie. Thirteen years earlier, Rosie had hooked up with a guy who sailed in on a yacht, stayed for four days, and then left. *The Pirate,* she called him. She had never seen him again. He was Maia's father.

"Anyway, I'm Cash," the hiker says, offering his hand. "As in Johnny."

"Ayers," she says. "As in Rock."

"And this is Winnie," Cash says. "As in the Pooh."

"So you found the petroglyphs," Ayers says. "What about Baker? He didn't make it?"

"He's not much of a hiker," Cash says. "He was by the pool when I left."

"Pool?" Ayers says. "Where are you guys staying? The Westin? Caneel?"

"Villa," Cash says.

"Nice," Ayers says. "North shore?"

"I'm really not sure," Cash says. He whistles to Winnie. "We should get back, though."

"Are you catching the boat?" Ayers asks. "Or hiking back up?"

"Hiking back up," Cash says. "I didn't realize there was a boat."

"You have to set it up with the park service," Ayers says. "Or maybe it picks up at certain times. I used to know, but I've forgotten." She shakes her head and, much to her chagrin, she starts to cry. "My best friend died a few days ago in a helicopter crash. That party you and Baker stumbled upon was her funeral reception..."

"I know," Cash says. He's carrying a small pack and he pulls out a navy bandana and an ice-cold bottle of water. He offers both to Ayers.

She accepts them gratefully. "I'm sorry," she says. "I heard it would be like this. You're fine one minute and not fine the next. It's just...I came down here to see the petroglyphs because Rosie loved them. She had this tattoo..." Ayers struggles for a breath. "She was just so pretty and so *cool,* such a good friend, my only friend, really, the best friend I've ever had. My parents...we never *stayed* anywhere. I would make a friend in Chiang Mai or Isla Holbox and then we'd *leave*..." She wipes her eyes with the bandana and takes a much-needed swig of water. "I'm babbling. This awful, horrible thing happened and now I'm bemoaning my entire existence." She tries to smile. "And you're a complete stranger."

"It's okay," Cash says. "Believe me, I understand being shell-shocked." He looks like he might say more but instead, he shakes his head. "It's just...I *do* understand."

That's not likely, but Ayers isn't going to argue. "Do you want to hike back up together?" she asks. "I have to get back, too. I have work at four o'clock."

"Sure," Cash says.

"Good," Ayers says. "I'm also worried about passing out on the way back up. I only brought one other bottle of water."

Cash grins. "Ah, the truth comes out. You need me to keep you alive."

He's cute, Ayers decides. Not rock star handsome like his brother, but cute. Compact, strong, sturdy.

But again, a tourist.

They start back up the trail, Cash leading, Winnie at his heels, Ayers following. Up is way harder, her hangover is gripping her head like a tight bathing cap. She has to stop and when Cash turns around to check on her—he's very sweet to do so—he stops, too.

"You seem like a pretty experienced hiker," Ayers says.

"I live in the mountains," Cash says. "Breckenridge, Colorado. Being at sea level is new for me. Honestly, I could probably go forever without getting tired. It's amazing how nice life is with an adequate supply of oxygen."

"Yeah," Ayers says. "I guess I take it for granted." That wasn't always the case, though. She and her parents had trekked to Everest Base Camp when Ayers was thirteen. The air in the Himalayas was thin; Ayers had crazy dreams that she still remembers to this day. She and her parents spent weeks hiking in Patagonia as well. She remembers sinking to her knees in scree, scrabbling over rocks, jumping down into her father's arms off a high ledge, eating ramen noodles cooked over a camp stove for days on end, waking up at three in the morning to see the sunrise set the Torres del Paine on fire. When they finally came out of the mountains, they stayed in a town called San Carlos de Bariloche, where they took hot showers and ate a breakfast of pancakes drizzled with chocolate sauce and a big bowl of fresh, ripe strawberries.

"So do you ski?" Ayers asks Cash. He's too far ahead for casual conversation, but Ayers wants him to know she's a normal person and not just some emotional basket case.

"I do," he says. "Do you?"

"I do. Haven't been in a while but my parents and I lived in Gstaad one winter so I got pretty good. I miss it." She gazes up into the trees. "You might not think it living here, but sometimes I really miss the snow."

"I've only been here three days and I miss it," Cash says.

"So you live in Colorado and your brother lives in Texas?" Ayers says. "And you're here for a family reunion?" She's proud of herself for remembering.

"Family reunion?" Cash says. "Is that what Baker told you?"

Is that what Baker told her? Yes, she's pretty sure that's what he said. "Um...?"

"I guess it is a family reunion of sorts," Cash says. "He's

right." With that, Cash seems to pick up his pace and Ayers takes the hint: he doesn't want to talk. Fair enough. She should conserve her energy and use it for making it up the hill.

This had been a stupid idea.

Once they reach the road, however, Ayers drinks the last of her water and eats a handful of the trail mix and immediately feels a sense of accomplishment. She didn't stay home and wallow. She hiked the Reef Bay Trail, wildly hungover.

"Want some trail mix?" she asks Cash.

He helps himself to a handful. "Thank you." He seems to perk up a little as well. "I don't want to pry, but your friend who died...do they know what happened?"

"Helicopter crash," Ayers says.

"I heard that," Cash says. "But do they know why? Or where she was going?"

"She was going over to Anegada for the day with her... boyfriend. The helicopter got struck by lightning."

"They both died?" Cash asks.

Ayers nods. "And the pilot."

"Do they know anything about the boyfriend?" Cash asks. "Does he have a family?"

"I don't care about the boyfriend," Ayers says. "At this point, I wish Rosie had never met him." Her voice is sharper than she meant it to be. "I'm sorry, bad topic. Listen, how long are you here?"

Cash looks at the ground. "Another couple of days, I guess," he says.

"Well, if you're free tomorrow, I'm crewing on a boat called

Treasure Island, and we're going on a day trip to the British Virgin Islands—the Baths on Virgin Gorda, snorkeling, lunch on Cooper Island. It's fun and I can bring you as my guest. Do you have a passport?"

"I do," Cash says. "I'm embarrassed to admit that I thought I might need it to come here. I wasn't sure. This trip was kind of thrown together at the last minute."

"If you have a passport, then you should definitely come," Ayers says. "Have you ever snorkeled before?"

"I haven't," Cash says. "I want to. But my mother might need my help tomorrow." He bends down to pat Winnie's head.

"Well, if you decide you want to come, just bring your passport and wear a bathing suit and come to the dock right across the street from Mongoose Junction at seven thirty tomorrow morning. I'll take care of everything else."

"Okay," Cash says. "I'll think about it." He waves as he leads Winnie back to his Jeep.

He'll think about it but he won't do it, Ayers knows. He thinks she's nuts.

And he's probably right.

CASH

There's no way Cash is going on a snorkeling trip to the BVIs, and yet he keeps thinking about Ayers and about the invitation.

Ayers is pretty, there are no two ways about it, and she was out *hiking by herself*, which turned Cash on in a big way. He had thought Denver and Breckenridge would be filled with women who loved the outdoors—who liked to hike and cross-country and downhill ski—and whereas that was sort of true, none of the outdoorsy women Cash had met had struck a chord with him.

None of them had been anything like Ayers.

And Winnie had been crazy about her. A good sign.

Cash doesn't tell Baker or his mother where he's been or who he's seen, and they don't ask. His mother had taken the other Jeep and gone into Cruz Bay—for what reason, Cash couldn't imagine. She sure as hell wasn't shopping for silver bracelets or bottles of rum. And Baker was being positively useless. He'd made two or three calls to the British authorities before declaring himself stonewalled, and so he'd spent the day "waiting for callbacks," which meant sitting by the pool, staring out at the spectacular view. He didn't even seem sad to Cash. Or maybe he was sad and just hiding it—which is exactly what Cash is doing. Cash wants to cry—to put his fist through a wall or break a vase, he wants to lose his shit, exorcise the bad feelings. But the problem is that his emotions are muddy. He's not purely sad about losing his father. Nor is he purely angry that his father was a wizard of deception. His feelings are a toxic combination of both, and to head off an explosion or tantrum, he is utilizing good, old-fashioned denial. Hence the hike today.

Cash takes an outdoor shower. The walls are encrusted with shells—conch, whelk, cowrie—and there's purple bougainvillea draping in overhead, and the water is hot and plentiful, and Cash has a view of the water. He decides it probably qualifies as the best shower he's ever taken. He gets dressed as the sun sets, then he offers to grill up some steaks.

Irene says she isn't hungry. "I think I'll go up to bed."

"Do you want me to call Milly, Mom?" Cash asks. "Just to, you know, check in?"

Irene turns around on the stairs and gives Cash a plaintive look. "Would you mind?" she asks. "I can't lie to Milly. I just can't do it. You know, she did a good job with your father. This isn't her fault. I don't ever want you to think that."

"I *don't* think that," Cash says. "Dad was a grown man."

"I'm beginning to wonder," Irene says.

"I'll call Milly," Cash says.

He dials the number for the Brown Deer retirement community, but the nurse who answers in the medical unit tells him that Milly is too weak to talk.

"What do you mean too *weak*?" he asks. "Is everything okay?"

"She's ninety-seven years old," the nurse says. "Her body is shutting down."

"Well, right," Cash says. "I know, but..."

"Call back tomorrow, Mr. Steele," the nurse says. "Until then, enjoy your vacation."

Cash and Baker eat steak and potato salad out on the deck. Cash knows he should tell Baker he saw Ayers, and he should tell Baker about Milly not being strong enough to come to the phone, and he should really tell Baker about losing the stores. But before he can broach any of these topics, Baker says, "So Mom told me she has a meeting tomorrow."

"A meeting?" Cash says. "With whom?"

"She wouldn't tell me," Baker says. "She came back from town and when I asked how it went she said it was productive and that she has a meeting tomorrow."

"What time?" Cash asks.

"In the morning," Baker says. "She wasn't sure how long it would take."

"Are you worried?" Cash asks.

"No," Baker says. "It's Mom."

Right, Cash thinks. They have never had to worry about Irene in the past. But now...things have changed, haven't they?

"What are you doing tomorrow?" Cash asks.

"Same thing I did today," Baker says. "Waiting for the phone to ring, but it's Sunday so I'm sure nothing will happen. I would like to get out tomorrow night, though. What do you think about that? I want to eat at La Tapa."

"La Tapa?" Cash says.

"Do you remember that girl, Ayers?" Baker asks. "From the reception?"

Cash's heart starts bobbing up and down. Yes. Ayers. Yes. He tries to keep his expression neutral. "Yeah, why?"

"She works there," Baker says. "And I want to see her again."

"See her why?" Cash asks.

"Because she was Rosie's best friend," Baker says. "She has information."

Cash clears the plates. Ayers *was* Rosie's best friend and she possibly *does* have information, but Cash gets a very strong feeling that that *isn't* why Baker wants to see Ayers again.

You're *married*! He wants to snap. To *Anna*!

But instead, Cash makes a decision. He's going to the British Virgin Islands tomorrow.

Cash avoids group tours for a reason: they turn even the most authentic experiences into a Disneyland ride. It's unavoidable, he supposes. This tour company, Treasure Island, which takes a group of twenty people on a three-stop adventure to another country, needs to make the experience safe and user-friendly. And fun!

"Most of all," Ayers says over her headset microphone to the assembled group, after explaining where the life preservers are kept, how to disembark at the Baths of Virgin Gorda (they have to jump off the boat and swim to shore), and how to defog one's mask for maximum snorkeling visibility, "we want you to have fun. In that spirit, the bar is now open. Come get your painkillers."

Painkillers, Cash thinks. *If only.* And yet he finds himself shuffling to the bar behind a big fat guy in a HARLEY-DAVIDSON OF SOUTH DAKOTA t-shirt. There's nothing wrong with this guy or any of the other couples or families aboard the boat, except that they are taking up Ayers's time and attention. It's like she's running a day care, Cash thinks. *Everyone* has questions: What if they aren't a strong enough swimmer to make it to the shore in Virgin Gorda? Will there be gluten-free options at lunch? Is it true that the Baths have been spoiled by too much tourism? Will there be sharks? What about barracudas?

Ayers answers all the questions, and Cash surreptitiously hangs on her every word while he sips his painkiller (it's rum, cream of coconut, pineapple juice, and orange juice, with nut-meg on top). He had to go online and look up what the Virgin Gorda Baths even *were*—when Ayers said it yesterday, he pic-tured a cavernous building populated by overweight Slavic men—so he knows it's a rock formation that has created vari-ous "rooms" that can be toured. After the Baths, they're stop-ping at Cooper Island for lunch, and on the way home they'll snorkel at a spot called the Indians.

"How're you doing?" Ayers has caught him back in line for a second painkiller; the first one went down way too easily on an empty stomach, and he knows that after his second, he should avail himself of the fresh sliced papaya, watermelon, and pineapple as well as a piece of the homemade banana coconut bread. Otherwise he's going to be one of the people who doesn't make it to shore.

When is the last time I did any real swimming? he wonders. Junior-year gym class at Iowa City High School?

"I'm good," he says. He knows he should engage some of his fellow adventurers in conversation—there's a gay couple about his age who look nice—so that Ayers doesn't think he's a snob or socially awkward. Cash has been too busy feeling jealous about Ayers's relationships with her two male crew members: James, the captain, and Wade, the first mate. James is a West Indian guy built like a Greek god and Wade must be a retired Hollister model. Both of them call Ayers "baby," and when Cash first arrived at the dock, he saw Ayers and James hugging, but then he realized James was offering his condo-lences. Still, Cash is discomfited by the physical attractiveness of the crew; it seems designed to make Cash and his fellow adventurers feel unremarkable.

"I'm sorry I don't have time to chill with you right now," Ayers says. "It'll be different on the ride home."

"No worries," Cash says. "I'm a big boy."

Ayers gives him a nice smile, one that targets his heart. Has he ever reacted this way to a woman? Geez, not since ninth grade with Claire Bellows, who ended up being his girlfriend all through high school until she went off to Northwestern, where she proceeded to hook up with Baker. His own brother. That had been devastating, Cash won't lie, and it had led to Cash hating Baker and being very mistrustful of women. Since then, Cash's romantic life has consisted of weeklong hookups and one-night stands, usually with the women he was teaching to ski.

Cash takes his second painkiller to the upper deck and chooses a seat near the gay couple. The sun feels good, and there is something about being out on the water that reminds Cash of standing at the top of a mountain. It's elemental, he supposes, communing with the earth. Ayers, over her headset microphone, gives the group some background history—the Danish settlers, the sugar plantation, the slave revolt in which African slaves from St. John swam to the British Virgin Islands to freedom. She points out Lovango Cay, where there used to be a brothel for pirates—the pirates called it "love and go," which was then shortened to Lovango; everyone laughs at that story. Ayers shifts her focus to Jost Van Dyke, home of the world-famous bar the Soggy Dollar (Cash has never heard of it), then to Tortola, on their left, and the "sister islands"— Peter, Norman, Cooper, Salt, and Ginger—on their right. Cash goes downstairs for another painkiller, and when he comes back up to the deck, he says to one of the members of the male couple (tall, balding, pale), "So is this your first time to the BVIs?"

"Affirmative," the other man (short, dark) says. "Chris's parents just bought a timeshare at the Westin so we thought we'd come down to see what the fuss is about. How about you?"

Cash needs to pick a story and stick to it. "Here for a week with my mom and my brother. Family reunion."

Chris says, "Did they come with you?"

"No," Cash says.

"My kind of family reunion!" the short, dark-haired guy says, and the three of them do a cheer.

Thanks to another painkiller or three (Could Cash really have had five drinks already? It's not even ten in the morning), the morning passes quickly, with soft, blurred edges. Once they reach Virgin Gorda, Cash's anxiety about jumping off the boat and swimming to shore melts away. He's an athletic guy, in good shape—that should count for something—and sure enough, he makes it with ease. Ayers leads the tour through the Baths. They're not like anything Cash has ever seen: huge granite boulders that form a series of rooms and formations with shallow pools of warm turquoise water in each. They start out viewing the Whale Gallery—a rock that looks like an orca shooting out of the water—then move on to the Lion's Den and Moon rock. Cash's favorite room is called the Cathedral because of the way the light reflects off the water, spangling the rocks with color and making it look like stained glass. Ayers not only offers charming commentary, she is attentive to the older and less agile members of the group who have difficulty negotiating the rough-hewn wooden steps and squeezing through narrow passageways. Cash helps out wherever he can, offering his hand and allowing a little girl, five or six years old, to jump down into his arms. He feels like a Boy Scout, but then again, he *was* a Boy Scout.

Ayers whispers in his ear. "Want a job?"

Does he want a job? Only five days ago, Cash made what he thought was a major life decision to return to the mountains. Now his father is dead and Cash's "life," or what's left of it, has been turned on its head. What remains that is solid and reliable? Winnie. His mother. In a pinch, he supposes, his brother. There's nothing to stop Cash from moving down here and working for Treasure Island. He could live in his father's villa. As outrageous as the thought is, it holds appeal. He realizes that Ayers is only kidding, but what if she's *not* kidding?

He's drunk, he needs to slow down, but when Chris and Mike ask him if he wants to join them for a beer—there's a bar at the exit of the Baths, of course—he says yes.

He has never before seen the appeal of day-drinking. Lots of people drink while skiing; many, many folks choose to do two or three runs and then hit the bar. Cash likes his daytime hours to be productive, and so he saves his drinking for the evening, which is probably a legacy of his strait-laced midwestern upbringing. Now, however, he understands how liberating it is to get intoxicated while the sun is out. It feels decadent in the best possible way. The world seems alternately kind, forgiving, absurd, and hilarious.

"You can't drink all day if you don't start in the morning," he says to Chris and Mike. "Am I right?"

* * *

They leave Virgin Gorda and motor to Cooper Island, where there is an eco-resort with a restaurant that serves large groups like theirs. Cash orders the blackened fish sandwich with fries, and Chris and Mike do likewise. They inform Cash with a certain solemn righteousness that they're pescatarians, which Cash hears as "Presbyterians," and he says, "I'm Presbyterian, too, though I hardly ever go to church anymore." This statement cracks Chris and Mike up and Cash is nonplussed until they explain that *pescatarian* means they eat only fish—no meat or chicken. Then Cash dissolves into laughter that he can't recover from. Every time he lifts his head to take a breath, he doubles over again.

"You look like you're enjoying yourself," Ayers says. She lifts Cash's rum punch and takes a discreet sip. "I'm not supposed to imbibe until after the snorkeling."

Cash tries to sober up a little. He introduces Chris and Mike to Ayers, and then their food arrives and it turns out there's a fish sandwich for Ayers as well, which she douses with hot sauce.

"God, I love" —Cash stops. He nearly says, "you," but he catches himself— "a woman who enjoys spicy food."

"Rosie loved spicy food," Ayers says. "And she could cook, too. She made the best jerk chicken. Mmmmmm."

Cash knows he should capitalize on the topic of Rosie, since Ayers brought her up, but he's too intoxicated to think it through strategically and he feels it would be awkward to include Chris and Mike in the conversation and rude to exclude them. He takes a bite of his own sandwich. It's delicious.

Food, he thinks. He needs food.

*   *   *

After lunch, they head to the Indians, three rock towers jutting from the sea, where they anchor to snorkel. Cash is feeling slightly more in charge of his faculties after eating, but he continues to drink because he doesn't want to risk becoming hungover.

Ayers puts her headset microphone back on and explains the rules of snorkeling—where they can go, where they can't go, what they can expect to see. "This is the best snorkeling in the Virgin Islands," she says. "You'll see it all—parrot fish, angelfish, spotted eagle rays, sea turtles, maybe even a basking shark. The sharks aren't dangerous to humans, but I'd advise you to leave them alone nonetheless. The only thing you need to worry about is the fire coral—it's easily identifiable by its bright orange branches—and if you rub up against it, you will develop a very painful burning rash. The other danger is sea urchins. The sea urchins have sharp black spines. Please do not touch or, God forbid, *stand on* any of the coral. James and Wade and I aren't just here to make a buck, people. We're here to educate you about the natural beauty of these islands and to spread awareness about just how precious and unique this eco-system is."

I love her, Cash thinks. She's everything he has ever wanted in a woman.

Once Cash is in his flippers, with his mask secured around his head and his snorkel poised a couple inches from his mouth, he feels like a world-class fool. Does everyone else feel this way? People seem excited, maybe a little anxious—there's nothing like jumping into shark-infested waters to inspire camaraderie—but generally the mood is positive, expectant.

It's all Cash can do not to just leap off the side of the boat rather than wait his turn to go down the ladder. Once he's in the water, he should be fine. He thinks back on the hundreds of people he has taught to ski. He recalls one girl in her twenties—a nanny for one of the fancy families with a house on Peak 7—who stared right into Cash's eyes and with the purest fear Cash has ever witnessed said, "I'm terrified."

And guess what? She had made it down the mountain just fine.

Cash waits his turn behind Chris and Mike, who look like frogs that mated with ducks, and then he lowers himself down the ladder into the turquoise water. He fits the snorkel into his mouth, takes a few breaths—all clear—and then lowers his head and swims behind his fellow adventurers.

How to describe what he sees?

He can't believe it's real. There's an entire universe under the surface of the water. The coral—purple, orange, greenish-yellow—are like buildings or mountains. Fish are everywhere: The parrot fish are shimmering rainbows, there are black angel-fish with electric blue stripes, schools of silvery fish that are as flat as coins, all of them swimming along, pecking here and there at the coral. It's astonishing that all this exists in pristine condition and that regular people like himself, without skills or specialized knowledge, can observe it. Why isn't everyone in the world talking about how *remarkable* this is? Why isn't a snorkeling trip to the Indians number one on everyone's bucket list? He's drunk, yes he is, but he's also blessed with a brand-new clarity. He is alive, on planet Earth, experiencing a natural wonder.

He lifts his head. Above the surface, life is the same. There's the coast of St. John in the distance, there's the boat a few hundred yards away. Cash likes the way his flippers give him buoyancy. He's barely treading water but he has no problem staying afloat.

Suddenly, there's someone next to him in a black mask. It's Ayers, he realizes. She's wearing a green tank suit, very simple and, on her, incredibly sexy. She takes his hand. They're holding hands? Or no, she wants him to swim alongside her. She wants to show him something. What? They swim for what seems like a while— away from everyone, away from the boat—then she points. On the smooth, sandy bottom, Cash sees a gargantuan silver platter with wings that ripple. It's a manta ray, gliding elegantly along the ocean floor. It's huge, way bigger than Cash expected.

Ayers stops to tread water and Cash does the same. She removes her snorkel.

"That's Luther," she says. "He's the biggest ray in the VIs. Five feet, two inches in diameter. He lives out here."

"Luther is . . . wow," Cash says.

"Let's follow him," Ayers says.

They trail Luther for a while, then Ayers makes a sharp turn—she must have seen something—and Cash kicks like crazy in an attempt to keep up. She's chasing what looks like a shark—it's sleek, silver, menacing. She takes off her silver hook bracelet and waggles it at him and he comes charging for it, then Ayers yanks it away and he darts past her.

Cash lifts his head. "What are you *doing*?"

She laughs. "Barracuda," she says. "A baby. He's harmless." She swims back in the direction of the boat and Cash follows.

They're back on the boat, headed home. Cash is bone-tired but energized. What a great day. What a transformative day. He's a convert: he loves the tropics.

"You're allowed to drink now, right?" Cash asks Ayers. She

nods and he grabs two rum punches from the bar and follows her to a bench on the shady side of the wheelhouse. The shade is a relief. He might be a convert in his heart and mind, but his skin is still that of his Scottish and Norwegian ancestors. He has been reapplying sunscreen every hour, but he's still pretty sure he's going to have a wicked sunburn.

He hands Ayers a rum punch and they touch cups. Ayers is wearing silver-rimmed, blue-lens aviators and her feet are resting up on the railing. She looks exhausted.

"To a job well done," Cash says. He takes a sip of his drink, his twentieth of the day. "You know, it's not so different from my job as a ski instructor."

"Aside from being completely different, not so different at all," she says. Together they look at the tired, sun-scorched, happy people below them on the deck — some snoozing, others forging bonds that will last all the way to the bar at Woody's, or the rest of the week or a lifetime. Cash has Chris's and Mike's numbers and promised to call them if he ever finds himself in Brooklyn, which secretly he hopes he never does.

Ayers sucks down the rum punch and seems to both relax and pep up. "You liked it, right?"

"Loved it," he says. "Can't thank you enough."

"Well, you basically saved my life yesterday by sharing your water. And you gave me your bandana. And you were nice to me when I was sad."

"Like I said, I understand."

Ayers leans her head on his shoulder. At the same time that he's experiencing pure ecstasy at her touch, he realizes she's crying again.

He hands her his damp cocktail napkin; it's all he has. "I'm happy to give you my shirt," he says.

She laughs through her tears. "I'm sorry," she says. "It's all lurking there, right below the surface. But I have to sublimate it. This job requires me to be peppy. I'm not allowed to be a human being, a thirty-one-year-old woman who lost her best friend." She sniffs and wipes at her reddened nose with the napkin. "At my other job it's different, because Rosie worked there with me, so we all lost her and every single person on the staff knows how close we were, so even though I have to smile while I'm serving, when I need a break I can hide in the kitchen and cry and do a shot of tequila with the line cooks."

Cash feels a surge of jealousy about the line cooks. He wants to ask if Ayers has a boyfriend or is married. He could be getting carried away for no reason. But instead, he asks if Ayers has a picture of Rosie.

"A picture of Rosie?" Ayers says.

"Yeah," Cash says. "I'd like to see what she looks like." It has occurred to him since their conversation yesterday that Ayers's friend Rosie might not be the same woman in the photograph with Russ. It would be better, so much better, if Rosie Small weren't Russ's lover. They would both still be dead, but maybe just friends or colleagues. It would be so much easier.

Ayers pulls out her phone. "Here," she says. "She's my screen saver." She hands Cash the phone.

On the left is Ayers in a canary-yellow bikini on a beach next to a tree that supports a tire swing. On the right is Rosie, the same woman in the photograph with Cash's father. She's wearing a white bikini and beaming at the camera.

"She's really pretty," Cash says. "Though not as pretty as you, of course."

"Oh, please," Ayers says. She tucks her phone back into the pocket of her shorts. "You know, I want to apologize about being short with you yesterday…when you asked about Rosie's boyfriend."

Cash holds his breath. *We don't have to talk about it,* he wants to say. When he'd registered for the trip, he'd been glad that Wade was handling the paperwork and not Ayers, because he didn't want Ayers to see his last name and make the connection.

He needs to tell her who he is, but he doesn't want her to know who he is. And he certainly can't tell her *now,* while she's at *work.*

"You don't have to apologize…"

"He was rich," Ayers says. "Some rich asshole who showed up every couple of weeks and completely monopolized Rosie's time, but that wasn't the problem. The problem was that he had this shroud of secrecy around him. They'd been together for six years and I'd never met him. And I was her best friend. The first few years I accused her of making him up, that's how bad it was. But he was always giving her things — silver bracelets, money, a new Jeep. He almost never left his property, and they never entertained or invited anyone over."

"Maybe he was hiding something," Cash says. "Maybe he was married."

"Maybe?" Ayers says. "Of *course* he was married. But the one time I brought it up, Rosie flipped out and wouldn't speak to me for three days. So that was the last time I mentioned it. She was two people, really: a very strong and independent woman, on the one hand — feisty, fierce, even. But when it came to the Invisible Man, she was a goner. She was so… blinded by him. So…in love, I guess you'd have to say."

"Well, then," Cash says. "He couldn't have been all bad." He tries a smile. "Right?"

HUCK

On Sunday, Huck cancels both of his charters. He'll reschedule them for the following week. Today, he just wants to go out on the water by himself, maybe see if there's any truth to Cleve's school-of-mahi story. He still has the coordinates written down, saved from New Year's Eve.

Back when Rosie was alive.

It's a cruel trick of the world, a person alive and well one minute, thinking harm will never come her way, and then dead the next.

Huck doesn't get as early a start as he would have liked, because he has to drive Maia over to Joanie's house. They are planning on starting a bath bomb business. They want to make bath bombs in tropical scents and sell them to tourists.

"Are you sure you don't want to come fishing?" Huck asks. Her company is the only person's he would relish, and he worries that Maia is returning to her regular twelve-year-old routine too soon. Tomorrow, Monday, she's going back to school.

"I'm sure," she says.

Huck reminds himself that everyone processes loss in his or her own way. After LeeAnn died, Huck had gone through a rough patch — smoking and drinking, and spending one regrettable night with Teresa, the waitress from Jake's, who everyone knew had a sleeping-around problem. And Rosie had handled LeeAnn's death by meeting, and then shacking up with, the Invisible Man.

He's going to let Maia be. If she wants to start a bath bomb business with Joanie, then Huck will be their first customer.

But today he's going fishing. And he's going to *catch* something, damnit.

He loads up *The Mississippi* with light tackle and his trolling rods, a chest of clean ice, a second chest that holds water, a case of Red Stripe, and two Cuban sandwiches from Baked in the Sun, plus one of their "junk food" cookies—the thing is loaded with toffee, pretzels, and potato chips—because those were Rosie's favorite. He's about to untie his line from the dock when he hears his name being called. His proper name.

"Mr. Powers? Sam Powers?"

He looks up to see a woman marching down the dock, waving her arm like she's trying to hail a cab. She's slender, with pretty hair—one fat chestnut braid hangs over one shoulder. She's wearing round sunglasses, so he can't get a good look at her, but as she grows closer he sees she's older than he originally thought, and her expression can only be described as All Business. That, combined with the fact that she's calling him "Mr. Powers" makes him feel like he's about to be reprimanded by his high school English teacher. What was her name? Miss Lemon. Miss Lemon had once caught Huck writing dirty limericks. Instead of tearing up the page, as he expected her to, she had insisted he go in front of the class and read them aloud.

Good old Miss Lemon, responsible for the most humiliating moment of Huck's young life.

And now here comes Miss Lemon reincarnated, although a sight better-looking. The original Miss Lemon, appropriate to her name, had a pucker face.

The reincarnated Miss Lemon marches right up to the edge of the dock. Huck has the line in his hand. All he needs to do is unloop it from the post and putter away. She can't very well follow him.

"Are you Sam Powers?" she asks.

"Technically, yes," he says. "But people call me Huck."

She nods once, sharply. "So I've heard. Mr. Powers, do you have a minute to talk? It's important."

Does he have a minute to talk? No. It's nearly nine o'clock now. He's going offshore, a forty-five-minute trip. He has to be back here by four thirty at the latest to pick Maia up from Joanie's by five. He wants to fish all day. To fish all day, he has to leave now. *It's important,* the Reincarnated Miss Lemon says, and he somehow knows this isn't a matriarch disgruntled by his postponed charters. This woman's face holds a certain tension in it that Huck recognizes. He has an idea, but he hopes to God he's wrong.

He cuts the motor, then offers the woman his barracuda hand. She takes in the sight of his half-missing pinky but doesn't flinch, which he supposes is a good sign.

"You want me to get into your boat?" she asks.

"You want to talk?" he asks.

She removes her sandals without being asked—she must be a boat person, how about that—and she takes his barracuda hand and nimbly descends into the bow.

Huck flips open the cooler. "I have water and I have beer."

"Nothing," she says. "Thank you."

Huck goes to reach for a water for himself when she speaks up. "Actually, a beer. Thank you."

Huck's eyebrows shoot up, but the Reincarnated Miss Lemon doesn't notice. Her eyes are scanning the dock. Who's watching? Well, the answer to that is: no one and everyone. The taxi drivers—Pauly, Chauncey, and Bennie—are lined up across the street from the cruise ship dock. Huck flips the top off two Red Stripes; he isn't about to let a lady drink alone, and if she needs a beer, then he probably does as well.

Huck hands the Reincarnated Miss Lemon a beer. "What can I do for you, Ms....?"

"Steele," she says. "Irene Steele."

Huck closes his eyes a beat longer than a blink. Irene Steele. His bad feeling has been proved correct.

"I guess that answers my question," he says. He offers Irene Steele one of the cushioned seats in the cockpit. He's a bit concerned about who will hear what; acoustics over the water are funny. He sits down a respectful distance away but leans in. It could still be an ex-wife, he thinks. Please let it be an ex-wife.

"Russell Steele was my husband," Irene says, immediately dashing Huck's hopes. "And I understand that you're the father of Rosie Small. Who was my husband's mistress."

Huck flinches at the word "mistress," although he realizes she could have chosen worse.

"I'm her stepfather," Huck says. "*Was* her stepfather. I married her mother, LeeAnn, nearly twenty years ago. LeeAnn passed five years back."

"But you're still close with Rosie? *Were* close with her? She lived with you?"

"You did your research," Huck says. "How did you find this out?"

"It wasn't easy," Irene says. "I don't know anyone here except for Paulette, from the real estate agency..."

Paulette Vickers, Huck thinks. He saw her at the funeral and the reception yesterday, but then again, he saw everyone.

"...but Paulette was out of the office yesterday." Irene pauses. "So I had to ask around, which didn't yield me much until I found the woman who sells mangoes next to Cruz Bay Landing."

"Henrietta," Huck says.

Irene shrugs. "She gave me the basics. When I asked if the girl who died had parents, she told me your name and the name of your boat and that you tied up here most mornings."

"I'm sorry about your husband," Huck says. He's not, though—not sorry one bit that sonovabitch is dead. He only cares about Rosie. But before Huck can tack on any more insincere statements, Irene says, "No, you're not. Nor should you be. You can tell me the truth, Mr. Powers."

"The truth?" Huck says. "I don't like being called 'Mr. Powers.' Also, I'm grieving just like you are and I plan to take today out on the water by myself so I can fish and drink beer and gaze off at the horizon and wonder what happens when we die."

"So you'd like me to leave?" Irene says.

Pretty much, Huck thinks. But he's too much of a gentleman to say it. "I'm just not sure what you want from me. I probably know as much as you do about what happened. They were traveling by helicopter from here to Anegada in the BVIs."

"Why?" Irene says.

"Day trip?" Huck says. "Anegada is pretty special. It's nothing more than a spit of pure white sand, really. It has a Gilligan's Island feel to it. There's almost nothing there, a few homes, a couple of small hotels, a few bars and restaurants, a native population of flamingos..."

"Flamingos?" Irene says flatly.

"And lobsters," Huck says. "Anegada is famous for its lobsters. So my guess is they were on a day trip. Go over, see the birds, walk the beach, eat a couple lobsters, fly home. People do it. I've done it. Of course, most people take a boat." He finishes his beer and deeply craves a cigarette. He needs this woman off his boat. He stands up, takes Irene's empty bottle from her, and throws both bottles in the trash. Hint, hint. What else could she possibly want to ask?

"Did you know Russ?" Irene says.

"No," Huck says, clearly and firmly. "Never had the pleasure. Rosie was…protective, I guess you'd say. I knew the guy existed, knew he had money…and a villa somewhere…"

Irene laughs. "Villa."

"I've never seen it, was never invited, don't know the address. Rosie kept all that private. She told me his name once, long ago. But after that she referred to him only as the Man and everyone else on this island refers to him as the Invisible Man. Because no one ever saw him."

"The Invisible Man?" Irene says. "That's ironic. I could have called him that as well." She stands up and Huck fills with sweet relief—she's leaving!—but then she opens the cooler, takes out another beer, and hands it to Huck.

He can't decide whether to laugh or cry. He needs to go. He wants to fish.

"Can we finish this conversation another time?" he asks. "I want to fish."

"Take me with you," Irene says. "I can pay."

"I had two paying charters today that I canceled," Huck says.

"But those people weren't me," Irene says. "They weren't the widow of your stepdaughter's lover."

Huck's head is spinning. He needs a cigarette and it's his boat, goddamnit, so he's going to have one. He opens Irene's beer and lights up.

"Do you fish?" he asks. "Where are you from?"

"Iowa City," Irene says.

Huck chuckles. "I doubt you're built for a day offshore."

"I most certainly am," Irene says. "I used to go fly-fishing with my father on a lake in Wisconsin. He called me…" She pauses as her eyes fill. "He used to call me Angler Cupcake."

Angler Cupcake: Huck hasn't heard that one before.

"I'm sorry," Irene says. "I don't mean to horn in on your day of solitude and reflection. It's just that I could use a day like you're about to have myself. Fishing, drinking beer, gazing at the horizon, and wondering what happens when we die."

Go to the beach at Francis Bay, he wants to tell her. Drive out to the East End—no one is *ever* on the East End. Hike to Salomon Bay. Sit at the bar at the Quiet Mon. St. John has lots of places to hide.

But instead he says, "You really think you can handle this?"

"I know I can," she says.

"Okay, then." Huck starts the engine and unloops the rope and steers them out into the harbor. There's instantly a breeze, and between the wind and the noise of the motor, the need for conversation evaporates. Still, Huck looks at Irene Steele, his stowaway, the wife of Rosie's lover—what the *hell* is he doing?— and says, "Angler Cupcake, huh?"

"I guess we'll see," she says.

Huck captains *The Mississippi* offshore to the south-southeast toward the coordinates Cleve gave him. Irene "Angler Cupcake" Steele is lucky, because the water is glass and the boat might as well have a diamond-edged hull. The ride is smooth and easy—and despite having an unwanted, unexpected passenger, Huck relaxes. Is he surprised this woman found him? He is. But then again, he isn't. He had guessed that she existed, though he never spoke the words out loud. He thought maybe a few months from now, someone from the secret life of the Invisible Man might surface.

Or was *this* the Invisible Man's secret life?

Yes, Huck thinks.

He might ask Irene some questions. Maybe by learning about Russell Steele, he'll learn about Rosie. But Huck knew Rosie. He *knew* Rosie. She fell in love with a man who had a wife elsewhere and now that wife was here on Huck's boat, expecting Huck to answer questions like he owes it to her.

Does he owe it to her? That's not a question he wants to explore right now.

He's less bothered by her presence than he ought to be. Why is that? Because she's hurting, too. Because she lost someone at exactly the same time he did, and so she also must feel like the gods have her by the head and toes and are wringing her out.

But enough. It's time to fish.

As Huck nears the coordinates Cleve gave him, he slows down. A little ways off he sees something floating on the water and directs the boat over until he can see what it is. A rectangular cut of carpet. Huck bends over to grab it.

"Someone tossed that?" Irene asks.

"Someone *left* it," Huck says. "As a marker. This is where the fish are. Or were. There's no telling now. I heard this back on New Year's Eve."

"Before," Irene says.

They're in the same emotional space. There's no way to think of New Year's Eve except as *before.*

Huck nods and grabs a rod for Irene and one for himself. He checks her lure and her line and hands it over.

"You know how to cast?" he says.

"Of course," she says.

"Would you like a beer?"

"If you're having one," she says.

Well, it's his day and he *is* having one. He happens to believe that beer brings the fish. He flips the cap off two Red Stripes and places one in the cup holder next to Irene's left hip. Then he retreats to the other side of the boat and discreetly watches Irene.

She lifts the beer to her lips and takes a nice long swallow. Then she holds the line, flips the bale, and executes a more than competent sidearm cast. *Wheeeeeeeeee!* The line flies.

Beautiful, Huck has to admit. He hasn't seen a woman — hell, a *person* — cast like that since ... well, since he's not sure when.

Nearly as soon as she starts to reel the line in, her rod bows.

"Fish on," she says. Her voice is calm and assured. Most women — hell, people — get a fish on and they shout like God lost a tooth. The rod is *really* bending; there's a fish on and it's big. Huck gets a rush. He has been skunked since Halloween. He's ready — more than ready.

"You want help with that?" Huck asks.

"Not yet," Irene says.

"Come sit in the fighting chair," Huck says. "I think you're going to need it." He leads Irene over to the chair and gets her situated, pole in the holder. Meanwhile, she's doing just the right thing, letting the fish take some line and then reeling when the fish rests. Huck would normally be offering verbal instructions, but Irene is making every move at just the right time. He can't be accused of "mansplaining," which has earned him the silent treatment from both Rosie and Maia in the past.

Huck moves Irene's beer to where she can reach it and she does, at one point, take a quick swig, then gets back to reeling.

She is one cool customer. Likely she has a monster on the other end of her line, and Huck has seen men twice her size give up on light tackle. It's difficult by anyone's standards.

"You're doing great," Huck says. He feels strangely useless, the way he felt at Rosie's bedside when she was giving birth to Maia. "Just let me know if you need help."

"I'm fine," Irene says.

She *is* fine, releasing, then reeling in, two steps forward, one step back, which is what a fish like this takes, and she doesn't seem to be losing patience. Fifteen minutes pass, then twenty. She's getting more aggressive with her reeling, which is what he would have advised. The fish is getting tired.

"Anyone else would have handed the reel over by now," Huck says.

"I doubt that," Irene says.

"I only meant to say you're doing well," Huck says. He can't believe it, but he thinks of the Invisible Man, Russell Steele. *You have a wife who fishes like this and you cheated on her?*

Huck should cast his own line, he knows, but he's vested in this fight and wants to see it through. Irene lets the line go and then she reels with a grunt — she's human, after all — and just like that, Huck sees the flash of gold fins beneath the surface.

"Here we go, baby," he says. "Don't give up now. Bring him in."

Irene lets out a moan that sounds like a bedroom noise, and Huck won't lie, he gets a bit of a rise. But no time to dwell on that, thank God, because here's the fish. Huck grabs the gaff and leans all the way over the side of the boat to spear the fucker and hook it up over the railing onto the deck of *The Mississippi,* where it flops around, making a tremendous ruckus. It has gorgeous green and gold scales, Huck's favorite color in the world, and the protruding forehead of a bull fish.

"Mahi mahi," he says. "I'd say twenty-five pounds, maybe forty inches long."

Irene takes a sip of her beer. "Can we eat it?"

"For days," Huck says. Without thinking, he raises his hand for a high-five and Irene slaps his palm, square and solid. He grabs her hand.

"Congratulations," he says. "That was some skillful rod work there, Angler Cupcake."

Irene looks at Huck and she breaks into a smile and then so does Huck, and for one second, they are two people standing in the tropical sunshine while one hell of a majestic fish flops at their feet. For one second, they forget their hearts are broken.

It doesn't end there—no, not even close. Huck puts the bull on ice and then casts his own rod, and Irene casts again, and they both get fish on. Two more mahi. Again, they cast. Huck gets a hit right away, Irene a few minutes later. Two more mahi. Irene asks if there's a head and Huck says, "There is down below. No paper in the bowl, please." Irene comes up a few minutes later, pops the top off a Red Stripe, and casts a line. She gets a fish on.

It's insane. Insanely wonderful. They have six mahi, eight, twelve. Huck brings in a barracuda, which he throws back, and Irene brings in a mahi that has been bitten clean in half.

"Shark," Huck says. He unhooks the half fish and throws it back.

"Oh yeah?" Irene says. He thinks maybe he scared her, but she casts another line.

Fourteen, sixteen, seventeen mahi.

Thank you, LeeAnn, he thinks. For the past five years, every time he's caught a fish, he's thanked his wife, because he believes she's helping from above. Silly, he knows.

They take a break and Huck offers Irene one of the Cuban sandwiches, which she accepts gratefully. He thinks maybe they'll talk, but Irene takes her sandwich to the bow of the boat, on the side with the shade, and Huck lets her be. He does wonder what she's thinking about. Is she contemplating the horizon, wondering what happens when we die?

He would like to explain to her how extraordinary today is. *Seventeen mahi!* Maybe she understands, or maybe she thinks fishing with Huck is always like this. At any rate, she returns to the stern, pulls a bottle out of the water, and casts a line.

At three thirty, he tells her it's time to go.

"Yes," she says. "I'm sure my sons will be wondering about me."

Sons? he thinks. She has sons. He wants to ask how many and how old they are—but there isn't time. He has to pick up Maia. Today has been magical, nearly supernatural, and restorative the way he'd hoped. But unfortunately, real life awaits.

Forty-five minutes later, he pulls up to the dock by the canary-yellow National Park Service building. He ties up and offers a hand to help Irene out of the boat.

"Oh wait," he says. "I owe you some fish."

"Don't worry about it," she says.

"No, no," he says. He doesn't have time to fillet any right now, and he can't very well hand her a whole mahi. "I could drop some off at your villa tomorrow. Or we could meet somewhere in town?"

"You don't have to give me any fish," Irene says. She takes a deep breath. "I can't believe how therapeutic today was. I managed...somehow...to step out of myself. And it's because you let me tag along. So I'm grateful. I will forever remember today and your kindness."

It sounds like she's saying good-bye, and Huck rejects this for some reason. "Are you...leaving? Soon? Leaving the island? Heading home?"

"At some point, I guess," Irene says. "I have a life at home. A job, a house, and Russ's mother, Milly, is still alive and I'm her...contact person, her point person, the one who makes decisions for her. My sons have lives as well. We can't stay forever. But we're still waiting for the ashes and for a report from the authorities about what exactly happened..."

"Bird got struck by lightning," Huck says.

"I guess they need to confirm that," Irene says. She presses her lips together, and Huck sees her fighting tears.

"Listen, what if we met in town sometime tomorrow? We could grab a drink and I'll bring you a bag of mahi fillets." Tomorrow's Monday, and it's also the night of the Gifft Hill School's annual overnight field trip to the Maho Bay campground. They'll sleep in tents and tell ghost stories. Maia had said she still wanted to go, and Huck wasn't particularly looking forward to a night alone.

"You said you've never been to the villa," Irene says. "Is that true?"

"That's true," Huck says. "I don't even know where it is."

"I don't know where it is, either," Irene says. "But why don't you bring some of that fish over tomorrow evening and we can grill it. I'll figure out the address and I'll text you. You do text, right?"

"Of course I text," Huck says. "I have a twelve-year-old granddaughter."

Irene stares at him a second and then pulls out her phone. "Give me your number," she says.

Huck watches Irene walk away. She's not a bad-looking woman, not bad-looking at all, and, boy, can she fish. If she were any-one else—*anyone* else—Huck would ask her out. As it is, they have a sort-of date tomorrow night.

If she remembers to text him.

Which she probably won't.

Why would she?

She might, though, he thinks. She just might.

BAKER

Both his mother and his brother return to the house in the late afternoon. Both are sunburned, and they won't tell him where they've been. Baker has been home, lying by the pool, waiting for his phone to ring with some news about...about anything. He's called VISAR and gotten transferred three times, so he's had to leave messages. Then he called the Pee-bles Hospital on Tortola, hoping they could give him some information about Russ's ashes, but the woman he spoke to, Letitia, said she didn't have any bodies by the name of Russell Steele.

"Really?" Baker asked. "It's my father...he was in that helicopter crash off Virgin Gorda on New Year's Day."

"I was off last week for the holidays," Letitia said. "All I can tell you, sir, is that name is not in the hospital database."

"The contact name might have been Todd Croft," Baker said. "Would you mind checking Croft?"

"Not a problem," Letitia said. He heard her typing. "I'm sorry, I don't have that name in the database, either. You might check with the Americans."

Baker called the Hurley-Davis Funeral Home in St. Thomas and spoke to Bianca, who was even less helpful.

"I'm looking for my father's remains. His name was Russell Steele. He was killed in the helicopter crash north of Virgin Gorda on New Year's Day."

"Virgin Gorda?" Bianca said. "You'll need to call Peebles Hospital, then. On Tortola."

Baker hung up, confused and agitated. He tried the number his mother had for Todd Croft next, but it was out of service. Next he went to his laptop to look up the Ascension website, but the site wouldn't load. Baker couldn't figure out if his service here on the island was the problem or if something was wrong with the website. He googled the names Russell Steele and Todd Croft—his Google worked, so it *wasn't* the service that was the issue—but none of the hits matched the men Baker was looking for. He tried Stephen Thompson next—there were probably only fifty or sixty thousand people in the world with that name—so he refined it by adding *pilot* and *British Virgin Islands,* but that was a bust. There was a

Stephen Thompson, Esquire, listed in the Cayman Islands—not exactly pay dirt, but Baker had nothing else to go on, so he called the number listed on the website and that number, too, was out of service.

Coincidence? Baker wondered. Or was this Stephen Thompson the same Stephen Thompson who piloted the helicopter? It was beginning to feel like someone was trying to erase the whole situation.

Before Baker could explore further, Anna texted, asking Baker when he was coming home. *Floyd misses you,* she wrote. Baker wanted to respond that Anna would be well served to put in some quality time with Floyd now that she was going to be a single parent. But instead, Baker channeled his best self—which was easier when he remembered how he felt when he'd set eyes on Ayers—and he said, *Things here are still in flux so I'm not sure. Tell Floyd I love him.*

To which Anna responded not *Ok* (her go-to) but rather, *Do you think you'll still be there on Wednesday?*

Yes, he said. *Definitely yes. If you need a sitter, call Kelsey.*

Don't need a sitter, she said.

Yeah, right, Baker thought. In his ruminations about Anna and Louisa, he has naturally wondered how long they've been together, and when it started, and what their plans for the future entail. They'll become a regular lesbian couple, he supposes, if two in-demand cardiac surgeons count as regular.

His pain and shock have been ameliorated by his own experience. When he set eyes on Ayers, he knew instantly it was love. Why shouldn't that have been true for Anna? She might have been discussing a case with Louisa when she realized: *This* is who I want.

Cash and Irene head off to opposite parts of the house to shower. Neither of them had expressed any interest in dinner, and frankly, they had both seemed kind of off, almost as if they'd been drinking.

Well, fine, Baker thinks. Clearly they aren't a bonded band of three in their grieving. If his mom and brother can go out on their own, then so can he. He grabs one of the sets of Jeep keys. He's going to dinner at La Tapa.

Baker heads to town slowly—the steering wheel is on the left, like at home, but here everyone drives on the left instead of the right—and the roads are steep, hilly, and poorly lit. Once he gets to town, he finds that the streets are alive with people out enjoying their Caribbean vacation. Baker has an urge to grab a father walking through Powell Park holding his wife's hand while he carries a little boy about Floyd's age on his shoulders. *Do you know how lucky you are?* Baker wants to ask. Baker's envy isn't limited to just that one guy. *Everyone* who isn't mired in an emotional crisis should be grateful. Baker, while he was at the playground with Floyd on Tuesday afternoon, should have been grateful, instead of bemoaning the state of his marriage. Why hadn't he been grateful?

La Tapa is easy to find. It's right next to Woody's, which has a crowd of post-happy-hour revelers still hanging out front. Baker parks the Jeep up the street and heads back to the restaurant. His emotions quickly shift from self-pity to nerves. It's been a while since he's pursued anyone romantically. But he's an okay-looking guy, maybe a little soft around the middle, thanks to life as a stay-at-home dad and all the late-night ice cream, but he can shed the weight with some exercise. He'll go for a run tomorrow, he decides.

He steps down into a tasteful, rustic dining room. The place is charming, with its candlelight and white linen table-cloths, rough-hewn wooden bar and fresh flowers. And it smells so good—rich, layered scents of butter and roasting meat and herbs.

Baker takes an empty seat at the end of the bar closest to the kitchen, next to where the waitstaff come to pick up their drink orders. Ayers, where is Ayers?

"Hey, man, welcome to La Tapa," the bartender says. "My name is Skip. Can I get you something to drink?"

Baker has become a big fan of the St. John beers but he opts for a vodka tonic. He's out of the house, this place is really nice, and he's going to act like an adult. His drink comes and he peruses the menu, using his peripheral vision to look for Ayers. There's a tall, slender girl with cropped dark hair hanging at the service station, flirting with Skip the bar-tender, and there are two male servers. But Baker doesn't see Ayers.

"Can I get you something to eat?" Skip asks.

Baker scans the menu. It all looks delicious, but he can't begin to think about food until he finds Ayers. He's in the right place: she said La Tapa, and she *asked* him to stop by…

"What's good?" Baker asks helplessly. If she's not here, he should leave and come back tomorrow. He'll bring Cash with him.

"The mussels are the best in the world, and the mahi was just caught today, if you like fresh fish," Skip says. "It's done with braised artichokes and a thyme beurre blanc."

Baker raises his head to look Skip in the eye. "Is Ayers working tonight, by any chance?"

Skip's eyebrows shoot up. "Ayers? She's off tonight. It's Sunday night—she works on *Treasure Island* on Sundays. She'll be on tomorrow night. Do you want me to leave her a message?"

"No, no..."

Skip leans over the bar and lowers his voice. "I hear you, man, she's really hot. A little psycho, but all chicks are psycho. She sometimes comes in here on her night off for a glass of Schramsberg, so you might want to stick around."

Baker's heart is buoyed even as his mind is racing. Stay or go? *Stay,* he thinks. She sometimes comes in here on her night off for a glass of the whatever. But what does Baker's new best friend, Skip, mean by "a little psycho"? There's a mom named Mandy at the Children's Cottage—Baker's school wives call her "psycho" because she's obsessed with the Houston Astros, especially Justin Verlander. She wears Astros merch *every single day,* and she got a vanity plate for her Volvo that says JV-35. Maybe Skip tried to put the moves on Ayers and she turned him down, so he has categorized her as "a little psycho" to soothe his bruised ego. Guys do that. For instance, Baker might be tempted to call Dr. Anna Schaffer "a little psycho" for leaving him for Louisa, even though Anna is the most mentally stable person Baker knows.

Maybe Ayers has foibles—of course she does, everyone does. Baker vows he will love her foibles.

"I'll have the mussels," Baker says. "And the mahi, at your suggestion."

"Good man," Skip says. The tall, short-haired girl comes back, and Skip says, "Hey, Tilda, this guy is here to see Ayers. Is she coming in for a nightcap, do you know?"

Tilda turns to stare down Baker. She shakes her head in disbelief. "You do *realize* that Ayers's best friend died, like, five days ago, right?"

"Uh," Baker says. "Right…"

Tilda snarls at Skip. "And no, I don't think Ayers is coming for a nightcap, since that was only something she did *when Rosie was working*!" Tilda's voice is so loud that the entire restaurant grows quiet.

Skip pours Tilda a shot of beer, and without a word she throws it back and storms off. A few seconds later the restaurant returns to its normal decibel level and Skip leans forward.

"Sorry about that, man. That's Tilda for you. She's a little…"

"Psycho," Baker says. "Got it."

The mussels arrive, they're outstanding, the best Baker has ever had, and then the mahi comes and it's even better, fresh and moist, just cooked through, perfectly seasoned, and the sauce is so sublime, he's light-headed.

But no Ayers.

"How was your food?" Skip asks as he clears the plates.

"Unbelievable," Baker says. "So good that I think I'll be back tomorrow night with my brother."

"Cool, man," Skip says. "I'll save you guys two bar seats, and, hey—I don't do that for just anyone."

"That's great, thank you," Baker says. He pays the bill and leaves Skip a very, very generous tip—nearly 40 percent—because he can't risk Skip telling Ayers that a guy came in looking for her who seemed a little…

* * *

The next morning Baker gets up early to go for a run. He was an athlete in high school, the classic three—football, basketball, and baseball—and when he got to Northwestern, he played on his fraternity's intramural teams. In Chicago, he belonged to Lakeshore Sport & Fitness, where he went mostly to meet women. He hasn't done much in the way of exercise since moving to Houston. There was one ill-advised 5K in Memorial Park; he thought he was having a heart attack—a great irony, because Anna was supposed to come cheer him on, but she'd been called in to work, so one of his thoughts as his vision went black and he stopped dead in his tracks, bent over his knees, was that at least Anna was in a position to save his life.

But today, Baker decides, will be different. Today he is motivated. He has a mission: he is going to sweep Ayers off her feet. He laces up his sneakers and heads out to the end of his father's driveway.

While he feels okay running down his father's shaded road, when he gets to the bottom and turns right, he's in the sun and it's immediately uphill. As if that isn't bad enough, a large open-air taxi comes blazing around a blind corner, nearly forcing him over the guard rail down the side of the cliff to the sea. Baker breaks stride to flip the driver off.

Ayers, he thinks. He keeps going, shoulders back, spine straight, face stoic. The sun is broiling, it's hotter than Houston in August, and suddenly he feels last night's vodka tonics and mussels and mahi churning in his stomach. The hill grows steep. Baker sets his gaze three feet ahead of his stride—otherwise he'll give up.

Ayers, he thinks. Do this for Ayers. He hears three low

resonant notes, like a foghorn. He raises his face to see an enormous water truck barreling down the hill toward him. He jumps aside.

That's it, he thinks. He's done. He turns around.

He gets lost walking back. How can he be lost when he's only been on one road? His father's driveway is hidden and unmarked, but Baker has been able to find it when he's driving because it's a few yards after the utility pole, which has two yellow stripes. Where is that pole? Baker can't tell if it's in front of him or behind him. He didn't bring his phone; he has sweat in his eyes.

A small lizard-green pickup truck pulls up next to him.

"Are you lost?" a woman asks.

"Maybe?" Baker says. He wipes the sweat off his face with the bottom of his t-shirt and starts to laugh in a way that he knows makes him sound unhinged. But really, what is he even *doing* here? And then it hits him: *his father is dead.*

He starts to cry.

"Baker?" the woman says.

Baker's head snaps up. He looks through the open passenger window to the driver's side. It's not some random woman in a funny truck. It's Ayers.

No, he thinks. Not possible. But yes, it's her, and she's even lovelier than he remembers. Her hair is in a messy bun; she's wearing a loose tank top and yoga pants and he can see she's driving in bare feet. Bare, sandy feet.

"Hey," he says, wiping at his eyes. "How are you?"

"Surviving," she says. "Listen, can I give you a ride somewhere?"

"Oh…no," Baker says. "I'm good. I was just heading back from a run and I seem to have gotten turned around, maybe. Or maybe not. I'm not sure. But I'll figure it out."

"You sure?" Ayers says. "I just took yoga on the beach at Maho and I don't work until four. I have plenty of time to take you wherever."

"I'm okay," Baker says. "Thanks, though."

"Was it you who came in to La Tapa last night?" Ayers says. "I must have just missed you. Skip said you'd been in."

"Oh…yeah," Baker says. "Yeah, that was me. Food was fantastic. Thanks for the recommendation." He realizes he sounds like he's trying to get rid of her—and he *is* trying to get rid of her. He can't *believe* she caught him here, now, in his weakest moment. On top of everything else, his bowels are starting to rumble. He needs her to move on. Why her, of all people? Did he conjure her by saying her name so many times in his mind? Or are there really only five people on this island?

"You're welcome," Ayers says. "Hey, are you sure you're okay?"

Baker straightens up against the troublesome clenching in his gut. He tries to look like the world conqueror he wants her to believe he is. "I'm great, thanks. Hey, listen, I may…" He wants to say he may come to the restaurant again that night with Cash, but at that moment a taxi pulls up behind Ayers and the driver lays on his horn.

"Okay, bye!" Ayers says, and she drives off.

It takes him a while but eventually he finds the pole with two yellow stripes and the nondescript dirt road that is his father's.

When Baker finally makes it home, he's depleted, physically and emotionally. What must Ayers think of him? He's going to have to roll into La Tapa that night and be his most impressive self.

He enters the kitchen to find his mother standing in front of the open refrigerator, sniffing the container of pasta salad, and he's transported back a decade or so.

"Mom?" he says. He's surprised to find her in this posture; his mother has expressed no interest in food the entire time they've been here.

Irene straightens up and closes the fridge. She has an inscrutable expression on her face. Baker almost feels like he caught her at something.

"I have to ask a favor," she says.

He goes to the sink for water. "Anything," he says. "What is it?"

"I need you and your brother to go out tonight," she says. "I have a dinner guest coming at seven and I'd like privacy."

Baker takes a second to process this. She has a *dinner guest* coming? It must be Todd Croft, he thinks. Who else could it possibly be? His mother doesn't know anyone around here. He realizes her request is fortuitous. Now Baker and Cash can go to La Tapa by themselves without seeming like they're ditching her.

"You got it," Baker says.

His mother appears relieved, not only at his answer but also because he hasn't asked any follow-up questions. She has a secret, he thinks. She knows something she isn't telling them. Which leads him to the nagging guilt he feels because he hasn't told his mother about what's happening with Anna. It seems inconsequential after everything that's happened.

His mother goes back to rummaging through the fridge, inspecting this and that.

"Oh, look," she says. "Camembert."

Baker handles the news of Irene's surprise dinner guest far better than Cash. Cash barely manages to conceal his indignation. Baker has to admit that it is a little disconcerting to see his mother wearing a black gauzy sundress, her hair freshly washed and combed out long and loose (honestly, he can't remember the last time he saw it out of its braid). The dress isn't anything *new,* he doesn't think, more like something she would wear when she and Russ used to entertain the Dunns and the Kinseys by the pool back in Iowa City.

Baker watches Irene bury a bottle of Cakebread chardonnay in an ice bucket. There's no mention of how twisted it is that Russ kept Irene's favorite wine—a *case of it*—in a house that she knew nothing about. She bids both boys good-bye with a kiss, seeming like a subdued version of her former self. But it's clear she wants them to leave. It's quarter to seven.

As soon as Baker and Cash get in the Jeep, Cash explodes. "What the hell is going *on*? Cheese and *crackers*? Wine? And did you see what she was *wearing*? And what's with the secrecy? She won't tell us who's coming for dinner?"

"It must be Todd Croft," Baker says. "Right? It has to be. Which is good, because he's been unreachable and the Ascension website is down. Something weird is going on."

"Then why not just *tell* us that?" Cash says. He's on his way to a five-flavor freak-out, which is how their father used to describe Cash's tantrums growing up. It makes no sense that Cash—who doesn't have an ambitious or competitive bone in his body, who *skis* for a living—is so high-strung emotionally, while Baker, who thrives on pressure and tension, tends to be pretty sanguine no matter what. And yet that's the way it is. Maybe Cash inherited more of their hotheaded Scottish ancestors' blood and Baker the sangfroid of the Norwegians. Maybe Cash was treated differently growing up because he was the "baby." Maybe it's simply one of the unsolved mysteries of human nature: how two siblings, born of the same parents and raised in the same house, can be complete opposites. Cash is clearly bent out of shape by Irene's behavior, whereas Baker doesn't care. What he *does* care about—immensely—is seeing Ayers.

Maybe Baker is just painfully self-absorbed.

"Do you trust Mom?" Baker asks.

"Yes," Cash says. "But then again, I trusted *Dad*…"

Baker cuts him off. "We're talking about Mom. You trust her. Do you think she's likely to do anything rash or self-destructive?"

"No," Cash says.

"No," Baker agrees. Irene Steele is the epitome of level-headed competence. Her behavior today harks back to her actions on Thanksgiving Day of his senior year at Northwestern, when he brought home his friend Donny Foley, from Skagway, Alaska. Baker and Donny had been in the front yard of the Steeles' Victorian playing the traditional game of tackle football with Cash and a few of the neighbors. Donny took a hard hit and started screaming that his shoulder was dislocated. Irene had come flying out of the house in her apron—she was cooking a turkey with all the trimmings for twenty people—and with one strong twist, she had popped Donny's shoulder back in place. The entire episode took all of thirty seconds, but his mother's composure and swift act would be forever emblazoned in Baker's mind.

His mother is, in today's parlance, a badass.

If she wants privacy for dinner, it's for a good reason.

"...but I trusted *Dad* not to do anything rash or self-destructive, and *look what happened*!" Cash shouts these last three words, and, as usual when confronted with Cash's episodes, Baker shuts down. He won't say a word until they get to dinner.

But Cash's words echo in Baker's mind. *I trusted Dad not to do anything rash or self-destructive, and look what happened.*

Look what happened.

At La Tapa, Baker and Cash take the seats at the corner of the bar that Skip has reserved for them. Skip lights up as though Baker is an old friend and offers a fist bump.

"Hey, man, back again, two nights in a row, now that's an endorsement, if ever there were one." He leans in. "And Ayers is here, man, you're in luck."

"Great," Baker says, and he immediately breaks into a light sweat. There's a guy with a guitar in the corner crooning Cat Stevens, and because of the live music, the restaurant is really crowded, much more crowded than the night before. Where is Ayers? Baker casts around, then sees her pulling a cork from a bottle of red wine for a middle-aged couple on the deck under the awning. Her hair is up and she's wearing the black uniform shirt with the black apron over it. She is...breathtaking. There's no other word for it.

"Hey, man, I'm Skip." Skip offers Cash his hand, and Baker says, "I'm sorry. This is my brother, Cash."

Skip asks Cash where he's from and Cash says Breckenridge, Colorado, and it turns out that Skip was a snowboarder in Telluride in his former life. Cash says (as Baker knows he's going to), "To hell you ride! No way, man!" And then they're off and running, talking about how Peak 7 compares to Senior's as Baker sits anxiously by, wondering when he can reasonably interrupt to ask Skip for a vodka tonic.

He feels a hand on his back.

"Hey," Ayers says. "You came!" She looks genuinely happy and surprised, and Baker experiences a surge of pure love like a sugar high or a hit of nicotine—but then Ayers turns her attention to Cash. "Hey, stranger!"

Cash stands up and gives Ayers a hug—more like an overly familiar, overly affectionate squeeze—and Baker is confused. He recalls introducing Cash to Ayers at the reception briefly, but had they said anything more than hello?

Ayers looks at Skip. "Buy these two a round on the house." She points to Cash. "Painkiller, extra strong, for this guy."

Cash laughs. "No, thank you."

"Aw, come on," Ayers says. "How about a rum punch, Myers's floater?"

"Stop!" Cash says.

Baker is lost. What is going *on* here? He's about to ask when Ayers rests a hand on his bicep. Involuntarily, he flexes.

"Are you feeling better?" she asks.

"I...uh, yeah, yes," Baker says.

"If you want to run, you should drive to Maho. There's a

four-mile loop to Leinster Bay. Skip can draw you a map, can't you, Skip?"

"On it," Skip says.

"Gotta get back to work," Ayers says. "Say good-bye before you leave."

"Thanks for the drink," Cash says. Then to Skip he says, "Don't listen to her. I'll have a beer. Island Hoppin' IPA is fine."

"Did you go out on *Treasure Island?*" Skip asks.

Cash nods. "Yesterday. Poisoned myself."

"That happens," Skip says. "Did you go to Jost?"

"Baths, Cooper Island, the Indians."

"Next time, you've got to go to Jost," Skip says. "You haven't lived until you've had a painkiller at the Soggy Dollar."

Baker says, "I'll have a vodka tonic, please." He pauses. Then, at the risk of sounding like a douche bag, he says, "Pronto." He's failed: He sounds like a douche bag. But he's learning that Skip is a talker and easily distracted. And Baker desperately needs a drink if he's to process what he thinks is going on.

Skip slaps the bar. "Pronto."

The drink does arrive pretty much pronto. Baker takes a long, deep sip before he turns to his brother, who is doing his best to look nonchalant—twirling his beer bottle, humming along to the guitar player, who is doing a fair rendition of "Promises," by Eric Clapton.

"Do you mean to tell me *that's* where you were yesterday?" Baker says. "You went out on *Treasure Island?* You went on a trip to the BVIs?" Baker lowers his voice and moves in on Cash. "Our father is *dead.* I sat home waiting to hear from Her Royal Highness's blasted coast guard or what have you. I called the crematorium trying to track down the *ashes,* and you're out getting *drunk* on a *pleasure cruise?*"

"Yep," Cash says. A smile is playing around his lips and Baker wants to punch him. He was out all day on a boat with Ayers, getting drunk, getting cozy. Baker's question is: How did Cash even know Ayers worked on *Treasure Island*? He hadn't been around for that part of the conversation. Was it just dumb luck—Cash needed something to do, stumbled across *Treasure Island,* and recognized Ayers? Or is something more going on? Baker knows that Cash has long wanted to get back at him for hooking up with Claire Bellows at Northwestern. Baker had bumped into her at a Sig Ep party when he was a junior and she was just a freshman. Quite frankly, Claire had thrown herself at Baker. She had drunkenly confided that the entire time she'd been with Cash she had harbored a painful crush on Baker. Baker had pretended to be surprised by this admission, although he had certainly noticed all of the moony looks and the way, whenever Irene had invited Claire to stay for dinner, she had always chosen the seat next to Baker and "accidentally" bumped knees with him under the table. When Baker saw her at Sig Ep, he had spent a few minutes deliberating with his conscience. Could he screw Claire Bellows? He wasn't a complete asshole, and he did love his brother, deep down. But Claire's fawning attention and the number of beers Baker had drunk that night won out. He had taken her back to his room. In the morning, consumed with guilt, she had called Cash.

Cash had been pissed enough to threaten getting on a bus from Boulder to Chicago and showing up to kick Baker's ass.

Baker had laughed and said, "I can't help it if chicks like me better, dude." He had meant this as a kind of apology, but Cash had taken it as exactly the opposite. Things between them had never been the same. Baker thought, *Fine, whatever.*

He wished they were closer or at least on less prickly terms, but they were adults—or at least Baker was, with a house and a wife and a child. Cash was still a punk, mooching off their father's magnanimity, and apparently still a sore loser. It could be that Cash has been waiting all these many years to get back at Baker.

"Really," Baker says now. "How did all that come about?"

"Ayers invited me," Cash says.

Baker finishes the rest of his vodka tonic in one swallow, then holds his empty glass up to Skip, and Skip says, "Pronto, man, as soon as I finish with the sixteen orders from the service bar," a response Baker knows he deserves.

"Invited you *when?*" Baker says.

"When I bumped into her hiking," Cash says.

"Hiking."

"Winnie and I hiked the Reef Bay Trail on Saturday," Cash says. "And we came across Ayers by the petroglyphs, crying and nearly out of drinking water."

"Stop," Baker says. He can all too easily picture the scene. Winnie probably approached Ayers; Cash was fond of letting his dog introduce him to women. And then Cash wooed her by being his well-prepared Boy Scout self. "Just so we're clear on this, I'm going to ask her out."

"What?" Cash says. "You can't ask her out. You're married."

"I..." Baker realizes he hasn't told Cash about Anna, so he most definitely sounds like a world-class jerk. "Anna and I have separated."

"*What?*" Cash says.

Baker can't explain right now. And he can't wait another twenty minutes for a drink. And he can't sit and eat a meal with his brother, who has seen Ayers two of the past three days and now has his own private jokes with her.

Baker stands up. He sets the Jeep keys next to Cash's beer. "I'm out," he says.

He expects Cash to protest, but all Cash says is, "Good."

Baker weaves between tables as the guitar player croaks out "Thunder Road." Baker scans the restaurant and sees Ayers taking an order out on the deck. He stands a few feet behind her until she finishes and then he whispers her name.

She spins around. "Oh, hi," she says. "Are you leaving?"

"I only came for a drink," he says. He squares his shoulders. "Listen, turns out I'm here for a couple more days. I'd love to take you out."

"That's sweet," Ayers says. "But I'm pretty busy. I work two jobs and I have…"

"When are you free?" Baker asks. "I can do lunch, I can do dinner…"

Ayers chews her bottom lip and peers into the restaurant. *Is she looking at Cash?* he wonders. That's just impossible.

"Seriously," Baker says. "I can do breakfast or late drinks. Or late dinner. How about tonight, after you get off?"

Ayers looks hesitant. She's wavering. There's no way she's into Cash; Baker rejects the very idea.

"Please," he says. "Just tell me what time."

"Ten o'clock," she says. "I'll be done by ten and we can go to De' Coal Pot. They serve Caribbean food."

"Perfect," Baker says. "I'll be back at ten."

Ayers nods and hurries inside, and Baker watches her go. *Just please don't invite my brother,* he thinks.

IRENE

What is she doing?

What is she doing?

What is she doing?

She is throwing away the rule book, she thinks. And it feels okay.

For the first fifty-seven years of her life, Irene stayed on script. She was a dutiful daughter, a good student in both high school and college. She got married, had children, took a job that was suited to her.

She had been a good mother, or good enough. The boys were fine.

She had been a good wife.

Hadn't she?

It's only at night, after Irene has taken one of the pills that Anna prescribed, that she allows herself to indulge in self-doubt. Where did she go wrong? She feels like she must have done Russ a huge, terrible injustice somewhere along the way for him to engage in a deception so wide and deep.

But she comes up with nothing.

She wasn't sure what to expect when she arrived here; the villa and the island are as foreign as Neptune. What she finds surprising are the small flashes of her own influence that she stumbles across. All of the beds, she's noticed, have six pillows, along with one oversized decorative pillow against the headboard, one small square decorative pillow in front, and a cylindrical bolster. This is exactly how Irene dresses the beds at home; she had no idea Russ had ever noticed. Also, the wine Russ keeps on hand—cases of it, on the ground floor—are her two favorites: Cakebread and Simi. It's almost as if Russ expected her to show up for a drink one day.

She wouldn't say these details made her feel at home, although they do provide a connection. This was her husband's house. *Her husband's house.* And now her husband is dead. These pieces of news that were, initially, so difficult to conceive, she's now finally processing.

This is Russ's house.

Russ is dead.

She's also becoming acclimatized to life here—the temperature, the surroundings, the particulars of the villa—kind of the way one gets used to the thin air at altitude after a few days. Irene remembers when she and Russ used to visit Cash in Breckenridge; she would suffer from shortness of breath, headaches, strange dreams—and then these symptoms would gradually fade away.

She supposes this goes to show that one can get used to anything.

Seeking out Captain Sam Powers—Huck—had been a bold move, Irene knows. She had desperately wanted to hold *someone* accountable. She can't confront Rosie, but why not Rosie's parents? Huck had been nothing like what Irene had expected. First of all, he was not Rosie's biological father but her stepfather, married to Rosie's deceased mother. Secondly, he was kind— gruff, yes, at first, and unenthusiastic about talking to her (can she blame him?), but he seemed to understand that they were in the same boat (so to speak). Irene had stunned herself by asking to go fishing, and Huck had further stunned her (and likely himself) by agreeing. He could easily have told her to go away and leave him alone. He owed her nothing. He had lost a daughter, and Irene could see that his pain equaled her own; he deserved a day out on his boat by himself. That they had enjoyed such a cathartic and successful outing and that this dinner had evolved from that says…what? That misery loves company, she supposes. That they are not enemies but rather casualties of the same sordid circumstances.

Huck likely has as many questions for her as she does for him, but of course, she has no answers.

She'd had such an easy time finding Huck first thing Monday morning that she tries to track down Todd Croft. Cash had checked with Paulette, who had no contact information for Croft. Paulette dealt only with Marilyn Monroe and with pilot Stephen Thompson—an associate, she said, from the British Virgin Islands.

Irene tries Marilyn Monroe's number again, but it's still disconnected.

She tries the Ascension webpage, but—just as Baker had claimed—it won't load. Someone took it down.

Russ's cell phone isn't in the house, though Irene has called it several times each day. Every time the phone starts ringing, her heart tenses in anticipation. Will today be the day that Russ answers? Is he alive somewhere? No: after two rings, it clicks over to generic voicemail. Irene doesn't even have the luxury of hearing Russ's recorded voice; if she did, she would likely scream at him each time.

She tries to access Russ's cell phone records. She knows his phone number, of course, but the phone bill was paid by Ascension, and she has no idea which carrier he used—she tries contacting AT&T, Verizon, and T-Mobile but gets nowhere.

She wonders if he used a carrier out of the British Virgin Islands, but here she grows frustrated. Even if she figures out the carrier, she doubts they'll give her access to his call log without a court order.

Russ said that he'd been acquainted with Todd Croft at Northwestern, so Irene calls the Northwestern alumni office to see if they have contact information. They don't. Irene could potentially ask one of Russ's other friends from Northwestern— Leo Pelusi or Niles Adrian—but she hasn't seen either of them since their wedding thirty-five years earlier. She has their mailing addresses—they exchange Christmas cards every year—but not phone numbers or email addresses. Russ doesn't go to reunions. The last time he went to Northwestern was eight years ago, for Baker's graduation.

A garden-variety Google of the name Todd Croft, paired with the name Ascension and then separately with Miami, yields nothing fruitful.

Irene grows frustrated. In this day and age, everyone has a digital profile. Someone just told her that, but who? Mavis Key! Mavis Key had explained to Irene and Irene's boss, Joseph Feeney, that with some new software they could learn a lot more about their subscribers' purchasing habits.

Irene is just desperate enough to do the unthinkable. She calls Mavis Key.

"Hey, Irene," Mavis says. She sounds both surprised and concerned. "I heard you had a family emergency. Is everything okay?"

Everything is the opposite of okay, Irene wants to say. *My husband is dead and he had a secret life.* She should have thought this conversation through before she dialed. She needs to convey that the family emergency is real without disclosing even a hint about what has happened.

"Things are difficult right now," Irene says. "Very difficult. But I can't get into it. I called you because I need help finding someone."

"Finding someone," Mavis says. "I'm at the Java House getting a chai." Before Irene can think that of course Mavis Key is downtown on the pedestrian mall, where all the hip university students hang out, ordering a "chai," whatever that is, Mavis adds, "Let me sit down with my laptop. I love detective work."

Irene feels herself relax. Mavis sounds self-assured. She's thirty-one years old, roughly the age of Irene's children, and she exudes both confidence and competence. Irene cherishes competence in everyone, even Mavis Key.

"The man's name is Todd Croft," Irene says. "He's in his mid- to late fifties. He's a banker—a businessman—in Florida, I think. Miami. His business is called Ascension. He went to Northwestern."

Mavis double-checks the spelling of Croft and of Ascension, then Irene can hear her fingertips flying across a keyboard. *LinkedIn*, Mavis murmurs. *Tumblr, Instagram, Snapchat, Twitter, Facebook.* This is a world Irene has actively resisted. People encouraged her to start a Facebook page about her home renovation, but she had been so immersed in the work itself that there had been no time left over to document it.

"I'm not finding him," Mavis says. "Do you know where he worked before Ascension? Do you know if he has kids, or where they went to school? Do you know where in Miami he lives? Do you know if he owns property?"

"I don't," Irene admits. She chastises herself for being so

impetuous; it isn't like her. Now Mavis will go back to the office and tell everyone that Irene is looking for a fifty-something banker from Miami—and what will people *think*?

Well, whatever they think, it won't be as awful as the truth.

"Never mind," Irene says. "I just called on a whim. I need to get a hold of this gentleman because he has some information that will assist with my family issues. But thanks anyway, Mavis."

"Oh," Mavis says. "No problem. When do you think you'll be back? The office isn't the same without you. We're kind of like a bunch of crazed teenagers when Mom is away."

Irene imagines Beyoncé and Drake playing at full blast over the office sound system, microwave popcorn ground into the rug of the common room, long, expensed lunch breaks at Formosa, and the entire staff cutting out early for craft cocktails in the name of "team building." Everyone at the magazine probably views Irene as a schoolmarm, smacking her yardstick into her palm. Irene offers a paltry laugh. "I'll be back next week to restore order," she says. "Thanks, Mavis." She can't hang up fast enough.

The boys leave for dinner. Irene asks them to stay out until eleven, a request that is met with blank stares. Neither of them has asked what she's planning. They're afraid of her, she realizes. They're afraid that at any minute she's going to crack and all of her ugly emotions are going to come flying out. That's fine—they can think what they want, as long as they give her privacy tonight.

She pulls things out of the fridge that she can serve with grilled mahi. Camembert with crackers to start, pasta salad and the makings of a green salad as sides. There's a fruit salad she can serve for dessert with packaged cookies. Food is the least of her worries.

She pours herself a glass of wine, the first since she left the Pullman Bar & Diner six days ago. Thinking about the Pullman and Prairie Lights leads Irene to thoughts of Milly. Cash called Milly on Saturday evening and Milly had been unable to come to the phone. What must Milly think? That they've abandoned her?

Irene grabs her cell phone and calls Milly while she sets the table for two. She debates setting out candles. They're more flattering than the outdoor lighting, but will Irene be sending the wrong message? The boys were kind enough not to ask why she was wearing a sundress and earrings (possibly they hadn't noticed). Irene wants to look nice and normal, though not like she's trying too hard. She has left her hair hanging down her back, still damp from the shower. No makeup; it's best if Huck sees her how she really is.

As she decides no to candles and then yes to candles—why deny herself the pleasure of candlelight?—Dot, the head nurse on the medical floor, answers.

"Dot, this is Irene Steele. I know I've been lax about calling this week…"

"Oh, Irene," Dot says. "Cash called and let us know that you all were taking a vacation. Are you back?"

"No," Irene says. "Not yet." She stands at the deck railing and looks out at the sky, striped pink as the sun sets out of sight to the left. The water has taken on a purplish hue, and pinpricks of light start to appear on the neighboring islands. This view is probably what someone like Dot thinks of when she thinks *vacation*. And yet.

"I haven't called you because I don't want to rain on your

parade," Dot says. "But Milly is failing, Irene. It's nothing dramatic, just a steady decline I've noticed since the first of the year. She's not going to die tomorrow—I don't want you running home—but I figured you ought to know."

Irene is silent. Milly has been failing since the first of the year. The day that Russ died. Her only child. It's almost as if she sensed it.

"Is she awake now?" Irene asks. "Can I speak with her?"

"She's been asleep for hours," Dot says. "But I'll tell her you called. Around lunchtime is best, if you want to try again tomorrow."

Try again tomorrow, Irene thinks. So she can lie to Milly and tell her everything is fine, Cash surprised her with a vacation, the Caribbean is beautiful.

"Okay," Irene says. "I'll do that."

Huck arrives a few minutes after seven. From her second-floor guest-room window, Irene watches his truck snake up the driveway. She checks her hair and hurries down the stairs to meet him at the door.

This is not a date, she tells herself, though her nerves are bright and jangly with anticipation. She will attempt to make Huck her ally. She needs one here on this island.

Irene opens the door. Huck has cleaned up a bit himself—his red-gray hair is combed, his yellow shirt pressed. He's holding a bag of fish fillets—more than they could possibly eat—in one hand and a bottle of...he immediately hands the bottle over to Irene...Flor de Caña rum, eighteen years old.

"Thought we might need that," he says.

Irene accepts the bottle gratefully. It solves the problem of how to greet him—air-kiss or handshake. Now neither is necessary.

"Come on in," she says. "Did you have any problem finding it?"

"You know I've lived here twenty years," Huck says. "And I never knew this road existed. Does it have a name?"

"Lovers Lane," Irene says.

"Seriously?"

"That's what the deed says." This is a development, new as of this afternoon. Paulette Vickers managed to produce the deed. The house, known as Number One Lovers Lane, is owned solely by Russell Steele. This news had come as a solid punch to the gut. Irene had secretly believed that they would discover the property was owned by Todd Croft or Ascension. If that had been the case, Irene could have believed Russ was a pawn, manipulated by his powerful boss. More than once after Russ had accepted the job from Todd, Irene had realized that he'd made a deal with the devil. But had she ever encouraged him to quit? Never. The money had been too seductive.

According to Irene's lawyer in Iowa City, Ed Sorley, Russ's will leaves everything to her should she survive him. *When had he signed the will?* Irene had asked Ed. She worried that another will would materialize, leaving everything to Rosie Small. But Ed said that Russ had come in to sign a new will in September, one that included a new life insurance policy he'd taken out, to the tune of three million dollars.

"September?" Irene said. This was news to her. She remembered them both signing new wills back when they bought the Church Street property.

"Yes," Ed says. "Why do you ask? Is everything all right?"

"Never better," Irene said, and hung up.

"Well," Huck says now, stepping into the foyer. "This is quite a place."

Quite a place. Huck follows Irene through the entry hall into the kitchen. She doesn't feel like giving him a tour—although there is something she wants to show him upstairs, after dinner.

"Let me get you something to drink," Irene says. "I have wine chilled or..." She looks at the rum; she's not sure what to do with it. No one has ever brought her a bottle of rum before. "Can I make you a cocktail? We have Coke, I think."

Huck opens a cabinet and pulls out two highball glasses; he pours some rum in each. "Let's do a shot," Huck says. "Then we can be civilized folks and switch to wine."

Throwing away the rule book. "Deal," Irene says. She lifts her glass, raises it to Huck, and throws the rum back. It burns, but not as much as she'd expected; it has a certain smoothness, like fiery caramel.

"Well," she says.

"Good stuff," Huck pronounces. "Now, if you can find me olive oil, salt, pepper, and a lemon, I'll marinate our catch."

Thirty minutes later, Irene is slightly more relaxed, thanks to the rum, a glass of the Cakebread, and a man who is as confident a cook as he is a fisherman. Irene sits at the outdoor table as

Huck grills, and when he brings the platter of fish to the table, she finds herself hungry for the first time since the call came.

Huck takes the seat next to Irene and then pauses a minute, looking at the food. It seems like he's about to speak— make a toast maybe, or say grace. Do they have anything to be grateful for?

Well, they're still here.

"To us," she says. "The survivors."

Huck nods. "Let's eat."

AYERS

The restaurant clears out by quarter of ten, as usual, though there are still a couple of people at the bar, including Baker's brother, Cash. Or maybe Ayers should be thinking of Baker as Cash's brother. She likes them both. Baker is hotter, but Ayers feels more comfortable around Cash.

She wipes down the tables, clears all the dishes, unties her apron, and throws it in the hamper. The chef hired someone to replace Rosie, an older gentleman named Dominic, which Ayers supposes is for the best. Skip pours Ayers a glass of the Schramsberg to drink as he counts out her tips.

"Ayers!" Cash calls across the bar. "Come sit!" He raises his beer aloft and Ayers drifts over but does not commit to sitting down. Baker had said he'd be back at ten, and Ayers plans on taking him to De' Coal Pot. She has been dreaming about the oxtail stew all night.

Rosie had loved the oxtail stew at De' Coal Pot. And the curried goat.

"So how was your dinner?" Ayers asks Cash.

"Wuss good," Cash says. He's slurring his words. From the looks of things, he's even drunker than he was on *Treasure Island.* Ayers notices the Jeep keys next to his place mat.

"Water here, please," Ayers says to Skip with a look. She wonders if her date to De' Coal Pot is in jeopardy. Baker will have to drive Cash home; he can't drive himself.

Ayers feels a hand on her back and turns, expecting to see Baker but—whoa! surprise!—it's Mick. He's wearing a sky-blue Beach Bar t-shirt and his hair is damp behind the ears. He's working, obviously, but what Ayers doesn't understand is why, if he's going to sneak off for a drink, doesn't he go somewhere *else*? Why not Joe's Rum Hut or the Banana Deck? Why does he have to come *here*?

"Hey," he says. He waves to Skip, and a cold Island Summer Ale lands in front of him.

"What?" she says.

"I came to see how you're holding up," Mick says. "Want to get a drink? I just got off. And actually I'm starving. Want to grab Chinese at 420?"

Chinese at 420: Their old ritual. 420 to Center is a dive bar next to Slim's parking lot where everyone in the service industry goes after his or her shift. It's owned by two guys from Boston; "420 to Center" is some reference to Fenway Park. They do whip up remarkably good Chinese food late-night. Time was, not so long ago, that Mick and Ayers were the king and queen of 420 to Center. But that time has passed. Ayers hasn't been to 420 once this season. She avoided it because she assumed Mick went there with her successor.

Speaking of which.

"Where's Brigid?" Ayers asks.

Mick shrugs.

"Trouble in paradise?" she says.

"It was never paradise."

Ayers thinks about this for a moment. Ayers would have called what she and Mick had paradise. Yes, she would have. They were in love in St. John, they had good jobs and the same days off, and they knew everyone; when they went out, it was hard to pay for a drink. They both loved the beach, the sun, sex, hiking, drinking tequila, and Mick's dog, Gordon. What could Ayers assume when Mick left but that Brigid—young, alluring Brigid—offered something *even more sublime.* To discover that this maybe wasn't true, that life with Brigid had somehow not lived up to expectations, is, of course, enormously satisfying. But only for a fleeting moment. Mick is here, she realizes, *not* to see how Ayers is "holding up." No, it's not about Ayers's emotional state, but rather, about *Mick's.* He wants her company or he wants sex—probably the latter—but Ayers doesn't have time for it.

"Oh, well," she says, and she turns back to Cash, who has consumed his water and seems reinvigorated, like the herbs in Ayers's garden after a rain. "You feeling better?"

"Yes," Cash says. "Do you know what time it is?"

"Nearly ten," she says. She can feel Mick at her back, watching her, and probably sizing up Cash. When they were a couple, Mick had been fiendishly jealous of every single one of Ayers's male customers—single or married, in the restaurant or on the boat—and yet, in the end, it was he who had put his head up someone else's skirt. "Are you calling it a night?"

"I wish," Cash says. "I can't go home for another hour. My mother has a guest for dinner and she wants privacy."

"Your mother," Ayers says. "Did she meet someone here? Or...do you know people?"

"Met someone," Cash says. "Apparently."

"So your parents are divorced?" Ayers asks.

"Divorced?" Cash says. He takes what seems like a long time to consider the question. "No. No." Another pause, during which Ayers hears Mick and Skip talking about a supposed surfable swell in Reef Bay. It was Ayers's least favorite thing about Mick: he professed to be a "surfer," and he used all the lingo, but the one time Ayers had watched him "surf," he'd fallen off the board and broken his collarbone. He'd blamed his accident on the waves. "My father is dead."

Because she's distracted thinking about the five hours she and Mick had spent in the waiting room at Myrah Keating, with Mick moaning and groaning while she smoothed his hair and brought water to his lips like a dutiful girlfriend, it takes her a moment to process this statement.

"Dead?" she says. "I'm sorry. Recently?"

Cash nods. "Really recently. That's kind of why we're down here."

Down here. Family reunion, maybe the first vacation since the father died, which is why the mother came along.

"You're still here?" a voice says.

Ayers turns around to see Baker standing behind her and also, of course, behind Mick. Baker is as big, tall, and broad as a tree. He's staring down his brother.

"Mom said stay out until eleven," Cash says. "Where else was I supposed to go?"

"Yeah, I don't know," Baker says. "But Ayers and I are going out and you're not invited." His tone is strong, nearly bullying, and Ayers feels bad for Cash. She understands now that both

Cash and Baker are interested in her, and she wished they'd sorted this out at home to save her from being stuck in the middle, although a small part of her is gloating, because what better situation for Mick to witness than two men fighting over her?

"Where are you guys going?" Cash asks.

"None of your business," Baker says, so harshly that Ayers winces, but then he softens and says, "Listen, just give us an hour, okay, man? I'll be back to pick you up at eleven. I promise."

"But where are you going?" Cash asks.

"De' Coal Pot," Ayers says. "It's Caribbean food. You're welcome to…"

Cash holds up a hand. "You guys go. I ate."

"De' Coal Pot?" Mick says. "I could go for some oxtail stew myself."

Not happening, Ayers thinks. *This is not happening.* She is smacked by a wave of devastating sorrow. The person she needs by her side right now isn't Mick or Baker or Cash. It's Rosie.

Can you see this? Ayers asks Rosie in her mind. *Please tell me you are somewhere you can see this.*

Baker swings around. "Who are *you*?" he asks Mick.

Mick, wisely, holds up his hands. "No one," he says. "I'm no one."

Baker and Ayers walk down the street toward De' Coal Pot, although Ayers finds she no longer has any appetite. She needs air, she needs space.

"I'm not hungry anymore," she says. "Let's go down to the beach."

"You lead," Baker says. "I'll follow."

Ayers takes him down past the Beach Bar to the far edge of Frank Bay, where it's dark and quiet. Out on the water, she sees the ferry making its way toward St. Thomas. On the far horizon, she spies a cruise ship, all lit up like a floating city. Ayers sits in the cool sand and Baker eases down next to her.

"Your brother is pretty drunk," Ayers says.

"I didn't realize you knew him so well," Baker says. "That came as a surprise."

"He didn't tell you we bumped into each other on the Reef Bay Trail?" Ayers says. "He saved my life, or at least it felt like it at the time. So, as a thank-you, I invited him to come on *Treasure Island* yesterday. I didn't think he'd show up, but he did."

"Of course he did," Baker says. "When a gorgeous woman invites you somewhere, you go."

Ayers smiles. She's flattered by the compliment—but then she chastises herself. She can't let herself be won over so easily.

"Your brother is nice," Ayers says.

"Very nice," Baker says. "I'm extremely jealous that he got to spend so much time with you. When I met you at the reception...I can't explain any way to say it except that I was bowled over. Blown away. I looked at you and...well, I'd better not say anything else."

"You don't even know me," Ayers says. "And I hate to tell you this, but I have a rule about dating tourists. I don't do it."

"That's good to know," Baker says.

"I'm serious," Ayers says. "Guys like you and your brother come here, you're on vacation, on the beach all day, hiking, snorkeling, happy hour, out to dinner, and that's all great. That's what you're supposed to do. But then you get back on the ferry to St. Thomas, where you board the plane home to your real life. And I stay here." She opens her arms wide, aware that the back of her right arm is now touching Baker's chest. He gently reaches around her and pulls her close. She lets him. She wants physical contact, meaningless though it may be. It's really not fair that Mick showed up and then admitted that life with Brigid was never paradise. It's not fair that Rosie is dead because *she* fell in love with a tourist—or if not a tourist exactly, then a visitor, and if not a visitor, then . . . Ayers doesn't quite know *how* to categorize the Invisible Man, but she does blame him for stealing her friend. And, just say it, for *killing* her friend. Her best friend.

Baker senses something in her breathing, maybe, or he reads minds, because he touches her chin and says, "Hey, are you okay?" And the next thing Ayers knows, she's kissing him. She tells herself to stop, this is irrational, self-destructive behavior; she knows exactly nothing about this guy. But the kissing is electric, just like it was the very first time she kissed Mick, maybe better. Chemistry, she has learned, is either there or it isn't and wow, yes, it's there, this guy knows what he's doing, his tongue, she can't get enough of it, his arms are so strong, his hands, every cell of her body is suddenly yearning for more. She's going to sleep with him, maybe right here on the beach— no, that would be bad, what if someone sees, it'll be all over town by tomorrow, but she doesn't want to break the spell to go to her truck and drive to her house, it's too far, she wants this now. Does he want it now? He's being shy with his hands, one is on the back of her head, one on the side of her neck, she wants him to put his hand up her shirt. She guides his hand, he just barely fingers her nipple, she groans, she reaches over into his lap, he's hard as a rock, practically busting through his shorts. Oh yes, she thinks, this is happening *right now*.

He pulls away, out of breath. "We have to stop."

"We can't stop," she says. She strokes his erection through his shorts and he makes a choking sound, then says, "You're killing me. But I like you, I like you so much, Ayers, and I don't want it to be like this, here on the beach, over quickly and then I go home and you go home and I'm just the tourist you let through the net because you're sad about your friend and because I told your ex-boyfriend off."

She draws back. She only had one sip of Schramsberg after service but she feels light-headed, not drunk exactly but addled, mixed-up, off-kilter, and yet she knows he's right. She's startled, in fact, at just how right he is.

"You knew that was my ex-boyfriend?"

"You pointed him out at the reception," Baker says. "He was with that unwashed trollop."

"Yes," Ayers whispers. "Brigid."

"Let's spend the day together tomorrow," he says. "Can we?"

"We can," Ayers says. "I have the whole day off tomorrow. Day and night—"

He squeezes her. "Beach during the day…"

"Wait," she says. She's supposed to take Maia tomorrow after school and overnight. It's the first time since Rosie died. Ayers can't cancel. She *won't* cancel. "Actually, I'm only free tomorrow until three."

He stiffens. "Hot date?"

"Something like that," Ayers says. She doesn't elaborate; she wants him to be jealous. "But we can still do beach. I'll meet you around ten, we'll get sandwiches. I know a place out in Coral Bay that's always deserted. I swim naked."

"Yes!" Baker says. "I'm in!" He stands up, offers her a hand, pulls her in close, and kisses the tip of her nose. "I don't want you to think I meant anything by stopping. I just want this to be memorable. I want it to be perfect. You deserve that."

He's saying all the right things. But he's a tourist. A tourist! He lives in . . . she tries to remember. He has a child somewhere and a wife who left him.

"How much longer do you have here?" Ayers asks. "When are you leaving?"

Baker pauses. "I'm not sure."

"You're not sure?" Ayers says. She suddenly gets the feeling he's hiding something, and she realizes that she felt that way while talking to Cash as well. As if not everything added up. They're here for a family reunion, the father is dead, but the mother has a date tonight. They don't know the address of where they're staying and Baker seemed pretty dead set against Ayers driving him home that morning. He was lost, he said. "Well, you rented a villa, right? How long is the rental?"

"It's not a rental," Baker says. "The villa belongs to my father."

He and Ayers have made their way back up to the road. At the Beach Bar, a band is playing a Sublime cover. "But isn't your father dead?" Ayers asks.

Baker stops in the street. "Did Cash tell you that?"

"Yes?" Ayers says. "He said your mother has a date tonight and I asked if your parents were divorced and he said no, your father was dead."

"Did he say anything else?"

"Anything else like *what*?" Ayers says. It's now more than a feeling; it's a certainty. Something is going on with these two guys that they're not telling her.

"Well, first of all, my mother does *not* have a date," Baker says. He takes Ayers's hand and they head back in the direction of La Tapa. "But we do, tomorrow at ten. Right?"

Ayers takes a deep breath of the sweet evening air. The problem, she realizes, is Mick. Mick has made her mistrustful. He cheated on her with Brigid and now Ayers is destined to think *everyone* is hiding something.

"Right," she says.

CASH

At five minutes to eleven, Cash finishes his beer, leaves a tip for Skip, and stumbles out to the front of the restaurant. He has called Baker three times but gotten no answer, which is really making Cash's blood boil, because while Baker is out putting the moves on Ayers—on *Ayers,* the first woman Cash has been attracted to in *years*—Cash has no way to get home.

What is he supposed to do? He has twenty-six dollars left to his name; all the rest of the cash from his now-defunct stores is gone. To live another day, he's going to have to ask his mother or brother for money. He can maybe pass off his flat-broke state as a logistical situation, claiming his bank card doesn't work down here, but there are enough cover-ups and lies in this family as it is. He needs to come clean: the stores are gone.

It seems like a minor problem. He tried to be someone he wasn't, he failed, and now he will go back to being the person he is. A ski instructor. For some reason, the idea doesn't hold as much appeal as it did before all this happened.

He tries Baker again: voicemail. He feels himself about to

snap. But then he hears his brother's voice and sees Baker waving an arm.

"Back in five!" Baker says. He's with Ayers; they're holding hands. They walk down the street to a green pickup and then Cash is treated to the sight of them kissing, really kissing. Cash feels sick.

"He's married!" Cash calls out. But they don't hear him.

On the way home, Baker is giddy. He sounds like a teenage girl. He kissed Ayers on the beach, he could have done more, way more, but he stopped her. *He* stopped *her*. She was totally into it, eager, ready, but with a woman like Ayers, a quick hookup on the beach isn't good enough. She deserves a bed. A suite at Caneel Bay. He's going to look into it.

"Look into a *suite* at *Caneel*?" Cash says. The words leave his mouth just as they happen to drive past the grand landscaped entrance of the Caneel Bay Resort. None of the resort is visible beyond the gatehouse, but Cash imagines it's pretty opulent. Like his father's house, only sexier. "You're married."

"I told you, Anna and I separated," Baker says. "She came home on New Year's Day, I kid you not, like five minutes before Mom called with the news, and she said she was leaving me. She said she was in love with someone else."

"Really?" Cash says. He has never thought of Dr. Anna Schaffer as someone who would be "in love" with anyone, Baker included. She had appeared decidedly unenthusiastic at the wedding, but Cash understood that Anna was in thrall to her work. People took a distant second. Irene had long intoned her concern that Anna didn't even have warm feelings for Floyd. Her own child. "Who is she in love with?"

"Dr. Louisa Rodriguez," Baker says. "Another cardiothoracic surgeon. Friend and colleague."

"Luis?" Cash says. He's confused. "Or Louisa?"

"Louisa," Baker says. "Woman."

"Really?" Cash says. "Anna's a lesbian? I guess I can see that."

"I'm not sure we need to label her," Baker says. "It might just be that she has feelings for Louisa in particular."

"Fair enough," Cash says. At that moment, his phone starts ringing and he thinks it must be his mother, calling to say the coast is clear and they are free to come home—because who else could it be? When he checks the display, he shakes his head. *Anna*, it says. Wait. He looks at Baker, then back down at his phone. It's almost as if she heard them talking about her.

"Hello?" Cash says.

"Cash," she says. "Hey, it's Anna. Anna Schaffer. Baker's wife."

"Hi," Cash says. It speaks volumes that she has to explain who she is. Still, he tries to keep his voice neutral. "How are you?"

"Do you know where Baker is?" she asks. "I've been calling him all night but he won't answer."

Cash nearly says, *Yeah, Baker is right here*—but something stops him. "Is everything okay?" he asks.

"Everything's fine," Anna says. "Would you please let Baker know that Floyd and I are flying down there tomorrow? We land at one fifteen and should be on the two o'clock ferry out of Red Hook that will get us to St. John by three."

To St. John tomorrow by three.

"Okay," Cash says. He can't believe this. Didn't Baker say he had a date with Ayers tomorrow?

"You really need to remember to tell him," Anna says. "Baker has no idea we're coming. It was basically impossible for me to clear it with work until the very last minute."

"Will do," Cash says.

"I can count on you?" Anna says.

"Absolutely," Cash says.

"Okay," Anna says, and she sounds happier, maybe even a little excited. "See you tomorrow!"

Cash hangs up the phone. He can't believe this is happening. He can't believe it.

"Who was that?" Baker asks.

"That?" Cash says. "No one."

HUCK

This is right up there with the craziest things Huck has ever done. A dozen times on the way over, he thought, *For the love of Bob, turn around, go home to your book and your beer. Getting mixed up with this woman, the wife, is going to be nothing but trouble. Rosie is dead and nothing will bring her back.* The voice in Huck's head was one of reason, loud and clear, and yet still he drove to the north shore and found the utility pole with the two yellow stripes. Still he ascended the steep, winding road—there were no other homes, only dummy driveways that led to nowhere, until you reached the gate at the top, which had been left open. Huck wondered if this bastard had enough money to buy up the entire hill, just to make certain he had no neighbors.

Still he knocked on the door.

Irene looks pretty. It's not a thought he should be having about Russell Steele's widow, but there it is, plain and simple. Huck is a man, built like other men, and so he appreciates Irene's chestnut hair hanging loose and damp down her back, and the black sundress that shows off her arms, her neck, and her pretty feet.

She's nervous, he can tell—her hands are shaking as she accepts the rum. Huck thinks, *Better do a shot right away.* Why did God provide humans with alcohol if not for situations like this?

They make casual chitchat while Huck prepares the mahi. Irene pours white wine, it's her favorite, from Napa, she says, and Huck makes a sound of general appreciation, as if he cares where the wine is from. Irene has set out cheese and crackers but she doesn't touch them, and Huck holds back to be polite. Or maybe it's rude not to eat? He can't tell; he should have reviewed his Emily Post before coming up here. Huck asks Irene if she has a job. She says yes, she's the editor of something called *Heartland Home & Style.* It's a glossy magazine, she says, with a hundred seventy-five thousand subscribers and a quarter-million in advertising each month.

"So it's like *Penthouse,* then?" Huck says.

This gets a laugh out of her, which must come as a surprise, because she claps a hand over her mouth.

"It's okay," Huck says. "You're allowed."

This is the exact wrong response, because Irene's eyes fill with tears, but she takes a breath, recovers, and says, "I'm sorry. It's kindness that undoes me."

"Understood," Huck says. "From here on out, I'll try to be more of a bastard."

Irene smiles. "Thank you. Anyway, a day or two before all this...I had something happen at work. They named me 'executive editor,' which is technically a rung up the masthead, but for all intents and purposes I was fired. They relieved me of all my important duties, my decision making..."

"Turned you into an editor *emeritus,*" Huck says.

Irene's eyes grow wide. "Exactly."

"They're giving you an honorary title, hoping you'll retire," Huck says.

"They couldn't fire me because then advertisers would have made noise, so they got sneaky instead."

"You should quit," Huck says. "Move down here. I'll hire you as my first mate. You're one hell of a good fisherperson."

Irene laughs again, not happily. "Not a chance," she says.

He gets back in her good graces once he sets down the grilled mahi. He waits until Irene takes a bite.

"Wow," she says.

"Really?" he says. "Good?"

She takes another bite and he takes the hint: she's not there to plump his ego. He tastes the fish: yes, perfect. Huck is something of a fanatic about grilling fish. In his opinion, you have a sixty-second window with fish. You take it off a minute too early, it's translucent and not quite *there*. But this is preferable, in his mind, to a minute too late. A minute too late and the fish is dry, overcooked, ruined. Three generations of Small women—LeeAnn, Rosie, and Maia—have been schooled in Huck's feelings about grilled fish, and they all reached a point where they were as discriminating as he was. Huck's fish is always on point, because he stands at the grill like the Swiss Guard and doesn't let anything distract him. He'd worried that tonight would be an exception, because there are a host of distractions here, but, praise be, the fish is correct.

Irene eats only the fish—the pasta salad and greens remain on her plate—then she helps herself to seconds. "I have no appetite," she says. "Except for this fish."

"Because you caught it yourself," Huck says. "Because you pulled it out of blue water." He catches her eye. "Angler Cupcake."

She pours more wine. They're at the end of the first bottle and without hesitating, Irene opens a second. Okay, then, it's going to be that kind of night. Huck has questions, but he won't ask them yet.

"Powder room?" he asks, standing up.

Irene says, "Through the living room to the back corner down a short hall."

Huck takes his time wandering. The house is grand but the furnishings are impersonal. He had hoped to see something of Rosie, some indication that she spent time here. There are no photographs; there's no art at all, really. It looks like any one of a thousand rentals. On the other hand, Huck is glad about this for Irene's sake. How unpleasant it would be for her to have to live, even briefly, in the love nest Russell Steele once feathered with his mistress.

Huck isn't sure when he started taking Irene's feelings into account. Probably when she took the second helping of fish.

As Huck washes his hands, he stares at himself in the mirror and asks himself the hardest question.

Did Rosie know the Invisible Man was married? Huck desperately wants to believe the answer is no, but...come on! Russell Steele shows up here a week or two per month; the rest of the time he's ostensibly "working," but he's never here at Thanksgiving or Christmas. Is he "working" on Thanksgiving or Christmas? No! He's with his family, his other family, his real family.

Rosie was sweet, but she wasn't naive.

When Huck gets back to the deck, Irene is standing at the railing with her wine, staring at the water.

It's time now, he supposes. He joins her.

"Tell me about your children," he says.

She shakes her head. No, she doesn't want to tell him, or she doesn't believe he deserves to hear. But then she says, "Baker is thirty. He lives in Houston. He's married to a heart surgeon and has a four-year-old son named Floyd. He's a stay-at-home dad, runs the household, does all the things I used to do when the boys were small. He day-trades in tech stocks, too, on the side, but Anna makes most of the money."

"Do we like Anna?" Huck asks. Something about the way she said the woman's name makes him curious.

"Oh," Irene says. "She's fine."

"That bad?" he says.

"She's an excellent surgeon. She makes all the Houston Best-of lists, and her patients love her. But you don't have that kind of demanding career without some personal sacrifice."

"The sacrifice in her case...?"

"She's never home. She isn't much of a mother to Floyd. She's a bit dispassionate. It's hard to pierce her armor, to get any kind of human response out of her at all. Now, in her defense, she deals with life and death all day, every day, so telling her about finger-painting projects or playground squabbles falls on deaf ears."

"That's too bad," Huck says. "I love hearing the day-to-day details about my granddaughter Maia's life. She and her friend Joanie are starting a bath bomb business. They're making them in tropical scents to sell to tourists. I had to order citric acid crystals from Amazon—the package will probably take several months to get here. But I treasure all the little stuff. Because then they get older and they stop telling you things."

"Amen," Irene says.

"I didn't mean to hijack the conversation," Huck says. "Tell me about your other son."

"Cash," she says. "Short for Cashman. The boys were given the maiden names of my two grandmothers. Cash owns and operates a couple of outdoor supply stores in Denver. Savage Season Outdoor Supply, they're called. Russ gave him the seed money. Russ wanted to see Cash do something with his life other than be a ski instructor."

"Nothing wrong with teaching people to ski," Huck says. "Honest living."

If Irene notices the archness in his voice, she doesn't let on. "So those are the boys. They're good kids. They don't know what to make of all this. They know about Rosie, although we haven't discussed it. I should tell them I know—it would probably be a weight off their minds. They want to protect me from it, I'm sure. I suppose I'll tell them in the morning."

"Always best to be open," Huck says.

"Is it?" Irene asks. "I made them leave the house tonight because you were coming. They don't know I've made contact with you. They don't know about the fishing." Irene throws back what's left of her wine. "It's like Russ had this giant secret, which, in turn, is causing the three of us to keep our own smaller secrets." She looks Huck in the eye for the first time, or the first time without her guard way up. Her eyes are steel-blue, the color of a stormy sea. "I can't believe this happened to me. And I can't believe I tracked you down, forced you to take me fishing, and then invited you to dinner."

"If it makes any difference," Huck says, "I'm glad you did."

"Are you?" she says.

He wants to kiss her. But he is too old and out of practice to know if she would welcome this or slap him.

Slap him, he thinks. She's been a widow for less than a week.

"Yes," he says. "I am." He rips his eyes away from her and focuses on Jost Van Dyke, twinkling in the distance. The view is quite something from up here.

"Tell me what you know," Irene says. "Tell me about Rosie."

"All right," Huck says.

Should he go all the way back to the beginning?

Huck is new to the island, but not brand-new. He has his boat and he has his best friend, Rupert, out in Coral Bay. Coral

Bay is different from town: folks out there keep to themselves,
West Indians and whites alike. Honestly, as soon as you came
down the other side of Bordeaux Mountain, it was as though
you were on a different island. When Huck wanted to see
Rupert, he had to drive to Coral Bay; Rupert simply refused to
come west. They would drink at Skinny Legs or Shipwreck
Landing and then, half in the bag, Huck would drive home.

Stay left, Rupert used to say. *And look out for the donkeys.*

It was at a full-moon BBQ at a place called Miss Lucy's that
Rupert introduced Huck to LeeAnn. There was a three-piece
steel band and she was right in front, dancing in the grass.
Love at first sight? Sure, why not.

LeeAnn had a daughter, fifteen years old and beautiful,
which meant trouble. Rosie's father was long gone, but his
people were still around, and while LeeAnn was working her
long hours as a nurse practitioner, Rosie sometimes visited her
Small aunties and cousins out in Coral Bay—or at least that's
what she said she was doing. Part or most of that time, she
was, instead, falling in love with a fella named Oscar from St.
Thomas who was twenty-four years old and bad news. Oscar
worked "security" for Princess cruises—Huck suspected he
also supplied the staff and passengers with drugs—and as
such, he was flush with cash that he liked to show off. He
drove a Ducati motorcycle and came over to St. John every
chance he got to take Rosie for a ride.

Rosie sneaked over to St. Thomas to attend the Rolex Regatta.
She had begged LeeAnn to be allowed to go and LeeAnn had

said no, she was too young, period. But Rosie had gone anyway. When LeeAnn found out, she dispatched Huck to find her and bring her home. Huck and LeeAnn had been together only a few months at that point, and Huck was still completely infatuated. He would do whatever LeeAnn asked without question, even though he knew he held no sway over Rosie.

He had loaded his truck on the car barge and driven to the St. Thomas Yacht Club, where he paid twenty-five dollars to park and another five for a couple of beers to walk around with while he hunted for LeeAnn's child. Because Huck had been born and raised in the Florida Keys, he was no stranger to regattas. They were only nominally about sailing; really, they were about drinking. Huck took in the well-heeled crowd holding their cocktails aloft as they danced to the band playing vintage Rolling Stones, and the pervasive sense of joy and revelry—because what better way to spend an afternoon than drinking rum and dancing under the Caribbean sun while a bunch of white guys in five-million-dollar boats negotiated wind and water in the name of an overpriced watch?

He was cynical because he was jealous. It looked fun, and he had come to be a buzzkill.

Huck found Rosie sitting on Oscar's lap at a picnic table crowded with other West Indians, all of them nattily dressed, all of them wearing Rolexes themselves. They were eating chicken roti and conch stew, drinking Caribes. Huck was bigger than Oscar, just barely, but there were some other gentlemen at the table who were bigger than Huck and Oscar combined, with Rosie thrown in.

Huck saw no way to tackle his assignment other than head-on. He approached the table—the men and Rosie were all speaking patois, Huck could barely decipher a word—and said, "Rosie, I've come to bring you home."

Rosie, he remembered, had blinked lazily, unfazed, and had burrowed like a sand crab into Oscar's arms. "I'm not going anywhere. I'm staying here."

"No," Huck said. "You're not."

"Hey, man," Oscar said. "You heard the lady."

"She's not a lady," Huck said. "She's fifteen years old."

This caught the attention of the other gentlemen at the table. They started lowing and whoa-ing. Oscar knew how old Rosie was—maybe he thought she was sixteen or seventeen. However, the others likely thought Rosie was nineteen or twenty, maybe even older. She was wearing iridescent-blue eyeshadow and a halter top the size of a handkerchief.

Huck squared his shoulders. "I'm not leaving without her." He hadn't been sure how intimidating he seemed, but he had been to Vietnam before any of these guys were born and he would remind them of that if he needed to. "I'm going to have a cigarette while you say your good-byes."

Oscar had eased Rosie off his lap and then held her face and talked to her gently while she cried. But it was clear Oscar wasn't going to put up a fight, and Huck felt proud of himself, thinking how relieved LeeAnn would be when both Huck and Rosie pulled in the driveway. As long as he found the girl some other clothes.

Huck was ready for Rosie's anger. She climbed into Huck's pickup and slammed the door so hard it nearly fell off. That hadn't surprised him. When they pulled up to Route 322, the sounds of the reggae band still wafting in through Huck's open window, Rosie said, "I hate you." That hadn't surprised him, either.

"I don't know who you think you are. Maybe you think you're some kind of god because you're white. But no white man tells me what to do."

Huck said, "There's a popular phrase that goes, 'Don't shoot the messenger.' I came at the request of your mother. She had to work, and so she sent me. Frankly, I think you got off easy."

"I still hate you," Rosie said.

Huck doesn't think Irene needs or wants to hear all this, so he just says, "I married LeeAnn when Rosie was a teenager. She was a rebellious child. She dated a West Indian fella, older, from St. Thomas named Oscar. That went on for too long, but it ended when Oscar went to jail."

"Lovely," Irene says.

"Tell me about it," Huck says. "He got drunk and stabbed one of his friends. Though not fatally."

"Did Rosie go to college?" Irene asks.

"She did, at UVI in St. Thomas. It's funny, some kids who grow up here can't wait to get away, and some can't bear to leave. Rosie was the latter. She loved it here. She and her momma used to fight like half-starved hens over a handful of feed, but there was a deep emotional attachment. So she stayed. For a long time, she waited tables at Caneel Bay. That's where she met the Pirate."

"The pirate?" Irene says.

"It was...let's see...thirteen years ago, Valentine's weekend. Some guy, rich, white, showed up on a yacht for the weekend and swept Rosie off her feet."

"What was his name?" Irene asks.

"Never learned it. He came and went. It was just a week-end fling. Rosie called him the Pirate, though, because he stole her heart."

"So she had a history of this?" Irene says.

"If by 'this' you mean poor choices in men, then yes," Huck says. "I actually suspected the Pirate was a made-up story. I thought Rosie was back with Oscar—this would have been after he was released from jail. But when the baby was born, she was very light-skinned. No doubt the father was white."

Irene backs away a fraction of an inch. "Baby?"

"Maia," Huck says. "Rosie's daughter. My granddaughter. She's twelve."

"Oh," Irene says. "I didn't put…I didn't realize…" She tears up, then starts to soundlessly cry. Huck pulls a handker-chief out of his pocket, which is actually just one of the ban-danas he likes to tie around his neck when he's fishing, and hands it to Irene. She shakes it out over the railing like a woman bidding her loved ones good-bye on an ocean liner, then dabs at her eyes. "I'm sorry. I didn't realize Rosie left behind a child."

"That's the real tragedy here," Huck says. "Me, I'm old. I've known loss. But Maia…"

"She's twelve, you say? And never knew her father? So Rosie was all she had?"

"Rosie and me," Huck says. "Now there's just me. But peo-ple will step up. Maia won't get lost. I won't let her get lost. I don't care if I have to keep myself alive until I'm a hundred years old."

"When did Russ come into the picture?" Irene asks.

"I couldn't be sure…"

"But if you had to guess," Irene says. "The deed says he bought this house three years ago. Had their relationship... been going on for *three years*?"

Here is where things get thorny, Huck thinks. Here is where he profoundly regrets his decision to let this woman ever set foot on his boat. They have been acting like they're on the same side. In some sense, they are. They're the bereaved. The survivors.

But Huck is Rosie's family and Irene is Russ's family. Irene wants this whole mess to be Rosie's fault and Huck wants it to be Russ's fault. Irene is making it sound like *three years* would be nearly inconceivable—but Huck knows that their relationship went on longer than three years. Rosie met the Invisible Man right after LeAnn died—five years ago.

"I'm really not sure, Irene," Huck says. "What I know about their relationship I could write on my thumbnail and still have room for the U.S. Constitution. Rosie told me next to nothing. And like I said, I never had the pleasure of meeting..."

"My husband."

"Mr. Steele." Huck clears his throat. "Your husband."

Irene steps back to the table, fills her glass with more wine, and regards Huck over the rim, as if trying to gauge whether or not he's telling the truth.

He is. He knows it sounds unusual. It *was* unusual. And part of what's at work in Huck is guilt. He should have nipped the relationship—or at least the secrecy about it—in the bud. But like he said, Rosie met the guy right after LeeAnn died, when Huck was in bad shape. LeeAnn had been sick, sure—her death hadn't come as a total shock. And yet Huck had been left feeling like his entire right side had been amputated.

He'd been glad that Rosie had found someone to distract

her from her grief. By the time he realized how pathological the relationship was, it was too late. Rosie was in love. All the way.

"I should have done more," he says. "I should have tried to stop it. I should have hired a private investigator."

Irene sets her wineglass gently down and lets her hands drop to her sides. "You showed up here," she says. "That's more than a lot of men would do."

True, he thinks. But he says nothing.

Irene reaches out…and takes his hand. "Will you come upstairs with me?"

He's speechless.

"There's something I need your help with," she says.

Huck follows Irene up the stairs, his mind racing. Is she making advances? Is the "something" that she wants help with getting out of that black dress? This is all moving a little fast for Huck. But he won't say no. She's a grieving widow and he has lost his daughter. Now that he has allowed himself to travel back in time, he realizes that Rosie became his daughter the second he yanked her out of the regatta. Or maybe it was when he paid twenty bucks for a regatta t-shirt to put on over the hankie she was wearing. Or maybe it was when she told him she hated him.

Irene needs physical contact and Huck needs it too, doesn't he? And she's a good-looking woman.

They walk down a long white hallway with a vaulted ceiling ribbed with exposed beams. There are rooms off to both sides, bedrooms. Huck peers into each one. They're similar; it feels like a fancy hotel. At the very end of the hall is a closed door. Irene turns the knob. Locked.

"When we got here on Thursday, the house had been cleaned out," Irene says. "Every personal item removed. Russ's clothes, gone. All the papers from his office, gone. Someone came and took it all away, probably his business partner, Todd Croft. Ever heard that name?"

Huck shakes his head. "No."

"This door is locked. And I was hoping you could force it open for me."

"Okay." Huck says. The door is solid wood, the handle is heavy. Nothing about this house is cheap. "Have you asked your sons?"

"I didn't ask them," Irene says. "And they obviously haven't been blessed with any natural curiosity, because neither of them has noticed. I'm afraid of what we're going to find inside."

Huck presses against the door. He's a big guy, but breaking down this door is beyond him; he'll have to pick the lock. The nice thing about owning a boat for forty years is that he can tinker with the best of 'em. He is a world champion tinkerer.

"Do you have a hairpin?" he asks. "Or bobby pin?"

"I do," Irene says. "Hold on."

She's back in a few seconds with an ancient, sturdy steel bobby pin that looks like it came straight from the head of Eleanor Roosevelt. It takes Huck a few moments of poking and twisting—he doesn't have his reading glasses, and the wine has gone to his head somewhat—but then, *click,* he gets it. Lock popped. He hesitates before turning the knob, because he's also afraid of what they're going to find inside. More dead bodies? Assault rifles and refrigerators full of money? Who was this guy Russell Steele, and what was he *into*? Irene clearly doesn't have the first idea.

* * *

Huck opens the door and the first words that come to him are those from "Sugar Magnolia," *Sunshine, daydream.* It's a bedroom with a huge white canopy bed decorated with turquoise and purple pillows. The wallpaper is a swirl of purple, green, and turquoise tie-dye. There's a white powderpuff beanbag chair, a desk, and a dressing table. Maia would love this room, Huck thinks. Then he sees the letters painted on the length of one wall. M-A-I-A.

"Oh," he says. "This is Maia's room."

Irene slips past Huck into the room and starts poking around. Hairbrush and pick on the dressing table, a bottle of shea butter lotion. A book on the nightstand entitled *The Hate U Give.* Huck thinks to speak up on behalf of Maia's privacy; she's only twelve, but she still deserves respect. Huck understands why the door was locked—it would have been impossible to "undo" this room on short notice.

How must Irene feel, knowing her husband decorated a room like this for his lover's daughter? Is it salt on the wound? Huck supposes so, although he, for one, is happy to see that Maia had a safe space of her own in this house. He will be Maia's champion to the end.

"There can't be anything too important in here," he says. "She hasn't mentioned it."

Irene spins around. "Do you have a picture of her?"

"Of Maia? Yes, of course." Huck takes his phone out of his pocket. There she is, a close-up of her face, his screen saver.

Irene takes the phone from Huck and studies the photograph. He expects her to comment on how pretty Maia is, exquisite really, and elegant in a way that belies her years.

But when Irene looks up, her steel-blue eyes are spooked. Like she has seen a ghost.

No, Huck thinks. *Please, no.*

BAKER

He can't have Ayers pick him up at the villa—he's savvy enough to realize at least this much—and so he plans to have her pick him up at the Trunk Bay overlook.

"I don't get it," Ayers says. "Why don't I just come to the house?"

For all he knows, Ayers has been to his father's villa with Rosie. He isn't willing to risk it. "I hate to be the bearer of bad news," Baker says. "But my brother, Cash, also has a crush on you, and I think you coming to the house to pick me up for our romantic beach date would be…uncool and probably also unkind. I'll be at the Trunk Bay overlook at ten."

Baker isn't completely lying: Cash *does* have a thing for Ayers. When Baker comes down dressed in swim trunks and a polo shirt, holding a couple of towels he lifted from the pool house, Cash shakes his head.

"I can't believe you."

"It's not like we're eloping. We're going to the beach."

"If you were eloping you'd be breaking the law. You're *married,* Baker."

Baker lowers his voice. He's not sure if Irene is awake yet or not. "I told you, Anna left me. She's in love with Louisa

Rodriguez. Do you not remember having this conversation? Were you too drunk?"

"I remember," Cash says. "But still."

Still, Baker thinks. You're jealous.

"She doesn't know who you are, does she?" Cash asks. "Who *we* are?"

"No," Baker says. "I haven't told her."

"If she knew who you were, she wouldn't go out with you," Cash says. "But she's going to find out sooner or later. You should cancel now to save yourself the heartache."

Baker feels an uncomfortable pinch of conscience. "Don't tell me what to do."

"Fine," Cash says. "What time are you going to be home?"

"She has a previous commitment at three. So I'll be home around then."

"Previous commitment meaning another date?" Cash asks.

"She didn't say."

Cash takes two bananas from the fruit bowl, pulls them apart, and hands one to Baker. "I have an errand to run around then. Why don't you have Ayers drop you at the ferry dock at that outdoor bar, High Tide? We can grab a drink and you can tell me about your date."

Something about this sounds fishy. "What kind of errand?" Baker asks.

"The only kind of errand there is," Cash says. "A boring one. I have to pick up something coming from the States."

Money, Baker hopes. Cash was ironically named because he's the brokest SOB Baker has ever known. However, meeting Cash at the ferry dock saves him from having to give Ayers another excuse about why she can't come to the house.

"Okay," Baker says. "I'll meet you at High Tide at three. And I'll tell you about my date."

As Baker hikes up the unreasonably steep hill to the Trunk Bay lookout in the gathering heat of the morning—the trade winds, he's learned, don't kick in until the afternoon—he has upsetting thoughts. His father is dead and the list of questions surrounding his death is long, and nearly all of them are unanswered. On the one hand, Baker feels like he's put in a good-faith effort. He's made calls, he's left messages, and he's followed up with more messages. Short of hiring a private investigator—which isn't a step his mother is ready to take—he has done all he can do. On the other hand, his efforts feel meager. He doesn't deserve a day at the beach. He should be at home to support Irene, whether she wants it or not.

There are the additional issues of Ayers not knowing who Baker is, and—as Cash so emphatically pointed out—of the pesky fact that Baker is still married to Anna and hardly in a position to jump into a new relationship.

To all of this, Baker says: *Too damn bad, I'm going anyway.* It's half a day of pleasure. Cash went out on *Treasure Island;* he has no right to point fingers.

Baker is panting by the time he reaches the lookout. He needs to get in shape! He has time to gaze down over the white crescent of Trunk Bay, backed by an elegant stretch of palm trees. He thinks about snapping a picture and sending it to Anna so she can show Floyd—half the fun of seeing something so breathtaking is letting other people know you've seen it—but he doesn't want Anna to question his real reason for being here on St. John while she's out saving people's lives. And there's no time, anyway, because at that moment, Ayers pulls up in her little green truck.

Baker folds himself into the passenger side. It's small; he's chewing his knees, even when he puts the seat all the way back.

"Your first ride in Edie," Ayers says. "I'm so happy you fit. I was a little worried."

He *doesn't* fit—he has to hunch over and his thighs are cramping—but he's so happy to be in Ayers's presence, he doesn't care. "Edie? That's the truck's name?"

"Short for Edith," Ayers says. "Rosie named her. She had a pet gecko named Edith when she was a kid that was this color."

"Gotcha," Baker says. There was no room for his backpack up front, so he put it in the back, and he checks the side view nervously, expecting it to go flying out when Ayers takes the steep, twisting turns at breathtaking speed.

"Don't worry," she says. "Your bag is fine. I stopped at Sam & Jack's for sandwiches. I got three because I wasn't sure what you liked, and I got some of their homemade potato chips and a couple of kosher dills. And I went to Our Market for smoothies!"

Baker looks down in the console to see two frosted plastic cups, one pink, one pale yellow. He was too nervous to eat the banana Cash gave him so he threw it to the iguanas on the way down the hill. But now he's both starving and dying of thirst.

"Which one is mine?" he asks.

"Take your pick," Ayers says. "There's strawberry-papaya and pineapple-mango." She turns up the music—it's Jack Johnson singing "Upside Down," and Baker surprises himself by singing along. Until this very moment, Baker *hated* Jack Johnson, harbored an almost personal vendetta against him, in fact, because one of Baker's former girlfriends from Northwestern, Trinity, had loved Jack Johnson so ardently. She would only have sex with Baker if Jack Johnson was playing in the background. Needless to say, this had made Baker jealous, and because of this jealousy, he declared Jack Johnson overrated. Now, however, sitting next to Ayers, who is singing along with gleeful abandon, sometimes in key, sometimes not so much, Baker fully understands the appeal. The music is happy, undemanding, and full of sunshine. It's going-to-the-beach music, the same way that Billie Holiday is rainy-Sunday-morning music and George Thorogood is drinking-at-a-dive-bar music. Thanks to the many hours Baker spent with Trinity in bed, Baker knows all the words. He chooses the pineapple-mango smoothie, it's delicious, and he finds a magic arrangement for his legs so that he can relax. He was right to come, he thinks. He's happy.

They twist and turn and wind around until they're somehow back on the Centerline Road. To the right is a stunning view of the turquoise water and emerald mountains.

"Coral Bay," Ayers says. "Fondly known as the Other Side of the World."

They cruise down hairpin turns until they reach a Stop sign, an intersection, a little town on a harbor filled with boats.

"Skinny Legs is that way," Ayers says, pointing left. "Legendary. I wish I could say we'll have time to stop for a drink on the way home but we probably won't." She turns right and they meander past colorful clapboard cottages, a convenience store called Love City Mini Mart, a round open-air restaurant called the Aqua Bistro. "Best onion rings on planet Earth," Ayers says. She hits the gas and they fly up around a curve and nearly collide with three white donkeys standing on the side of the road.

"Donkey!" Ayers cries, and at first Baker thinks she's as

surprised to see them as he is. What are three donkeys doing on the side of the road? Ayers pulls to the shoulder and the donkeys leisurely clomp over to the car. Ayers reaches across Baker, grazing his leg with her arm, which sends an electric current right to his heart, and she pulls a withered apple from the glove box.

"Do as I say, not as I do. We're not supposed to feed them." Ayers sticks the apple out and the alpha donkey eats it from her outstretched palm. She looks at the other two and sighs. "I wish I had three. Sorry, guys!"

When they pull back onto the road, Baker says, "Whose donkeys are those? Do you *know* them?"

"There's a population of wild donkeys across the island," Ayers says. "I do have one favorite. I call him Van Gogh—he only has one ear, and I keep the apple for him. But I wanted you to see them up close. You haven't been to St. John until you've seen the donkeys!" She throws her hands up. She seems positively radiant, and Baker hopes it's because of him. She's wearing a crocheted white cover-up with a white bikini underneath and her blond hair has been wrangled into a messy bun. She is so pretty it hurts, and she keeps an apple in her glove box for a donkey with one ear. Baker can't imagine anyone being more infatuated than he is with Ayers Wilson right now.

He feels a buzzing against his leg and the sound of bongo drums. It's his phone. He has to re-contort himself to slide it out of his pocket. He checks the display: *Anna.* He hurries to silence it, then to turn the phone off completely. He'd like to chuck it out the window. When he got home the night before, he saw he had six missed calls from Anna, but there was not a single voicemail. Anna doesn't believe in voicemail; it can too easily be ignored.

What's up? Baker had texted first thing that morning, but he had received no response. That was Anna's way of punishing him for not answering his phone. But Baker didn't *want* to talk to Anna on the phone and now that she had confessed to falling in love with Louisa Rodriguez, Anna no longer got to say when and how they communicated.

"Who was that?" Ayers asks.

"My brother," Baker says quickly. "He probably wanted to remind me that I'm meeting him at High Tide around three, or whenever we get back. I forgot to ask you, is that okay? Can you drop me at High Tide?"

"Works for me," Ayers says.

Finally they reach the beach, and, as promised, theirs is the only vehicle around.

"Sometimes there are snorkelers," Ayers says. "But hopefully not today."

In the back of her truck, she has two beach chairs, the picnic, and two pool rafts. She and Baker carry everything out onto the "beach," which is a half-moon of smooth blue cobblestones. Baker has never seen a stone beach like this one before. It's tricky to walk, but Ayers strides ahead sure-footed and Baker attempts to follow suit. She places the chairs down, hides the picnic in the shade of the chairs, and slips off her cover-up; it's like a veil falling off a piece of art.

She picks up one of the pool rafts and heads for the water, which is a bowl of crystalline blue.

"Come join me when you're ready," she says.

"Oh, I'm ready," Baker says. He shucks off his polo shirt, takes off his watch, puts his phone and his watch in his backpack, rubs sunscreen on his face, hoping he worked it all in. There is nothing less attractive, Baker's school wives have informed him, than a lapse of personal grooming in a man— back hair, yellow teeth, unclipped toenails. It has led him to become overly sensitive about how he presents himself. Anna, of course, wouldn't notice if he had hot dogs growing out of his ears, but now there is someone new to impress.

Baker grabs a float. The water looks inviting, but there's a slight downward incline and the rocks are difficult to negotiate, and they're burning hot besides. Baker decides to run for the water, praying he doesn't break an ankle, and then throw himself and his raft facedown onto the water's surface. This works, sort of, he's in the water now, half on the raft, half off. He probably looked like a buffoon. He made a huge splash and now there's a wake undulating through the water that reaches Ayers. She laughs.

"Come over here," she says.

He paddles over to her and flips onto his back without too much trouble. Ayers reaches for his hand. They hold hands, drifting across the surface of the bay. From here, Baker can better appreciate the beach. The stones are backed by scrub brush and the occasional palm tree, and on either side of this bay are rocky outcrops. It's silent and deserted. They might be the last two people on earth.

Baker closes his eyes, feels the sun warm his skin. This is delightful. He doesn't go to the beach enough. Why is that? Probably because the closest beach to Houston is Galveston, with its sour brown water. Floyd loves it, of course, and clamors to go whenever there's a break from school. But that's because he doesn't know any better. When Baker and Anna were in Anguilla on their honeymoon, she was stung by a jellyfish during their first dip into Meads Bay, so for the rest of the week they hung by the resort's pool.

When he and Cash were kids, Baker remembers, their family went to Jamaica. Russ had been keen to go, but this was back when he was still a corn syrup salesman, and so they had traveled on a budget; even at ten years old, Baker had realized this. They had stayed at a hotel not far from the airport, and for the first few days, it poured rain. Baker remembers watching television, exactly as he would have done at home. His father walked out onto the balcony every time the rain abated, thinking it would clear, but it never did. Finally, Russ had broken down and given the boys each three dollars for the arcade in the lobby, even though Irene believed video games corrupted children. Baker and Cash had quickly tired of the pinball and Ms. Pac-Man, and they decided to sneak out of the hotel. They darted across a busy road to a real Jamaican village, where people were selling crocheted hacky sacks and bootleg Bob Marley tapes. A goat was being grilled on a half-barrel grill, and a man was playing the guitar and singing in a language Baker and Cash didn't quite understand. Irene and Russ had shown up a little while later, Irene plainly frantic at first and then relieved and teary, then more furious than Baker could remember ever seeing her. When the sun came out the next day, it didn't matter: Irene stayed in the room. But Russ, not wanting the vacation to be a complete loss, had rented a car and driven the boys all the way to Dunn's River Falls; on the way home, they stopped at Laughing Waters beach. Baker remembers racing for the waves, screaming and splashing, with Russ right alongside him, giddy as a little kid. Later, they had dried off with the threadbare towels they'd taken from the hotel and stopped at Scotchie's for jerk chicken and rice. Baker can practically see Russ, glowing from a day in the sun, throwing back a Red Stripe to cool the spice of the chicken. His father had been happy. His father had loved the tropics.

"My father loved the tropics," Baker murmurs.

"Oh yeah?" Ayers says. "What did your father do?"

"I'm not really sure," Baker says. "He was in business."

Suddenly Baker hears a splash. He opens his eyes. Ayers has flipped off her raft into the water. Before Baker can blink, Ayers's bikini top lands on the raft and another second later, her bikini bottom.

"Whoa," Baker says. "Wait a minute."

She swims away, leaving Baker to grab hold of her raft and glimpse the curves of her naked body beneath the surface. He scans the beach—no one around.

"Come back here!" he says.

She floats on her back so that her breasts break the surface of the water. They're small and firm, her nipples hard. Baker is so aroused he aches. Her gorgeous wet breasts glisten in the sun; this is happening in real life—he can't believe it, but he isn't quite sure what to do. He decides to sacrifice the rafts; he'll swim after them later. He flips off his raft, takes off his trunks underwater and enjoys the feel of being naked in the Caribbean. It's liberating. He belongs here. He swims after Ayers. She treads water, waiting.

They kiss in the water for a while and then Ayers reaches down to stroke Baker; the sensation of her warm hand in the cool water is almost too much to bear, he's about to pop, but no, he doesn't want it to go this way.

"Let's swim back to shore," he says. He heads for the beach, hoping she's following, but once he clambers out of the water onto the hot stones, he sees this is going to be a logistical nightmare. Why couldn't she have picked a sandy beach?

Probably because sandy beaches are populated, whereas stone beaches—nearly impossible to walk on and impossible to have sex on—are unpopulated.

Baker sits in one of the beach chairs and spins Ayers around to sit on his lap. She slides right down on him and the sensation is too amazing to describe. He has never more fully inhabited his body; every cell swells with desire, every nerve ending is shimmying.

"Don't move," he whispers. He reaches forward to gently touch her breasts. He pulls her down onto him and groans. She is a goddess. He wants her to crush him, to subsume him; he wants to become her.

She lifts herself an inch then slides back down, and Baker tries to control himself, to feel the sun on his back and neck, to move his hands down to the curve of her waist.

She is divine.

And then, without warning, the earth shakes, it slams up to meet them and Baker is thrown backward. There is pain, instant and rude.

The chair has broken under their weight. Ayers scrambles away, reaches for towels, tosses one to Baker. *NO!* he thinks. They can't just stop. He feels nauseated. Ayers wraps herself up; her head is turned. Sure enough, another car has pulled into the small dirt lot.

"You stay here," Ayers says. "I'm going to make a dash for it." She walks to the water's edge, drops her towel, and executes a shallow dive into the lapping waves. She swims for the rafts, which have drifted to the right side of the beach, out near the rocks.

Meanwhile, Baker secures a towel around his waist and fixes the chair, waving to the approaching couple, who are all decked out for snorkeling. Ayers has reached the floats; Baker watches her put her suit back on.

The couple is approaching him. "Beautiful day," the man calls out. Baker has never hated anyone more in his life.

"Isn't it?" he says.

Plan B: Baker and Ayers pack up and drive the short distance to Salt Pond.

"The good news is we can snorkel with the turtles!" Ayers says.

"Great," Baker says, but he can't conceal his crushing disappointment. Sex, he wants sex. The thirty or forty seconds inside her weren't enough. But where can they go? Her truck isn't an option; it's way too small. Baker's spirit sags as Ayers pulls into a different sandy parking lot, this one packed with cars.

"Let's snorkel first," Ayers says. "Then we'll eat." She seems unfazed by their reversal of fortune, and Baker tries to discern if this is a good thing or a bad thing. Maybe she didn't like the way it felt, maybe the position was uncomfortable, with her feet resting on burning rocks. Maybe she was so mortified by the collapse of the chair that her way of dealing with it is just to pretend it never happened. Baker is with her on this final option. They should reset, start over. Third time's a charm. As soon as Baker gets to High Tide, he's going to call Caneel and book a room.

His mood improves after the short hike to Salt Pond. He has always been a reasonably good sport, able to deal with pitfalls and move on, and today will be no exception. He's carrying the chairs and his backpack; Ayers has the picnic and the snorkeling gear. She has a mask, snorkel, and fins for Baker, left behind when her ex-boyfriend moved out of her apartment. Baker is such a good sport he's going to calmly accept the fact that he's using Mick's old snorkel equipment. He's going to relish it, even. After all, it saves him from having to rent, and the fins fit.

Ayers wades into shallow water, secures her mask, and grins at Baker. Then she takes off swimming and Baker follows. He has used a mask before in swimming pools growing up but never in open water. (They were supposed to go snorkeling on a day trip in Anguilla, but Anna had nixed it.) If Cash snorkeled, then Baker can snorkel. Cash is the better skier, but Baker is a far better swimmer. He takes off after Ayers and soon is right by her side.

The water is clear; the bottom is white sand covered by a carpet of sea grass. They swim a little farther and Baker expects the scenery to change. Cash described "cities" of colorful coral and thousands of multicolored fish. Baker sees only sand and sea grass and Ayers's body, which is sweeter than anything Jacques Cousteau could dream up.

And then he hears Ayers make a sound. She's gesticulating wildly, pointing—and Baker will be damned: A few yards ahead of them, nibbling on the sea grass, is a turtle! A real turtle, one that looks exactly like Crush from *Finding Nemo*. That's backward: Crush is a cartoon and this is nature—this is real! Floyd would... well, his little mind would be blown.

Ayers swims on and Baker follows, waving to Crush, studying the pattern on the back of his shell, watching the way his neck stretches as he feasts on the grass. Ayers finds a second turtle and this one has a baby turtle with him—Crush *and* Squirt! Floyd would love this! Ayers swims alongside the father-and-son turtles and soon Baker is, too. He is so close he could reach out and touch the back of the father's shell, but he's guessing that's against the rules, like feeding the donkeys. He's content to just glide along with the turtles and Ayers until the turtles dive to eat again and Ayers takes Baker's hand. They both surface. Ayers lifts her mask and says, "Cool, huh?"

"So cool!" he says. "I can't believe they're just ... hanging out."

"This is where they live," she says. She pulls Baker in to kiss him, which makes Baker very, very happy, and then she says, "I'll race you back. I'm starving."

They sit on a towel in the sun and eat their sandwiches— turkey with arugula for Ayers, rare roast beef with BBQ sauce for Baker. When she's finished, Ayers lies back on her towel and says, "I'm going to take a nap. Then we should probably head out."

Head out? Baker thinks. But she's right: It's quarter of two already. The day flew by and now their date is almost over, so he will have to ask her about Caneel on the way home. Tomorrow night, if she's free.

Ayers closes her eyes and Baker props himself on his elbow and watches her sleep.

On the way home, Baker feels a leaden sense of melancholy. Despite the mishap with the chair, it was a great date and he doesn't want it to end.

"Are you sure you can't go to dinner tonight?" he asks.

"Positive," she says.

"Because you have another date," Baker says. "Just tell me one thing, is he bigger than me?"

Ayers's laugh is musical, like a bell. He loves her laugh. He loves her smooth tan arms. He loves her jangling silver brace- lets. There are five, all variations of the St. John hook, including one she had custom-made with an "8" and a hook because every February she runs a race called "8 Tuff Miles"—the length of the satanically hilly Centerline Road from Cruz Bay to Coral Bay. The race ends at Skinny Legs, hence the name of the bar. (Things here are finally starting to click for Baker.) He loves her blond curls, her sense of adventure, her taste in music, and her enthusiasm about the natural world.

"I have another commitment," she says. "And I'm not telling you what it is, but you don't have to feel threatened."

"I do feel threatened," Baker admits. "I don't want to share you."

"Hey now," she says. "Aren't things moving a little fast?"

"Sorry," Baker says. "I just had a really good time today. I enjoy being with you."

"I had a good time, too," Ayers says. "But you're a tourist, so we can't get too serious. Let's just have fun while you're here, okay? Let's not attach too many feelings to this."

Baker takes this like a poison dart to the throat. No feelings? He is nothing *but* feelings.

"Let's not *not* attach feelings," he says. "Besides, I don't know when I'm leaving. I might be here for a while yet."

"I guess I don't understand that," Ayers says. "Do you not have a return ticket?"

"It's open-ended," he says.

"Really?"

"Really."

"Why did you get an open-ended ticket? I mean, I realize you don't have a traditional job, but you do have a child, right, and a life in... Austin?"

"Houston," he says.

"We had a wonderful day," Ayers says. "And it was exactly

what I needed. But we barely know each other. And I also don't understand why you don't want me to come to your villa. It's like you're hiding something."

"*You're* hiding something," Baker says. "You won't tell me what you're doing tonight."

Ayers takes an audible breath. "My ex-boyfriend, Mick? He cheated on me. He told me he was working late 'training' Brigid, and I went down to the Beach Bar at two in the morning and found them together. *Very* together. So I'm sorry, but I can't handle a man who isn't absolutely forthcoming and transparent. If you have secrets, that's fine, that's great, good for you, but I'm not interested." She grins at him. "I'm dead serious. I will never let myself get hurt like that again."

"I would never," Baker says. "Will never." He needs to keep himself in her present, in her future, but her words make him realize that he needs to tell her about his father. It will take just one sentence: *My father was Russell Steele.* Baker worries she will freak out, maybe even leave him on the side of the road and drive off. The time to have told her was right at the beginning, at the memorial service, when they were sitting on the branch. But the situation had been so raw then; they had been at Rosie's funeral lunch. He had been right to keep quiet. He could have told her last night on the beach. That was a missed opportunity. He doesn't want to tell her now because she hasn't quite fallen for him yet. He'll take her to Caneel Bay, he decides, he'll consummate the relationship properly, he'll make her fall in love with him, and *then* he'll tell her. And she'll have no choice but to process and accept the news. It might not even matter.

All right, he's not naive, it will matter. But he still thinks it's best to wait.

"I want to take you to Caneel Bay," he says. "Take you to dinner, get a room, spend the night. Would you do that with me? When's the next night you're free?"

"Caneel?" she says. She drops the tough-girl attitude and lights up. Baker has stumbled across the magic words, apparently. "I've never stayed there, though I've always wanted to. And ZoZo's, the restaurant, the osso buco is…wow, are you sure that's what you want to do? It's not exactly cheap."

"Who cares?" Baker says. "It's a splurge. You're worth it. I would love to stay a night away from my mother and brother."

"I would love a night with reliable air-conditioning," Ayers says. "Can we turn it all the way up?"

"All the way up," Baker says. "What night are you free?"

"Tomorrow night," Ayers says. "I work on *Treasure Island* tomorrow, I'll be back around four."

"I'll make a reservation," Baker says. "And meet you there around five."

"I probably shouldn't go on such an extravagant date with a tourist," Ayers says. "But it's too tempting to resist. And I don't have to be at La Tapa on Friday until four, so maybe we can sleep in, get a late checkout?"

"Anything you want," Baker says. "Breakfast in bed, midnight swim, a marathon of Adam Sandler movies…"

Ayers grabs his hand. "I can't believe it. Thank you. I'm…"

"Say no more. It's happening. Caneel Bay, tomorrow night."

At three o'clock, the traffic in town is at a standstill. A ferry has just unloaded, and some of the all-day charters have come in, and happy hour at Woody's is beginning and...yeah. Cruz Bay is a blender.

"Is it okay if I just drop you here?" Ayers asks. They're in front of a restaurant called the Dog House Pub. "That way I can avoid going all the way around the block. I really have to be somewhere."

"No problem," Baker says. "I'll grab my backpack when I get out, so don't drive away." He leans over to kiss her good-bye and the kiss goes on and on until the taxi driver behind them honks his horn. Ayers pushes Baker away. "Go," she says. "I'll see you tomorrow at five."

"Thank you for lunch," he says. He doesn't want to get out of the truck.

"Yeah, yeah," she says. "Go!"

He hops out of the truck, grabs the backpack, blows Ayers a kiss, then blows a kiss to the disgruntled taxi driver. He is so happy that he floats around the corner and down to the ferry dock. Next to the dock is High Tide.

Caneel, he has to call Caneel. What if they're fully booked? It's high season, but at least it's after the holidays. They'll have a room. He'll pay whatever it takes.

Baker strides into High Tide, half hoping that Cash is a little late—that way he can order a drink and regroup, maybe even take care of the hotel reservation right there at the bar. But no such luck, he sees Cash right away—that bushy blond hair is impossible to miss. Baker blinks. Next to Cash is a woman who looks a little like Anna. The woman has long, dark hair like Anna, but it's loose and she's wearing a lavender tank top, drinking what looks like a margarita.

Not Anna.

But then Cash waves and the woman turns and a wave of

nausea rolls over Baker. *Run!* he thinks. *Hide!* He hears a familiar voice and feels a pair of small arms wrap around his legs.

"Daddy Daddy Daddy, we're here!" the voice says.

Instinctively, Baker bends down to pick up his son.

IRENE

After Huck leaves—the door to Maia's room closed and locked again for the time being—Irene does the dishes, takes an Ativan, takes a second Ativan, then goes to bed.

She wakes up early, very early; the sky is just beginning to turn pink. She slips from bed and heads down the eighty steps to the beach. She sits on one of the orange-cushioned chaises. Now at least, she understands why there are three chaises—one for Russ, one for Rosie, one for Maia.

Russ's daughter.

Irene takes off her tank top and sleep shorts. She steps into the water. And then she starts to swim.

She learned to swim in Clark Lake, in Door County, Wisconsin, which is also where she learned to fish. The water of Clark Lake has little in common with the Caribbean, and yet the swimming clears Irene's mind, just as it used to the summer she was sixteen. That was the summer she witnessed her family falling apart. Her grandmother, Olga, was dying of lung cancer in the gracious old lakefront cottage where Irene had spent every summer of her life. Irene had wanted to go to bonfires with her best summer friend, Caris, and listen to Lynyrd Skynyrd and talk to Davey Longeran, who had just bought his first car, a Pontiac Firebird. She had wanted to ride through the back roads of Door County in Davey's Firebird more than she wanted the sun to rise in the mornings. But she was stuck in the house with her mother, Mary, and her mother's sister, Aunt Ruth. Mary and Aunt Ruth fought nonstop about who was doing more for Olga, and who Olga loved better. Irene was assigned the bottom-rung jobs: emptying the bedpans and the bucket Olga coughed into, washing the soiled sheets and hanging them on the line and riding her bike — two point nine miles each way in the hot sun — to the pharmacy, where Mr. Abernathy would occasionally ask Irene to "spin around" so he could see how big she'd gotten.

When Irene's father showed up on the weekends, they went out on the boat to fish for smallmouth bass and walleye, and he took over Irene's unpleasant tasks so that she could swim in the lake. She swam the crawl, arms pulling, legs like a propeller, breathing every third stroke, alternating sides.

The movement comes right back to Irene, even though it has been a while since she really swam. She spent nearly a hundred thousand dollars on the pool in her Iowa City back-yard, forty feet long, but she only did what Russ called the "French dip" — into the water to her neck and then back out in a matter of seconds. She would hold her braid up so that it didn't get wet; the chlorine gave her hair a greenish tint. There had been a time — in the mid-nineties, maybe — when she had gone to the community pool on Mondays, Wednesdays, and Fridays to do laps—thirty-six laps, half a mile, in the name of physical fitness. But that lasted only a couple of months, the way those things do.

Irene swims out at first, toward Jost Van Dyke. Then she finds a calm swath of water and starts to the east. When she catches sight of the neighboring bay, she turns around and heads back.

There isn't time to think while she's swimming except about her heart, her lungs, her eyes, which are stinging, and her arms and legs.

She misses her father. He was a man of few words but he loved her; she is named after his favorite song, "Goodnight, Irene." Irene even misses her mother, though her mother had turned bitter and hard after Olga left the house on Clark Lake to Aunt Ruth. Irene's mother had never forgiven Olga or Ruth; her last words to her sister were at Olga's funeral. Irene has often wondered why Olga made the decision to leave the house to one daughter instead of the other. Did she, in fact, love Ruth more? Or were they simply closer, the way Irene is closer to Cash and Russ was closer to Baker? Or did Olga feel sorry for Ruth because she was single and childless, while Mary had a husband and a daughter? Maybe the house was meant to be an attempt to make up for the bad luck life had dealt Ruth. Irene, of course, will never know, just as she will never know why Russ engaged in such a tremendous deception. It's newly astonishing to Irene that as much as we know about the world, we still can't see into another person's mind or heart.

Irene remembers when she introduced Russ to her parents. His ardor for Irene had been on grand display, and Irene wondered how her emotionally reserved parents would view a man who was so outspoken about his feelings. Mary, Irene recalls, had said, "That young man certainly wears his heart on his sleeve."

Before the cataclysmic revelations of this past week, Irene had agreed with that statement: Russell Steele was a man who wore his heart on his sleeve. But, as it turned out, it wasn't his real heart.

Russ loved Rosie. To deny this in the name of self-preservation is folly. Fine, then, Irene thinks. She can accept it but she is allowed to be hurt and angry.

And now, for the next revelation.

Maia is Russ's daughter.

Irene had looked at the picture on Huck's phone and she had very nearly fainted. The girl, although only twelve years old and half West Indian, *was* Russ. She looked *exactly* like him. She looked more like him than either of the boys did.

That's Russ's daughter.

It can't be, Huck said. *It was years before…*

Huck had calculated back. Maia was seven when his wife, LeeAnn, died, and the one thing he knew for sure was that Rosie started seeing "the Invisible Man," Russ, *after* LeeAnn died. The other fella, Maia's father, was years before.

That's Russ's daughter, Irene insisted. She showed Huck the photograph she'd found wedged under the mattress in the master bedroom, but in that photo, Russ was wearing sunglasses, and so Irene had pulled up a picture from off her phone. She had to scroll all the way back to the summer before, a picture of Russ and Irene at the magazine's annual cookout. Before handing the phone over, Irene marveled at how normal they looked—Russ with his silvering hair and his dad shorts, Irene with her braid, wearing the very same dress she had on right then. Did she remember anything peculiar about that cookout? Not one thing. The cookout was always potluck. Irene brought her corn salad with dill, toasted pine nuts, and Parmesan, and people raved over it; she told them the secret was just-picked corn. *Go to the stand just off I-80*, she said. *It's so much better than the Hy-Vee!* She drank the fruity sangria that Mavis Key brought in an elaborate glass thermos with a nickel-plated spout and a cast-iron stand. Irene had gotten a little tipsy. She and Russ had danced to the bluegrass band; Irene fell asleep on the way home. It was one night of a thousand nights where she was just a regular married woman, maybe one with a grudge against the shiny, newfangled ways of Mavis Key.

When Huck looked at that picture, he pressed his lips into a straight line.

Irene swims until it feels like her arms might break and then she heads for shore. She staggers out of the water, wraps herself in a towel, and bends over, staring at her feet.

Maia is twelve, born in November. The story that Rosie told Huck is that the Pirate came in on a "big yacht" over Valentine's weekend and stayed for four nights. Rosie was working as a cocktail waitress at Caneel Bay. She served the Pirate and his "friends," the Pirate took a liking to her, things went from there. The Pirate left on Tuesday morning, never to be heard from again, according to Rosie. A month or two later, when Rosie discovered she was pregnant, this was the story she told. She had never given the man's name. Huck said that, on the birth certificate, the father's name was left blank. *I was at the hospital when Maia was born,* he said. *I was there.*

Thirteen years ago next month. February. Irene squeezes her eyes shut and tries to concentrate.

When had Russ taken the job with Todd Croft? Thirteen years ago? Irene and Russ had bumped into Todd in the lobby of the Drake Hotel in Chicago. They had been in the city for the Christmas party given by Russ's biggest corn syrup client. So that would have been December…and Todd had called Russ up a few weeks later.

Yes. Irene raises her head. Russ flew down for an interview in February. The meeting was at Todd's office, which Irene understood to be in southeastern Florida somewhere—Miami, Boca, Palm Beach. It *had* been over Valentine's Day, which also fell during Presidents' weekend; they had planned to drive up to St. Joseph, Michigan, to ski. Irene had ended up taking the boys alone. Baker met a girl and vanished, Cash took half a dozen runs with Irene the first morning, and then he went off to snowboard. Irene had headed back to the hotel, wishing she were in Vail or Aspen and that she were returning to a lodge with a roaring fireplace instead of the Hampton Inn. She had wished she could get a hot stone massage instead of taking a lukewarm bath in a cramped fiberglass insert tub. She had indulged these longings because Russ was away, interviewing for a new job, a whole new career. Irene had prayed he would get an offer. She had prayed so hard.

The following Tuesday or Wednesday, Russ had come home, with the first of many suntans, triumphant.

They're going to give me a bonus just for signing the contract, he said. *Fifty thousand dollars.*

Irene had let out an uncharacteristic whoop. Her entire view of Russ had changed in that moment, *because of the money.* Their struggle was over. Irene could throw away the envelope stuffed with grocery store coupons in the junk drawer; she didn't have to steel herself for Russ's reaction when the Visa bill came and he saw that Irene had bought Cash a new pair of ski goggles for fifty-five dollars.

That was what she had been thinking of thirteen years earlier—her liberation from coupon clipping, the dread she felt every time she handed her credit card to a merchant. She hadn't asked Russ how his weekend was, where he went, what he did. She didn't ask if he'd sailed to the Virgin Islands on a yacht, met a cocktail waitress, and impregnated her.

But that, apparently, is what happened.

What Irene does *not* want is to become a slave to her rage and her jealousy. She does not want to become her mother.

I will forgive them, Irene thinks once again. *If it's the last thing I do.* And it might be the last thing. Because the burden keeps getting heavier.

A daughter. A twelve-year-old daughter, Maia Rose Small. In sixth grade here on St. John at the Gifft Hill School. A good student, Huck said, and an entrepreneur. She's starting a bath bomb business. She's making them in tropical scents to sell to tourists.

Russ had never wanted a daughter. He had been hoping for

a boy both times Irene was pregnant, and both times he got his wish. The person who had wanted a daughter was ... Irene. Irene had wanted a daughter.

She climbs back up the eighty steps, wrapped in just a towel; her legs are so fatigued they're shaking. Both the boys are in the kitchen, but Irene walks right past them, up to her room.

She had told Huck she wanted to meet the girl, Maia. *Please,* she'd said.

He told Irene he would think about it. *Give me a couple days*, he said. Which Irene knows was the right answer.

AYERS

She pulls up in front of the Gifft Hill School just as Maia is emerging. Maia sees her and breaks into a shy smile. Ayers lets go of the breath she has been holding since she pulled out of town onto the Centerline Road. She thought she was going to be late, late for her first sleepover with Maia, late because of some incredibly handsome, charming, and sexy *tourist*.

But no. She is here as she said she would be. She is a reliable, steady force during this tumultuous time for Maia.

Another mother—Swan Seeley is her name; Ayers has served her at the restaurant—comes over to Ayers's open window and squeezes her forearm. "You're here to pick up Maia? You are. Such. A. Good. Person." Swan's eyes shine. "I asked Beau just last night: *Who* is going to be the female influence in Maia's life? She needs one, you know—every girl needs a positive role model. Especially. These. Days. I'm so glad it's you, Ayers. Rosie was lucky to have a friend like you. This community is lucky to have you."

Ayers blinks back her emotion. Secretly, Rosie found the other mothers at Gifft Hill a little too touchy-feely for her taste, although it was unfair to criticize them because they were all. Just. So. Nice. They wore no makeup, bought organic produce, dressed in natural fabrics in neutral colors, volunteered at the animal shelter, lobbied for more efficient recycling, and were generally tolerant and thoughtful. Every so often, one of these mothers would show up at La Tapa and have a couple of glasses of wine and loosen up, and that was when Rosie liked them best. Swan Seeley, Ayers happens to know, even enjoys the occasional Marlboro.

"Thank you. There was no question. Maia is" — Ayers grabs Maia's ponytail because now she has climbed into Edith beside her — "my best girl."

"Well," Swan says. She's clearly overcome, and her son, Colton, is tugging on her arm. But Swan seems hesitant to end the conversation, and Ayers fears the question that might be coming. *Have they figured out what happened?* Ayers refuses to address that topic in front of Maia, or at all, and so she just gives Swan a wave and backs Edie out into the street.

"Thank you for saving me," Maia says. She pulls out her phone. "I'm tired of people asking me how I'm doing."

Ayers is astonished by, and maybe even a bit uneasy about, how well-adjusted Maia seems. Ayers was expecting a sadder girl, possibly even a broken girl. She hopes Maia isn't burying her feelings, which will then fester and come spewing forth later in some toxic way, like lava out of a volcano. Ayers wants to ask Maia how she's doing, but then it will seem like Ayers isn't listening. Maia is sick of that question. She probably doesn't want to be seen as a twelve-year-old girl whose mother just tragically died; she wants to be seen as a twelve-year-old girl.

"Mrs. Seeley was lending her support," Ayers says. "She thinks I'm a positive role model in your life. Ha! That shows how little *she* knows!" There's no response. Maia is down the rabbit hole. Ayers grabs Maia's phone away without taking her eyes off the road and says, "Hey, where to? Happy hour at Woody's?"

"Pizzabar in Paradise," Maia says. "Then Scoops."

"Pizza and ice cream on opposite sides of the island," Ayers says. "I feel like you're taking advantage of me because you know I would do absolutely anything in the world for you. What did Huck pack you for lunch?"

"What do you think?" Maia says.

"A leftover fish sandwich on buttered Wonder bread?" Ayers says.

Maia pulls a greasy paper bag from her backpack and Ayers can smell the fish. "First order of business, throwing that away."

"Facts," Maia says. She reclaims her phone, and Ayers understands what it's like to be the parent of a teenager.

They pull into Pizzabar in Paradise at three thirty, which is a time that nobody other than a sixth grader with a stinky lunch wants to eat, and so they have the place to themselves. Maia orders the margherita pizza. "Why mess with perfection," she says.

Ayers nearly orders the bianco, which was Rosie's favorite. She thinks it might be a tribute of sorts, but she doesn't want to seem like she's trying to *be* Rosie, and besides, she isn't hungry at all. She had a turkey sandwich on the beach with the tourist.

She says, "Will you think I'm a bad influence if I order a glass of wine?"

"You're my surrogate mom now, right?" Maia says. "Moms have wine."

"Perk of the job, I guess," Ayers says, trying to keep things light. She waves to the owner, Colleen, and orders a glass of the house white with a side of ice to water it down. She's keyed up and she needs to relax. She should ask Maia about school, about things at home, about her *feelings,* but Maia is into her phone, which gives Ayers a few minutes of freedom to think about the tourist.

Baker.

She rummages through the factoids: Houston, son Floyd, wife left him, brother Cash, mother here at the mysterious villa, father dead, father loved the tropics. Ayers realizes she doesn't know Baker's last name. She remembers that at the reception, he signed only "Baker" in the guest book. Ayers had made a joke about it. Madonna. Cher.

Had *Cash* mentioned their last name? Ayers doesn't think so. But they'll have it in the files at the Treasure Island office. Ayers will have to remember to check tomorrow.

She sips her wine, watches Maia scroll through other adolescent girls performing lip-sync on musical.ly, and tries to talk herself out of her feelings for the tourist. Yes, he's tall and super-hot; yes, he's charming and a really, really good sport.

The circus act of trying to have sex on Grootpan Beach, the slapstick of the chair collapsing — that might have sapped anyone's confidence. But Baker had rebounded like a champ.

And now they have a date at Caneel Bay. Ayers is embarrassed about how excited she is, and she issues herself a stern warning: she is *not* to fall in love with the tourist! And yet, an overnight date at a five-star resort like Caneel, with a candlelit dinner at ZoZo's first and a midnight swim and uninhibited, unimpeded hotel sex and a breakfast in bed of percolated coffee and banana French toast might tempt her down that forbidden path. Ayers's life is so devoid of luxury and, even some days, comfort, that the allure of a splurge is strong. Baker wants to treat her like a queen, and that is a powerful aphrodisiac.

That, Ayers thinks, is how the Pirate stole Rosie's heart. And later, the Invisible Man. It's not necessarily the creature comforts themselves, it's that someone thinks you deserve them.

Maia's pizza arrives, fresh and hot.

"Want a slice?" Maia asks.

"Duh," Ayers says, because who can resist a piping hot pizza?

Ayers lifts a slice, and strings of cheese stretch all the way to her paper plate. Then she feels something warm and hairy crawling around her ankles and she shrieks and looks down. It's Gordon, Mick's dog. Ayers watches Maia's eyes widen. She fully expects to find Mick and Brigid behind her. A split second later, the stool next to Ayers's is yanked out and Mick sits down. He helps himself to a slice of pizza.

"Hey!" Quick surveillance tells Ayers there's no Brigid. "That's Maia's."

"It's okay," Maia says to Mick. "You can have some."

"It's okay," Mick says to Ayers. "I can have some." He chucks Maia on the arm. "How you holding up, bae?"

Maia turns pink and Ayers remembers that Maia has always been smitten with Mick. He's nowhere near as good-looking as Baker, but Mick has that something, a magnetism, a masculinity, a sly sense of humor that makes him appealing to women of all ages.

"I'm okay," Maia says.

"Oh yeah? Really? I'd say you're better than okay. I'd say you're the coolest young lady on the whole island." He winks at her. "And of course, the prettiest."

Maia fist bumps him. "Facts."

This makes Mick laugh. He turns to Ayers. "Yeah, I'd say she's okay. Self-esteem fully intact."

"What are you doing here?" Ayers asks. Without thinking about it, she finds herself rubbing Gordon's sweet bucket head, and he closes his eyes in ecstasy. Gordon feels about Ayers the way Maia feels about Mick: pure devotion.

"Hangry," Mick says. He devours his slice in three bites and reaches over to take what's left of Ayers's slice, and she lets him. "I have to be at work in an hour."

Right, Ayers thinks. The only other people who eat at three thirty in the afternoon? Everyone in the restaurant business.

"So how was your *date* last night?" Mick asks.

"What date?" Maia asks Ayers.

"Friend of mine, Baker," Ayers says. "We went to dinner."

"I call shenanigans," Mick says. "I swung by De' Coal Pot. You weren't there and you hadn't been there. I asked."

"We went somewhere else," Ayers says.

"Where?" Mick says.

"Who's Baker?" Maia asks. "Do I know him?"

"You don't," Ayers says. "He's visiting."

"He's a tourist," Mick says.

Maia tilts her head. "I thought you didn't date tourists."

"There's an exception to every rule," Ayers says.

"So you're *dating* that guy, then?" Mick asks. "Seriously? He looks like...a banker."

Ayers throws back what's left of her wine. Oh, how she would love to order another, but she can't. She has to drive all the way across the island to Scoops, and then drive home.

"He's taking me to Caneel Bay tomorrow. The hotel. Overnight."

Mick cocks an eyebrow. "Really? So he *is* a banker."

"None of your business," Ayers says.

"Are you jealous?" Maia asks Mick. "Do you still love Ayers?"

"Maia!" Ayers says.

"Yes," Mick says. He turns to Colleen and orders a pizza — the pepperoni and ham, which Ayers could have predicted. Mick is a devout carnivore. "Yes, I do still love Ayers."

"Mick, stop," Ayers says.

"Do you really?" Maia asks.

"Yes, I do, really."

"Oh," Maia says. "I thought you broke up with her."

"I did something wrong and Ayers broke up with me," Mick says. "I made a huge mistake and I'll regret it for the rest of my life. But just because I made that mistake doesn't mean I don't still love Ayers."

"Love is messy," Maia says. "My mom used to tell me that. She said love is messy and complicated and unfair." Maia rolls her eyes. "I'll take a no-thank-you helping."

Mick laughs again, and Ayers asks Colleen for a box to take the rest of Maia's pizza to go.

"On that note," Ayers says. "We're leaving."

"Ayers...," Mick says.

Ayers bends down to kiss Gordon between the eyes. Then she turns to Maia. "Ready for ice cream?"

"Facts," Maia says.

CASH

He is so juiced about taking Baker by surprise with the arrival of Anna and Floyd that he has ignored the fact that they will have another situation on their hands.

That situation is named Irene.

But first, *first,* Cash takes a moment to savor Baker's shock and obvious discomfort at seeing his wife and son. He looks *caught.* He *is* caught. The only thing better would have been if Ayers had come with Baker to the bar. But no — that would be cruel to Floyd. Cash will avoid compromising Floyd at all costs. He's learning what it's like to be the son of a philanderer.

If it were only Floyd who had arrived unexpectedly, the scene would have been touching indeed. Floyd grabs Baker around the legs and Baker, although seeming disoriented at first, squeezes Floyd tight, kisses the boy on the cheek, then squeezes him again. Cash has to admit: Baker is a good dad, very open with his affection, just like Russ used to be.

Baker and Floyd go down to look at the water, and Cash turns to Anna. She seems different here, on the island. Her hair is down and she's into her second margarita, so she is super-relaxed. Has Cash ever seen Anna relaxed? Maybe once, when she and Baker came to Breckenridge, but that time, Cash remembers, she had turned her hyper-competitive nature toward skiing. She was faster than Baker and more technically sound than Cash, and she had taken great pride in her superior speed and prowess. Now, she is only competitive about her margarita drinking, and Cash can get behind that— especially since Irene, who is unaware of Anna and Floyd's arrival, waits at home.

"Floyd missed him," Anna says to Cash. "It wasn't until Baker left that I realized how much he does—the cooking, the cleaning, the shopping, the laundry. He coaches Floyd's basketball team, takes him to chess club on Sundays, and he's on the fund-raising committee of Floyd's school, so the phone kept ringing with people donating things for a silent auction that I knew nothing about. I haven't given him nearly enough credit."

"He told me you left him," Cash says. He eyes his own second margarita, half gone.

"*Am* leaving," Anna says. "I told him just seconds before your mother called with the news."

"Ah," Cash says. He finds he's disappointed that Baker was telling the truth. "It's a...colleague of yours?"

"Louisa," Anna says. She raises a palm. "Don't ask me why, because I don't know. I like men, I'm attracted to men. This came out of nowhere, but it's big and it's real."

"No judgment here," Cash says. "Any chance this might be a phase? Any chance you might salvage the marriage?"

"Nope," Anna says. "But we can salvage the family, I'm pretty sure. We can have a functional divorced relationship, with shared custody."

Baker and Floyd reappear. "I'd love to join you two for a

drink," Baker says, "but I think we should get Floyd home. He's overheated."

Anna pulls out a fifty and leaves it on the bar, much to Cash's relief. "I made a reservation at a place called St. John Guest Suites," Anna says. "I didn't want to assume there would be room for us at the villa."

"Oh, there's room," Cash says. "You can cancel your room." He then thinks of Irene. "Or keep it — you may want privacy, and you probably won't get your money back anyway."

"Nonrefundable," Anna confirms. "But I'd love to see the place. And to see your mom, obviously."

"Obviously," Cash says.

He tries to text Irene about their impending arrival, but his phone has no service on the north shore road. *Oh well,* he thinks. His mother has been through a bigger shock than this; she'll be fine. Then again, his mother has been through such a big shock that it feels unfair to pile on more. Cash is sitting in the backseat of the Jeep with Floyd as though he, too, is a child — but he is also the architect of this mess. He alone knew Floyd and Anna were coming. He could have — *should have* — given Baker and Irene fair warning.

Baker turns right and they wind up the hill and pull up to the gate, which they've left open since their arrival. The house comes into view.

"Wait," Anna says. She turns to Baker. "This is where you're staying?"

"This is the villa," Baker says flatly. "My father's villa."

"I don't believe it," Anna says.

Baker doesn't respond. He parks and gets out of the car. "Come on, buddy," he says to Floyd. "You want a tour?"

Baker and Floyd head up the stone staircase to the main deck, with Anna and Cash following a few steps behind. Anna is plainly floored. Cash tries to remember what he felt like six days ago when he saw this place for the first time. He had been gobsmacked. Now he takes it for granted.

"Outdoor kitchen," Baker says. "Pool, hot tub…"

"The pool has a slide!" Floyd shouts. "To another pool! This house has two pools, one on top and one at the bottom!"

Anna stands on the deck and takes in the view. "What was going on?"

"We're still not sure," Cash says. "The helicopter crashed in British waters. Dad's boss, Todd, signed off to have his body cremated. We're waiting for the ashes and for a report from the crash site investigators, but it's tricky because the Brits are the authority, not the FAA or the coast guard. The pilot was killed—he was British—and a local St. John woman."

"Local woman?" Anna says. "Did your father have a mistress here? Was he *that* cliché?"

"I think he might have been, yes," Cash says.

They step into the kitchen, where Irene is sitting at the table. Her head is buried in her arms. She's asleep.

"Your poor mother," Anna says. "Don't wake her."

Irene raises her head, blinking. "Oh," she says. She gets to her feet and offers a hand. "Hello, I'm Irene Steele."

"Irene," Anna says. "It's Anna. Anna Schaffer. Baker's wife."

Irene steadies herself on the back of a chair. "Anna," she says. "What are you doing here?" The question comes out as accusatory, just as Cash feared it might, but Anna wears a heavy suit of armor, so Irene's tone bounces right off of her.

"I brought Floyd down," she says, and she opens her arms. "I am so sorry about all of this. How awful it must be for you."

Irene stares at Anna for a moment and then she walks right into Anna's arms and the two women embrace, and Cash is as amazed that his mother is accepting comfort as he is that Anna is offering it—but he is also relieved.

Baker and Floyd enter the kitchen, Floyd gets a hug and a kiss from Grammie, and Baker announces that he's taking Floyd down to look at the beach.

"That's fine," Anna says. "Then someone should probably drive us to our hotel."

"Hotel?" Baker says.

"I got a suite at a boutique place in Chocolate Hole," Anna says. "I'm sorry, I wasn't sure how big this home was."

"There are nine bedrooms," Irene says. "Stay here, please."

"Floyd will stay here," Baker says. "Anna can go to the hotel." With that, he takes Floyd's hand and leaves the kitchen, shutting the side door firmly for emphasis.

Irene raises her eyebrows. "Is something going on?"

Anna says, "Baker and I are splitting. I've met someone else. Another surgeon at the hospital, actually. Her name is Louisa."

Cash wishes he'd had a third margarita, or even a fourth, although he admires Anna's ability to just come out with the plainspoken truth. Her tone is matter-of-fact and holds not even a hint of apology.

Irene opens her mouth, then closes it, then starts to laugh. Cash cringes. Why is *he* the one who has to bear witness to this confession? Why didn't he go to the beach with his brother and nephew, or run upstairs to the guest room he has claimed as his own and hide under the bed? Why does he have to be standing here, watching his mother laugh at Anna's moment of coming out? Irene laughs so hard that tears leak from her eyes. She's trying to stop herself; she struggles to catch her breath.

"I'm sorry," Irene says finally. "It's just I didn't think anyone else in the whole world could take me by surprise, but you've gone and done it. You're leaving Baker for a woman?"

"A person," Anna says, and Cash wants to applaud. "Another doctor, who also happens to be female, yes. I'll apologize for being the one to break up the family, Irene, but I won't apologize because Louisa is a woman."

Irene nods. "I didn't mean to laugh at you. I'm a bit self-absorbed these days, but I appreciate your being direct. Would you like to stay for dinner?"

"I'm tired," Anna says. "But thank you for asking."

"It's just as well," Irene says. "I have a delicate matter to discuss with the boys."

"Delicate matter?" Cash says. "Did you get news?"

"Something like that," Irene says. She smiles at Anna. "Thank you for bringing Floyd down. It's a lovely surprise. Now, if you'll excuse me." Irene leaves the kitchen.

When Anna turns to Cash, he expects her to be angry or offended—but she's beaming. "That went much better than I expected," she says.

* * *

Baker and Floyd come up from the beach and the adults agree that the best course of action is for all of them to drop off Anna at the St. John Guest Suites and then for the menfolk to pick up dinner at Uncle Joe's B.B.Q. Baker seems nervous and agitated. He drives like a bat out of hell all the way to Chocolate Hole, and when he pulls into the driveway to drop Anna off, he says, "How many nights did you book?"

"Two," Anna says. "And I thought you would come back with us."

"No!" Baker says, his voice like a hammer. "As you can see, my mother needs me."

"Cash is here to care for Irene," Anna says. "But you have a child who needs you. I need you."

"What you mean is that you need me to come home and be a parent because you're too busy to do it."

Cash glances at Floyd. He has earbuds in and is fully engrossed in his iPad, but still.

"Don't do this here," Cash says. "I don't want to hear it, and neither does you-know-who."

"Cash is right," Anna says.

"I'm not leaving in two days," Baker says.

"We'll discuss later," Anna says. She gets out of the Jeep, grabs her bag, pokes her head in the backseat window. "Thanks for coming to get us, Cash. Floyd, I'll see you at some point tomorrow." Floyd doesn't look up. Anna removes one of his earbuds. "See you tomorrow."

"Okay," Floyd says. "Bye."

Maybe she's not the most maternal presence, but Cash still finds his sister-in-law impressive. He notices her posture as she goes to greet the owners, trailing her roller bag behind her, the picture of extreme self-confidence, uncompromising in her principles.

A person, Anna said to Irene. *Another doctor, who also happens to be female.* Cash chuckles and moves to the front seat, next to Baker.

"Don't kill me," he says.

Turns out Baker isn't angry. Scratch that: he is angry, but his anger is secondary to his panic. He had told Ayers he would take her to Caneel Bay the following night — dinner, hotel, the whole enchilada.

"I had to text her and cancel," Baker says. His voice is low, even though Floyd still has his headphones in. "I told her our sister showed up unexpectedly."

"Our *sister*?" Cash says. "You *lied* to her?"

"I didn't lie," Baker says. "She's your sister."

"She's my sister-in-*law,*" Cash says. "She's your wife."

"I couldn't very well tell Ayers my wife showed up."

"Estranged wife," Cash says. "You could have said your estranged wife showed up with your child out of the blue and you need a few days to deal with it. Ayers is cool. She would understand."

"*Ayers is cool,*" Baker mimics. "You have no idea whether she's cool or not cool. Stop pretending like you know her better than I do."

"I wasn't saying that. But I have spent time with her, and I do happen to think she's cool. I hiked with her, and we went on *Treasure Island* together. I'm sure it comes as a crushing blow, but she likes me."

"She may like you just fine," Baker says. "But she likes me more. All women like me better, Cash, starting with that sweet little...what was her name?"

Claire Bellows, Cash thinks.

"Claire Bellows," Baker says. "I bet you still haven't forgiven me for Claire Bellows."

"Claire Bellows was my girlfriend," Cash says. "And you slept with her—not because you liked her, but because you wanted to prove to me that you could."

"You knew Anna and Floyd were coming," Baker says. "And you didn't tell me."

"If you'd answered your phone, you would have known."

"You're in love with Ayers yourself," Baker says. "And that's why you didn't tell me Anna was coming."

"You shouldn't have been on a date with Ayers," Cash says. "You're pretending you're a single man, but you're far from it."

Baker pulls up in front of Uncle Joe's B.B.Q. and puts the car in park. "Get chicken and ribs," Baker says. "And a bunch of sides."

"I need money," Cash says.

"You've got to be kidding me," Baker says. "I've paid for everything on this trip. You haven't paid once."

"I told you my bank card doesn't work down here."

"That's bullshit and you know it," Baker says. "What's the issue? You own a business, right? A business that Dad handed you on a silver platter. Are the stores not making money?"

Cash stares at the dashboard. He's going to punch his brother. He clenches and unclenches his fists. They are right downtown, people are everywhere, Floyd is in the backseat, he has to control himself.

"The stores failed," Cash says. "They're gone. The bank owns them now."

Baker throws his head back to laugh. Cash gets out of the Jeep, but instead of going to Uncle Joe's B.B.Q., he storms off toward the post office and the ferry dock.

Baker yells from the car. "Cash! Where are you going, man? Listen, I'm sorry."

Cash doesn't turn around. He ducks behind a tree and watches Baker drive past, looking for him.

Cash isn't flat broke. He still has twelve dollars, which, because it's now happy hour at High Tide, will buy him another margarita.

An hour later, he's buzzed and indignant. The heinous things Baker said roll through his mind, one after the other. *You're in love with Ayers yourself...a business that Dad handed you on a silver platter...she likes me more. All women like me better...Are the stores not making money?* Baker thinks he's better than Cash. He has always thought that, and maybe Cash had thought it, too. But Baker isn't going to win this time, not if Cash can help it.

He calls Ayers's cell phone. He vaguely recalls that she's busy tonight, not work, some other commitment—but she answers on the second ring.

"Cash?" she says. "Is that you? Is everything all right?"

He breathes in through his nose. He tries to sound sober, or at least coherent. "Baker canceled your date for tomorrow night?" he says. "He told you our sister arrived on the island?"

"He did," Ayers says. "I didn't realize you guys had a sister. Neither of you mentioned her before…"

"We don't," Cash says. "We don't have a sister. Baker was lying."

"Oh," Ayers says.

"The person who showed up was his wife, Anna. And she brought their son, Floyd."

"Oh," Ayers says. "He told me they'd split. That she left him."

"She's leaving him, yes," Cash says. "That part is true. For another doctor at the hospital where she's a surgeon. But she's here now, with Floyd. Baker didn't know they were coming."

"He didn't?" Ayers says.

"He didn't at all," Cash says. "He was blindsided and he didn't want you to know, so he lied and said it was our sister."

"I see," Ayers says.

"I'm pretty drunk," Cash says. He's standing in Powell Park near the gazebo. The sun is setting and the mosquitoes are after him. "Do you think you could come give me a ride home?"

"I wish I could," Ayers says. "I'm busy, I'm sorry."

Cash takes a breath. He's come this far; he might as well go the rest of the way. "Ayers, I have something to tell you. I'm in love with you."

"Oh, Cash," she says. "Please don't make this complicated. You're a great guy, you know I think that…"

"But you have the hots for Baker," Cash says. "Because that's how things always go. Women think I'm a great guy but they have the hots! For! Baker!" He's shouting now, and he has attracted the attention of a West Indian policewoman, who crosses the street toward him. "You really shouldn't be interested in either of us. Do you know why?"

"No," Ayers says. "Why?"

"Russell Steele? Rosie's boyfriend? The Invisible Man?" Cash says.

"Yes?" Ayers says. She sounds scared now. "Yes?"

"He was our father," Cash says. And he hangs up the phone.

HUCK

Hard things are hard. And there's no instruction manual when it comes to parenting—or in Huck's case, step-grandparenting—a twelve-year-old girl.

His dinner with Irene, instead of heading in an amorous direction, as he had hoped, ended with a quandary. Irene was dead certain Maia was Russ's blood daughter. Huck had been skeptical. Why wouldn't Rosie have just said so? Why make up the story about the Pirate and then pretend the Invisible Man was a different guy? Rosie *was* prone to drama; maybe she *wanted* her life peopled like a Marvel comic.

To prove her point, Irene brought Huck a framed photograph: Rosie with an older gentleman, lying in a hammock. Russell Steele. But in the photo, Russ was wearing sunglasses. There was something in his face that was replicated in Maia's face, but without seeing his eyes, Huck couldn't be 100 percent sure. Then Irene scrolled through the pictures on her phone and found a good, clear picture of her husband's face.

Yes, Huck thought. There was no denying it. Maia had the

same half-moon eyebrows, the same slight flange to the tip of her nose, the exact same smile.

"Uncanny," Huck said.

"She's his," Irene said.

"Yes."

"Yes, you see it?"

"Impossible not to see it." Huck remembered back to when he and Ayers told Maia that Rosie was dead. She had asked about her father. She knew. They'd told her, maybe. She was twelve, old enough to understand. It also explained why Russell Steele paid for Rosie's living expenses and Maia's tuition. Huck had checked Rosie's bank account balances. She had seven thousand in her checking and a whopping eighty-five thousand in savings, and it looked as though she might have some kind of account in the States. Huck would need to hire a lawyer to get access to that money on Maia's behalf, and he supposed he would need to legally take custody, although his distrust of lawyers and his distaste for paying their exorbitant fees had kept him from doing anything just yet. The custody question was a moot point—or so he had assumed. No one on this island was going to dispute his claim to the girl, not even the Smalls, Rosie's father's people. So there was no sense of urgency. Until now. Maybe.

"I'd like to meet her," Irene said.

Huck could not put the inevitable off any longer: he needed a cigarette.

"I'd like to smoke," he said.

"I'll join you," she said.

They stepped out onto the deck and Huck lit up. He took a much-needed drag, then handed the cigarette to Irene. "Or I could light you your own."

"A whole cigarette would be wasted on me," Irene said, though she inhaled off his deeply. "I know she's not related to *me*."

"Just let me think a minute," Huck said. "I need to consider Maia. Maia's emotional state, Maia's best interests."

"I don't think there are blueprints for this," Irene said. "The circumstances are unique. I, for one, can't accept the information that Russ has a child, a daughter, without wanting to meet her."

"What do you hope to get out of it?" Huck asked.

"I'm not sure," Irene said. "I loved him. She's his. I think my motives are pure."

"You *think*?"

"The boys — Baker and Cash — are her brothers."

"Half brothers."

"Fine, half brothers. But that's still blood. That's still family."

Huck didn't like where her reasoning was headed. *He* was Maia's family! He had been the third person to hold her after she was born. He had taught her how to cast a line, bait a hook, handle the gaff. He drove her to school, packed her lunches, signed her permission slips. It rankled him that "the boys, Baker and Cash," shared blood with Maia when he did not.

Irene was a perceptive woman. She put a hand on his arm. "I'm not going to take her from you, Huck. I just want to meet her. Let her know we exist. She's twelve now. Even if we don't tell her, she'll find out eventually and there will be resentment. Aimed at you."

"Let me think about it," Huck said. "I'll call you by Wednesday night."

"Thank you, Huck," Irene said. "Thank you for even considering it." She gazed up at him, her eyes shining; she looked, in that moment, as young and hopeful as a woman in her twenties. Huck flicked the butt of the cigarette over the railing. It was time for him to leave.

Irene stood on her tiptoes and kissed his cheek. It was official. Despite the bizarre, twisted chain of events that had brought them both there, he liked her.

On Wednesday, he picks Maia up from school at noon. She has a half day and he didn't schedule an afternoon charter because they have an important mission.

They stop by home to grab the things they need. Huck loads the buoy, rope, and anchor into the back of the truck. Maia emerges with a paper lunch bag.

Thirty minutes later, they are in *The Mississippi,* heading for the BVIs. It's a clear day, cloudless; the sun is so hot it paints fire across the back of Huck's neck. He pulls his bandana out and imagines it's still damp with Irene's tears. He hasn't been able to think of much besides Irene—half because he's starting to feel something for her, half because she has asked him to make an impossible decision.

"How was your night with Ayers?" Huck has been so preoccupied with Irene that he has neglected to ask until now.

Maia is facing into the wind, wearing an inexpensive pair of plastic sunglasses that she decorated with seashells she and her mother collected on Salomon Beach. "Impossible-to-reach-Salomon-Beach" had been Rosie's favorite. Maia has a faraway expression on her face, and Huck wonders what's going on in that mind of hers. He nearly repeats the question, but then Maia says, "It was fine. I think Ayers is having man problems."

"Oh really?" Huck says. "Someone new, or is she still hung up on Mick?"

"Someone new," Maia says. "A tourist, I think."

"Bad news," Huck says. He casts a sidelong glance at Maia. "You're not allowed to date until you're thirty, by the way."

"We saw Mick at Pizzabar in Paradise," Maia says. "He told me he still loves Ayers."

"Oh boy," Huck says. "Sounds like you had an educational night."

"She likes the tourist," Maia says. "But they had a date for tonight, and he canceled. She was upset. I told her she should go back out with Mick. I like Mick."

"I know you do," Huck says. Huck likes Mick, too. Mick always buys him a round at the Beach Bar, and he buys Huck's fish for the restaurant. But Mick had gotten mixed up with one of the little girlies working for him and Ayers gave him the boot.

Now she's interested in a tourist? No, Huck thinks. Not a good idea. Although Huck, of course, has no say.

Huck steers the boat past Jost and up along the coast of Tortola. He's in British waters now and he expects to be stopped by Her Majesty's coast guard; Huck isn't allowed to be over here without going through customs. But the border control and BVI police boats must all be at lunch or at the beach, because he moves toward their destination unimpeded.

North of Virgin Gorda, southeast of Anegada. It's a haul—

which, he supposes, is why Russ and Rosie decided to take a bird. It was only an irresponsible decision because of the weather; it must have seemed like a good gamble, though, and if Huck had all the tea in China and a bird at his disposal, he might have chanced it as well.

They pass *Treasure Island,* which is on the way from Norman Island to Jost Van Dyke, and Maia starts waving her arms like crazy.

"Ayers is working today," she says.

"Does she know what *we're* doing today?" Huck asks.

"I didn't tell her," Maia says. "I didn't tell anyone." *Treasure Island* is past them now, and *The Mississippi* catches some of her choppy wake. The boat bounces, but Maia enjoys it the way she might a ride at the amusement park. She's his girl.

Hard things are hard. Maia asked to see the place where the helicopter went down. At first, Huck had resisted. What good would come from seeing the place where Rosie died so violently? But then Huck reasoned that any real-life visual would likely be less horrific than the pictures Maia held in her mind.

They reach the general area of the crash, according to the coordinates Huck had gotten from Virgin Islands Search and Rescue when they had delivered Rosie's body—a huge favor pulled by Huck's best friend, Rupert, who grew up in Coral Bay with the governor; bodies are notoriously hard to recover from the Brits—and Huck cuts the engine. The water is brilliant turquoise; the green peaks of Virgin Gorda are behind them. Huck picks up the mooring—a white spherical buoy that Maia painted with a red rose and Rosie's name and dates.

Huck had told Maia that the mooring isn't legal; it will likely be pulled within twenty-four hours. Maia doesn't care. She wants to go through the ritual of marking the spot.

"We're here," Huck says.

Maia stands, holding the buoy, and kisses it. Huck picks up the rope and tosses the anchor overboard. Maia throws the buoy over. The rose is pretty; she did a good job.

"Should we say something?" Huck asks.

"I love you, Mama," Maia says. "And Huck loves you, too, even if he is too manly to say it."

"Me, too manly?" Huck says. He clears his throat. "I love you, Rosie girl. I'll love you forever. I just hope you're with your mama now. My precious LeeAnn."

"Amen," Maia says.

Huck smiles, though a couple of tears fall. LeeAnn was the only one of them who ever went to church—Our Lady of Mount Carmel: she loved the priest, Father Abraham, who has an enviable charisma—but some of the faith must have rubbed off on Maia.

She opens the paper lunch bag and produces a pink sphere. She holds it above the water with two pincer fingers and lets it go right next to the buoy. The water fizzes, just as it used to back in the day when Huck would make himself an Alka-Seltzer.

"What is that?" Huck says. He's an ecologist by nature, so he's concerned.

"Bath bomb, rose-scented," Maia says. "Don't worry, it's organic."

They both peer over the side of *The Mississippi* until the rose-scented bath bomb dissolves.

"For you, Mama," Maia says.

Huck waits a respectful moment. Just as he's about to start the engine, Maia pulls out a second bath bomb, this one pale yellow.

"What's that?" Huck asks.

Maia brings it to her nose and inhales deeply. "Pineapple mint," she says. "My favorite. It's for Russ." She drops it in the water. "For you, Russ."

He couldn't hope for a more natural segue, and yet when he starts to speak there's a catch in his throat. He's about to change this kid's entire life. But he won't live forever. He's sixty-one now, and who's to say he won't drown or get struck by lightning, or die of a heart attack, or get bitten by a poisonous spider, or have a head-on collision on the Centerline Road? If there's one thing Huck can say about Rosie, it's that she firmly believed she would live forever. And she didn't. So it's best to err on the side of caution. If Huck dies, the girl will have no one. Ayers, maybe, if Ayers doesn't move to Calabasas or Albany, New York, with some tourist—but Ayers has no legal claim of guardianship.

Maia needs family—a chance at family, anyway. And Irene is right—if Huck doesn't tell her now, she'll find out when she's older. And hate him.

"Speaking of Russ," Huck says.

"Uh-oh," Maia says. She puts her elbows on her knees, rests her chin in her hand.

"Back when I told you the news," Huck says, "you said that Russ was your father."

"He is," Maia says. "Was. They told me the truth on my birthday, back in November. Russ is the Pirate. We have the same birthmark."

Huck shakes his head. "Russ has the birthmark?"

"The peanut," Maia says. "In the exact same spot on his back."

"No kidding," Huck says. Maia's birthmark, on the back of her shoulder, is the shape and size of a ballpark peanut.

"No kidding," Maia says. "He was my birth father after all. I kind of already knew. We have the same laugh, we both love licorice, we're both left-handed."

"Do you know...anything else?" Huck asks. *Like where the guy was the first seven years of your life?*

"No," Maia says. "Mom said she would tell me the whole story when I was older. Fifteen or sixteen. When I could handle it better, she said."

"Okay," Huck says. His job has been made both easier and more difficult. On the one hand, there's no need to pursue a DNA test if the birthmark story is true—Irene should be able to confirm—but on the other hand, Maia may not want to know the truth about her father. "Well, I've made a new friend recently."

"Seriously?" Maia says. "I thought you hated people."

Huck gives a dry laugh. "My friend, Irene, Irene Steele, actually, used to be married to Russ."

Maia's face changes to an expression that is beyond her years. It's wariness, he thinks, the expression one gets when one senses a hostile presence. "Used to be?" she says.

"Honey," he says. "Russ was married. While he was with your mom, the whole time, he was married to someone else. A woman named Irene. She flew down here when she learned he was dead, and she found me. She has two sons, one thirty years old, one twenty-eight. They are your brothers."

"My brothers?" Maia says. "I have brothers?"

"Half brothers," Huck says. "Russell Steele is their father and he's your father. Their mother is Irene. Yours is . . . was . . . Rosie."

"Okay," Maia says. She bows her head. "Wait."

Wait: Huck has done irreparable damage. Something inside of her is broken . . . or altered. Innocence stolen, spoiled. She now knows she's the daughter of a cheat and a liar.

"He loved Mama," Maia says.

"I know," Huck says.

"But love is messy, complicated, and unfair," Maia says, like she's reciting something out of a book.

"That's a dim view," Huck says. "I loved your grandmother very much. We were happy."

"Mama used to say that."

Rosie might have known about Irene—must have known, Huck thinks. It was one thing for Russell Steele to keep Rosie a secret from Irene. Could he really have kept both sides in the dark? "Did they ever explain where Russ went when he wasn't around?"

Maia shrugs. "Work."

"Did they ever say what kind of work?"

"Business," Maia says. "Finance, money. Boring stuff."

"Boring stuff indeed," Huck says. He takes a sustaining breath. He has not ruined her. She had a clue, an inkling, that Russ was keeping secrets. Huck is grateful that Rosie and Russ didn't see fit to burden Maia with any information about Russ's business, even though Huck is dying to know what the guy was into. "Okay, now for the tricky part."

"Tricky?" Maia says.

"My new friend Irene, Russ's wife, wants to meet you. And

she'd like you to meet her sons. They aren't taking you from me, they're not taking you anywhere, they just want to meet you."

"But why?" Maia says. "Wouldn't they hate me? I'm the daughter of Russ's girlfriend. Even though Mama is dead, wouldn't they want…I don't know…to pretend like I don't exist? Wouldn't that be easier?"

Easier, for sure, Huck thinks.

"Part of it is that they're curious. Part of it is that…well, your mother was right about love being complicated. Irene loved her husband and you're his child, so" — Huck can't quite make the transitive property work here, much as he wants to — "she's interested in you."

Maia blinks. If she were any older, she might take offense at how objectifying that sounds: "interested," the way one becomes interested in astronomy or penguins.

"Okay, let me ask you this. Let's say we found out that your mom had another child, a son, say, that you never knew about until now. You love your mother and maybe you feel betrayed that your mother kept this big, important secret. You would still want to meet your brother, right?"

"I guess," Maia says. "Do I have a secret brother?"

"Not on your mother's side," Huck says. "I can vouch for the fact that your mother was pregnant only once, and that was with you. But what I'm telling you is that you have two brothers. They want to meet you and their mother, Irene, wants to meet you. But you're in control. If you say no, I'll politely decline."

"Will they be upset if we decline?" Maia asks.

"Maybe," Huck says. "But that shouldn't affect your answer. You wouldn't be meeting them so they feel better. You'd be meeting them because you want to." Huck pauses. The sun is bearing down on him. "I know that may sound selfish, but you have to trust me here. If you want to meet them, we'll meet them. If you'd rather not, that's fine. More than fine."

Maia leans over the side of *The Mississippi* and peers into the water. Both the bombs have dissolved; all that remains, on the surface, are soap bubbles, like one would find in dishwater. Huck doesn't want Maia to contemplate this particular spot for too long—the depths of this sea; the darker water below, where Rosie's body landed.

"I'll meet them," Maia says. "But if I don't like them, I don't ever have to see them again, right?"

"Right," Huck says.

"You promise?"

"I promise." Huck is proud of her. She is brave and fierce and incorruptible. Huck can't believe he thought that either he or Irene Steele or her sons could ruin Maia Small.

No matter what happens with all of this, Huck thinks, Maia is going to be fine.

BAKER

At eight thirty at night, after Floyd and Baker have eaten the barbecue—chicken, ribs, pasta salad, coleslaw with raisins, rice and beans, and fried plantains—there's a knock at the door. Somewhere in the house, Winnie barks.

Who could it be? Baker wonders, and he wishes they'd left the gate down. He feels ill. He just indulged in some world-class stress eating, shoveling food in without even tasting it, and he can't imagine who could be at the door this late. It's not Cash; he would have sauntered right in. Maybe the police have shown up with Cash in custody? Maybe something happened to Cash: he hitchhiked home with the wrong person, or he was trying to hitch a ride and a driver didn't see him and mowed him down. Maybe he did something desperate. Baker shouldn't have teased him about Ayers, or about Claire Bellows, and he should *never* have forced a confession about the business. *The stores failed. They're gone.* Even though Baker had predicted that would happen, he feels no joy in the reality. Poor Cash. He just wasn't meant to run a business.

It could be Anna at the door, Baker supposes, although she would have to be a homing pigeon to find this place in the dark. There are no neighbors on this road.

He asks Floyd to run upstairs, brush his teeth, and put on his pajamas.

"No," Floyd says.

Normally, Baker has a deep well of paternal patience, but he senses that this knock means bad news of some kind. "Please, buddy," Baker says.

"I'm scared," Floyd says, and Baker realizes that Floyd has every reason to be scared. This is a huge, unfamiliar house. Even Baker can't recall which room he put Floyd's suitcase in. Baker wants to tell Floyd that he, too, is scared—of things far more terrifying than shadows and strange noises.

It's probably a taxi driver who picked up Cash and now is demanding to be paid.

Baker opens the door to find a tall, hulking West Indian man, and initially he thinks his guess is correct.

"Hello?" Baker says. He searches the darkness beyond the man for signs of his brother.

The man thrusts forward a square cardboard box. "For you," he says. "Mr. Steele's remains."

Mr. Steele's remains? Baker reaches out to accept the box and the man turns to go.

"Wait," Baker says. "Who are you? Where did you come from?"

"I'm Douglas Vickers, Paulette's husband," the man says. "Those came to her office today and she asked me to deliver them here."

"Oh," Baker says. In the moment, this makes sense. "Thank you." Douglas gives Baker and Floyd half a wave and disappears down the stone staircase, leaving Baker to hold what remains of his father. The ashes have been delivered to the door like a pizza.

"Daddy?" Floyd says. There is likely a barrage of questions coming as soon as Floyd can figure out what to ask, but for now, he just seems to need reassurance.

"Everything is okay, bud," Baker says. "I'll be back in one second. You stay right here." Baker turns to check that Floyd is standing in the doorway, then he goes flying down the curved stone staircase after Douglas. He catches the man just as he's climbing into a white panel van. "Excuse me? Mr. Vickers, sir?"

Douglas Vickers stops, one leg up in the van, one on the ground, his face framed by the open driver's-side window. "Yes?"

"You were the one who identified my father's body, is that right?" Baker asks.

Douglas Vickers nods once. "I did."

"You . . . *saw* him?" Baker asks. "And he was dead?"

Douglas Vickers gives Baker a blank stare, then he hops into the truck and backs out through the gate.

* * *

Once Baker gets Floyd to sleep—thankfully, Anna remembered to pack a few picture books, including *The Dirty Cowboy*, which reliably knocks Floyd out by the end of page six—he heads down the hallway to the room Irene has been using and knocks on the door.

"Come in," Irene says.

His mother is sitting on the side of the bed, fully dressed, as if she has been waiting for Baker to knock.

"Is Floyd asleep?" she asks.

Baker nods.

"Good," Irene says. "Because I have to talk to you and your brother."

"Um, okay?" Baker says. "Cash isn't home. I left him off in town when I got the barbecue."

"Whatever for?" Irene asks.

"He jumped out of the car, actually," Baker says. "We had an argument. I wasn't very nice. I was upset…he knew Anna and Floyd were coming and he didn't tell me."

"He didn't tell me, either," Irene says. "I had no idea who Anna was when I saw her. I *introduced* myself to her. She was so out of context and I haven't laid eyes on her for so long…"

"Three years," Baker says. Anna hasn't been back to Iowa City since just after Floyd's first birthday. "Listen, Mom, Anna and I are getting a divorce."

"She told me," Irene says. "She's fallen in love with a person named Louisa."

Baker's eyebrows shoot up. "She told you that?"

"She did."

Well, yes, Baker thinks, she should have. It was Anna's

news. The dismantling of their family was Anna's doing. "I'm sorry. I'm sure you're disappointed."

"Hard to register any kind of feeling about Anna, I'm afraid," Irene says. "She's always been a mystery."

"You should probably also know…if he hasn't told you already…that Cash lost the stores. They went belly-up."

Irene gives Baker a sharp glance. "He hasn't told me, no. I figured as much, but it's Cash's responsibility to tell me, not yours."

"Right," Baker says. He knows his mother favors Cash, or feels more protective of him than she does of Baker. "None of my business, sorry. So listen, Mom, a gentleman just stopped by…"

"Gentleman?" Irene says. "Was he older, with a reddish beard?"

"Huh?" Baker says. His mother is on her feet now, at the front window, searching. "No, it was a West Indian gentleman. Paulette's husband, Douglas. He brought Dad's ashes."

"Dad's ashes?" Irene says. "Where are they?"

"Downstairs," Baker says.

They get to the kitchen just as Cash stumbles through the door. Baker can smell him from across the room—tequila.

He opens the refrigerator door. "Any barbecue left?"

"Plenty," Baker says. He's relieved that Cash seems to be either numbed or neutralized by alcohol and that there will be no rehashing of their earlier argument.

As Cash pulls the various to-go containers out of the fridge, Irene cuts open the cardboard box.

"Actually, Cash, you may want to wait on eating," Baker says.

"Fuck you," Cash says. "I'm starving."

"How'd you get home?" Baker asks.

"That tall chick that works at La Tapa picked me up outside Mongoose Junction," Cash says. "Tilda, her name is."

"Yeah, I know who you mean," Baker says.

"I guess she has the hots for Skip, the bartender," Cash says. "Funny, we've been here less than a week and we know everyone else's personal drama…"

There's a sound.

It's Irene, wailing in hoarse, ragged sobs. She's holding a heavy-duty Ziploc bag that contains white and pale-gray chunks. Without warning, she collapses on the kitchen floor.

For an instant, both Baker and Cash stare. They are grown men and they have never seen their mother act like this. Baker, although not surprised—he's been wondering if his mother would break, if she would finally act like a woman who has tragically lost her husband instead of a woman moving around in an extended state of shock—doesn't know what to do. Cash is holding the take-out containers of food and a bottle of water, seemingly paralyzed.

Cash is better at dealing with their mother. *Do something!* Baker thinks.

Cash sets the food down and approaches Irene cautiously, as if she's a ticking bomb or a rabid dog.

"Mom, hey, let's get you up. Can you sit at the table?"

Irene cries more loudly, then she starts to scream—words, phrases, Baker can't make sense of much. He keeps checking the stairs; the last thing he wants is for Floyd to wake up and see his grandmother like this.

"...I trusted him! Bad back...clients in Pensa*cola*! I never checked! Never questioned! Never suspected a thing...greed... the money...the house! I was married to the house! Secrets are lies! They're lies! I never suspected...why would I suspect? Your father was so...effusive...so loving...it was too much, sometimes, I used to *tell* him it was too much...I told him to *tone it down,* it was *embarrassing...*" She stops. "Can you imagine? I was embarrassed because your father loved me too much. Because I wasn't raised like that. My parents told me they loved me...once a year, maybe, and I never heard them say it to each other. Never once! But they did love each other...they just showed the love in their actions, the way they treated each other...honor, respect. They didn't keep secrets like this one!"

"Mom," Baker says, but he doesn't know what to add. She's right. Their father was demonstrative, verging on sappy. He exuded so much *I love you, please love me back* that Baker at least, and probably Irene and Cash as well, saw it as a weakness.

Had it all been an act, then? Baker wonders. Or had the three of them done such a pitiful job of returning Russ's love that he'd sought affection elsewhere?

Irene holds up the plastic bag. "This is all that's left. All! That's! Left!" She flings the ashes across the kitchen. The bag hits the cabinets and slaps the floor. Thank goodness the seal held, Baker thinks. Otherwise they would be sweeping Russ up with a broom and dustpan.

Cash gets Irene to a chair at the kitchen table while Baker picks up the ashes. Across the label of the bag it says: STEELE, RUSSELL DOD: 1/1/19.

Baker sits down beside his mother. Cash has brought a pile

of paper napkins to the table. He's trying to put his arm around Irene, but she's resisting—possibly because he smells like a Mexican whorehouse.

"Just let me...just let me...," Irene says.

Baker studies the contents of the plastic bag. The pieces are chalky and porous; the "remains" look like a few handfuls of coral on the beach in Salt Pond. It's a sobering, nearly ghastly, thought: You live a whole life, filled with routines, traditions, and brand-new experiences, and then you end up like this. Baker can't let his mind wander to the mechanics of cremation—your body, which you have fed and exercised and washed and dressed with such care, is pushed into a fiery inferno. Baker shudders. And yet there is no escaping death. No escaping it! Every single one of us will die, as surely as every single one of us has been born. Baker is here today, but one day he will be like Russ. Gone.

He, for one, is glad the ashes have finally arrived. They all needed closure.

Baker checks the cardboard box for the name or address of the funeral home but finds neither. It's just a plain box, sealed with clear packing tape. The bag is just a bag, labeled with Russ's name and date of death.

How do we know this is even Russ? he wonders. It could be John Q. Public. It could be coral from Salt Pond. Baker had asked Douglas point-blank, Did you see my father, was he dead? And Douglas had stared. Now, maybe he'd stared at Baker like that because he thought the question was rhetorical. Maybe he thought the question was coming from a man half-crazed with grief, ready to grasp at any straw. But maybe, *maybe,* the stare meant something else.

Irene blots her nose and under her eyes with a paper napkin. "I need you boys to promise me something," she says.

"Anything," Cash says. But Baker refrains. Cash can be his mother's acolyte, but Baker is going to hear what Irene is asking before he commits.

"What is it, Mom?" Baker says.

"Don't be like him," Irene says. "Don't lead secret lives."

Cash laughs, which Baker thinks is in poor taste.

"No one *intends* to lie," Irene says. "But it happens. Sometimes the truth is difficult and it's easier to create an alternate reality or not to say anything at all. I can't imagine how soul-shredding it must have been for Russ to...to go back and forth. Rosie here, me in Iowa City."

Baker looks at his brother. Irene knows about Rosie. Did Cash tell her?

"Mom...," Baker says.

Irene barks out a laugh. "I found the photograph. Winnie helped me. And then I did some sleuthing. It must have destroyed your father deep inside to know he was betraying me and betraying both of you..." She stops. "Just promise me."

"Promise," Cash says.

"Promise," Baker says.

"And yet, you've both spent the better part of a week with me. Baker, you didn't tell me that you and Anna had split. Cash, you didn't tell me you'd lost the stores."

The kitchen is very, very quiet for a moment.

Baker says, "I didn't want to make you even more upset..."

"I thought it was irrelevant," Cash says. "Petty, even, to bring it up when you had so much else going on..."

"So you said nothing, time passed, and I had no idea about

either thing. Which is why I'm asking you now to please not keep any secrets. Secrets become lies, and lies end up destroying you and everyone you care about."

"Okay," Baker says.

"Okay," Cash says. He rises to fetch Irene some ice water. He is such a kiss-ass, Baker thinks, but really Baker is just jealous because he's better at anticipating Irene's needs.

"Thank you," Irene says. "I haven't exactly been forthcoming, either, as I'm sure you both realize..."

Cash says, "Mom, you don't have to..."

"Let her finish," Baker says.

"I tracked down Rosie Small's stepfather," Irene says. "He's a fishing captain by the name of Huck Powers. He was the one who came for dinner last night. He helped me jimmy the door to the bedroom at the end of the hall."

"What bedroom at the end of the hall?" Baker says.

Cash shrugs.

Irene says, "The door at the end of the hall was locked, and I wanted to see what was in it. I thought maybe I would find something that would explain all...this." She holds up her arms.

"What was in it?" Cash asks.

"A bed," Irene says. "Furniture."

"Oh," Baker says. "With that kind of buildup, I thought maybe you'd discovered something."

"I did," Irene says. "Because painted on the wall, in decorative letters, was a name: Maia."

"Who's Maia?" Baker asks.

Irene takes another sip of her water. "Maia is Russ's daughter," she says. "Your sister."

* * *

Funny, we've been here less than a week and we know everyone else's personal drama...

Those words, spoken by Cash, contain some truth, but who are they kidding? Nobody can hold a candle to the Steele family when it comes to personal drama.

Russ has a daughter, twelve years old, named Maia.

He was not only hiding this home, a mistress, and whatever it was he did for a living—he was hiding a child.

Okay, fine, it happens. Baker knows it happens. There was a guy in Iowa City—Brent Lamplighter, his name was, he used to belong to the Elks Lodge—who had gotten a waitress in Cedar Rapids pregnant. That child was in kindergarten before anyone realized that he was Lamplighter's son.

But Russ with a daughter? It's a punch to the gut. Another punch to the gut.

Russ's deception knew no bounds.

The only thing more shocking than the news of Russ's daughter, Maia, is the revelation that Irene wants to *meet* Maia. She wants them *all* to meet Maia. Irene has asked Huck, Rosie's stepfather, if that would be possible. He's going to let her know by tomorrow.

Before Baker goes up to bed, there is something he has to do.

He steps out to the deck beyond the pool to call Ayers. The call goes straight to voicemail, which isn't surprising, given the hour. It's nearly eleven. It also isn't surprising because when

Baker texted Ayers—*My sister showed up out of the blue and I can't do Caneel tomorrow night. What's the next night you're free?*—there was no response. Maybe Ayers was busy with her other "commitment," or maybe she was angry. Maybe she thought Baker was just another tourist who made pretty promises he had no intention of keeping.

Baker can't let himself care why Ayers hasn't responded. He has feelings for her, but those feelings are cheapened because he hasn't been honest.

"Ayers, it's Baker. I'd like you to listen carefully to this message. I lied today when I said my sister showed up out of the blue. It wasn't my sister. It was my wife, Anna, and my son, Floyd. Anna and I are estranged. She's staying at the St. John Guest Suites, so there was no reason I couldn't be honest about that other than I thought you'd be angry or think some kind of reconciliation was going on—which, I can assure you, is *not* the case."

Baker takes a breath. He hates when people leave him lengthy voicemails. He should hang up now and explain the rest when she calls him back.

But what if she doesn't call him back?

"The bigger issue is more than a lie. It's a deception. I never told you the real reason I'm on St. John. The real reason I'm here is because I'm Russell Steele's son. Russell Steele, your friend Rosie's lover, was my father. Cash and I had no idea he owned a villa here, no idea about Rosie…it's been a confusing time for us, and for my mother. Despite the lie and the deception, I want you to know that my feelings for you are genuine. It was love at first sight."

Baker wonders how to sign off. *Call me if you want to? Talk to you later? Good luck and Godspeed?* In the end, he just hangs up.

When he steps back inside the house, he's surprised to find his mother is still awake. She's at the kitchen table in her pajamas, with the bag of ashes and her phone in front of her. When she hears the slider, she raises her head.

"I just got a text from Huck," she says. "He's going to bring Maia by tomorrow after school."

"Great," Baker says. He has no idea if this is great or not, but his mother seems buoyed by the news. "I'm happy to meet Maia tomorrow. But I'm flying back to Houston with Anna and Floyd on Friday."

Irene nods. "That's the right thing to do."

It *is* the right thing to do, Baker tells himself. No matter how much it feels like just the opposite.

PART THREE

Love City

MAIA

"What's a love child?" Maia asks.

Ayers hits the brakes and they both jolt forward in the seats. She reaches an arm across Maia.

"Sorry, Nut," Ayers says. "That just surprised me. Why are you asking?" She seems halfway between horrified and amused. This is one thing Maia has noticed about adults: they never feel just *one* way. Kids, on the other hand, are simpler: they're angry, they're sad, they're bored. When they're angry, they yell; when they're sad, they cry; when they're bored, they act out or play on their phones.

"I overheard someone say it, and I think they were talking about me."

"Who?" Ayers says. "Who said that?"

Maia doesn't want to get anyone in trouble. It was Colton Seeley's dad. He was talking to Bright Whittaker's father in the parking lot of Gifft Hill and he said something about the "love child of Love City," and Maia had felt that the words were aimed at her. "Just tell me what it means, please."

"It means what you'd think it means," Ayers says. "A child conceived in love."

"But does it have a negative connotation?" Maia asks.

Ayers laughs. "You know what's scary? How precocious you are."

"Tell me."

"Well," Ayers says. "I think it's often used to describe a child whose parents aren't married. So, way back in the olden days, having children was seen as a biological function to propagate the species. People got married and had children so that mankind survived. Whereas a love child is special. Its only reason for being is love."

"And so that's what I am?" Maia asks. "A love child? Because my parents weren't married?"

"I've got news for you, chica. My parents aren't married, either."

"They're *not*?" Maia says.

"Nope. They've been together a long, long time, thirty-five years, but they never got officially married. And guess what? I never think about it. Nobody cares."

Maia loves that she is still learning new things about Ayers. Ayers is *interesting*—and Maia's greatest desire when she grows up is to be interesting as well. She knows that to become interesting, she must read, travel, and learn new things. Maia is pretty much stuck on St. John for the time being, but she does love to read and she watches a fair amount of YouTube, which is how she and Joanie learned to make bath bombs.

"So if you and Mick had a baby, it would be a love child?" Maia asks.

"If Mick and I had a baby, it would be a grave error in judgment," Ayers says, and she turns in to Scoops. "I'm getting the salted peanut butter. What are you getting?"

"Guava," Maia says. Before she gets out of the truck, she notes that she must be growing up, because she feels two distinct emotions at this moment: She is happy to be getting her favorite ice cream with Ayers. She loves Ayers. And she feels empty—like if someone did surgery and cut her open, they would find nothing inside her but sad, stale air. Her mother is dead.

Maia's mother, Rosie, is dead. Some days, Maia can't accept this truth, and so she pretends her mother is on a trip, maybe the trip to the States that Russ was always promising but which never came to fruition. Or, she pretends that Rosie and Russ made it to Anegada, have gotten a beachfront tent at the Anegada Beach Club, and are so taken with the flat white sands, the pink flamingos, and the endless supply of fresh lobster that they have simply decided to stay another week.

Other times, reality is dark and terrifying, like the worst bad dream you can imagine, only you can't wake yourself up. Rosie is gone forever. Never coming back.

Lots of people offered their support—Huck, obviously, and Ayers. Also Joanie's parents, especially her mom, Julie. Julie pulled Maia aside to talk to her alone.

"I lost my mother when I was twelve," she said. "She died of a brain hemorrhage while she was asleep. So as with Rosie, there was no warning."

Not knowing what to say, Maia just nodded. The no-warning part was important. No-warning was the worst. LeeAnn had died, but she had been very sick, and they'd all had time to prepare. They said good-bye. LeeAnn knew they all loved her.

Maia worries: Did Rosie know how much Maia loved her? Did she know she was the start and end of everything for Maia? Did she know she was Maia's role model?

Julie continued. "It's going to be hard for the rest of your life, but it'll also define who you are. You're a survivor, Maia."

There have been plenty of moments when Maia hasn't felt like a survivor. There have been moments when she wished she'd gone down in the bird with her mother, because how is Maia supposed to go through *the rest of her entire life* without Rosie? It feels impossible.

"But it'll get easier, right?" Maia said. Other people had reassured her that the nearly unbearable pain Maia was feeling now—worse than a side stitch, more torturous than a loose molar—would mellow with time. Maia repeated that word, *mellow.*

"Yes, it'll get easier," Julie said. "But certain days will be more difficult than others. Mother's Day is always tough for me. And when Joanie was born"—here Julie welled up with tears, and Maia wanted to reach out and hug her—"...when I had Joanie, I wanted my mom. I wanted her to see her granddaughter. I wanted her to tell me what to do." Julie had then taken a deep breath and recovered. "What helped me was looking outward, and thinking about the other people who missed my mom. You're mature enough for me to suggest that you keep an eye on Huck and Ayers, because they're hurting, too, and they're trying to stay strong for you. But you have something they don't. You have your mother inside of you, half her genes, and as you get older, you'll likely become more and more like your mother, and that will bring people comfort. It'll be like getting Rosie back, in a way."

Maia liked that idea enormously. Her mother was alive inside of her. Maia was her own person, but she was also a continuation of Rosie.

"But don't put pressure on yourself to be perfect in order

to make your mother proud," Julie said. She lifted Maia's chin and gave her a very nice smile. "I assure you, Maia Small, your mother was proud of you every single second of every single day, just for being you."

Maia has never been religious, but now it's helpful to imagine her mother and her grandmother in the sky, in a place Maia thinks of as heaven, where they lie back on chaise longues, like the ones they used to relax in on Gibney Beach. Maia's grandmother, LeeAnn, was friends with Mrs. Gibney, and she was allowed to sit in the shade in front of the Gibney cottages whenever she wanted.

"I hope heaven looks like this," LeeAnn used to say. White sand, flat, clear turquoise water, the hill of Hawksnest and Carval Rock in the distance.

When Maia can keep her mother and grandmother in those chaises in the sky, watching over her, cheering her on, keeping her safe, then she can move—nearly seamlessly—through her days.

She tries to remember her mother in full, fleshy detail, because one of the things she has heard is that once people die, they fade from memory and become more of an idea than a person. Maia and her mother were so connected, so attached, that Maia can't imagine forgetting her, but she replays certain moments and images again and again, just in case.

Her mother was beautiful—short, trim, perfectly proportioned. She had cocoa skin, darker than Maia's, and a flash of orange in her brown eyes, which caused people to stare. Her eyes were *arresting*, Russ said once, meaning they made you stop. Maia didn't inherit the orange; her eyes are regular dark brown like her grandmother's. LeeAnn claimed the orange was a Small trait—it meant fire, and the fire meant trouble.

Rosie worked four evenings a week at La Tapa. She was a great server, the kind returning guests requested when they called to make their reservations. Having dinner at La Tapa wasn't enough of a tradition; they had to have dinner at La Tapa with Rosie as their server—otherwise their trip wasn't complete. Rosie knew a lot about wine and even more about food, and she liked to hang out with the kitchen crew to see how they prepared things. Rosie was a really, really good cook, and at home she made mostly Caribbean food, recipes she had learned from LeeAnn and that LeeAnn had learned from *her* mother—conch stew, jerk chicken, Creole shrimp over rice. She put peas in her pasta salad and raisins in her coleslaw just like everyone else in St. John, but Rosie's versions of these dishes were better because she added a teaspoon of sugar.

Maia is old enough to wonder if her mother had aspirations. She sometimes talked about opening a food truck, but she thought it would be too much work. More than anything in the world, Maia knows, her mother had been passionate about the Virgin Islands—the USVI and the BVI—and when she was working at La Tapa, she was always giving people at her tables excellent tips, such as go to the floating bar, Angel's Rest, in the East End; don't miss the lobster at the Lime Inn; there's yoga on the beach at Cinnamon and a really cool church service on the beach at Hawksnest. She could have been a tour guide, Maia thinks, or a yoga instructor, or owned a food truck, but Rosie had lacked ambition, whereas Maia has ambition to spare. She will need two or three lifetimes to reach all of her goals. Maia doesn't like to think badly about her mother, though, so instead of believing her mother *lacked* something, she has decided to categorize her mother as content. She was so happy with her life—in love with Russ, absorbed with Maia, good at her job, and living in a place she adored, with friends everywhere she turned—that she had no reason to make any changes.

Maia tells Huck about her plan for a memorial ceremony out on the water, in the place the bird went down, and he agrees, as she knew he would. Huck has always been Maia's favorite. Her mother and grandmother loved her because they had to. Huck loves her because he wants to.

Originally, she was only going to honor Rosie, but at the last minute, she chose a bath bomb for Russ as well.

Maia's feelings about Russ are mixed. She first remembers him as the man with the lollipops—flat, oval Charms pops, strawberry, Maia's favorite. Then Maia remembers him teaching her to swim at their private beach. Then, when she was nine, he let her decorate her room in his house however she wanted. But there was a part of Russ that made Maia uneasy. He didn't stay on St. John; he came and went. When he came, Maia's mother was happy—ecstatic, even. Impossible to bring down! And when Russ left, Rosie was devastated. It broke her every time, she said, and the leaving, the worrying that he would never be back, never got any easier.

Normally when he came, Rosie and Maia went to his villa. They swam in the pool or at the beach, they ate at the house— food Mama fixed or that Miss Paulette dropped off from different restaurants. Russ liked the lobster tempura from Rhumb

Lines and the key lime chiffon pie from Morgan's Mango. They read books and watched movies and played shuffle-board. But they didn't go anywhere, and once they returned to their own lives, to the house where they lived with Huck, Maia wasn't allowed to talk about Russ or the villa at all. She had heard Huck and other people refer to Russ as the Invisible Man, and it did sometimes seem to Maia that Russ only existed for Rosie and Maia. It was as if they and Miss Paulette and her husband, Douglas, and the man who came to do the landscaping and service the pool, were the only people who could see him. Maia wondered how Russ got on and off the island. Did he take the ferry, like everyone else? It seemed inconceivable. Maia had asked her mother, and Rosie had said, "Sometimes he takes the ferry, yes. Sometimes he flies in a helicopter. Sometimes his business associates pick him up by boat down on the beach." The helicopter and the private boat sounded reasonable; Maia could not imagine Russ waiting in line at the ferry dock, or sitting on the top deck, the way Maia liked to, or disembarking in Red Hook. She thought Rosie was trying to make Russ seem like a normal person, when it was quite obvious to Maia that he was not.

When Maia got older and had friends and activities and plans of her own, she started opting to stay at Huck's when Russ came. But she still wasn't allowed to talk about him or the villa, or the location of the villa.

I deserve privacy in one area of my life, Rosie would say. *I don't need every damn person all up in my business. And you know that is what would happen.*

Maia *did* know. If the citizens of St. John found out about the huge villa overlooking Little Cinnamon, they would treat

Rosie differently; they would ask for favors and loans—especially Rosie's Small relatives.

Love is messy and complicated and unfair, Rosie would say—but only on the days that Russ left.

The last time Maia saw her mother was midday, New Year's Eve. Rosie had come home from Russ's villa, where she had been staying for the past few days, solely to give Maia "the last kiss of the year." Rosie looked supremely gorgeous, like a goddess, in a new cream-colored sundress (Christmas present from Russ) and a new leather and black pearl choker (ditto). Seeing these gifts made Maia check out her mother's left hand, but it was still unadorned, which Maia knew meant that, deep down inside, her mother was disappointed. What Rosie wanted from Russ, more than anything, was an engagement ring.

Maia and Joanie hunkered down in Maia's room, making a list of tropical scents for their nascent bath bomb business. They were also talking about a boy in their class, Colton Seeley, because Joanie was obsessed with him. Joanie had been snapchatting with Colton, using Maia's phone. Joanie's parents were strict and protective; they treated Joanie like she was six years old instead of twelve. Joanie had a *flip phone,* for phone calls only. It didn't even text.

When Rosie knocked and then entered Maia's room without waiting for a response, Maia made a noise of protest.

"What?" Rosie said. "You hiding something?"

"No," Maia said defensively. She had never hidden anything from her mother. There was no reason to: her mother was a very lenient and permissive parent. But Maia didn't want to give away Joanie's secret. Joanie only pursued her crush on Colton while she was in the free world that was Maia's house.

But Joanie seemed eager to tell the truth. "I'm snapchatting with Colton Seeley," she said. "He's so hot."

"Colton *Seeley*?" Rosie said. "I've known that child since he was in his mama's belly. Let me see what's so hot."

Rosie sat on the bed between them and inspected picture after picture of Colton while both Maia and Joanie snuggled up against her. Maia was happy that Joanie felt comfortable admitting her crush to Rosie and proud of Rosie for being the kind of cool mom that her friends could confide in. For those few moments on the bed, Maia's world was golden.

Then Rosie stood up. She told the girls she was going to "the villa," shorthand for Russ's house, and that she was headed to Anegada the next day. So she was there to give Maia the last kiss of the year.

"What if *we* want to come to Anegada?" Maia asked. She knew she was pressing at a boundary by asking, because Russ didn't socialize with anyone, not even Joanie. But Maia thought maybe this year would be different.

"Sorry, Nut," Rosie said. "We're taking a helicopter." Rosie had caressed Maia's cheeks and kissed her flush on the lips. "I love you and I'll be back late tomorrow night. Happy New Year." Then she turned to Joanie. "You're right, Joan, Colton Seeley is a hottie in the making. Bye, girls. Be good."

Joanie had fallen back on the bed, returning to her rapture over Colton. She didn't see Rosie peek her head back in the room to mouth to Maia, *I love you, Nut.*

Love you, mama, Maia mouthed back.

Rosie blew a kiss and was gone.

* * *

When Huck tells Maia, as they're bobbing out on the water that claimed Rosie, that Russ had a wife and other children, sons, Maia is stunned breathless, but on the other hand it feels like Huck is telling Maia something she had already guessed. All Rosie had wanted was an engagement ring. But Russ was already married.

"They want to meet you," Huck says.

Maia has an adult moment: she wants to meet them because she's curious. At the same time, she doesn't want to meet them because she's scared.

In the end, she decides to meet them. Otherwise, she'll always wonder. But she has a couple of conditions. She wants Huck there, obviously, but she also wants Ayers there.

"This may be putting Ayers out of her depths," Huck says.

"I need her," Maia says. "The two of you are my squad."

"Joanie is your squad," Huck says. "But you would never invite Joanie, because she's not family."

Maia considers this for a moment. When she tells Joanie that this is happening—she's meeting her father's wife and his sons, who are, in fact, Maia's half brothers—Joanie will be fiendishly jealous. A secret in Joanie's family is that her father, Jeff, occasionally goes to Greengo's in Mongoose Junction for carnitas tacos. Joanie has to whisper *carnitas tacos* so Julie doesn't overhear.

My father is only pretending to be vegan, Joanie said.

"Ayers is family," Maia declares. "I need her there."

"I'll ask her," Huck says, but he still seems uneasy.

"*I'll* ask her," Maia says with a martyr's air. She sends Ayers a long text, the gist of which is that it has been revealed that Russ (the Invisible Man) has a wife and two sons and they just found out about Maia and want to meet her, and Maia would like Huck and Ayers to go with her tomorrow after school.

Kind of like a king needs tasters, Maia says. She's proud of herself because she just learned about this courtly detail that very morning—the tasters sampled the king's food to make sure it wasn't poisoned—and now she is applying it to her own life. *Only you won't die.*

I have work at four, Ayers texts back initially. But then, a few seconds later, she says: *I switched nights with Tilda. Ask Huck to pick me up at home.*

Yay! Maia responds. *TYVM!* She's relieved Ayers is going, but she also feels guilty that she has to miss work. Having adult feelings is exhausting, she realizes.

Driving to the villa the next day, Maia is petrified. She's shaking, a phenomenon she has never experienced before but that is beyond her control. She holds her hand out, palm facing down, and tries to steady it—but to no avail.

"Do you want me to turn around?" Huck asks.

"No," Maia says with more certainty than she feels. She won't back away from something because she's afraid of it.

"If it makes you feel any better, I'm nervous, too," Ayers says.

"And me," Huck says.

What is Maia afraid of, exactly? Last night, on the phone,

Joanie helped Maia break it down. They were taught in school that fear often derives from ignorance. Once you understand a situation, it becomes far less intimidating.

"What's the worst that could happen?" Joanie asks. "They aren't going to *hurt* you."

Maia had written a list:

1. They're mean.
2. Awkward silence.
3. They don't like me.
4. They will say unkind things about Rosie. They will call Rosie names. They will say the crash was Rosie's fault.

Bingo: It's the last one. Maia can't bear to hear her mother maligned by people who didn't even know her. And yet that's also why Maia has to go. Someone has to defend Rosie's honor.

Huck makes the turn—he knows where it is without Maia even telling him—and they crawl up the hill.

"Come on, chipmunks," Huck says, but his heart isn't in it, Maia can tell. He would probably be okay with the chipmunks quitting altogether.

Finally, they pull into the driveway. The gate has been propped open; that never happened when Russ was here. Of course, the people Russ was hiding from are now inside the house.

Maia takes a deep breath. Ayers is squeezing her hand. "You're okay," Ayers says. "You've got this."

When Maia climbs out of the truck, the enormity of what

is about to happen strikes her. She runs over to the bougainvillea bordering the driveway and throws up her lunch—fish sandwich. Huck hands her a bottle of water from the fishing trip supply he keeps in the back of the truck.

Tomorrow, she'll tell Huck she's becoming a vegan. She'll accept only peanut butter and jelly for the rest of the year.

That decision made, they ascend the stone staircase.

Before they enter the house, Ayers takes in the view. "It's so weird," she says. "This is Little Cinnamon, or close. The house has this view and yet you can't see it from the road."

"Only from the water," Huck says. "I'm sure that was by design." He strides right up to the slider, knocks on the glass, and opens the door. "Hello!" he says. "We're here."

There are three people sitting at Russ's kitchen table—a woman and two men. When Maia, Huck, and Ayers walk in, they all stand.

One of the men, the really tall, good-looking one, says, "Ayers?"

"Here we are," Huck says. He strides over to the men and offers a hand. "Captain Huck Powers."

"Baker Steele," the tall one says.

Baker: Maia has heard this name before. Then it clicks. Baker is the tourist, Ayers's tourist.

"Cash Steele," the other man says. He's shorter, with a head of bushy blond hair like a California surfer. His face is sunburned, which makes his eyes look fiercely blue.

"This is our friend Ayers Wilson," Huck says. "And this is Maia."

The woman steps forward and offers Maia her hand. "I'm Irene," she says. "It's nice to meet you, Maia. You're even prettier than the pictures your grandfather showed me."

"Oh," Maia says. "Thanks." She gives Irene her firmest grip and manages to look her in the eye. She's old, Maia thinks, way older than Rosie. She's pretty, though in a mom/grandma kind of way. Her hair is reddish-brown and styled in a braid. She's wearing a green linen sundress, no shoes.

Baker looks at Ayers. "I didn't realize you'd be coming."

"Last-minute decision," Ayers says.

Irene says, "Do you two know each other?"

The other brother speaks up. Cash. Cool name, Maia thinks. She loves last-names-as-first-names and has long wished her name, instead of Maia, was Rainseford. Or Gage. Maia is boring and soft.

"Baker and I met Ayers when we went to dinner in town," Cash says. "She works at La Tapa."

"Guilty as charged," Ayers says, but her tone sounds forced.

Did Ayers know the tourist was Russ's son? Maia wonders. Her mind goes one crazy step further: If Ayers and the tourist get married, Ayers will be Maia's half sister-in-law!

This thought serves as a distraction from Maia's prevailing emotion, which is one of bewilderment. This is the kitchen of the villa, in some sense Maia's kitchen, or at least a kitchen where she has spent a lot of time—and maybe as much or more time pretending it didn't exist. If she opens the cabinet on the far left, she knows that she will find half a dozen cans of SpaghettiOs, which Maia loves but which Huck doesn't allow at home because he had to eat them cold out of the can in Vietnam. Now, Maia is here with Huck. And Ayers. If Rosie is watching from her beach chaise in heaven, she is very, very upset. Maia is suffused with a sense of disloyalty. She's betraying her mother—and her father—by being here.

But maybe not. Maybe Russ, anyway, is happy his two families are finally meeting each other. Maybe this was supposed to happen.

Maia studies the three strangers, and she can tell they are studying her.

What do they think? she wonders.

IRENE

The girl is beautiful and she has a grace you can't discern from a picture. She is light-skinned, her hair gathered in a frizzy ponytail. She has brown eyes, but her nose and smile are all Russ, and more than Russ, they're Milly. Looking at Maia is like looking at Milly at age twelve, if Milly were half West Indian.

Irene needs to get a grip, offer everyone a drink and put out some snacks, but she is hobbled by thoughts of Milly. When she goes home—which will be very soon, maybe as soon as the weekend—she will go to see Milly. That morning, she decided that she needs to tell Milly the truth: Russ is dead, Russ had a home and a second family down in the Caribbean. Irene lectured the boys about not keeping secrets, and she can't be hypocritical. Milly needs to know. Milly needs to know, too, that she has a granddaughter who so strongly resembles her.

"What would you like to drink?" Irene asks Maia.

"Ginger ale, please, if you have one," Maia says, and she places a hand on her stomach. "I'm feeling a little green."

Poor thing, Irene thinks as she pulls a ginger ale out of the fridge. This defines what it feels like to be thrown for a loop.

Winnie saunters into the kitchen, wagging her tail. She heads straight for Ayers, who bends down to rub Winnie under the chin. Irene isn't quite sure who Ayers is or why she's here. She's a friend of Rosie's, maybe? If so, she may have some of the answers Irene is looking for.

Cash says to Ayers, "You've never been to this house before?"

"Never," Ayers says. "I didn't even know where it was."

"I'd never been here before, either," Huck says. "Until the other night, when Irene invited me for dinner."

"Really?" Baker says. "Didn't either of you wonder...?"

"You've been here before, right, Maia?" Irene asks. She catches a warning look from Huck. He told her that under no circumstances was she to grill the child.

"Yep," Maia says. "I have my own bedroom here, upstairs at the end of the hall."

Irene knows she's pushing her luck but she has to ask. "Do you have any idea what Russ did for a living? Who he worked for or what kind of business he was in?"

"Not really," Maia says. "Money or something. All I know is he was away a lot."

This last statement makes Irene laugh, but not in a funny ha-ha way. "You mean he was home a lot."

Maia blinks, uncomprehending.

"At home in Iowa City," Irene says. "With me. His wife. Us, his family..." She nearly says *his real family*, but she stops herself. She will not vent her anger at the girl. The girl is innocent.

She wants to ask, *Did your mother know about me?* Did she know about the woman she was betraying? Did she know about Baker and Cash, Anna and Floyd? Did. She. Know. Irene realizes she can't ask; Huck will whisk Maia out of here faster than you can say Jiminy Cricket.

However, Maia is intuitive.

"My mother used to tell me that love was messy, complicated, and unfair."

"Well," Irene says. "She was right about that."

"Amen," Baker says.

"Amen," Ayers says.

"Amen," Cash says.

Winnie stands at the sliding door and barks.

AYERS

Thank God for dogs, she thinks. No matter how tense a situation humans find themselves in—and the situation in the kitchen of the Invisible Man's villa, with his decidedly visible wife and his *sons,* Baker and Cash, is an eleven out of ten on the stress scale—a dog lightens the mood.

When Winnie enters the kitchen, she comes right over and buries her nose in Ayers's crotch, her tail going haywire.

Everyone is trying to act normal, to pretend this visit isn't completely messed up. Irene says she'd like to talk to Huck and Maia alone, and Baker takes the opportunity to invite Ayers outside. Cash follows with Winnie.

"Go away," Baker says to him. "Please."

"Cash can stay," Ayers says. "I'd actually like to talk to you both."

They wander over to the pool. There's a shallow entry where they can all sit with their feet in the water. Winnie lies down between Ayers and Cash, and Ayers strokes her head.

"Let me start," Baker says. "I owe you an apology."

"Stop," Ayers says. She marvels that her parents took her to the rice paddies of Vietnam, the red desert of the Australian outback, and the snow-capped peaks of the Swiss Alps, all with the aim of making her "worldly," and still she has no idea how to negotiate this emotional landscape.

"Ayers is talking now, Baker," Cash says. "Respect."

"Thank you," Ayers says. She bows her head and smells Mick's scent on her clothes. When she'd gotten off the phone with Cash the afternoon before—*You really shouldn't be interested in either of us*—she had flipped out. She had been blindsided. But once that piece clicked, everything else made sense.

Baker and Cash came to Rosie's memorial lunch on purpose—because they wanted to gather intel on the woman their father was keeping on the side.

Even saying that phrase in her head fills Ayers with fury. Rosie was nothing more to Russell Steele than a side piece, a baby mama, an island wife. What can she think but that Russell Steele was a despicable human being? And yet she has to be careful, because he was Maia's biological father. The Invisible Man was also the Pirate, which is sort of like finding out that Santa Claus is the Tooth Fairy.

"You're both liars," Ayers says. "Like your father."

Cash holds up his palms as if to protest his guilt, and Ayers pounces. "Neither of you told me who you were at the memorial reception. You let me believe you were crashing."

"We *were* crashing," Baker says.

"And then I bumped into *you* on the Reef Bay Trail," Ayers says to Cash. "Did you *follow* me there?"

"*Follow* you?" Cash says. "No, that was a coincidence."

Ayers narrows her eyes.

"I swear," Cash says. "I've never been here before, I'm an outdoors person, I wanted to get out of the house, *see* something, take Winnie for a walk. Bumping into you was totally random. How could I possibly have followed you?"

Fair enough, Ayers thinks. Maybe it was just really terrible luck. "But you came on *Treasure Island* because you wanted to ask me questions about Rosie. Admit it."

"I came on *Treasure Island* because I wanted to see *you*," Cash says. "Because I thought you were pretty—scratch that, I thought you were *beautiful,* and I thought you were cool. And you invited me."

"Sheesh," Baker says.

"And you!" Ayers says. "You were so much worse."

"I admit, we went to the reception to do some detective work," Baker says. "But when I saw you, Ayers…I could barely remember my own name. It was love at first sight."

"You *used* me," Ayers says. The sun is directly in her eyes so she squints, which suits her mood. "You say you like me, you say you love me, but both of you lied to me about who you were or weren't. And the thing is...I *knew* something wasn't right. I *knew* it." She drops her voice. "I never met your father, but he spent years lying to my best friend. All I can think is not only did he have no scruples, he had no soul."

"Whoa," Baker says.

"She's right," Cash says. "I offer no excuses for my father. None."

Ayers wants to land one more punch. "The two of you are just like him. You're sneaky."

"I called you and told you the truth," Cash says.

"You did not," Baker says. "I did."

"You did?" Cash says. "I did, too."

"Too little, way too late," Ayers says. She never wants to see either of them again, and this really hurts because she liked them both. She's also worried that she'll never be rid of them now because *they're Maia's brothers.* "It doesn't matter, anyway. I'm back together with Mick."

"No," Baker says.

"Yes," Ayers says. "I was with him last night."

She relishes saying this, even though a part of her is ashamed about taking Mick back so readily. She called him, and he was at her house half an hour later with an order of oxtail stew from De' Coal Pot, plus a side of pineapple rice, plus one perfect red hibiscus blossom, which he stuck in a juice glass. He'd begged her for another chance. He'd made a mistake and it would never happen again.

Ayers had succumbed, even though she knew it *would* happen again—just as soon as he hired the next girl who looked like Brigid. But unlike these two, Mick was a known quantity. And he lived here.

Tourists, she thinks, are nothing but heartbreak.

CASH

The bad news is, he can't have Ayers.

The good news is, Baker can't have her, either.

She hates them both.

It's a knockout punch, but Cash admires Ayers's principles. He would hate them, too, if he were her.

They leave the pool and head back to the kitchen, where Irene, Huck, and Maia are sitting at the table in silence. It feels like they've interrupted something, or maybe they came in on the tail end of a conversation.

Huck stands. "We should probably go."

"But wait," Irene says. "The ashes."

"I'm leaving," Ayers says. "I'll walk to the bottom of the hill and call my boyfriend to come pick me up."

"I'll drive you home," Huck says. He looks at Irene. "I'll run Ayers home and then I'll come back to pick up Maia. Forty minutes. Will that be enough time to do what you have to do?"

"Plenty," Irene says.

Cash, Baker, and Maia follow Irene down the eighty steps to the private beach. A few minutes later finds the children of Russell Steele, along with the wife he betrayed for thirteen years, tossing chunks and silt into the Caribbean. No one says anything. No one cries.

Irene saves a handful of ashes in the bag. "I'm taking these home for Russ's mother." She smiles at Maia. "Your grandmother. She's ninety-seven."

"Really?" Maia says.

"And you look just like her," Irene says.

Cash has tried not to study Maia's face too carefully—he doesn't want to make her uncomfortable or self-conscious—but he agrees with Irene: there is something about Maia that strongly resembles Milly.

He replays Ayers's words in his head. *I never met your father, but he spent years lying to my best friend. All I can think is not only did he have no scruples, he had no soul.*

Cash feels that's too harsh. He wants to think that Russ was more than just what happened down here. Russ had spent years and years providing for their family in a job he disliked, and he had always been an involved, enthusiastic father. When Cash was little, Russ would hold on to his hands, let Cash walk up his legs, and then flip him over in a skin-the-cat. Two years ago, Russ had handed Cash the keys to two prime pieces of Denver real estate. He hadn't objected to the name Savage Season Outdoor Supply; he had even come to Denver for the ribbon cuttings. He had believed in Cash more than Cash had believed in himself.

And yet there's no denying that Russ made a terrific mess of things. The money for those stores had come from . . . where?

Cash is the first one back up the stairs.

He may feel differently at some point, but for now, he's glad to be rid of the man.

HUCK

When Huck and Maia are alone with Irene, she says, "I want to talk about money."

"Maybe you and I should have that talk privately," Huck says.

Irene ignores this suggestion. "I'm guessing Russ probably gave Rosie support," she says. "And I just want you to know that I want to continue. Do you go to private school?"

Maia nods. "Gifft Hill."

"And do you want to go to college?" Irene asks.

"Of course!" Maia says. "My first choice is NYU and my second choice is Stanford. I'm interested in microlending. That's where you lend a small amount of money to help people get local businesses started. I want to help Caribbean women."

"Well," Irene says.

"I'm an entrepreneur," Maia says. "My friend Joanie and I started a bath bomb business. They're six dollars apiece, if you'd like to buy one."

"I'd like to buy several," Irene says.

"Let's keep the transactions simple, like that," Huck says. "I'm perfectly capable of supporting Maia and sending her to college."

"Of course," Irene says. "I didn't mean to offend you."

"Not offended," Huck says, though he is, a little. The emotional terrain here is difficult enough without bringing up money, although he understands that Irene is trying to provide reassurance: She isn't a witch, she isn't vindictive. Maia will continue to have what she needs.

"I don't want to impose myself on your life," Irene says.

"But I wanted to meet you, as strange or unconventional as that choice might have been. I want to stay in your life, as little or as much as you want me. Maybe I leave here on Friday and I don't see you again until you're on your way to NYU or Stanford. But I want you to know I'm here, and if you ever need anything, I want you to be comfortable asking me. I would be *honored* if you asked."

"Thank you," Maia says.

"You're leaving Friday?" Huck says.

"I am," Irene says. "The boys and I will spread most of the ashes today and Maia, I hope you'll join us, but then I need to get back."

"What are you going to do about the house?" Huck asks.

"Nothing, for the time being," Irene says. "I have a lot of decisions in front of me, but, thankfully, they don't have to be made today." She reaches over to squeeze Maia's hand. "I am so glad you came today, Maia. You are a very special person."

"Thank you," Maia says. "I try."

Irene laughs then, for real, and she says to Huck, "You have your hands full with this one."

"Wouldn't have it any other way," Huck says.

Their conversation must have been far more pleasant than the one going on outside, because Ayers, Baker, and Cash walk into the kitchen looking like three kids whose sandcastle just washed away.

Huck offers to give Ayers a ride home so that Maia can scatter the Invisible Man's ashes with Irene and her brothers.

Irene and her brothers. Huck wonders how long it will be until he gets used to the way things are now.

When they reach the north shore road, Huck turns to Ayers. "You okay?"

"I guess," Ayers says.

"I'm sorry if that was awkward for you," Huck says. "Maia really wanted you there."

"I met both the boys this past week," Ayers says. "I went on a date or two with Baker."

"Is he the tourist Maia was telling me about?" Huck says.

"He's the tourist," Ayers confirms. "I knew better, but I fell for him anyway. And he's leaving tomorrow."

"Irene is leaving Friday," Huck says, and he realizes he sounds wistful.

"I guess it would be easier if we didn't like them so much," Ayers says.

Huck nearly clarifies that he doesn't "like" Irene, at least not in the way Ayers is describing, but then he thinks, *Why lie?*

"I've decided to get a tattoo of the petroglyphs," Ayers announces.

"One like Rosie had?" Huck asks. Rosie's tattoo, which she got without permission when she was fifteen — before Huck came on the scene, he would like to point out — was just above her left ankle.

"Yes," Ayers says. "I used to think I didn't deserve one because I didn't grow up here, I don't have family here..."

"You loved someone deeply here," Huck says. "And you lost her. I think that makes this home for you."

"Thank you for saying that." Ayers is openly weeping. "Would you come with me when I get it?"

"I would be honored," Huck says.

IRENE

She sits in the same spot on the plane home, next to Cash, with a scant cup of Russ's ashes in her purse. She has been in the Virgin Islands for seven days and eight nights. She knows more now than she did when she arrived, although far from everything she needs to know. When she gets home, she has to call Ed Sorley, her attorney. She has to let everyone know that Russ is dead. She has to hire a forensic accountant and, most likely, a private investigator.

The Virgin Islands used to be rife with pirates, or at least the lore of those charming swashbucklers, with their skulls and crossbones and their hidden treasure. An aura of lawlessness still pervades the islands: that much Irene has learned. It's as if the sun has melted away the rules, and the stunning beauty of the water and the islands has dazzled everyone into bliss. The soundtrack says it all: "The Weather Is Here," "You and Tequila," "One Love."

Before she left, Huck had insisted on taking Irene out on *The Mississippi* again. She knew he had most likely canceled a charter in order to do so. He said he wanted to give her a proper island good-bye.

If I do a good job, you might even find you like it here, he said.

There wasn't enough time to fish, because Huck had to pick Maia up from school at three, so instead, Huck gave Irene a round-the-island tour. They puttered out of Cruz Bay harbor and headed northeast. Huck pointed out each beach and provided a running commentary.

"First on your right are Salomon and Honeymoon. You'd think Honeymoon would be the nude beach, but you'd be wrong. Salomon is nude, and Honeymoon has water sports."

Irene couldn't help herself: She squinted in the direction of Salomon, but it was deserted.

"There's Caneel Bay, the resort. If we had more time, we could dock and go in for a bottle of champagne."

"You don't seem like much of a champagne drinker," Irene said.

"True," Huck said. They rounded the point. "On the right is Hawksnest, popular with the locals, although I wouldn't be caught dead there, and on the left is Oppenheimer, named after Robert Oppenheimer, father of the atomic bomb. He used to own the land. Coming up is Denis Bay, below Peace Hill. My first mate, Adam, calls it 'Piece of Ass' beach."

Irene shook her head and smiled.

"There's Trunk Bay, our pageant winner, followed by Peter Bay, where all those fancy homes are…and now we are approaching…Little Cinnamon."

"Little Cinnamon?" Irene said. "Where's the house?"

Huck had to cut the engine and pull out his binoculars. He studied the hillside for a moment. "There. The outside of the house is meant to blend in with the surrounding bush, but if you look closely and hold the glasses exactly where I have them, you'll see it."

Irene accepted the binoculars. She had a hard time finding anything resembling a house, but then she picked out the curve of the upper stone deck. A man and a dog were outside: Cash and Winnie.

They proceeded past Cinnamon to Maho and went around Mary's Point to Waterlemon Cay ("great snorkeling—we'll have to do that the next time you come") and Francis Bay ("buggy"), and all the way around the East End ("nothing out there but a great floating bar") to Coral Bay. They headed back along the south-facing beaches: Salt Pond ("guaranteed turtles"), Lameshur Bay, Reef Bay, Fish Bay. Irene followed their progress on the map. She was awed by the size of the island and by the homes she saw tucked into crevices and hanging from cliffs.

There were a lot of places to hide in St. John.

Huck guided the boat toward an island called Little St. James. "What do you like on your pizza?" he asked.

"My pizza?" Irene said.

He pointed a few hundred yards away to a sailboat flying a pizza flag. PIZZA PI, the sign said. As they got closer, Irene could see a menu hanging on the mast. It was a pizza boat in the middle of the Caribbean.

"Let's have a lobster pizza," she said. "Just because we can."

"Woman after my own heart," Huck said. "All the pizzas are made to order, but the lobster is my favorite." He dropped the anchor, shucked off his shirt, and swam over to place their order.

Irene vowed that if she ever came back, she would bring a bathing suit.

She and Huck devoured the entire pizza, then she lay back in the sun. She was about to doze off when she heard Huck start the engine.

"Are we leaving?" she asked. Her heart felt heavy at the thought.

"We have one more stop," Huck said.

He drove them due west, pointing out Water Island, "the

little-known fourth Virgin," and then he cut the engine, threw the anchor again, and fitted on a mask and snorkel.

"Back in a sec," he said.

Irene leaned over the side of the boat to watch his watery form shimmering beneath the surface. At one point he swam under the boat, and just as Irene started to wonder if she should be worried, though she couldn't picture Huck as the kind of man who would ever need to be rescued, he popped up.

"Got a beauty!" he said.

What kind of beauty? Irene wondered.

He climbed up the ladder on the back of the boat with a brilliant peach conch shell in his hand.

"Oh!" Irene said. The shell was perfect; it looked like something she would buy in a gift shop.

Huck brought out the cutting board that he used to fillet fish and pulled the live conch from the shell and sealed it in a clean plastic bag.

"Maia loves my conch fritters," he said. He then dropped the shell in a bucket of water and added bleach. "That'll be clean by the time we dock."

"You're giving the shell to Maia?" Irene asked. She thought how wonderful it must be to have a grandfather who produced surprise gifts from the sea.

"No," Huck said. "It's for you."

It turned out Huck was giving Irene more than just a conch shell. With a few flicks of his fillet knife, he transformed the shell into a horn. He held his lips up to the hole he'd just cut, wrapped his fingers into the glossy pink interior, and blew. The sound was far from lovely. It was low, sonorous, mournful. It was the sound of Irene's heart.

Huck handed Irene the shell. "Take this home," he said. "And when you need a friend, blow through it."

"You won't hear it, though," Irene said.

"No, but you'll hear it, and you'll remember that there's a tiny island in the Caribbean, and on that island you have a friend for life. Do you understand me, Angler Cupcake?"

Irene nodded. She forced herself to look into Huck's eyes and she thought back to her last innocent hour, ten days and another lifetime ago, when she was at the Prairie Lights bookstore and noticed Brandon the barista gazing at her dear friend Lydia. Huck was gazing at Irene now in much the same way. She wasn't an idea or an outline or a mere distraction from a younger, prettier woman.

Huck saw her.

He saw her.

When Irene and Cash land in Chicago, Irene sees she has three missed calls from the Brown Deer retirement community and one voicemail.

"Milly," Irene says to Cash.

She listens to the voicemail. It's from today. "Hi Irene, Dot from Brown Deer here. I'm not sure if you're still on vacation? But I needed to let you know that Milly has lost consciousness and Dr. Adler thinks it's likely she'll let go tonight." There's a pause; Irene can practically hear poor Dot trying to choose the right words. "I didn't want to have to deliver this news while you were away, but I also can't have you not knowing. Thanks, Irene, and I'm sorry. Call anytime."

* * *

It turns out that Milly Steele does not let go that night. She holds on until Monday morning. By Monday morning, Irene and Cash have unpacked, thrown their clothes in the laundry, and made it over to Brown Deer to take turns sitting with Milly in case there's a miracle and she wakes up.

Irene and Cash have also had time to talk. Cash confided that Baker had feelings for the woman, Ayers, who was such good friends with Rosie, but that Cash liked her, too.

"Women always pick Baker over me," Cash says.

Irene shakes her head. "Baker isn't a free man yet, and you are. You are every bit as handsome and charming as your brother." Irene brightens. "If I remember correctly, Ayers seemed quite fond of Winnie. I think you should pursue her." Irene doesn't offer any thoughts about how Cash might go about this when Ayers is on St. John and Cash is in the American Midwest.

It just so happens that both Cash and Irene are sitting at Milly's bedside on Monday morning. It has been an arduous overnight vigil and now the eerie breathing known as the death rattle has set in. It won't be long now.

Irene is relieved that she has been spared telling Milly the truth about her son.

Because there are no cell phones allowed in the medical unit and certainly none allowed in a room where a ninety-seven-year-old woman is trying to seamlessly transition to the next life, neither Irene nor Cash sees the calls come in from an unknown number with a 787 area code: San Juan, Puerto

Rico. The call to Irene's phone comes in at 8:24 a.m. The call to Cash's phone comes at 8:26 a.m.

Missed.

Milly passes away at two minutes past ten in the morning. Dot comes in to record the time of death.

"Life well-lived," she says.

Irene and Cash make the necessary arrangements. Milly's body will be cremated. Her ashes, along with what remains of Russ's ashes, will be buried together in the cemetery at the First Presbyterian church once the ground thaws in the spring.

"What do you want to do now?" Irene asks Cash.

"Honestly?" Cash says. "I want to go back."

Irene nods. She doesn't have to ask what he means by "back." She knows.

"Me too," she says.

At 8:27 on Monday morning, Baker is having breakfast at Snooze in Houston with his school wives: Wendy, Becky, Debbie, and Ellen. They had been very worried about him. Baker had been gone for over a week without warning and they had seen Dr. Anna Schaffer herself delivering Floyd to school *and picking him up.*

"I knew something was wrong," Debbie says. "I didn't want to pry, and Anna isn't approachable even if I *had* wanted to pry."

Baker told his friends that his father died and he'd taken a week with his mother and brother. That's why they're all at breakfast. They want to comfort him.

"Your mother lives in Iowa, doesn't she?" Becky asks. Becky is in HR and remembers every personal detail Baker has ever told her. "How'd you come back with a suntan?" She is also, like any good HR executive, naturally suspicious.

Baker can't begin to explain that his father was killed in a helicopter crash in the Caribbean, where he happened to own a fifteen-million-dollar villa, keep a mistress, and have a love child. Baker also can't say a word about the beautiful woman — body and soul — that he fell in love with during his week away.

He can, however, tell them the truth about Anna. They're going to find out sooner or later.

"I have more bad news," Baker says. "Anna announced that she's leaving me."

"Whaaaa?" Debbie says. "Just as you found out your father was dead?"

"She found someone else," Baker says. "Another doctor at the hospital." He waits a beat. "Louisa Rodriguez."

There is a collective gasp, then some shrieking, then a declaration from Ellen that this is, hands down, the best gossip of the entire school year. Baker gets so caught up talking with his friends that he misses the call that comes in to his phone from an unknown number, area code 787, San Juan, Puerto Rico, at 8:32 a.m.

At 8:34 a.m. on Monday, Huck is dropping Maia off at school. They're four minutes late, but better late than not at all, which was what Maia was lobbying for. She was tired, they both were, because they'd accompanied Ayers over to Red Hook in St. Thomas the evening before so that she could get her petroglyph tattoo.

The tattoo had taken longer than they'd anticipated, but it was a beauty—an exact replica of the petroglyphs of Reef Bay, left there by the Taino three thousand years ago.

"It's so *cool*," Maia said.

"Don't even think about it," Huck said. After the tattoo adventure, he'd treated both of them to dinner at Fish Tails, next to the ferry dock. Ayers had been a little subdued at dinner, as had Huck. He couldn't pinpoint the exact cause of his malaise. If it wasn't such a cockamamie notion, he would say he missed Irene. But how could he miss someone he'd only known a week? He wondered if Ayers was suffering from a similar affliction, if she missed either or both of Irene's sons. She *said* she was getting back together with Mick. However, she didn't sound too excited about it.

Noting their glum faces, Maia had reached out for each of them and said, "I want you guys to know I'm here for you if you ever need to talk."

She had sounded so earnest that both Huck and Ayers had been helpless to do anything but smile.

"What?" Maia said. "What?"

Maia is gathering her things—backpack, lunch, water bottle—when Huck's phone rings. It's an unknown number, 787, San Juan, Puerto Rico. It's probably Angela, the travel agent who sends Huck group charters, which is all well and good. He needs to get his head back into his business.

"Hello?" he says. He shoos Maia out of the truck; she's dawdling.

"Mr. Powers?" a woman's voice says. The voice is too young to be Angela's; she's a grandmother of fifteen and her voice is raspy from cigarettes and yelling. "Mr. Sam Powers?"

"Yes?"

"My name is Agent Colette Vasco, with the FBI, sir. I've just had a call from VISAR in the British Virgin Islands. They were investigating a helicopter crash on January first, a crash in which your daughter was one of the deceased?"

"Yes," Huck says. Reluctantly, Maia climbs out of the truck. She eyes him through the windshield as she walks to the front gate of the school.

"That investigation has been passed on to us," Agent Vasco says. "What was initially thought to be a weather-related incident now looks like it involved foul play."

"Foul play?" Huck asks.

"Yes, sir," Agent Vasco says. "Any chance you're available to answer a few questions about your daughter and her friend Russell Steele?"

Huck puts the window down. He needs air. He notices Maia standing at the entrance of the school, staring back at him. She senses something.

Huck sets the phone down on the passenger seat. Agent Colette Vasco can wait. Right now, Huck has to tend to his girl. He is her Unconditional. He is her No Matter What.

"See you at three!" he calls out. "I'll be right here, waiting."

ABOUT ELIN HILDERBRAND

Elin Hilderbrand is: the mother of three 3-sport athletes, an aspiring fashionista, a dedicated jogger, a world explorer, an enthusiastic foodie, and a grateful three-year breast cancer survivor. She has called Nantucket Island her home since 1994. *Winter in Paradise* is her twenty-second novel.

...AND *WHAT HAPPENS IN PARADISE*

Irene Steele is still recovering from the shock of her life: her loving husband, father to their grown sons and a successful businessman, was killed in a helicopter crash. But that wasn't Irene's only shattering news: he'd also been leading a double life on the island of St. John, where another woman loved him, too.

Now Irene and her sons are back on St. John, determined to learn the truth about the mysterious death—and life—of the man they thought they knew. Along the way, they're about to discover some surprising truths about their own lives, and their futures.

Lush with the tropical details, romance, and drama that made *Winter in Paradise* a national bestseller, *What Happens in Paradise* is another immensely satisfying page-turner from one of America's most beloved and engaging storytellers.

IRENE

She wakes up facedown on a beach. Someone is calling her name.

"Irene!"

She lifts her head and feels her cheek and lips dusted with sand so white and fine, it might be powdered sugar. Irene can sense impending clouds. As the sun disappears, it gains a white-hot intensity; it's like a laser cutting through her. The next instant she feels the lightest sprinkling of rain.

"Irene!"

She sits up. The beach is unfamiliar, but it's tropical—there's turquoise water before her, lush vegetation behind, a rooster and two hens strutting around. She must be back on St. John.

How did she get here?

"Irene!"

A man is calling her name. She can see a figure moving toward her. The rain starts to fall harder now, with intention; the tops of the palm trees sway. Irene dashes for the cover of the tree canopy and wishes for a towel to wrap around her naked body.

Naked?

That's right; she forgot to pack a swimsuit.

The man is growing closer, still calling her name. *"Irene! Irene!"* She doesn't want him to see her. She tries to cover up her nakedness by hunching over and crossing her arms strategically; it feels like an impossible yoga pose. She's shivering now. Her hair is wet; her braid hangs like a soggy rope down her back.

The man is waving his arms as if he's drowning. Irene scans the beach; someone else will have to help him because she certainly can't. But there's no one around, no boats on the horizon, and even the chickens are gone. There will be a confrontation, she supposes, so she needs to prepare. She studies the approaching figure.

Irene opens her mouth and tries to scream. Does she scream? If so, she can't hear herself.

It's Russ.

She wipes the rain out of her eyes. Russell Steele, her husband of thirty-five years, is slogging toward her through the wet sand, looking as though he has something urgent to tell her.

"Irene!"

He's close enough now for her to see him clearly—the silvering hair, the brown eyes. He has a suntan. He's had a constant tan since he started working for Todd Croft at Ascension, thirteen years ago. Their friends used to tease Russ about it, but Irene barely noticed, much less questioned it. He was on business in Florida and Texas; the tan seemed logical. She had chalked it up to lunch meetings at outdoor restaurants, endless rounds of golf. How many times had Russ told her he would be unreachable because he'd be playing golf with clients?

Now, of course, Irene knows better.

"Irene," he says. His voice frightens her; she digs her heels into the sand. Russ's white tuxedo shirt is so soaked that she can see the flesh tone of his skin beneath. His khaki pants are split up one leg. He looks like he's survived a shipwreck.

No, Irene thinks. *Not a shipwreck. A plane crash. A helicopter crash, that's it.*

"Russ?" she says. He's getting pummeled by rain, and Irene flashes back twenty years to a Little League game of Baker's that was suspended due to a violent midwestern thunderstorm. All the parents huddled in the dugout with the kids, but Russ, in a show of gallantry, ran out onto the field to collect the equipment. Another father, Steve Sonnet (Irene had always rather disliked Steve Sonnet), said, *Reckless of him, picking up those metal bats. He's going to get himself killed.*

There was another time she remembers Russ soaking wet, a wedding in Atlanta. The Dunns' daughter Maisy was marrying an executive at Delta Airlines. This was five or six years ago, back when Irene and Russ found themselves attending more weddings than they had even when they were young. The reception was held at Rhodes Hall, and when she and Russ emerged from the strobe-lit dance floor and martini bar, it was to a downpour. Again, Russ insisted on playing the hero by tenting his tuxedo jacket over his head and dashing across the parking lot to their rental car. When he'd pulled up to the entrance a few moments later, his shirt had been soaked through, just like this one is now.

"The storm," Russ says, "is coming."

Well, yes, Irene thinks. *That much is obvious.* It's a proper deluge now, and the darkest clouds are still moving toward them. "I thought you were dead," she says. "They told me..." She stops. She's speaking, but she can't hear herself. It's frustrating. "They told me you were dead."

"It will be a bad storm," Russ says. "Destructive."

"Where should we go?" Irene asks. She turns to face the trees. *Where do the chickens hide from the rain?* she wonders. Because she would like to hide there too.

At eight o'clock on the dot, Irene wakes Cash. He has started calling her Mother Alarm Clock.

"I had another dream," she says.

Cash props himself up on his elbows in bed. His blond hair is messy and he's growing a beard; he hasn't shaved since they left the island. Irene has put him in the grandest of her five guest rooms, the Excelsior suite, she calls it. It has dark, raised-panel walls with a decorative beveled edge at the chair rail and an enormous Eastlake bed with a fringed canopy. There's also a stained-glass transom window that Irene got for a steal at a tiny antiques shop in Solon, Iowa, and a silk Persian rug in burgundy and cream that Irene purchased from a licensed dealer in Chicago. (She'd thought Russ might veto a five-figure rug, but he told her to go ahead, get it, whatever made her happy.) Irene's favorite piece in the room is a wrought-iron washstand that holds a ceramic bowl edged in gold leaf; above it hangs a photograph of Russ's mother, Milly, as a young girl in Erie, Pennsylvania, in 1928. Irene remembers the joy and pride she'd felt in refurbishing this room—every room in the house, really—but at this instant, she can't understand why. The Victorian style seems so heavy, so overdone, so tragic.

Irene has abandoned the master bedroom; she will never be able to sleep there again. Since she returned from St. John, she's been using the smallest guest room, originally meant to be quarters for a governess. It's up on the third floor, across from the attic. The attic is crammed with the bargains Irene scored at flea markets but couldn't find a place for in the house along with all the furniture from their former home, since Russ refused to let her take it to Goodwill. Russ had remarked many times that he would have been just as happy staying in their modest ranch on Clover Street, and Irene had thought him crazy. Of course, that was before she realized that Russ had a second life elsewhere.

The governess's room had been all but neglected in the renovation. Irene had simply painted the walls sky blue and furnished it with a white daybed and a small Shaker dresser. Now she appreciates the room's simplicity and its isolation. She feels safe there—although she can't seem to hide from these dreams.

"Dad was alive?" Cash asks.

"Alive," Irene says. This is the third such dream she's had since returning from St. John. Irene and Cash and Irene's older son, Baker, all traveled down to the Virgin Islands upon receiving the news that Russ had been killed in a helicopter crash off the coast of Virgin Gorda. He had been flying from a private helipad on St. John to the remote British island Anegada with a West Indian woman named Rosie Small. Irene then discovered that Rosie was Russ's lover and that Russ had left behind a fifteen-million-dollar villa and a twelve-year-old daughter named Maia. It was a surreal and traumatizing trip for Irene and her sons, and yet now, a week later, all of these shocking facts have been woven into the tapestry of Irene's reality. It was incredible, really, what the brain could assimilate. "He was talking about a storm. A bad storm, he said. Destructive."

"Maybe he meant the lightning storm," Cash says.

"Maybe," Irene says. The helicopter had been struck by lightning. "Or maybe it's what lies ahead."

"The investigation," Cash says.

"Yes." The week before, only a couple days after they'd arrived home from St. John, an FBI agent named Colette Vasco called Irene, Cash, and Baker to let them know that the Virgin Islands Search and Rescue team had contacted the Bureau with suspicions that there might be more to the helicopter crash than met the eye.

What does that mean, *exactly?* Irene had asked.

The damage to the helicopter doesn't match up with a typical lightning strike, Agent Vasco said. *There was lightning in the area, but the damage to the helicopter seems to have been caused by an explosive device.*

An explosive device, Irene said.

We're investigating further, Agent Vasco said. *What can you tell me about a man named Todd Croft?*

Next to nothing, Irene had said. She went on to explain that she had tried any number of ways to reach Todd Croft, to no avail. *I probably want to find him more than you do,* Irene said. She gave Agent Vasco the number that Todd Croft's secretary, Marilyn Monroe, had called Irene from. Agent Vasco had thanked her and said she'd be back in touch.

More to the helicopter crash than met the eye. An explosive device. This was turning into something from a movie, Irene thought. Yet she suspected that it was only a matter of time before the next dark door into her husband's secret life opened.

"Also, there were chickens in the dream," Irene says to Cash. "A rooster and two hens."

Cash clears his throat. "Well, yeah."

Well, yeah? Then Irene gets it: Russ is the rooster, Irene and Rosie the two hens.

* * *

Other than Cash and Baker, no one here in Iowa City knows that Russ is dead; Irene hasn't told anyone, which feels like a huge deception, as though she stuffed Russ's corpse into one of the house's nineteen closets and now it's starting to stink. Irene quiets her conscience by telling herself it's her own private business. Besides, no one has asked! This isn't strictly true—Dot, the nurse at the Brown Deer Retirement Community, asked where Russ was, and, in a moment of sheer panic, Irene lied and told Dot he was on a business trip in the Caribbean.

And he couldn't get away? Dot asked. *Even for this?* Dot was fond of Russ; she cooed over him at his every visit as though he had forded rivers and climbed mountains to get there, although she took Irene's daily presence at Brown Deer for granted. Irene perversely enjoyed watching the shadow of disillusionment cross Dot's face when she learned that Russ had put work before his own dying mother.

Russ's footprint in Iowa City all but disappeared after he took the job with Ascension thirteen years ago. Russ used to know everybody in town. He worked for the Corn Refiners Association and was a social creature by nature. He would drop off Baker and Cash at school and then go to Pearson's drugstore on Linn Street for a cup of coffee with "the boys"—the four or five retired gentlemen known as the Midwestern Mafia, who ran Iowa City. Russ's coffee break with the boys was sacred. They were the ones who had encouraged him to run for the Iowa City school board, and they'd suggested he join the Rotary Club, where he eventually became vice president.

All of the boys were now dead, and Russ hadn't been involved with local politics or the Rotary Club in over a decade. Irene occasionally bumped into someone from that previous life—Cherie Werner, for example, wife of the former superintendent of schools. Cherie (or whoever) would ask after Russ and then add, "We always knew he would make it big someday," as though Russ were a movie star or the starting quarterback for the Chicago Bears.

But who from Iowa City remained in Russ's everyday life? No one, really.

Now that the business of Milly's death has been handled—her body delivered to the funeral home, her personal effects collected, the probate attorney from Brown Deer enlisted to settle her estate—Irene has no choice but to face the daunting task of contacting the family attorney, Ed Sorley, to tell him about Russ.

"Irene!" Ed says. His voice contains cheerful curiosity. "I didn't expect to hear from you again so soon. Everything okay?"

Irene is in the amethyst-hued parlor, pacing a Persian rug that the same Chicago carpet dealer who'd sold her the Excelsior-suite rug had described as "Queen Victoria's jewel box, overturned." (Irene had bought it immediately despite the fact that it cost even more than the other rug.)

"No, Ed," Irene says. "It's not." She pauses. Russ has been dead for ten days and this is the first time she's going to say the words out loud to someone other than her sons. "Russ is dead."

There is a beat of silence. Two beats.

"What?" Ed says. "Irene, what?"

"He was killed in a helicopter crash on New Year's Day," Irene says. "Down in the Virgin Islands." She doesn't wait for Ed to ask the obvious follow-up question: What was Russ doing on a helicopter in the Virgin Islands? Or maybe: Where *are* the Virgin Islands? "When I called you last week to ask about Russ's will, he was already dead. I should have told you then. I'm sorry. It's just... I was still processing the news myself."

"Oh, jeez, Irene," Ed says. "I'm so, so sorry. Russ..." There's a lengthy pause. "Man... Anita is going to be *devastated*. You know how she adored Russ. You might not have realized how all the wives in our little group way back when thought Russ was an all-star husband. Anita used to ask me why I couldn't be more like him." Ed stops abruptly and Irene can tell he's fighting back emotion.

Anita should be glad you weren't more like him, Irene wants to say. Anita and Ed Sorley were part of a group of friends Irene and Russ had made when the kids were small—and yes, Anita had been transparently smitten with Russ. She had always laughed at his jokes and was the most envious on Irene's fiftieth birthday when Russ hired an airplane to pull a banner declaring his love.

"I need help, Ed," Irene says. "You're the first person I've told other than my kids. The boys and I flew down to the Caribbean last week. Russ's body had been cremated and we scattered the ashes."

"You *did?*" Ed says. "So are you planning a memorial, then, instead of a funeral?"

"No memorial," Irene says. "At least not yet." She knows this will sound strange. "I can't face everyone with so many unanswered questions. And I need to ask you, Ed, as my attorney, to please keep this news quiet. I don't even want you to tell Anita."

There was another significant pause. "I'll honor your wishes, Irene," Ed says. "But you can't keep it a secret forever. Are you going to submit an obituary to the *Press-Citizen?* Or, I don't know, post something on Facebook, maybe?"

"Facebook?" Irene says. The mere notion is appalling. "Do I have a legal obligation to tell people?"

"Legal?" Ed says. "No, but I mean...wow. You must still be in shock. I'm in shock myself, I get it. What was...why..."

"Ed," Irene says. "I called you to find out what legal steps I need to take."

There's an audible breath from Ed. He's flustered. Irene imagines going through this ninety or a hundred more times with every single one of their friends and neighbors. Maybe she *should* publish an obituary. But what would she say? Two hours after the papers landed on people's doorsteps, she would have well-intentioned hordes arriving with casseroles and questions. She can't bear the thought.

"When I called you before, Ed, you said Russ signed a new will in September." Irene had shoved this piece of information to a remote corner of her mind, but now it's front and center. Why the hell did Russ *sign a new will* without Irene and, more saliently, without *telling* Irene? There could be only one reason. "You said he included a new life insurance policy? For three million dollars?" She swallows. "The life insurance policy...who's the beneficiary?" *Here is the moment when the god-awful truth is revealed,* she thinks. Russ must have made Rosie the beneficiary. Or maybe, if he was too skittish to do that, he made a trust the beneficiary, a trust that would lead back to Rosie and Maia.

"You, of course," Ed says. "The beneficiary is you."

"Me?" Irene says. She feels...she feels...

Ed says, "Who else would it be? The boys? I think Russ was concerned about Cash's ability to manage money." Ed coughs. "Russ did make one other change. After you called me last week, I checked my notes."

"What was the other change?"

"Well, you'll remember that back when you and Russ signed your wills in 2012, you made Russ the executor of your will and Russ made his boss, Todd Croft, the executor of his. In my notes, I wrote that Russ said his finances were becoming too complex for, as he put it, a 'mere mortal' to deal with and he didn't want to burden you with that responsibility. He said Todd would be better able to deal with the fine print. Do you remember that?"

Does Irene remember that? She closes her eyes and tries to put herself in Ed Sorley's office with Russ. She definitely remembers the meeting about the real estate closing—she had been so excited—but the day that they signed their wills is lost. It had probably seemed like an onerous chore, akin to getting the oil changed in her Lexus. She knew it had to be done but she paid little attention to it because she and Russ were in perfect health. They were finally hitting their stride—a new job for Russ, a new house, money.

No, she does not remember. She doubts she would have objected to Russ making Todd Croft the executor of his will. Back then, Todd had seemed like a savior. *Todd the God.*

"So Todd was the executor," Irene says.

"And when Russ came in to sign the new will this past September, he changed it," Ed says. "He made you the executor."

"He did?" Irene says.

"Didn't he tell you?" Ed says.

"No," Irene says. Then she wonders if that's right. "You know what, Ed, he might have told me and I just forgot." *Or I wasn't listening,* she thinks. It's entirely possible that back in September, Russ said one night at dinner, *I saw Ed Sorley today, signed a new will with extra life insurance protection, and I made you executor.* And it's entirely possible that Irene said, *Okay, great.* Back in September, this information would have seemed unremarkable, even dull. Life insurance; executor. Who cared! It was all preparation for an event, Russ's death, that was, if not exactly inconceivable, then very, very far in the future.